OKLAHOMA

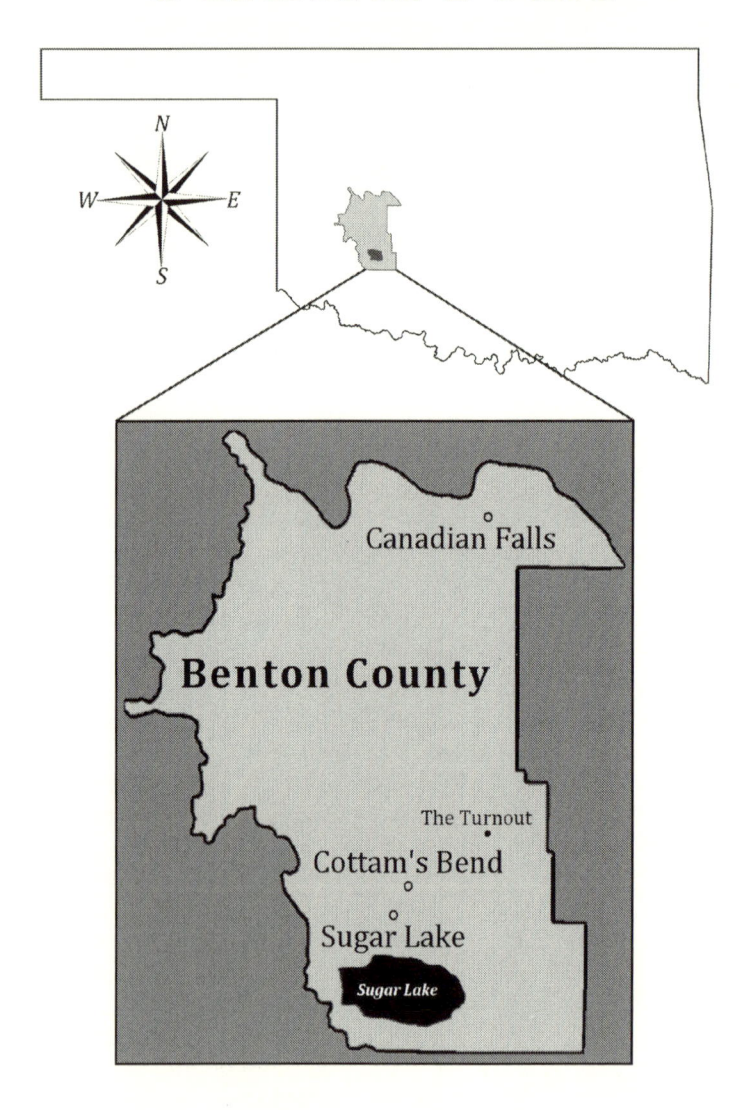

Benton County

- Canadian Falls
- The Turnout
- Cottam's Bend
- Sugar Lake

Sugar Lake

HYMNS

VOLUME ONE

† ALSO BY ERNEST SEWELL †

Greatest Hits - 2017

HYMNS

VOLUME ONE

ERNEST SEWELL

51st Street House Publishing
New York | Oklahoma

51st Street House Publishing
New York | Oklahoma

HYMNS Volume One by Ernest Sewell

Copyright © 2018 by Ernest L Sewell, IV

All rights reserved. In accordance with the U.S. Copyright Act of 1976, the scanning, uploading, and electronic sharing of any part of this book without the permission of the publisher constitute unlawful piracy and theft of the author's intellectual property. If you would like to use material from the book (other than for review purposes, which is allowed using only short excerpts), prior written permission must be obtained by contacting the publisher directly. EBooks are not transferable. All rights are reserved to the author.

HYMNS Volume One is a work of fiction. All names, characters, locales, and incidents are products of the author's imagination and any resemblance or similarities to actual people, places, or events is entirely coincidental. No familiarity should be inferred.

First Edition

Paperback & eBook simultaneously published October 2018 by
51st Street House Publishing.
Senior Advisor: Karen Bays-Winslow
Associate Editor: Michele Hamilton
Illustrations: Patrick Stephenson | Find more at www.thebearpad.com
Cover and interior design: Ernest Sewell
Manufactured in the United States of America.
Find more at www.ernestsewell.com

Set in Cambria 11 and Lucida Console 9.

ISBN-13: 978-0-9994328-2-2
ISBN-10: 0-9994328-2-6

*To all the men who made this book possible.
And to the women who did, too.*

*David met Jonathan, the king's son.
There was an immediate bond between them, for Jonathan loved David. Jonathan made a solemn pact with David because he loved him as he loved himself.*
1 Samuel 18:1, 3

Now Jonathan again caused David to vow because he loved him; for he loved him as he loved his own soul.
1 Samuel 20:17

† Canon of Hymns †

† Matthew	5
† Mark	19
† Luke	45
† John	69
† David	91
† Eli and Daniel	121
† Cain	147
† Abel	165
† Nicolaus	191
† Thomas	211
† Simon and Peter	235
† Paul	281
† Acknowledgements	307

† Matthew †

I worked with Andrew at a fast food joint. From day one he and I became fast friends who shared a lot of sarcasm, musicals and a particular penchant for men. Andrew was a swing manager, and I was but a mere wage worker. I had never aspired to work in fast food on a long-term basis but the place was within walking distance of my apartment, and the rent was cheap enough that a fast food restaurant's meager paycheck would cover my expenses and leave me some pocket change. Being stuck in the southern suburb of Sugar Lake, Oklahoma without a car was no one's ideas of success, nor was it particularly sexy. It was survival, but it worked. I was virginal, twenty-two and sharing a flat with my stepbrother. I was also on my way to serving more beef sandwiches and coiled-shaped, over-seasoned, deep-fried potatoes than I cared to think about on any given day. And while many might not admit Oklahoma a prime location to capture the frivolities of one's homosexual youth, one must consider that for decades Oklahoma had the largest gay population per capita. Clubs, restaurants, hotels, and dive bars were owned by gay proprietors and were ripe with homosexual men.

Andrew took me under his proverbial, glitter-tinged rainbow-soaked wing and slowly cranked open my gay closet door. He had no shame in who he was as a gay man. For me, a virgin in suburban Oklahoma, his life was a much-desired future as much as it seemed like a pipe dream. He took me to my first gay club, watched musicals together (Ms. Brice, table for three), talked trash about the high school girl coworkers and their proclivity for thick eyebrows, overdrawn pouty lips, and hair scrunchies. The fun moments manifested when we all rubbernecked at the same hot men that came by our drive-thru window. Cops got free coffee and a turnover; that was a company policy. Hot guys in a truck or jeep got a wink and sometimes extra fries if they happened to be shirtless; that was my & Andrew's policy. Over our intercom headsets, we would put out a pseudo-APB about which one we would let handcuff us on a Saturday night. Andrew and I would talk on the phone every afternoon when he got home from Culinary College, following his dream of being a chef. Then we hung out at work that evening. In between taking the orders of soccer moms asking for large sandwiches, side salads with bleu-cheese dressing, small diet colas, and the worn-out father picking up dinner for the kids on visitation night, Andrew and I would discuss all the more delicate details of men and what we liked about them. My admiration of Andrew's seemingly vast experience with men grew as much as my young twenty-something dick did every night. I knew nothing about the things he described to me in his encounters with other men. The feel of my left and right hands on my dick had been my only point of reference in conjuring an orgasm.

We often went cruising together which, back in those days, meant driving to different scenic turnouts along the interstate outside of town late at night. They were crawling with men. Gay, straight, and otherwise. Anyone who wanted their dick sucked could easily leave fifteen minutes later very satisfied. Some guys hung out to service multiple men while others dipped in to get taken care of and then head home. There were no lights to turn on so it was about as anonymous as sex could get without the use of a glory hole in the back room of an adult bookstore. The rule of thumb was that once you took the exit for the turnout area, you turned off your headlights. Anonymous sex locations like this demanded an unwritten rule of discretion. Driving into a den of iniquity on the eastern fringe of Cottam's Bend - what many of the religious types in our town would consider sexual perversion - was never supposed to be advertised with high-beams or a parade.

Andrew and I maintained a platonic relationship, although I had developed a crush on him early in our friendship. It is almost embarrassing to admit that fact. But at twenty-two and still quite green around the gills – and virginal around the crotch - it is understandable to crush on someone so quickly.

We traveled to one scenic rest stop northeast of Sugar Lake unofficially called The Turnout. We hopped in Andrew's Subaru station wagon (the Dragon Wagon, as he proudly called it – and somewhat of a ploy to deter the fact that he did not have a typical trendy gay vehicle), and off we went to meet men. I did not tell him, but I was just along for the ride. My fear of the unknown overrode my desire to have actual sex. It was not until a bit later that I realized Andrew had a plan that night to get me laid. I wanted to get fucked. I had experimented with many things on my own, but another man's penis inside me was still sitting on my bucket list. I felt like I was already bordering on gay-pathetic if I did not do something soon. I was young, had an average and quite a workable cock, was slightly stocky with a high libido. I would do plenty with myself and had had plenty of things up my tight virgin ass. Cucumbers, toothpaste pumps, hairspray cans - the list grew monthly. But never on the list, so far, was another man's meaty, slightly musty, cock.

Within just under three-quarters of an hour after Andrew picked me up, we arrived at The Turnout. As soon as we took the exit, Andrew turned off the car lights. No one wanted to be physically illuminated while deep throating a trucker; and if they did there were studios for that. The Turnout was a general rest stop during the daytime. It was on a hill, out of sight of traffic especially at night. No toilets but a couple of picnic tables and trash bins. It looked east toward counties I had never visited, as well as part of the Arkansas River. It was a beautiful view at night time. The city lights lit up like amber lightning bugs. It was fall, but in the mid-south, that means maybe a windbreaker at best. Andrew hopped out of the car ready for action. However, I had no idea how to proceed. We leaned against the car and talked a bit. Andrew either knew a lot of these guys, or he was just super friendly. He said hi to just about anyone who walked by us. There were so many guys at The Turnout than I expected. Older, younger, muscle-bound, average, bearish, cub-like, silver daddy, twinks, jocks, and more. They all had one thing in common: they were horny and wanted to cum. We were not there to trade brownie recipes. We were there to get some action. Well, they were, at least.

"Why are you just standing there? Go mingle," Andy barked at me as only a gay friend could without sounding like they wanted a fight.

"These dicks are not going to suck themselves." I suppose he had a point there.

"I am happy just hanging out here," I lied. I did feel like the front end of the Dragon Wagon, with my ass planted firmly on it, was my safe place. But that could not last for long. I was scared to death. I was the epitome of awkward. It was highly probable that I was the only virgin in fifty square yards. The whole thing sort of spooked part of me. I was a virgin in a new territory. This time, I was the fresh blood. I am surprised the men there did not smell it sooner. I could feel my balls shrinking up inside my gut; the way they do when you are frightened or anxious. I could feel butterflies in my stomach, and my knees were knocking, all due to the possibilities of future sex. Imminent sex, surely. To boil it down, I was a nervous girl on her first prom night sans the crepe paper streamers and balloons. Nope, this would not be that sort of celebration if I went all the way with someone tonight.

"I will be back. Go do something already," Andrew said.

He bounced off to a dark area along the walking path and was out of my view. I hated that he left me there by myself. At the same time, I admired him for being so bold as to have sex so openly and unapologetically.

Yeah, I will get right on that.

The small hiking path down the side of The Turnout had lots of trees and bushes, and no doubt lots of men getting their dicks sucked, or their asses fucked hard and fast. A couple of guys nodded at me while passing by but I was putting off a "do not touch me" vibe. Perhaps it was a bit on purpose, but it was working.

After what seemed like an eternity, Andrew came back around, and this time he was not alone. He brought a friend back with him.

Good God, what is he doing?

Standing next to Andrew was Matthew. Matthew was tall like me, a good six feet, dark hair, ruddy skin, and a bit on the feminine side. No purses were falling out of his mouth when he spoke, but he was not going to be winning an award in a Mr. Butch contest either. He was a good-looking guy, and who was I to be picky? Being gay in the mid-south at the start of the 1990's was a long way from marriage equality or starting a family. I did not have to invest much in this – except my cherry.

After some small talk, Matthew and I ended up in the backseat of the Dragon Wagon. It was like a bad scene out of a 1950's movie. We talked a bit, and I was as nervous as I would ever be in my life. Matthew seemed a lot more seasoned in the gay hookup realm than me.

"You are cute. Where do you live?'

"Oh, just outside town," I lied. Technically, Sugar Lake was a suburb, but it was not outside of anything.

"Love your brown hair; it is all wavy. I might have to touch it," he teased.

"Okay," I gulped.

He tousled my hair. Tingles went down my spine, up the back of my neck, and right into my cock. Being affectionately touched by another gay man was way more arousing than I bargained for in the backseat of the Dragon Wagon.

Almost immediately, my cock was hard. As Matthew and I started to kiss, my first kiss by the way – outside of a love peck from a girl when I was about eleven-years-old – and it felt weird and magical and fantastic. I had no idea what I was doing, but I just kept trying. I put my shaking hand on his chest, and he put his hands on my legs. It was sort of awkward in the backseat of a car, but we did the best we could with the situation.

"Are you nervous, hon? You are trembling."

"Yeah, I guess. I ... I have...um.." I was a stammering fool with a boner in his jeans.

"Let me guess. You have never done this before, huh?"

I was mortified. I was not Catholic nor was I looking to be in a confessional box right now.

I nodded.

"Aww, that is cute," he continued. "Everyone has a first time. It is okay."

I could only let out a nervous chuckle.

"We do not have to do this if you ..."

"No, it is okay. I am... this is new."

"Do not worry, baby. I will be gentle."

I am pretty sure I had heard that in a movie.

Matthew's hand eventually made its way to my zipper. I could feel the warmth of his hand through my jeans. No doubt he felt my rigid, young throbbing cock, hard as steel pressing upward for air. He gently, but firmly grabbed it and squeezed it through my jeans.

"Mmm, wow, nice," he proclaimed.

My body noticeably twitched from his touch. My dick was about to burst out of my pants. I could feel the viscosity of pre-cum between my dick and my underwear.

He moved his hand under my shirt and felt my chest. I thought this could be a moment where I could copy what he did and at least pretend I was not bumbling my way through the breaking of the cherry.

"Oh, I love a hairy guy," he confessed. I had never thought of myself as hairy or furry, but he was the professional here, not me. I did not counter his summation.

I put my hand under Matthew's shirt and felt his soft, squishy skin. He had a hairy chest, but it was sparser than my own. It felt nice against my shaking hand.

"Do you like my chest?" he asked.

"Yes, I do," disclosing the truth to the stranger. I realized his chest was the only other man's chest I had ever felt, other than my own. While I had wrestled with my stepbrothers, played tackle with friends, and hugged other men, this was easily the first time it was sexual.

We continued to kiss and rub each other's chest. I felt myself becoming more relaxed around him. He was tender and patient. He pulled his shirt over the back of his neck with it still around his arms. I pulled my jacket off, with his help, and I did the same. He leaned down and started exploring my chest with his mouth, sucking on my nipples. In between, he came up to kiss me deeper.

"Can I suck your cock, baby?"

"Um...okay. If you want to," I said, trying to be nonchalant in a very non-nonchalant situation. He was eager to get his mouth on my dick, and part of me was keen to let him. I reached down and unzipped my pants. Matthew took my hand and moved it out of the way. He pushed me back towards the door, so I was reclining. He leaned in towards me, and his hands quickly maneuvered my young meat out of its cage of denim and underwear.

"Relax. You are going to feel good, I promise."

Before I knew it, I felt something warm, wet, and utterly new on my cock. He licked the underside of my shaft. It sent shivers through my body.

"Oh fuck..." I could not help but exclaim.

"Are you okay, baby? Does it feel good?"

"Yes, I just was not..."

"...expecting that? Relax, honey. Just enjoy it. You do not have to do anything but stay hard."

"I can do that," I confessed.

He maneuvered my jeans and boxer briefs down more so my whole belly button-to-thigh area was fully exposed. He centered his mouth squarely on my rod, slowly working his tongue up and down my shaft. He teased the head of it with his tongue, sucking on its purple helmet, all while his hands would come in and cup my furry balls or rub my bare chest. Every stroke of his tongue not only felt like the first – it *was* the first. Sooner than later, I found myself lost in the abundance of his work. I went from being a hermit leaning on the side of a car to now getting my first full-on blowjob. I knew he had sucked a lot of cocks because he knew what he was doing. I wondered if Andrew had told him this would be my first blowjob. Even if not, he knew by this point that his mouth was the first ever to gobble my dick. He locked his mouth around my hard shaft like he was sucking a milkshake through a straw. No hands, just mouth, and pure suction. I thought I would blow in the first few seconds, but he read my body's messages. He could feel when I was getting close, pulling back on his oral vigor then returning to his task with a spirited advance. He read me like a dime-store paperback.

For some reason, I kept looking at the clock on the dashboard. I was not in a hurry, but I did not know how long blowjobs in a back seat were supposed to last. I just knew I did not want this to go too fast. I wanted it to continue as long as possible.

Matthew did not seem to mind the time. He loved my dick with his mouth; I loved him sucking it. He swallowed it down to the balls with every gulp. I relaxed even more. I grabbed his head and pushed his face down on my tool guiding him up and down as it pleased me. The more my shaft throbbed against his tongue, the more he took every inch of it. The muscles in my legs tightened up while face fucking Matthew. My hips started to find their natural groove and thrust. My fingers tangled themselves in Matthew's soft, brown wavy hair.

The windows had fogged over in the car, which, in the back of my mind, I found more than a little amusing.

A little stream of sweat had started working its way down my collarbone and into the hair of my chest. I was getting the hottest blowjob ever! Of course, I had no real reference point, but I was pretty sure it was up there in history's echelons of great blowjobs.

I grabbed the hair on his head, soft and wavy like his belly, and shoved his face down on my meaty white member, making him swallow it even when he probably wanted to gasp for air. I let him do all the work while I leaned back and tried my best to take in the experience of my first blowjob from a beautiful Latin-American cubby.

After forty-five minutes of Matthew continually swallowing my cock, he wanted me to cum. He poured on the tongue and mouth action. He did not let me pull back when I felt I was getting close to exploding my seed.

"Oh my God, I might cum!"

All I heard was a muffled affirmation. He wanted it. I could not hold it anymore. I felt the tingling in my groin grow. I felt like it started in my toes and the top of my head. The feeling rushed from both ends of my body and headed to a scheduled meeting in my dick. My heart was racing. My breathing was heavy, and my chest was heaving in sync with the pulses of the veins in my cock. Oh shit! It is going to happen. I am going to cum in this guy's mouth. I was so close to cumming and Matthew sensed it. I had never cum in front of anyone before, and I was about to blow a wad down his throat. The whole thought made me even harder if that was even possible. I pumped his face without regard, and he loved it. He grabbed the base of my dick to hold it in place. His other hand grabbed onto my chest with more aggression than I had seen from him. The moment of no return arrived.

"Oh God, oh God. I am cumming! I am cumming!" I shouted a warning. Matthew did not heed it as a warning as he did an invitation. My jizz was his reward for being so diligent at sucking my young rod. He settled into letting me squirt right down his throat. Then it happened. I came.

I came. So. Fucking. Hard.

My legs locked up, my chest flexed without recourse, and I had nowhere to go but down his soft and willing throat.

When I came, it felt as though it lasted for hours. I could hear Matthew choking on my cock as I held his head on my dick while all of my orgasmic tinglings left me. I heard him swallowing my cum with every shot. All of the hot, white, creamy jizz I had in me was still making its way to his belly. I collapsed against the door of the car, my dick still hard, and slightly bobbing up and down from my heavy breathing. It was perfectly in sync with the deafening heartbeat in my eardrums. I glanced down, and there was not a drop of cum on it.

I moved my hand from Matthew's hair and head, and he slowly came up, pausing for a second. He looked up at me like a kid who just ate all the cookies. His dark brown eyes and askew hair made him look scrappy and subservient. He smirked at me. I instantly filled with embarrassment and accomplishment. It was done. Another man had finally blown me.

"That was so hot," he said. "Your dick is beautiful."

"Thanks," I said, finding no other words to break the ice or lighten the moment.

I grinned in agreement. Despite feeling fantastic as ever, I felt slightly exposed and embarrassed. We were, after all, in a car with my friend right outside maintain a quick vigil. I pulled my boxers and jeans up over my rapidly declining dick but not before taking a minute to enjoy the moment. The gravity of what just happened sat on my lap. It fucked with my head. At twenty-two, had I finally done it? Yes. Yes sir, I had. I felt like maybe I should return the favor, although I am not sure I could have sucked a dick as well as he did. Matthew was here to suck a dick. Mission: accomplished. I did not know if I was I his first hookup that night or the last. I gathered my senses about me, fastened up my pants, and we both pulled our shirts back over the front of our bodies.

Within minutes, Matthew and I could see a dark figure walking up to the car window. Matthew wiped the sweat off his face and any other possible leftovers from our oral adventures. I almost giggled out loud. It is not like he had any of my jizz on the outside of him. He had swallowed every bit of it just moments earlier.

We were jarred back into reality by a knock on the window. It was Andrew.

"You in there, girl?! It is cold out here."

Matthew and I both laughed. We opened our doors and got out of the car.

"Goddamn, you look done for," Andrew said upon a quick visual examination of me.

"Shush," I said under my breath. "Give me a minute, asshole." I did not mind Andrew ribbing me about my experience. I did not want to do it in public.

Andrew got in and started the car. I walked around to the passenger side where Matthew waited for me.

"That was fun, right?" he asked.

"More than I expected, yes."

"I guess that makes me your first, huh?"

"Yeah. I guess it does."

"Too bad we do not have a drink to toast," he said, laughing at the silliness of the moment.

"I should go," I said, wanting to get back in the car.

"Have fun, baby." He kissed me goodnight.

"Thank you."

"Oh sweetie, it was my pleasure," he said.

"I am pretty sure I got the better end of the deal," I bargained. I was sure sucking dick was just as fun as getting sucked. I did not have another point of reference.

"See you later," he said. I knew I would probably never see him again. The Turnout was never on our short list as a team. Andrew was a regular visitor. But I was not. I got in the front seat, and off we went. Matthew traipsed off to conquer another dick, but I bet he would not find another virgin that night. I was the prime meat out there. However, at a turnout-turned-hookup-spot, it was a target-rich environment.

On the drive home, I had a million things race through my head and still had a few things racing through my crotch. It was quiet in the car for a few minutes before Andrew started questioning me about everything. He was genuinely curious about my first experience. I did my best to answer him. It was all very real and very unreal at the same time. To say it was surreal could not be more cliché but having sex in the back of a car was just as cliché. Andrew's questions had me giggling in the car, and we laughed about the whole thing all the way home.

Andrew dropped me off at my apartment, and we said our goodbyes for the night. I tip-toed in as not to wake up my stepbrother. He worked in retail and was up nearly every day it seemed. I was not done yet. I showered and got to bed. I did not find sleep until I jerked off and came one more time all while thinking about Matthew's mouth.

And, thus, began my journey into the beautiful and erotic world of man on man sex. It was my initial leap out of the closet and into the bedroom or the backseat of the Dragon Wagon. I did not go out that night expecting to receive my first blowjob. I thought I would hang out and enjoy the scenery in the dark. I am glad I did not protest when Andrew showed up with a willing contestant on *Can He Get Laid Tonight?* Starring yours truly. I loved every fucking minute of it.

18 † Ernest Sewell

† Mark †

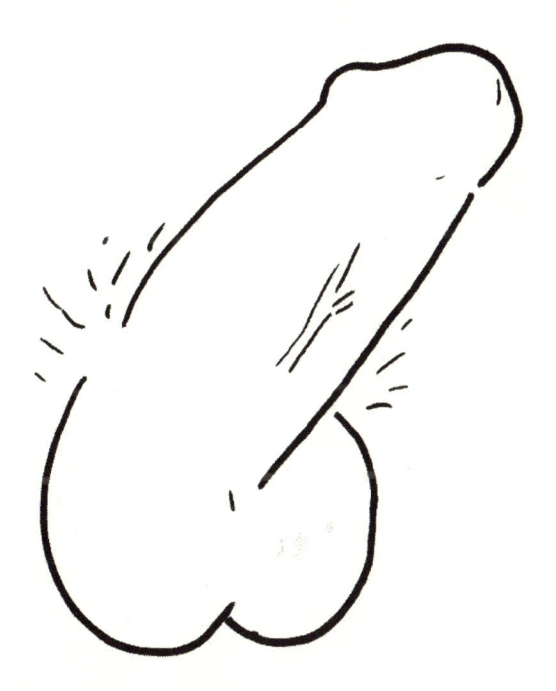

I was not necessarily a jock type. I did not have a six-pack of abs, run or play sports, and I certainly did not go to the gym. I did, however, have a thirty-six waist, and I could tie my shoes and not hold my breath. To think that a twenty-year-old jock would go for me seemed unusual, if not absurd. He had a locker room full of dicks to choose from for that sort of thing. I had not quite grown into being a bear, or even a cub body type. I was just a pasty white guy with a big sex drive. With only one awkward experience with a girl and one blowjob from a guy under my belt, I had little knowledge of who liked what, or what to expect from anyone. I always had the idea that you had to look like the person you wanted to sleep with for them to want to sleep with you. Jocks sleep with jocks, twinks fucked twinks, and bears shagged cubs. None of that is truthful in the slightest.

Mark was a jock. He was just a couple of years younger than me. As a teenager, he had played football in high school, drummed in marching band, and worked out in his parent's garage every evening. As an adult, he shuffled his gym routine with music practice at home. He loved perfecting his music as much as he loved sports and being physical. I always internally debated if it was hotter having a roommate who worked out in general or one that played drums shirtless while listening to classic rock or played guitar with the likes of Clapton, Page, Zappa, or Satriani over the stereo in his room. He practiced a lot, as much as he worked out to build his already perfect body into a godlike state. I would soon find out he was good at perfecting a lot of things.

Throughout about six months, Mark and I had a steady friendship and an intense sexual relationship. The kicker is that Mark was straight. Now while some might think "oh sure, while he is fucking another dude," but in reality, he had not been with a guy before or since I was with him. He trusted me for some reason. I had no ill will toward him, so if something sexual was going to happen, it was a perfect setup. No one would ever know. We had a blast fucking. It was six months of straight jock realness encompassing every muscle, locker room, bromance testosterone-driven fantasy I could muster.

See, it started when Mark and I decided on sharing an apartment. We had both moved back to the area, and friends put us in contact, knowing we both were looking for a place to call home. We decided to share expenses. It was a good call because living was pretty cheap overall with two of us in a small two-bedroom apartment. He biked to work, keeping his already perfect bubble butt tight and firm. I walked a few blocks up to my job in food service. Walking to work held my body right on the brink between healthy and chunky. I maintained a slimmer body, but I also was not soon fitting into skinny jeans.

One night, Mark and I were lounging around on the living room floor with some music in the background. We could not afford cable television, so we listened to an album or the radio, talked, or played video games. Sometimes he worked out, and I would read a book for a while. That is unless he was out on the prowl or bringing some kitty girl home. On this night, the music was low key; he was doing something with a notebook, probably writing down a new workout routine or song lyrics. I was feeling very relaxed. I had dozed off in the middle of the living room floor, my head and chest already propped up on a big throw pillow I had snatched earlier from the pit group seating area, but the cat nap did not last long. As I started to wake up, I could hear Mark somewhere in the room behind me breathing and flipping pages to his notebook. I was on my stomach, facing away from him. I was conscious but not ready to get up just yet.

At first, it started as a joke. I decided to mess with Mark a little bit. While my eyes were still closed, I pretended to have some weird dream. I gripped the carpet or moaned like I was in distress. Nothing too dramatic mind you, just something to get his attention. Tonight, I felt like I needed his attention and this was the vehicle to fuck with him a little bit. We played small pranks as roommates do, but we were not jackasses about it. Cold water over the curtain while the other was in the shower, fake vomit or dog puke in his bed; kid's stuff.

Mark towered over my six-foot frame by a couple of inches. His chest was big, his waist was thinner, and tanned all over (although I suspect he must have had some Greek or Italian in him, as he never really "faded" in the winter months). He had hairy legs and a moderately hairy chest. Long fingers, a size twelve shoe, beautiful light brown hair, and a smirk that could melt me at the knees – this is what I lived with every day. He was proud of his body but not a jerk about it. He was raised well to stay humble yet confident. He was not arrogant or conceited about how he looked. He just was who he was, which was adorable. It was not unusual to have him be in a pair of shorts or track pants without a shirt. The guy did not like shirts. He was shirtless more than not, by far. I did not mind the view, and he did not hesitate to soak up my quiet admiration. I think we both knew we were eyeballing the other. It was a win-win. I had never flirted with him or did anything that would make him uncomfortable. We were buddies, roommates, and friends. He had a girl over here and there, and I gave him space. When he brought home some bird, I could almost always hear him and her going at it. He got loud at times, apparently not shy about living in the moment, neighbors and roommate's peace be damned. I often went to bed at night and jerked off thinking about him - this big, oaf of a jock that had a kind heart and not a bad bone in his body - fucking me – arguably the least attractive thing on his radar whether straight or gay - with all his testosterone-driven libido. I used to cum so hard thinking about him – even hearing him – fucking. And since he was straight, I quickly settled into accepting it would never happen. As long as he kept puttering around the apartment shirtless, I was a happy dude. And in Sugar Lake, Oklahoma, who needed a damn shirt anyway? It was hot more than it was cold. Even with the breeze off the lake, we saw little relief from the heat between April and early October. Some people have a no-shoe rule in their homes. We did, too. But we also had an unwritten shirt-optional policy.

I could feel Mark grab my arm as if he was trying to save me from hurting myself in my faux-bad dream. For a moment, I felt terrible about what I was doing. But with

Mark bringing home girls all the time I figured I owed him some payback.
Wow, his hands are so warm!
"Yo dude. Hey, wake up," he said firmly as he shook me awake. "Wake the fuck up, bro."
I opened my eyes a bit.
"You must have had a nasty one," he snickered. "You were punching the floor as if you hated it. I hope you kicked someone's ass."
I giggled to myself. What a silly joke.
"I do not remember." I rolled over onto my back, sprawled out on the floor feeling oddly more comfortable than I ever had around him. He had squatted next to me. He was still in his black track pants and shirtless as usual.
"You are a dork sometimes you know that?" he grinned. He gave me a very light slap on the cheek almost like a big brother would to a little brother.
"Guilty as charged, asshole." I quipped. I made a fist and lightly play-punched him in one of his rock-hard pecs. Jesus, they felt like a brick wall.
I expected him to stand up and return to whatever he was doing. A moment passed.
He put his hand on my chest. Shit, did I tick him off with the faux punch? Not all guys take that thing with a grain of salt. It is aggression, but it is just guys being guys. Some want to wrestle or play fight, while some do it to show dominance or test another's submissive nature. Being a guy is eighty percent finding out who is in charge, it seems. If there were ever a zombie apocalypse, Mark would be in charge.
"You sure you are okay?" By natural reflex, I reached up grabbed his hand at the wrist.
"Yeah...I am... I am fine. Weird, huh?"
He was staring at me. What was happening? Was he mad? Did I say something that pissed him off? It was one of those moments where time just stopped for a minute. My

heart started racing and jumped into my throat. His hand on my chest felt like electricity coursing through me. I took a deep breath.

As I raised my head and upper torso with the intention of resting on my elbows he leaned in closer. He clasped his fingers grabbing my shirt, and some chest hair. He leaned in further. Before I knew it, his lips were on mine. We were kissing. My fucking hell, we were making out! Was he kissing me or was this payback for trying to play a stupid joke on him? I felt my cock get hard really fast. I was not sure what to do. Should I pull away? Should I keep going? He is straight, right? He is kissing me. I do not want to freak him out with my dick springing to action in what might be just an off moment between two guy friends doing something crazy.

Motherfuck, his lips were firm, soft, and he knew how to kiss. I felt inadequate in my kissing compared to his, but I was a willing student. I did my best to pretend like I knew what to do.

Fake it until you make it.

My nerves probably did not help. Suddenly, he stopped and pulled back. He let go of my shirt and pushed himself up from his haunches.

"I am sorry, man. I do not know what came over me. I am sorry," he offered.

"No. Um, it is okay." I struggled to find a way to have him get back to kissing me without spooking him. Maybe he was just curious. I did not want him to feel wrong about anything natural that happened.

"You are good, man. I mean, I am not offended." I was the opposite of being offended. I was so fucking turned on that I could have cum with one touch on my dick. I never touched my dick because this was not a sexual situation. Or was it? I had never been so erect. Well, at least not since that blowjob by Matthew.

"I am not gay," he continued.

"No, I know, man. I did not mean to ..." Did not mean what? What had I done to make him kiss me? Well, nothing. But before I could finish my thought, he squatted beside me again and kissed me even harder. He gave into his urge and took it out on me.

"Fuck, is this weird? I am not a homo, man. No offense."

"None taken, bro. I get you, man. It is okay." He always seemed to respond to words like bro or buddy. Ours was a bro thing, I guess. He was one of the guys and wanted everyone else to be that as well.

We kissed like two men should kiss, hard and soft, firm and supple. I slowly put one of my hands on his shoulder, and gently pulled him back towards me as I laid back down on the floor. He hiked one of his legs over one of mine and hovered over me. His biceps seemed to go on for days. He held most of his body just over mine, so his arms were fully engaged and flexed. When I reached up to grab his other shoulder, my hand reached his arm first. I kept it there, and he did not seem to mind. I was not sure if Mark wanted to fuck, get fucked, get a blowjob, wrestle, write song lyrics, or practice a few licks on his Fender six-string. What the fuck was he doing? God, please do not let this be a weird make-out session because I will bust before he gets a nut.

I decided to take a chance and make my intentions known. I slowly opened my legs, my khaki shorts tighter than they should have been. While still kissing me, he slowly lowered his body onto mine. He nestled himself between my legs. He had done this before but with women. Was it only women? I did not give a shit, it was my turn, and I was taking it. His chest rested on mine. I felt his crotch lay against mine. My God, his dick was huge! Fuck! I will never measure up to that! Now I was nervous. Very nervous. Guys in the locker room walk around naked all the time and are just guys. I was not that guy. I was more modest, shy; almost a wallflower.

I threw my hesitation to the wind, and slowly let my legs wrap naturally around his beefy waist and thighs. He was slowly and methodically grinding his groin into mine. Through his track pants and my shorts, I could feel our cocks fighting for dominance; a fight I could quickly lose.

I reached behind him and gently dug my fingertips into his back. I wanted to touch his body more and more. He pulled away from kissing me, and before I knew it, he grabbed my t-shirt and wiggled it off of me. Without missing a beat came back to kiss me again. Now his jock-type aggression started to kick in, and I found myself loving it. There is nothing sexier than a man in just a pair of jeans or pants, especially Mark. I had seen him near naked before, being roommates and all. I had seen him wet with a towel on, sweaty after a run, and dressed up to go out with his girlfriends. But never this close, and this aggressive. Never this horny. He held himself up with one arm on the elbow. He leaned to one side a bit, and then I felt his massive hand on the snap of my shorts. I do not know if unhooking a bra is anything like unsnapping a pair of khakis, but he had my shorts open before I knew it. But he did not go right for my fully engorged cock. Instead, he ran his hand up my treasure trail, from my waist and right onto my chest. I am sure he felt my stomach quiver. His hand reached my torso, and he rested the palm of his hand in the middle of my chest. I could feel the strength behind it. If he ever punched someone in the chest, they would end up in a less-than-desirable state. Luckily, his intentions toward me rose above anything violent or reactive.

"Your heart is pounding," he made a note.

"It is your fault." I shot back.

"You have done this before, yes?" he noted.

"Well, I got a blowjob," I said, almost ashamed. I did not have as long of a list of conquests as Mark, I was sure.

"I bet it was your first, right?" he teased.

"No," I lied. I realized I was not hiding it. "Yes."

"So, is this your second time doing it?"

I sheepishly replied in the affirmative.

"That is so hot," he lit up like a match against a brick.

"Really? I guess I am just a late bloomer," I said, trying to excuse my lack of experience and egg him on more.

"I bloomed at fifteen years old. By sixteen, I was fucking girls left and right."

I assumed his perception was slightly off as not all girls are as willing to be sexually active as much as a boy going through adolescence with hormones raging. I also did not doubt that he had conquered plenty of pussy in his life.

"Yeah, I have noticed. There is a worn path to your bedroom from the front door. And it is mostly high heel marks. We should put one of those deli counters on the front porch for your conquests."

"Guilty, man. No shame in getting some pussy."

He both had a quick giggle about my gentle chide.

I reached down and started to pull down his track pants. They were not tied, so it was an easy task to accomplish. He had on a pair of square-cut briefs that were small on him, barely keeping his massive meat in check. Fumbling around with a purpose, we quickly pulled off each other's bottoms leaving me in my generic boxer briefs, and him in his Hilfiger square-cuts. He settled his body back onto mine, and I propped my legs up on my feet, my bent knees around his chest. When he laid on me, he grabbed my hair and held my head in place while kissing me and shoved his tongue into my more-than-willing mouth.

He stopped a minute and said, "Do not open your mouth so wide. It is kissing not bobbing for apples."

It was a gentle reminder that I had not done this a lot, and he was a good teacher.

"Sorry."

"It is ok. Got to learn sometime."

I readjusted my mouth, and he came back in for more. I heard him let out a little moan.

"That is better, right?"

"Yeah, it is. Thanks."

Thanks? Did I say thanks *while making out with a hot jock? Seriously?*

"You want to suck me?" he asked. The guy is a mind-reader now. I did not want to come off too eager or desperate, so I tried my best to be sexy-casual.

"Sure."

He rolled over on his back with his arms lifted above his head. His chest muscles pulled the skin tighter over his torso and his abs. His muscles were accentuated and had no place to hide beneath his surface. His six-pack stared me down with a vengeance. His hips were slightly narrower but expanded again at his thighs. Leg day was as much as a priority as arm or chest day to Mark. His running routine kept his legs defined, trimmed, and meaty. His calves looked like perfect cuts of meat, and his thighs could probably pop a watermelon like a peanut. His legs were hairy from the lower thigh down to his ankles. His natural light olive skin tone was consistent over his whole body. His chest hair was dark, wavy but not kinky. His armpit hair was minimal but present. Laid out on the floor in front of me he looks like the letter Y with what promised to be a beautiful dick.

I propped myself up and rolled, so my face landed square in his crotch. He grabbed my pillow and put it behind his head. He was making himself comfortable. The outline of his dick through his skivvies was alarming and enticing. What was I going to do with that anaconda? I pulled the briefs down, and his dick sprang up like a spitting cobra ready for something to happen to it. My mouth was dry from nervousness. I licked my lips and tried to garner some saliva while I stroked his cock. I put the head of his monster tool in my mouth while grabbing the base. Immediately, he moaned with approval.

"Aww fuck, bro."

I could feel the heartbeat pulses in his cock against my tongue and on the inside of my cheeks. I wanted to give him all of me, and I started with my eager mouth. Instead of holding his meat in place with my hands, I used my mouth to swallow his colossal member. I did my best to disguise my lack of blowjob experience, a task I was never sure I was accomplishing as well as I hoped. My hands reached up and grabbed his chest, pressing myself against him to hold my body and neck in place. His hands were strangers for a while, but he eventually palmed the back of my now-sweaty head and guided me up and down his veiny shaft.

"That is good, man. Yeah, use your tongue."

I swear he was going to cum at any moment, and I was ready for it. It seemed forever, yet only a minute, that he pushed my head, aggressively yet gently, toward his groin as he slowly fucked my mouth. I pulled my mouth off his cock and put his balls in my mouth. Every guy is tender there, but it can also be an erotic spot. For him, it proved to be true. It was a dreamland being between his legs, making him groan. I caught glimpses of his face, eyes closed and enjoying my newly developing oral skills. His stomach and chest blustered in response. His thighs were hard and thick. He could have probably squashed my head between them.

I got a rhythm going and was in the zone. I was sucking Mark's cock, using my hands to either stroke his abs or chest, or cup his balls, and appreciate his body as much as I could. Sometimes I used a hand to simultaneous jerk him off while sucking his dick. It gave my jaw a break for a few minutes before going hog wild on it again.

As if on a mission, he pushed me off his cock.

I thought to myself, "Shit! He is over it."

I was wrong.

I sat up on my knees, looking at him the only way I knew how. Before I could even form words, he grabbed me around my waist, and practically picked me up, and forcefully body slammed me to the floor. It was like two guys wrestling with their dicks swinging. I could take some of his aggression because I knew he would never hurt me. I was not a jock, but I was not a total wimp either. He put his legs between mine and with one swoop had me spread eagle face down on the rug. His right hand was on the back of my neck, the other holding my left arm. I was not fighting it much, although I probably did have a couple of quick wiggles to feign weakness. I felt him beat his steel-hard dick on top of the cheeks of my ass. He lowered his chest and abs against my back. He was strong. His legs, his arms – they were not giving me any space to move. He easily overpowered me. His mouth was over my left ear, as the right side of my head was against the floor.

"I am going to fuck you, dude."

My mouth went dry. I tried to swallow, and it probably looked like I was nervous.

"You sure. You do not have to..." Of course, he did, but why was I giving him an out?

"Tell me you want me to fuck you."

"Mark, I want you to fuck me like you want, man! Fuck me! Fucking do it!" I said as I raised my voice. If iron sharpens iron, then testosterone would engage the same. His hand slightly jarred my head.

"Now make me believe it." His queue was shameless.

I felt drops of sweat from his body land on my back.

I decided to raise my rancor.

"If you think you are man enough why not put your dick in me, or else we are going to have a fucking problem, *buddy*." I was almost mean about it. I was not lying – after all that foreplay and dick sucking, I would have a problem if he did not fuck me. I emphasized the buddy to him as if arguing over road rage or something equally stupid. You know how people argue and they will cap a sentence with "*honey*" or "*pal.*" I was trying to incite him.

"I still do not believe you, fucker," he implied, slightly pushing his cock into my ass cheeks a bit more. It made me hungry as fuck for him to be inside me. I knew it might hurt; I knew he would fuck me six ways and sideways. I knew I did not care.

I decided to get him upset, at least a little.

"What are you stupid? Do you want a written invitation? Why are the pretty ones always dumb fucks? Maybe you cannot handle another guy. A hole's a hole, right? You going to pussy out on me?"

I heard the aggression in his voice rise. "What the fuck did you just say to me?"

His hand tightened around me as he leaned into me more from behind, no doubt trying to be intimidating. He was puffed up and showing off to me. I could tell that while he might be feeling more testosterone than usual, he was turned on by it. He was as mad as he was horny.

"Are you stupid or something, motherfucker? You want me to beg for it? Is that what you want?" I started to roll over to face him. If he wanted a fight, I would give him one without pause. His hand on the back of my neck had already tightened its grip, and now it suddenly bared downward. There was no moving, at least for a moment.

"How about I make you beg me to stop?!" My neck was free of his grip. His left hand was now pressing into the middle of my back, and I could feel his right hand around my butt. He, like any jock, grabbed his dick and beat it against my ass a few more times.

"You can try, big man. All I hear is a lot of talking. You are scared, I knew it. You do not have the balls to do it."

That set him off, big time. He saw it as a challenge and the encouragement he needed to continue. He spit into his hand, wet his dick with his saliva, then I felt it. That big, fat purple head that had been in my mouth moments ago was now pressing against the other side of me. He moved his cock around to feel for my puckered canal flexing with unprecedented anticipation.

He found it.

"You talk like a bitch; now I am going to fuck you like a bitch." He was still challenging me.

"You are not shit," I huffed back. But before I got the sentence out, and with no real regard, if it would hurt or not, he pushed the head in, still holding his other hand against my back to keep me in place. Instinctively, my hands clawed at the carpet, and I tried to push myself forward away from him. The pinch of pain coupled with a mounting pleasure that would prove to be the tip of the iceberg. I did not want him ripping me apart, but I did want him to take it as he wanted. I squirmed by instinct to try and relieve the pangs coursing through my ass.

The head stayed in, and with both hands, he grabbed either of my wrists, pulled my arms to my lower back.

"Where are you going? You wanted this. There is no backing out, buddy."

I let out what probably sounded like a whimper. I am not sure what it was, but it was in no way a disagreement.

"You are not going to cry, are you?" he taunted.

His hands were big with long fingers. I remember thinking his fingers wrapped all the way around the back of my head earlier; as a basketball player palming a ball. He put both my hands together, and with one hand, held them in place. He used his other hand to brace himself, and then it happened. He pushed the rest of himself into me. Not slowly, not fast, just consistent. His dick was huge, and it felt like it was sliding in me forever. I kept waiting for his balls and his pubes to reach my ass.

They finally did.

He let out a huge groan.

"FUCK!" I thought. Had he cum already?

"Your ass is tight as fuck, man." I squeezed down as much as I could. He slowly pulled out and pushed back in, his measured pace slowly and steadily building.

"Do not tell me you have never been fucked before now."

"Not by some meathead jock."

He had a one-breath chuckle and continued to fuck me. God, he was fucking me! I could not believe it. This guy, my roommate, this friend who loves pussy and brags about his conquests was fucking me. He liked to be in control. He let my hands go, but as I tried to reposition them, he grabbed them again, one hand on either of my arms, held me in place, leaned forward, pressing his waist against the small of my back, and continued to split my willing hole open. I returned the favor by squeezing his dick when it was all the way inside me. Sometimes he would let out a moan when he felt it. I knew he felt it, and he knew I knew. It was one of those unspoken "do not stop" moments. Our bodies were communicating. He took turns laying on my back; his arms hooked undermine, his hands on the back of my neck almost like I was in a vice grip. Sometimes his legs were between mine, other times he would straddle my ass and keep fucking me. My butt bounced against his body slamming into it. We were in a groove. He was not stopping anytime soon. I could only hope his stamina would support his bravado.

The warm summer air making its way through the open windows proliferated his abundant sweating. Unwisely, we had kept the air off for the evening. Even with a few random fans throughout the house, the temperature outside was the same on this side of the walls. Two bodies thrashing about raised the temperature in the house. I was not sure if the sweat on me was his or my own. It was as good as an aphrodisiac.

He raised up to get on his knees behind me, grabbing my hips. "Raise your ass up, man. Get on your knees."

I did without missing a beat. I got on all fours, my hands on the floor, my knees spread just far enough apart so he could nestle up behind me. He shoved his dick right back into my hole without hesitation. He grabbed my hips hard while fucking me. His thrusts were furious, his chest was sweaty, and his big muscle-boy balls were slapping against my ass. My cock marched to its own percussive rhythm against my furry treasure trail.

When he had me face down earlier, my dick was hard, pressed against the floor under me. I could not play with my dick. I could not touch myself. I had only hoped that the friction he was giving me would not make me cum. I had been close so many times. His dick was hitting my prostate straight on, and it was good.

But on all fours, I was wide open. My legs were apart; my body was now fully exposed, I had nothing to hide. You cannot act inhibited when your brotato chip is fucking you. There are no dark rooms or subtleties when big Broseph is pounding your hole. My dick bobbed up and down under me as I took jolts from the jock. He was unapologetic, and the force of his fucking was remarkable; my whole body surged with verve.

"Let me see you."

"What?" he asked, in between his thrusts.

"Mark, let me see you fuck me."

He paused, pulled his dick out of me.

"Hurry up, man." I knew he wanted to cum, and soon. But I wanted to see that massive fucking chest heaving, flexing and tensing up while he pounded me.

I quickly rolled over, on my back, and moved downward toward him. I pulled my legs up, and in the same motion, he grabbed my ankles. He looked down, and with just his hips, he maneuvered his cock into place and pushed it into my hole. I could see on his face that he loved it. I reached up and grabbed his abs, or his chest, or wherever my hands landed.

"I am fucking you like a bitch; you know that?"

"I was just thinking the same thing about you, fucker."

He smirked and kept fucking me. In his head, he probably did think of me as a bitch at that moment. A submissive bottom that he owned with his massive meat (not far from the truth); yet someone who could still hold their own with him. He liked the back and forth; it was petrol to him. God knows I was trying to maintain my own with him as much as possible. Mark worked out five or six days a week. He was one of those jocks that ran, instead of just lifting weights to bulk up his body. His cardio kept him looking damn near ripped, but not with that look where you think steroids were involved. He bulked up in the winter and trimmed down in the summer. Seeing his ever-changing body had always been my self-indulgent secret whenever he walked through the house. Like most guys, he liked to show off and pretend shirts did not exist. That all worked to my advantage and I had plenty of spank bank material when I masturbated. He would run ten to twelve miles every other day, plus lift weights. I had seen him do things that left me winded while he barely blinked. To me, he was a machine. He was nice, too, so living with him was more than tolerable. Tonight though, his stamina was incredible. He loved to sweat, he told me once. He loved to work his body and feel the rush of endorphins. He used to say that pain was weakness leaving your body, and that sweat was purging the toxins. He liked to compete and win. He loved a challenge. I had no idea my ass would be tonight's challenge. But thus far, he was in blue ribbon territory.

His hips were like a machine, rhythmic, steady, purposeful. His dick was as hard as it had been all night, and my ass was fully accepting. He knew how to fuck like it was the first thing he did when he came out of the womb. The more he pounded me, the more I wanted to cum. I reached down and grabbed my dick. I was afraid to jerk it, or even touch it, knowing he had me near cumming the whole time he was inside me.

"Go on – you going to cum, bro?"

"Not yet. I want you to tell me when I can. I want to cum when you do," I said as an upright bottom does.

"So intense." It tumbled out of his mouth awkwardly. I did not say anything about it. This was not a moment I wanted to ruin. But him saying us cumming together would be intense was just adorable and endearing. Mark was everyone's pal, but right now he was my main squeeze – for a moment.

"Goddamn, you feel so good inside me," I blurted.

"Yeah? You ever had a dick this big before? I bet not."

He was correct. I had not a dick nearly as big as his nor one attached to a near perfect body like his, and he knew it. Hell, I had never been fucked, but I was too embarrassed to reveal my lack of experience.

"I do not want you to stop. I want you to fuck me as long as you want to, bud."

"Oh yeah? I am not sure you can take it, bro."

"Try me, fucker. I have handled you this long."

For whatever reason, that challenge sent him into fifth gear. He was going to cum, and it was going to be soon. I could feel it. You know how when you are fucking and you get close and you just sort of phase out of your own body? You are right there. The intensity is so overwhelming you just let loose of your thoughts and inhibitions and go for gold. It is that moment where nothing else in the world matters.

A few more minutes went by, just fucking and sweating, his body engorged with blood and testosterone; for a straight jock, he seemed to enjoy being a man fucking another man. He had gone from holding my ankles to bracing his hands on the back of my thighs, my legs pressing against the sides of my torso. He would watch his dick go in and out of me. He had to be watching my dick, rock hard as it was, bouncing around with every push he made inside me. My balls filled beyond their average capacity, and I was aching to cum. My body shivered with anticipation.

"I am getting close, dude," he said.

"I am going to cum with you," I demanded.

"Then get ready, because I am close. Fuck, I am close, man. I am so fucking close!"

I grabbed my dick with a tight grip. I surprised myself at just how rigid and hard my cock had become through it all. I had not lost my erection at all. I started jerking in sync with his thrusts. He began to moan with each push.

"Oh, fuck man. I am going to cream your hole!"

"You cumming?" I was eager for him to fill me.

There was that split second before a guy cums when he is silent when the first waves of orgasm hit him. I knew where he was at, because I was there, too. It is a moment when we are the closest to the universe.

He let out a primal roar. His body was beautiful with his flexed abs and tensed chest. The sweat made him like a Norse god with a hammer coupled with a Nasty Pig model between my legs. He kept fucking while he was cumming. Some guys stop for a second and let it happen. He wanted to feel it all and kept pushing in and out of me. I could feel him breeding me with every inch of that thick dick that he insisted on slamming in my hole.

It only took a few jerks before I knew my end was coming. My load suddenly spilled out onto my belly and my chest. I let out the massive groans that only an orgasm this intense could bring me. My legs tightened up and pressed back against Mark's arms. He was in the throes of cumming, resisting the push of my legs with no effort. His strength was evident. My ass was squeezing down on his dick, while we were both cumming. Our muscles, our breathing, our screams of ecstasy were out of sync, but concurrent. He had thrown his head back while cumming, his hands tightened their grip on my legs, which only enhanced the feelings I had, too.

His rhythm slowed a bit. I was still milking my dick, wads of semen popping out of me. He was breathing heavy; he looked down with a smile on his face. He kept his dick in me. I could feel it pulsing against the inside of my hole. I squeezed as best I could to lock my grip on his cock. His expression was a mix of being embarrassed by what he had done as well as a great sense of accomplishment. Was he in disbelief that he had readily and voluntarily fucked another dude and seeded in his asshole?

"Holy shit, Mark!"

"Dude, I just fucked you so hard." He was a champ.

"Yeah, you did!"

"Fuck – should I have cum inside you?!" He seemed worried, and I believed in his concern. "Oh fuck, was that wrong? I am sorry, man! Should I have done that?"

"Mark, you are okay. It is fine. We are both good. It is okay. We are safe."

"Good, because it was super hot cumming inside a dude. No way was I going to pull out of you."

"I could feel it when you did."

"No way! Shut the fuck up!"

"No seriously, I could feel your spunk when you came." I was telling the truth.

"Wow, that is pretty cool. No girl has ever said that to me," he confessed. I could not tell if he was disappointed or stating a fact.

"Well, I am not one of your birds either."

"No. No, you are not. But fess up," Mark's dick was still hard, and inside me, "you have been fucked before me." He was still slowly pumping my ass as if to milk any of his DNA out of his cock and into my hole.

"Not really, man. Just a blowjob or two. I told you I am a late bloomer," I said. With those words, I realized my hunch was right. I did feel slightly shamed by my admission to having a short resume.

"You could have fooled me, Brocephus." He looked down at my chest and belly and saw the puddles of my cum. I glanced at the clock. Ninety minutes had passed since he initially tackled me.

He was still slowly pushing and pulling his dick in and out of my ass. He was so masculine and full of testosterone. I swear I felt every vein on his dick inside my hole. He was getting off on the tease. I could not fight the moment. I felt comfortable and trusted him.

"Kiss me," I said.

"Come up here and get it," he challenged me. He sat back on the floor and spread his legs out while scooping his hands around my back and lifting me toward him. I sat on his crotch and hovered over his dick. I sat back down on it as he guided it in me, my legs wrapped around his waist. His dick was still just as hard as it was before he came. We sat there, facing each other in the middle of the floor, him inside me entangled in a sweaty, cum-ridden mess. I held onto him by his sweaty shoulders, pulled myself up and we met in the middle for a kiss. I kept my legs wrapped around his midsection, and he responded by pushing my hips down on his dick more. He was all the way inside me while we made out together. How long was he going to stay hard? I could feel his balls against my ass. I rode his dick while we made out like teenagers. I wondered if this was going to be round two.

I stroked his head with my fingers, feeling the sweat on his body. He held me in place with his big arms around my midsection, holding me up from my backside. God, he was a good kisser! The jizz on my stomach was now covering his abs. It was acting like glue between us.

He raised up and looked at my belly again. "You are covered in it, man."

"Yeah, and you are too. I bet you have never had another dude's cum on you."

He just smiled. Had he?

"I guess I should shower, huh?" I coyly asked.

"Dude, you do not want to wear that all night." he joked.

"Uh, probably not." I lifted up and pulled myself away. His dick slid out of me and was already starting to soften. My hole was still resonating from being stretched out for so long. It was a perfect way to get my indoctrinating fuck. I braced myself on his shoulder and pushed my way to stand up on my feet.

"I hope you had fun," I said.

"Goddamn, right I did!" he said without apology. He hopped up in front of me like he had not even fucked me in beast mode for the past hour and a half.

"Did you?" he asked, almost coyly.

"I would give it a strong seven out of ten."

"Shit, I gave you a solid eight, and you know it."

"You did that, for sure," I admitted, still glowing.

"But listen," he continued. "Do not take this the wrong way, but can we keep this between us? I am straight."

Right. Of course, you are bro.

I knew what he meant. I had no plans of broadcasting it to the neighbors or anything.

"We are good, Mark. We are buds."

"Yeah, we are. You are a good friend."

"Thanks, man. But let us be honest. You are, at least, a raging bromosexual."

He laughed so hard his abs flexed as he had just finished five hundred sit-ups.

"You got me there, Hans Brolo."

"Oh wow, you are ridiculous, Bro Diddly." I could do this shit all night.

"You can call me Broseidon, king of the Brocean."

"Okay, you are done, Brosie Berez. I am going to shower. I will save you some hot water," I said. In any other situation, I could do that silly bro shit all night. But after the fucking he had just given me, I had no more witticism.
"Please do! I am covered in sweat."
I headed to the bathroom, feeling like I could barely walk. I am sure I looked wobbly as I disappeared from his view. He went to grab something from the fridge.
I half-assed closed the door behind me when I got to the bathroom. There was no master suite, but there were two bathrooms in the apartment, one with just a shower stall. We both kept to our own spaces, but mine was the one with only the shower. I turned on the shower and let it get warm. I pissed, as guys tend to do after they cum. I tested the water, and it was hot. I stepped in, closed the translucent gray shower curtain, and stood quietly under the rainforest shower head. The hot water felt good. I almost could not tell it was hot because my body temperature was still high from the ravages of Mark's looking-at-me-bro-driven ass pounding.
I stood there for a minute, my eyes closed, the hum of the vent fan running, the water hitting my head, running down my back, over my shoulders, and around my neck onto my chest. I did not need to check the mirror to know I had a smile on my face which probably did not fully mimic the one inside me. Without looking, I reached up and grabbed my shampoo. I squeezed some out and lathered up my whole face and head. The smell of it calmed me. I felt masculine. I felt like a fucking man. I also felt like a man who just got fucked by another man. It is not that I had felt unmanly before, but hell, I just had some of the best sex of my life thus far (although the notches in my headboard were arguably a bit on the sparse side). The endorphins were doing their job.
I leaned back toward the water more to rinse my head, just letting the water do its thing. I stood there, thinking

about what just happened. My eyes were closed, but my mind flashed images of moments with Mark in and out as quick as lightning in an Oklahoma storm.

What was that? I heard something. Or did I?

I felt those warm hands on around my waist. I realized was not alone anymore.

I tried to pull back from the water, blinking my eyes open, trying to see through the water, and the glaring light from the vanity. The light refracted through the water in my eyes, rendering me temporarily blinded. I was able to clear enough to focus to see I had a visitor.

"Hey there, Bromeo. Can I join you?"

Mark had decided to hitch a ride in my shower time. I stood there, wet, still had some cum on my belly, my dick was ever so slightly hard, but on its way out of service. I felt even more vulnerable now than when I had while being fucked by him.

"Does that make you Juliet?" I asked.

"Aww, fuck you. You were the bottom, not me."

"All in good time," I scolded.

"Here, I brought you a beer," he offered.

"What, no water?"

"Oh, sorry man, did you just want water?"

"I am fucking with you, Mark. Beer is fine. I need it."

"I always rehydrate after a workout." It was a typical gym rat vaunting, but I loved it.

"You rehydrate with a beer?"

"Shut up and drink it," he said. We both took a big swig.

"So, is that what we did out there? 'Work out'?" I asked with finger quotes.

"I think it is safe to say it was a cardio session with a fusion. Maybe a little weight lifting."

That last line came with him slightly pinching at my midsection. My body involuntarily jerked back since I was ticklish at the slightest brush of a finger.

"Oh, fuck you, Mark. You were not straining in the least!" I poked back.

"True, but it did get my heart rate up some. You were breathing heavy too, man."

"Yeah, but that is because I am not as in shape as you."

"You could be. I can show you how to work out anytime you want. I could be your trainer!"

"You mean my gay-ner?"

He let out a big laugh that echoed through the shower. "Funny. Now move over, asshole."

Almost instinctively, he grabbed my hips as we pivoted positions. I stood at the other end of the shower, beer still in hand while my roommate rinsed his body. The water cascaded over his inflamed muscles like south American waterfalls hiding Escobar's pesos. Every ripple of his excruciatingly developed mid-section became a virtual mirror, glistening with water, accentuated by compact fluorescent bulbs and his hand slowly dragged over them as if congratulating himself on his body and his most recent sexual conquest. He ducked his head under the water, which laid the short hair on his head flag against his scalp. Water ran down his V-shaped back in perfect formation as dominos would fall in succession, tipped by one purposeful flick of a finger. He turned around to wet his back. He tilted his head back - his strong neck supporting it without strain – and the water again found a home across his face and down his chest. His dick was long and unapologetic as it jaunted from the front of his groin. The same dick that had been inside me moments ago was red with blood and still slightly firmer than it would have been otherwise. His thighs were thick, holding him in place.

Was this happening? Was I having a porn moment in the shower with my jock roommate and friend?

"You are not going to fuck me again, are you?" I joked. "I mean, do you not normally 'workout' twice a day?" I asked with finger quotes.

We both chuckled at the absurdity of it. We shared the water and traded off soaping up and rinsing. Just two guys hanging out in the shower. Nothing to see here, folks; move along, now. No big deal.

I leaned out of the vinyl curtain to sit my beer on the floor outside the shower. I stood back up and pulled the curtain closed again. Before I knew what was happening, Mark pushed me against the cold tile, held my arms over my head with his big hands. Was he going to frisk me, pat me down? Check me for weapons? But there I stood, just a pale guy still tingling from being split open like wet lumber ten minutes ago. I did not even try to break free of his grip because it was pointless. The damp tile was not a place to engage in a wrestling match. He stared at me with a sinister look on his face. He kissed me. I could feel his dick against mine. We were both getting hard.

"Why? Do you not normally jerk off twice a day?" he said, giving my sass back to me.

"No. Just did not know if you could handle another round so quickly, being a dumb jock and all."

And that is all it took.

† Luke †

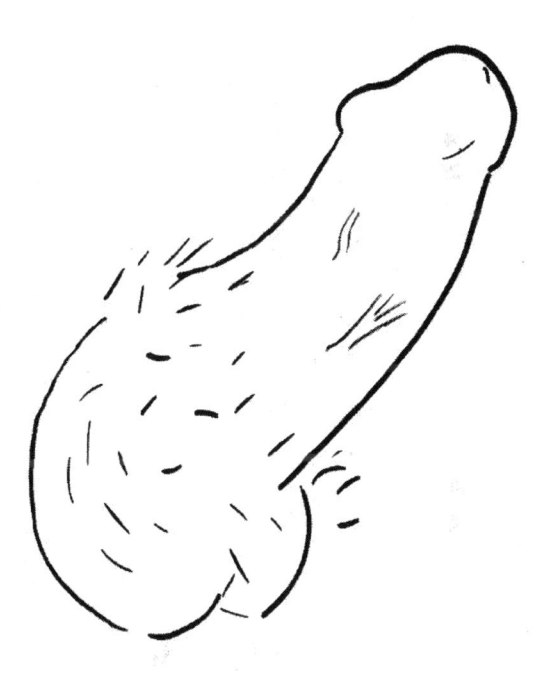

I started masturbating at around fifteen years old. Like most guys, I just sort of figured it out once the hormones started to kick in during my early teenage years. It was glorious. How did I not know about this before?! Every day after school I would come home, have a snack, then jerk off my teenaged putz. I soon learned to save the meal until after the orgasm because that is what us men do. We cum and get hungry.

It was during those younger years of self-exploration that I started to have, what some would call, deviant imaginations. I am not sure where they came from, but I have a good idea. One of my fantasies was to be tied up and taken advantage of sexually. I had significant feelings for a specific dynamic superhero and a younger charge whose episodic shows repeated every weekday afternoon. When they were tied to some device, helpless and vulnerable, legs spread apart and facing certain peril; those were the moments I found it to be key boner material. As I started to reach adolescence, it became a regular fantasy. I could put myself in that situation and find something erotic about it. Those images fed fantasies for my newly developing libido. I would lay on my bed, naked, and wrangle my feet on either side of my footboard pretending they were bound and spread eagle. My legs were unable to close to protect myself. It made me feel vulnerable. I would wiggle around as if trying to get loose from my pseudo-shackles. My dick quickly gained stiffness to the point of relentlessly throbbing. The fantasies never left either of my heads. I never knew much about the world of dominance or submissiveness. In my early adolescent development, exploring my darkest fantasies, I almost always seemed to be in a submissive position. It often played out in my adult life.

Fast forward to the early days of online internet services which proved to be an exploratory goldmine of potential dicks; good and bad. Once you learned the ins and outs of a service provider's chat rooms, you could field for cock all day. Whether you wanted your dick sucked or you wished to glob onto a few mushroom heads yourself, it was all there for the taking.

It was while living in the Twin Cities that I first experienced the joys of online cruising. Men, men, men! Dick for days. I popped in a chat room for BondageM4M, or something as equally sinister, and watched the scrolling conversations peppered with titillating exchanges. Almost immediately, I had a few private messages pop up on my monitor. Some were asking the a/s/l question, which I always thought was a shitty opener. Age, sex, location? Be original, or at least try. Most conversations ended with little fanfare, but a few ended up being more engaging.

Having stuck to my rule of "no clothes at home," I had already gotten damn near naked when I got home earlier that afternoon. I settled into my evening routine which included opening my webcam and snapping a few revealing but not X-rated photos to spread amongst the people. I did that about once a week because I never wanted to be a guy with an old picture. I always made it a point to keep current photos on hand. Too many times I had met guys who had photos from a decade prior. I did not want to be that guy. I logged into a couple of chat rooms and watched the conversations scroll.

One guy caught my attention. He called himself Sir Luke. We traded a few photos and talked the typical gay small talk. He told me he was the IT manager in a physician's office right where Cottam's Bend and Sugar Lake shared a city line. Today, as luck would have it, he was not working. Whoever this Sir Luke fellow was, he seemed to enjoy what he saw in my pictures. He continued to push the conversation into a possible meeting between us.

I was upfront and told him I had never had anyone dominate me but was willing to try it with a man I felt I could trust. As I typed the words on the screen, I found myself astounded admitting those fantasies out loud (or at least on a computer screen). Was I finally going down this road? I had long considered it, watched porn with it, dreamed about it, and saw others talk about it. Now, I found myself willing to try it. He seemed to be just as keen to show me the ropes. I had a few restrictions. I was not going to be pissed on, or anything else I thought to be out of my wheelhouse. To each his own but I needed to take it a bit slower. Some elements were never going to be my thing. He respected that and assured me he was a

good judge of just how far to take a newbie. Our conversation soon ended with us agreeing to meet at my place. I did a quick rinse in the shower, and I slid into a pair of jeans. I had always found men in just jeans to be a fetish. No shirt, no shoes or socks, maybe the top snap unfastened. God, there is something so masculine and raw about that view. I did my best to emote that fetish when I could, even with myself. I was not fooling myself either. No magazines were calling for a photo shoot anytime soon. But half of a good time is feeling sexy.
Additionally, I could not answer the door in the nude.

∞

Twenty or so minutes later, I heard a car pull in the driveway. I knew my visitor had arrived.
Oh boy, here we go.
I peeked out the window to get a glimpse of this Luke guy having seen only a couple of photos from our chat. He was a bit shorter than my six-foot build but not much. He was lean and toned, wearing jeans (score), a leather vest with no shirt underneath, a steel-toed black work shoe, and had a wallet chain hanging from his belt loop that no doubt connected to a sturdy carryall in his pocket. His hands were enveloped in leather gloves with the fingertips cut out of them. His dark sunglasses hid his eyes but did not obscure his face. He got out of his Jeep, on which he had removed the hard top. It was summer, so there was no need for anything but open-air freedom. I always found it sexy for just about any guy in a Jeep with the hardcover removed. Those men gave no fucks, and that was as sexy as any day at the gym. Luke swaggered with confidence, an equally hot trait. He knew who he was and what he was here to accomplish. I watched as he made a quick survey of the neighborhood. The car alarm chirped, and he buried his keychain in his

pocket. He made his way to the porch. Just before he could knock, I opened the door to greet him.

"Come on in, stud!" I spouted.

"Whoa, you caught me off guard there, slick." I saw him look me up and down even through his dark glasses. "Damn, you are a cute pup! And topless," he replied.

"Well, thanks," I blushed. "It looks like you are not far behind me," I continued, pointing to the chest hairs peeking out from the vest. If he was going to be inside me within the half-hour I assume formalities take a back seat and my lack of a shirt did not matter.

I shut the door behind him.

"Can I get you something to drink? Water, a beer? Do you want to hang out upstairs? I was watching some TV." I lied, but I did want to get him upstairs.

"Nah, I am good for now. Yeah boy, lead the way."

Boy? Well, I can not hate him for that. This was undoubtedly going to be a dominant and submissive situation. I was as ready as I could ever be for it.

He followed me upstairs to my bedroom. The television was on some weather channel but muted.

"Make yourself comfy. I must inform you that item number 3A has been expedited to the top of my To-Do list." He had a curious look on his face and was waiting for the punchline.

"I need to pee," I said, delivering the clincher with perfect comic timing.

It took him a second to realize I was messing with him. I was not sure what he was thinking about my stupid humor, but I did need to piss. He finally let out a chuckle under his breath. I assumed we both, now, got the joke.

I do not know why I always had to pee right when someone visits. I could clean myself up inside and out and go through that whole ritual of preparing to bottom, and I would still have to pee when a guy walked in the door. Nervous bladder, maybe.

"Go ahead," he took a beat, "and lose the jeans, boy." He was in bossy mode already.

"Roger that," I said.

"What do you call me?"

"Sir, yes sir I understand." I quickly got the hint. If anything, I was a fast learner.

"Good. Now hurry."

Fair enough. Under my jeans, I had slipped into a pair of square cut boxers made from that Spandex/cotton blend that hugs your nuts and lets them breathe at the same time. I was not sure if I should lose the boxers, too.

The plus of having the master suite is that the bathroom is never far either for business or pleasure. I did not bother entirely closing the door while I dropped my pants and let loose. I finished what I was doing and got out of my jeans. I tossed them on top of the wicker hamper near the sink. I adjusted my junk and made one last check in the mirror. As I approached the door, I could not see him in the room.

Did he leave? Fuck, did he jet on me?

I ambled over the threshold and BAM! Before I could see him, I felt him. He tackled me and threw me to the floor. For a moment, I was shell-shocked. What in fresh hell just happened? He took advantage of me being stunned and had somehow maneuvered one hand on the back of my neck, and the other holding one of my arms by the bicep. His legs were straddling my ass. I remembered back at my first session with Mark, the jock roommate, and that he initiated a similarly aggressive & dominant position. I was in familiar territory.

"You are mine, now, boy," he announced. He was stronger than I thought. I felt his leather vest against my exposed back. He was right. I was not getting out of this quickly.

I tried to move a little bit, and his grips got stronger. He was not fucking around today.

"Where are you going?" he taunted.

"Nowhere."

"Nowhere, what?!" He demanded his respect.

Nowhere right now? Nowhere yet? Nowhere without you?

"Nowhere, Sir," I replied.

"That is better." The hand on the back of my neck moved up to my head, and he turned my head sideways so I could see him out of the corner of my eye. He leaned down, taking off his sunglasses, and held me in place.

"I am going to make you beg me to stop. It is going to hurt, and you are going to want me to stop, but I will not. Do you understand me? You are mine until I release you."

Gulp.

"Yes, Sir, I understand."

He raised himself up, and stood up, simultaneously grabbing me by the back of my neck, and pulling me around to face him.

"Get on your knees, boy."

He put his hand under my chin and raised my head to look at him. I could smell the leather of his gloves. It made me drunk for his commands.

"Now, unzip my jeans and suck my dick. Do you understand?" he queried.

"Yes, Sir." I obeyed him.

He had one hand on his waist, cocky like – waiting for me to obey. His other hand rested on the back of my head while I schemed to get his belt undone, and his zipper released from its grip. I grabbed the sides of his jeans at the waist and pulled them down exposing his black jock strap. Across the thick elastic waistband, between two thin white border stripes, read "OBEY" in white block letters. His dick was getting hard. Mine was already harder than I expected it to be and felt it struggling for a place to be in my now-too-tight boxer shorts. With his hand still on the back of my head, he shoved my face into his crotch, my nose right in the middle of his jockstrap. He was musty like he had been walking a while in the heat. Not overpowering, but in a blind test, you knew he was all man. I admired his ample bulge against my face.

"Smell that, pup? That is the smell of a real man. Sniff it. Deep." I complied and took a deep breath through my nose. I gave in to his redolence.

With my mouth open, I took another breath. I put my lips around his now-larger-and-harder offshoot. I sucked it through his funky jock. He was already enjoying himself feeling my hot breath against his groin. I knew he took great seeing me kneel at his feet while obeying his commands. I heard his occasional groan or deep and throaty "yeah" coming from above me. He was grinding his muscular hips into my face, holding my head in place with both of his hands. I looked up at him when I could to show him I was complicit.

He reached down and pulled his jockstrap to the side, letting his meat loose from its stretchy prison. He was a solid seven inches. It was thick, veiny, and stone-like. He waved his hips side to side taunting my mouth. His dick wagged back and forth in front of my face. If this guy had been a cop, then his dick was the long arm of the law. I was helpless to resist anything about him. If he had kept swinging his cock in front of me, it would have been a strong case for hypnotism. That is not to say I was not already dick-ma-tized by this manhood.

"Look at that dick, boy. You want to suck it? Beg me for it. Beg me to suck my dick."

"May I please suck your dick, Sir?" I plead. I did want to swallow his rod. I looked up at him with my best sexy-meets-puppy-dog eyes while still knelt in front of him.

"Please Sir, put your beautiful dick in my mouth. I want to suck you. Your dick is ..."

He had had enough of my imploring him.

He grabbed my chin.

"Open your fucking mouth." I did. "Wider." I opened expecting him to slide his dick into it.

He spat in my mouth.

"Keep that," he commanded. I did not swallow and kept it on my tongue as best I could with my mouth wide open.

He guided the head of his dick into my mouth, put both hands on my head, and shoved all seven inches right into my throat. Our mutual sputum acted as lube, and I started to suck him. He immediately started pumping his crotch into my chops. I sat there, squatted on my knees, my hands on his meaty, hard thighs, and just let him face fuck me. My dick was solid and poking into my boxer briefs. I did not dare touch my dick because he was in control. I could tell I was oozing precum. The front of my boxers was getting wetter and wetter. I wanted him to tell me when to cum. Or suck. Or breathe.

His leather gloves stayed on the whole time, sometimes holding my head in place and sometimes under my chin guiding my mouth around his shaft. I looked up at his face and caught his eye. He was intently looking at his cock going down my mouth. He was enjoying every inch of his dick he was putting down my throat. Me staring submissively and helplessly at him seemed to make him more dominant and aggressive, as he turned to more pointed thrusts of his hips into my face.

I was in awe of him. His body was mature, toned and littered with tattoos, each having a story. The Americana collage on his left arm had Vegas dice, a pin-up girl, gears to a machine, an American flag, the Twin Towers, a couple of hearts, an eagle, and more than I could not fully recognize. His black jockstrap matched his vest and gloves. His stomach was flat and hard, but his abs were not over-developed like a gym rat. He was a man with muscle gained from working on cars, cutting down trees, or otherwise lifting heavy stuff. The landscape of flesh, hair, tattoos, and muscle from his dick to his face was every bit of nothing I could have imagined. I let his tanned body abide in my gaze as every inch of his cock pulled out and pushed back into my eager mouth. The black garb made him some dark god standing over me demanding worship and celebration of his manhood however he saw fit. He stood there, in front of me, one-hundred percent man. I was one-hundred percent submissive to serving and pleasing him.

I sucked his dick for as long as he wanted and he was in no hurry. If my jaw became sore, I would sometimes just let him fuck my mouth. Other moments after I rested a few minutes, I would lock down my lips and mouth more, creating suction around his stem, and edge him closer to wanting to cum. We both felt him getting close and would relax the intensity. He would slow his thrust if he was getting close and I would pull back on my energy. We began to learn each other's bodies. But even through all of this, it was just a warm-up.

"Damn, your mouth is hot, baby boy. I want to know how that ass of yours feels." He pulled his cock out of my mouth leaving me gasping for air and wanting more.

"Fuck me, and find out, Sir. Please."

"Get up!" I quickly stood up, my knees popping as I did. He spun me around, facing away from him, grabbed my shorts, and yanked them down to my ankles. He pushed my body forward onto the bed. I landed awkwardly but did not attempt to move. My legs flailed out behind me which permitted him to pull my precum-filled boxers from my ankles. He threw them on the bed next to me, almost to taunt that he owned me.

He did.

"Get up there, boy," he motioned toward my bed.

I crawled up onto the bed on all fours in my best doggy position. I heard him struggle to take his jeans and shoes off, but somehow, he did it.

Oh my God, he is going to fuck me. Should I scream or take it without saying a word? Am I in the right spot? Should I ask him if he needs anything? What is he doing back there?

God this is going to hurt. I hope I do not kill the moment. Is he making tea back there? Fuck me already!
SMACK!
His hands, still in his leather gloves, met the bare skin of my ass with a jolt. He crept up behind me. His fingers explored the curve of my blanched white butt, his thumb teasing the entrance to my hairy crack. He spread my cheeks apart with one hand and beat the head of his dick against my hole. Holy fuck it felt enormous.
Shit. I can survive without walking for a week, right?
He ran his dick up and down the pit of my ass, not penetrating, just teasing. He moaned as the coarse hairs in my ass rubbed against his man pole. I tried to push back to let him know I wanted that magnificent cock inside me. The more he toyed with my willing ass, the more I clawed into the bed linens. He spit on my asshole, then buried his face in it. His tongue felt as strong as his arms. It was a luxury I had not nearly enjoyed enough in my sex life. I was tingling with goosebumps. My thighs quivered. His tongue knew right where it was going, and it went right to my hole. He tightly gripped, and occasionally slapped my ass. Each time felt better than the last. He licked my balls from behind and grabbed my dick from between my legs, sucking it to tease me. It was never long enough for me to get into enjoying having my dick sucked. It is just sufficient to keep me on the edge of glory. His constant changing up what he was doing drove me crazy. He could see that. He was grooming me for the next stage. The more I got eaten out by him, the more I was ready for him to fuck me senseless. It was precisely the frenetic heights where he wanted to take me. I could not endure it anymore. I was overwhelmed with the euphoria that was surging through my body.
I would wait no longer.
"Please Sir, will you fuck me now? I want your cock inside me," I yelled. "Please fuck me, Sir!"

"Oh, my God. You want it bad, boy." he taunted, as he stood behind me.

"Sir yes, Sir! I want you to fuck me, Sir!" I meant it. He leaned down, and again spit right on my eager and freshly eaten out hole.

"You want me to fuck your hole, boy?"

"You own me, Sir. Please fucking use me."

"Move up, son." I moved more into the middle of the mattress to make room for him to join me fully. He positioned himself dead center behind my hole.

"Move your ass down some, boy." I obeyed, readjusting myself. My legs were longer than his, so spreading my knees further apart brought my hips down and lined up my hole right to his massive rod bobbing on the front of his firm, mature body.

"So perfect. Look at that hole. You need to be fucked, boy. You need to be shown what a real man feels like fucking you. Not one of your pussy faggot friends."

How did he know my friends were pussy faggots?

He put the head of his dick on my asshole. I took a deep breath, preparing for whatever was about to happen and how it would feel. He teased me more by pressing the head of his cock on my eaten-out hole. He threatened to push the head inside me. My ass muscles seized. I did my best to breathe and relax. My dick jumped with an involuntary reflex from the pressure against my brown eye. He pushed the swollen purple head of his cock into me. He knew that his cock was big and that he had to maneuver enough to show his dominance but not send me to the emergency room. We both groaned, and he kept it there for a minute. I leaned back just a bit to let him know I was ready for all of him. Whether my ass was fully ready or not, I was ready.

Then it happened.

He reached up and grabbed my hair with one hand and my shoulder with the other. Without missing a beat, he shoved his massive member in me. Not just a little; he pushed it in all the way until I felt the warmth of his balls and body against my butt cheeks.

Fuck, I was right. It hurt like a motherfucker. I let out a huge scream, but he was not going to let up on me. He held it there and let me work through the pain.

"I told you it was going hurt, boy," he taunted, tightening his grip on my hair and my shoulder.

"Yes Sir, you did." I almost whimpered, equally embarrassed and aroused.

"Are you going beg me to stop now?"

"No Sir. But it hurts."

"It hurts?!" he almost seemed annoyed.

"Yes, it does."

SLAP!

The blow of his leathered hand on my bare ass was enough to put me back in my place.

"You are a pussy ass faggot; I should have known."

"I am not, Sir. Your cock is just huge."

It was, but him using it to impale me on my bed was worth the wage of pain.

"What do you want?" he jabbed.

"I want what you want, Sir. Use me. I am nothing. You own me, Sir. It does not matter what I want."

"Fucking right."

Goddamnit, it hurt, but I was relaxing little by little. Somehow the pain drove me to want more. As much as I wanted a minute to regain my senses, he did not stop. He was showing no mercy in his anal attack. Asking for mercy would have been pointless. He was not only enjoying the tightness of my ass and my struggle to stay above the pain, but he was genuinely enjoying fucking me. His thrusting became more purposeful and more comfortable for him. I thought I might get an occasional moment to regroup while he caught his breath or just paused. I was mistaken. He was a machine, focused on his task, and not pulling out anytime soon.

"Fuck damn son; your ass is tighter than some pussy I have had." High compliments from someone who had felt, and tasted quite a few asses. And cunts.

"Yeah, you are a fine boy."

"A boy for you, Sir?"

"I might have to make you one of my regular boys. You think you want to be at my call whenever I need to fuck some ass, boy?"

"Yes, sir, I can be yours. It would be an honor, Sir." It was starting to feel a lot better.

"You work hard enough, and I might let you be my number one or number two."

"Fuck me, Sir. Just fuck me however you want to, Sir. I will not cum until you let me," I pleaded, unintentionally auditioning for the role of number one or two.

"You are goddamn right you will not," he co-signed as he kept pounding my hole. My willingness to submit to him only made him hornier to keep fucking me. He grabbed my shoulders again, pulled me back toward him and kept pushing his shaft into me.

The summer heat made us sweat like whores in church. We could not have been more cliché than we were right now. A younger guy with a slightly more mature man, the former void of tattoos and any semblance of sexual experience in comparison; the latter full of tattoos, more experience than could ever fit on any resume, zero body shame, and a fetish for younger men as well as their asses. We might as well have been in a porn film, him being a maintenance guy and me being the young renter who had air conditioning trouble. He makes advances; we sweat it out on my bed, then he goes back to work all in under a half hour. Fucking is cliché, but we were trying to put an edge on it. We were taking much more time than your average porn scene.

"Flip over, boy, let me see you take this dick."
I quickly flipped onto my back. I could feel the sheets immediately stick to my sweaty back. I raised my legs to invite him closer. He hopped off the bed to remove his jockstrap leaving only his leather half-fingered gloves on his person. He walked up on his knees closer to me.
"You are so hot, Sir."
"Tell me you want my dick in you," he ordered.
"I want you to fill my hole, Sir. Please, Sir, fuck my hole with your hard cock."
"I changed my mind," he countered.
He grabbed his jockstrap and shoved it into my mouth.
"I want you to be quiet and obey me."
The scent of his man funk was abrupt in my nostrils. I could taste the sweat that had soaked into the oversized elastic OBEY jockstrap band. I had no choice but to endure and enjoy the cotton and latex gag I had been given; a situation that made me arguably more erect. I looked up at him, towering over me in control of every single nuance, with the best helpless eyes I could muster. I had no reservations when considering that my powerless stare only made him want me more.
"Put your hands under your ass."
I raised the small of my back with my legs and put my arms to my side, my hands behind my back. I rested my body back on my hands and arms leaving me helpless.
"Much better. A quiet faggot is a good faggot."
He raised my legs up with his gloved hands and centered his cock against my gaping hole.
He started fucking me like it was his last time. Sweat droplets ran from my brow to the sides of my head, soaking the bed under my pale body. He almost exclusively used his hips to fuck me. His upper body was steady and fully engaged. His chest easily flushed red while working so hard. He had beads of sweat collecting on the hair of his firm pecs. A few rivers of sweat ran

down his man cleavage right through his treasure trail. I could feel his sweat escaping from his body to mine. I loved that with every drop I had more of him on me. Eventually, I would have more of him inside me.

"Move, boy."

"What?" I asked, muffled by his jockstrap still dutifully in my mouth. He pulled it out – the jock from my mouth and his dick from my asshole.

"Ride me. If you want the rest of this dick, then you are going to work for it. My boys are not lazy."

What have I been doing until now, baking bread?

I moved over and let him lay on his back. I crawled on top of him. He looked up at me, and I drank in his sweaty body with my eyes.

"Let me clean you up, Sir." Without waiting for a response, I leaned down, still straddling his rock-hard cock, and started to lick his chest. I licked the hairy area between his pecs, and sucked on his nipples, licking the sweat off of them. It was salty. I could smell his natural stench, and it only turned me on more. He raised up one of his arms and without saying a word I moved my face right into his smelly armpit. His hips were shifting back and forth, up and down, his dick searching for a place to hide. I moved to his other pit and licked it clean.

"Good boy, now ride it."

I readjusted my ass over his dick and sat down on it. My ass was wet from his spit, and our sweat. Goddamn it, his cock felt amazing inside me. My dick seemed to consistently get harder, although I do not know how that was possible. I steadied myself with my arms on his chest, and using his legs, he thrust his hips directly into mine, fucking me as hard as he could. I rode him in the same rhythm that he was fucking me. He grabbed hold of my dick with one hand, and just squeezed it.

"Please do not make me cum Sir," I begged him. I wanted this to just last forever. "I am so close if you touch it I might explode too soon." I was serious. I had been near the edge the whole time.

"Then do not cum, boy. You control your cum. Be stronger than that. My boys are not weak."

I was not entirely sure I could obey him. He had me so riled and turned on that I could have cum with just the wind blowing.

"I am trying, Sir. You make me feel so good. I only want to cum when you want me to, Sir."

I tried to silently tell him with my eyes that I was super close and I did not want to cum yet. He showed mercy and let loose his grip. It would be the only consolation I would receive from the Sir. I was thankful he let go of my dick. Given another thirty-second stretch and it would have been too late to hold back any longer.

My pleas for mercy seemed to rile him up another ten notches noted by the intensity of his fucking increasing exponentially. His dick was hitting my prostate in just the right way, and I thought I would cum at any moment. His steady hand teased my dick, jerking it at times, then letting go, slapping it, twisting my nipples. I refused to touch my cock, and it continued to bounce between my stomach and his nearly-flat belly. His brawn was his allure. He may have dressed in khakis and a buttoned shirt at the doctor's office where he worked in the daytime, but at night he was a leather daddy full of the energy of a horse, the muscle of a gorilla, and reeking of a man's natural odor head to toe.

I yelped, and moaned, and let out every other kind of vocalization that came to mind. It was a free flow of expression. While it lasted, we went full force.

"I am going to cum in you, boy!" he announced.

I looked at him and could tell he was close. "Can I taste your seed, Sir?"

"Fuck yeah, you can!" His eyes brightened immediately. He pumped me for another minute or so, but he also grabbed my dick again. He started jerking it.

"I want to see you cum, boy. I want to see you cum just for me, pup."

"Yes, Sir. Can I cum now, Sir?"

"You better," he commanded. He continued to fuck me and jerk my dick. I could not handle both sensations much longer; so tenacious, so evident. I braced myself, hands on my thighs. I leaned my head back and closed my eyes to concentrate.

"Look at me when you cum!" he barked at me.

I obeyed him. I started into his eyes. He was jerking my dick without recourse. I wanted to cum so badly, and there was no turning back. I felt it coming.

"I am ready to cum, Sir. I am going to cum!" I shouted as I looked at him right in his face.

"Then fucking do it, faggot! Let it out!"

His thrusting did not miss a beat. My body started to shake and convulse only motivated him to fuck me harder. My thighs tightened up around his waist, and my torso hunkered forward shadowing his body. I had to use both hands to brace myself on his steel-like chest.

My dick exploded warm, gooey ribbons all over his stomach. I could not even say "oh god." I had lost all vocalizations. All I could do was cum. It seemed as though I would not stop cumming. I believed I was going to lose my breath. I might have for a second or two.

"Yeah boy! Holy fuck, look at all that puppy milk! You were backed up!" He continued to drain my dick.

"Oh, yeah. You got lots of cum for Sir, huh?"

I could only let out a slight grunt. I was not sure if he cared that my response was guttural rather than words. I was not sure if I was holding my breath or breathing. I only knew my orgasm was one of the hardest I had even procured thus far. He chuckled at my awkward euphoria, but I paid no mind to it.

Once I gathered my senses, I answered him.

"Yes, Sir. You made me cum hard." I do not know how I said anything. I was delirious and buzzed. I was still tingling all over from my massive orgasm. He let go of my cock, still resonating and still oozing white semen from my piss hole. His dick was still inside me, and he had no intentions of removing it. His tool vehemently pushed back against every constricting anal muscle God issued me. There was little doubt he was feeling my orgasm as much as I was, if not more and in a different way.

"Now suck my dick, boy. Help me cum," as if he needed any real assistance. He just wanted to finish in my mouth. A task I was more than happy to provide him.

I hopped off his dick, which was red and visibly pulsing with his heartbeat. I could almost see the energy bubbling on his skin. His body was kinetic; his muscles twitched, fingers wiggled in mid-air, and his legs shifted. His orgasms were just under the surface like fresh crude oil. One only had to drill a bit further to find it. I got on my knees between his legs and licked his stomach on my way down to his piledriver dick. He watched me in quiet splendor while I cleaned his torso, lapping own mess from his furry gut. Every touch of my tongue causes his body to flinch involuntarily. There, on his person, I sensed a fine line between begging and craving.

He suddenly grabbed my head with one hand and guided his dick with the other. I savored his briny precum oozing onto my taste buds.

"Get on your back, boy."

Oh fuck, is he going to fuck me again?

"Sir?"

"Get on your back, now."

I obeyed him. He moved out of the way, and I got into the position he demanded.

"Put your arms to your side."
He straddled my torso and arms which rendered me utterly helpless. I could not move or readjust if his dick became too much. He braced himself against the headboard with his hands and heaved his body into my face. He aimed his dick like a starship zeroing in on a runaway meteor. I was submissive to his desires.
"Open your mouth, son."
I did. Luke slid his dick into my mouth to face fuck me.
I met his challenge with new-found vigor. Most guys lose their arousal once they cum. Today, I was not that guy. I wanted nothing more than for him to use me to the natural end. I vacuum sucked my jaws closed around his shaft so I could feel every vein, wrinkle, and pulsating artery against my tongue. My mouth was his to use. He fucked my face as mightily and intently as he had violated my ass. I could smell our combined scent on his crotch. It lingered in my nostrils while the bush that surrounded his dick tickled my face. I felt no gag reflex as his bulging cock rammed down my throat. His hard body was so close it was hard to see any other part of him in full; only catching glimpses of his sweaty muscular anatomy as it prepared to release all his energy into my mouth.
His legs suddenly hardened with an internal quiver. His whole torso tightened up, showing his natural brawn in the most conspicuous way possible. He let out a loud non-verbal noise which alerted me his release was imminent. At this point, it could not be stopped.
His dick erupted in my mouth. I clamped down even harder to extract every bit of his tasty nectar that I could ingest. He could barely control himself, nor did he try. He was taking everything he wanted. The ribbons of cream shot down my throat giving no pause to my ability to swallow them purposely or by accident. As he came, he rested his pubes on my face while his dick kept residence

on my tongue. The head of his dick teased the back of my throat as it continued to fertilize my gorge.

The drum of his dick lightened. I kept my mouth open and pliable. He slowly pulled his dick out then pushed it in to savor ever bump on my tongue and every groove in my mouth. I was guaranteed to make this a blowjob he would never forget. The more he came, the more I drank it taking great pleasure in this robust and mature man's white gift was now inside me.

He slowly pulled his dick out of my mouth, and it was still hard as a rock. His eyes were closed, and his breathing was still thick and deliberate. I spotted some of more of milk on his paunch, so I leaned forward and licked it clean. He twitched at the surprise of my tongue and lips finessing cum off of his body. He smiled and let me continue. A lick, and another, and another, and one more. On the last one, he scooped up some of the spunk on his belly and shoved it in my mouth. He leaned down and kissed me, deep. His tongue invaded my mouth, and I returned the favor. He kissed me and did not seem to mind mixing our cum in our mouths.

"Did you like that fucking, pup?"

"Yes Sir, I did. I have never been fucked quite like that before," I confessed. I had not.

"I wanted to cum without touching my dick. But I love that you controlled when I came. I wanted to give you everything I had, Sir."

As a bottom, I could be submissive and take care of the top. I had great times as a bottom, but Sir Luke had taken me to a new place with his verbal dominance, unapologetic daddy status, and his innate genius ability to fuck like a beast. It was not about the dominance so much as just playing submissive to my version of a cigarette ad man. But who am I kidding? While our liaison would have been equally passionate and intense without any verbal queues, the added saltiness of his commands cranked up the inherent eroticism twenty notches. His ripe supremacy over me was everything.

He removed his gloves. His hand, already calloused, warm, sweaty, and firm, cupped the side of my face. I leaned in again for another kiss. He collapsed beside me motioning for me to join him closer. I laid on top of him, my legs straddling him. Our soft and wet dicks smashed gently against each other perfectly content to stay that way for a while; although he was arguably still harder. His hand ran down my back. He caressed me and comforted me. My sweaty skin prickled with elation. A feeling of security washed through me, a sense only an experienced top worth his weight could offer.

It was a sweet moment.

"You get off on giving up control, I can tell," he said in softer tones, chuckling at the very idea.

"And you get off on taking it all for yourself," I quipped.

"Well," he continued, "I told you what to do, and you obeyed quite well. Maybe you will again sometime."

"Yes. Maybe, I will. I remember your offer in the heat of passion," I half-joked.

"It would be nice," he offered as a matter of fact.

"I trusted you, and you did not disappoint. You pushed me to new places there," I conceded.

"It is what a good dom does, pup. They push for a deeper connection and more intense fun." His daddy mode was flexing right now giving me his best-unsolicited insight.

"Well that, it certainly was. No lie."

"You had fun, did you not?" he asked, as his arm tightened around me as if to reassure me my answer was already accepted.

"Absolutely. You were amazing," I said, truthfully.

"I could feel you trusting me more. I am glad. If there is a next time, then maybe I will bring some toys with me."

"Or a couple of friends," I offered with a coy giggle.

What did you say? Did you invite yourself to be gang-banged by the Sir and his friends?
If I am telling the truth, I was not entirely lying. I threw my penny in the Luke pool openly making a wish. This guy had the potential of showing me some great things. I had every intention of giving him my control.
"I have equipment in my car."
"What? Like a lug wrench?" I joked.
"No. *Equipment*." He leered at me until I got it.
"Oh. OH! Okay." It hit me. He came prepared.
We drifted off into a post-coitus nap for over an hour. It was a welcomed refresher. We later woke up in the same position we fell asleep. With him on his back, I snuggled next to Luke, my leg over his, and my arm over his midsection. His one arm wrapped around me from the back. My pair of floor fans kept us cool and relaxed as we slept. The sun had long since put itself to bed.
We riled ourselves awake and took a piss. He grabbed his jeans and slipped them on his thick legs.
"Are you leaving me?" I taunted.
"Nope. Just running out to the Jeep to get something."
"Oh."
"I told you I had gear. I am always ready."
The rest of the night, I realized just how prepared he was.

† John †

Bathhouses are one of the gay's fabulous creations. A place to work out, shower, hang out with other gay men, do some naked hot-tubbing, and not get kicked out for hitting on someone while they were in a towel. That shit did not fly at a regular mainstream gym, but it was an unwritten rule at a bathhouse. The Creek Court Club was just that place. (We often called it the 3C or C^3 because we were dorks like that.) The city government and local cops knew about it. Some police often visited off the clock because even cops need a blowjob. I am not sure if I ever blew a cop there, and I never tried to find out either. I did not typically conduct in-depth interviews before I let my oral skills loose on someone's cock. Thanks to the cooperation of the city it made for a much more peaceful and relaxed place to hang out with other guys. It was always clean, there were few rules, but the ones that existed were quietly enforced. All this resides in a juxtaposition to the bathhouse raids in the seventies and eighties where open rooms and tubs of solid vegetable shortening were around every dusty corner. Those were seedier days. They had their "we can just get a shot to clear this up" charm. To its credit, I never saw a tub of solid vegetable shortening at 3C. Not to say there was not any there at some point but we had to advance as a people, right? The mess factor alone was enough to push those who were selling, and buying, sexual pleasure to invent new mediums to grease a hole.

The 3C had a sauna, steam room, hot tub, showers, locker room, private rooms, a lounge area with a television (sometimes with porn, sometimes with daytime trash talk shows), a computer area, a coffee & tea bar, and a full gym. The cost was minimal to get into the place. One would typically pay a fee to get in, then pay for either a locker, a private room, or one of the two deluxe rooms. The deluxe rooms included a larger bed, more room to move around, and a television and DVD player. It was not a four-star hotel, but it was not motel-turned-crack-house. The caretakers and owners took great strides to keep it in check, clean, and run by the rules. It was worth the "no sex in a public space" rule to be able to spend a few hours walking around in a towel with other men, suck some dick, get sucked or fucked, and sit in the hot tub and solve the world's problems.

This particular afternoon I had my usual spot in the hot tub. I liked to sit on the far side, so my back was facing the wall allowing me to see everyone passing the tub. A good-looking fellow kept cruising by and staring at me then acting like he did not look at all. It is all a cat and mouse game, visual and physical. It is part of the fun in the hunt. The mental part is figuring out who inadvertently caught your eye and who is purposely trying to send out signals. Most times men were as subtle as sunshine in July. While part of me wanted to trail this guy to his room or lead him to mine, the other side of me was relaxed and enjoying the hot tub. Two other guys were in there with me. We were all keeping to ourselves aside from the casual chit-chat that only naked men can maintain. I figured the guy would be somewhere if he still wanted to get together later. Of course, 'later' was defined as fifteen or twenty minutes in the future.

I knew one of the other guys in the tub. Gad and I both frequented the club quite a bit, so our familiarity with each other was based solely on being club mates. We had never played with each other directly, but we had both been part of a larger orgy in one of the deluxe rooms the year prior. We had gotten to know each other on a casual "I did not recognize you without your towel" basis.

"Seems John has the hots for you, buddy," he offered.

"You know him?" I asked, still curious about the no-nonsense guy making his rounds.

"Oh sure, his brother is my boyfriend. I guess you could say he is a pending brother-in-law."

"Wow. So, um...." I was confused. He had a boyfriend and was sitting naked in a hot tub in the middle of a bathhouse. I was not judging, but I was judging.

"It is okay. We have an open relationship. Simple rules. No kissing, only blow jobs or hand jobs, no anal. I do not fuck anyone but him, and vice versa."

"Oh. Well, cool. To each his own."

"It works for both of us. It is just a little side play whenever we want to fill a need," he explained.

"What is John's story?" I wondered.

"He is a great guy, single as a dollar bill. He seems to love being a bachelor. The dude is thirty-two. I have known him for almost twelve years. Not once has he ever thought about settling down with someone. I think he likes his freedom. He is a freak sometimes. We all head down to the Gulf coast with friends almost every summer. John would disappear for hours, or a couple of days, at a time. We had no idea who he was with or what he was doing, but he always came home with a smile on his face. Sometimes my boyfriend and I would wake up in the middle of the night and hear these crazy noises coming from his bedroom in our beach rental."

"How the heck do you sleep after that?" Frankly, I would have stayed up and jerked off or tried to sneak a peek. Not everyone wants to watch their brother-in-law fuck.

"White noise machine. We dragged it everywhere on vacations and did so mostly for that reason. He has had more ass in his time than I have to this point," he offered.

"Well, I am not exactly here looking for a husband either," I retorted. I was open to any possibility, but when you are in a hot tub full of men, marriage is not on your to-do list.

"Dick is easy to get. Marriage is not for everyone. I got tired of the chase, so I finally asked his brother to marry me. Thank God he said yes." He laughed.

"That could have been awkward," I joked.

"You got that right!"

"Not sure a bathhouse is a place to pick out wedding invitations or potentials anyway," I prodded.

"No shit."

"I did not mean to sound like I was judging earlier," I offered. "Just sort of threw me for a second."

"Hey, cool beans, man. No harm, no foul. You are not the first to have that reaction."

"You and John come here together?"

"No. I drop in on my day off sometimes. I use the gym upstairs. It comes out cheaper than any regular gym, especially with the extras. Then, I hang out and see if anything gets my attention. John does his thing. I do mine. The funny part is, once we both leave here, it is likely we will end up in the same place for dinner with my fiancé or hanging out watching a movie."

"Does that get weird?" I was genuinely curious.

"At first, yes. We respect each other's privacy so whatever happens here stays here. If my fiancé asks what I did, I will tell him. I carry no secrets from him. He does not care what his brother does in here."

"Sounds like you guys have a nice system worked out between you." I was puzzled. He seemed accepting of it.

"We do. Not to say we have not all ended up in the same hotel room with a couple of locals down in New Orleans or Mykonos on a summer trip. I figure there is almost never a time not to have some fun. We love playing with others when we can, but I love the one-on-one time with my fiancé the most. We trust each other."

If anything, Gad was verbose and gregarious even naked in a hot tub. It certainly beat the low-tone chatter you usually strain to hear in these kinds of places.

"It is nice that you guys have that worked out for you," I said. "Not everyone can handle an open relationship like that. I have plenty of friends that broke up because of it. The worst part is for the rest of us is that we are almost forced to choose a side when it ends. I would like to think that if I were ever in an open relationship, I could handle the open part of it."

Gad and his fiancé could handle it, but I had yet to test those waters for myself.

"Hey, a little tip about John?" he prompted.

"Sure." I leaned in to catch every bit of Gad's confession.

"Old John boy loves to have his salad tossed, you know what I mean?" he said, stuttering his eyebrows.

"Oh, he is the toss*ee*, not the toss*er*," I joked.

"Every time he talks about a hookup, he talks about how he got the guy to tongue his hole. He can be submissive about that. He is all about the ass. Get your tongue in there, and he is yours for as long as you want."

Not that I had planned on hooking up with your future brother-in-law but thanks for the cheat sheet.

"Sounds fun. I can get with that." I did not mind the idea of eating his butt. John was adorable. He was in his early thirties going on early twenties, easily. He had that grown boyish look about him. Fresh-faced, great body, unashamed. I had seen him shower earlier when he arrived at the club, so I knew he was clean.

"You should. Trust me," Gad pushed.

"I think I might do that. I am turning into a raisin in this thing anyway."

"Good luck, man."

"Thanks, have a good one if I do not see you," I offered, as I got out of the tub.

We were no longer alone as three other men had since joined us in and around the tub. I excused myself, dried off, wrapped my towel around me and headed to my room. I wanted to swap towels, as mine was now wetter than usual. It happened every time. Thank God for the club issuing two bath sheets.

I decided to take a moment to myself to cool down again. The heat from the tub can be a bit much. I took about fifteen minutes to relax on the bed in my private room. I still had more than enough time to play around and could afford the luxury of a nap. I closed my door, laid on the bed and let the air conditioning sweep over my overly steamed and soaked body. For a few moments, I forgot about Gad, John, and how they all knew each other. I set the alarm on my phone and rested my eyes.

∞

I took a swig of the bottled ice tea I had bought from the vending machine, wrapped a fresh towel around my waist, put my elastic keyring around my wrist, locked the door behind me, and went for a walk around the club. I needed to stretch my legs. I still had a couple of hours on my four-hour limit and wanted to make the most of it. Instead of circling near the hot tub again, I did a quick tour upstairs. The lounge and computer area were occupied with a baker's dozen more mostly mature gentlemen talking about whatever, all of them loosely wrapped in towels, or nude. The television was nothing more than white noise in the background. Another guy was making good use of the free coffee and tea bar. I hung out near the entryway for just a few minutes then decided to head back down to the dark places. I enjoyed the downstairs more anyway. It was darker, more mysterious; it just felt sexier. The upstairs had large glass block windows from the building's days as a public business. When 3C took over, no changes were made to the exterior, but the interior got a whole makeover. The afternoon sun lit up the lounge and gym areas, which were adjacent to each other separated only by the computer tables. It could be less than flattering light when looking for dick.

I rounded a corner and took a passing peek through the sauna's glass-windowed door. I saw Gad was holding court with two comrades. They were perched on the built-in cedar benches like naked gangsters, missing only cigars and a bottle of Scotch. It was a great visual, and I chuckled to myself at the thought of it. Next door was the steam room. The steam room was too hot for so many guys, but I enjoyed sweating out the weight and grime of the week. It beat the sauna, for me. It was hard to focus on anyone through the steamy mist and the dim lights. It was nice to sit in a hazy bubble and let the heat wash over my body. My pores thanked me later as I always walked out of the club with that steamed and freshly fucked glow on my skin. It beat a $75 spa facial.

After almost a half-hour in the steam, I decided to make another round in the bowels of the club. I passed the hot tub and saw John again. He was sitting on the ledge talking to the guys in the hot tub. They were enjoying the bubble jets, and John was enjoying the men. He and almost a half-dozen other good-looking men were holding court having the same conversations as the men upstairs. I did want to get with John, so I had to make a big move to get his attention. As I passed him, amid all the conversation, moaning from some distant room, and blaring disco music, I slipped the elastic keyring off my wrist. As I walked by him, I tossed it on the floor. It landed right near his feet. The chink of the metal key on the tile floor caught his attention. He quickly leaned down to grab it for me. I leaned down at the same time. I let him grab the key before I got to it.

"Here ya go, man."

"Hey, thanks."

It was an old move, but it worked every time.

He handed my key to me, and I held onto his hand a moment longer than would have been normal. I leaned near his ear to not be heard by the gaggle of gays in the hot tub. Although they were deep in their conversation, I wanted some level of privacy.

"I am in fifteen if you want your butt eaten."

It seemed to catch him off guard, and rightly so; I was calculating like a viper. (That is what I told myself.)

I winked at him. Then noticed the guys in the tub. The key dropping grabbed all their attention.

"Sorry fellas, just saying hi. I am all thumbs today."

I did not wait for an answer. I put my keyring back on my wrist and made my way to my room at the end of the hall hoping John would soon follow. If Gad was right then my room would quickly be a target-rich environment.

When I arrived, I fiddled around with the stuff on the little table in the room to look busy. The door to room fifteen always had a mind of its own. I do not know if it was the humidity or if it was possessed. I could push the door almost closed, and it would open. Other times I could walk in and leave it open, and it would close itself two-thirds of the way leaving a slight crack for someone to look in my room. I liked this particular room because the square footage was more substantial than other rooms on the ground floor. The rub to getting the bigger room was that fucking door. I never really paid much attention to it. I certainly was not going to start today. My focus was on my faith in John coming to visit me for a while. And unlike the door, John did not disappoint. Only a couple of moments would pass before John darkened the threshold. He stepped inside the door.

"Hey there, John." His face showed I caught him off guard knowing his name before he knew mine.

"Hi, how are you?"

"I am great; please make yourself at home."

He sauntered in a couple of steps.

"Ignore the door. It is sentient."

He seemed perplexed but ignored it.

"You are one hot dude. I saw you looking at me earlier," I said. I was not sure if he was genuinely cruising me, but I figured he was not going to deny it and risk hurting a stranger's feelings. He had taken me up on my invitation.

"Thanks. But how did you know my ..."

He paused to figure out how I had a leg up on him. I could only smile watching his gears turn. I let out a chuckle.

"Fucking Gad," he realized.

"We were chatting in the tub earlier..."

"I knew it."

"Hope you do not mind."

"He is a talker; I will give him that. He is my future brother-in-law."

"He told me. I think he was pimping you out, man. Do not be offended, John. It was all in fun."

"Do you know him?" he asked.

"Not really. Just from coming here. He seems like a good guy. We are not like friends or anything outside of the club. We are club buddies."

"He is funny, and he treats my brother well."

I took a step toward him grabbing his towel at the waist, feeling his treasure trail against the back of my fingers.

"Does anyone treat you right, John?"

"Men have tried," he joked. "But I do alright."

"I had an idea if you are game."

"Sure."

"I want to kiss you and lick your hole." It was one of my bolder moments.

"Oh yeah?" he asked.

I yanked my towel off, and it fell loose around my ankles.

"Yeah, I do."

I pulled him against my body. I initiated the first kiss. I wrapped my hands around his body and grabbed his ass. I reached under his towel and let one of my fingers tease his crack a little bit. It seemed like his whole body came alive. I knew what he felt, having had so many men toy with my hole over the years; a couple even right in room fifteen, my favorite haunt. I loved to bottom, but life is always about fun. I always thought it was too short to be just one thing. I purposely stayed versatile in my life to have as much fun as I could with handsome men like John. He had a perfect little bubble butt. I cupped my hands on either of his cheeks over his towel. I could feel both our dicks getting hard through the terry cloth that separated us. I slid both my forefingers into the crack of his ass. I could feel the bits of hair, the rougher skin, the warmth of him having been in the hot tub. It left his hole damp and supple to the touch. It was inviting to my fingers which continued their trek into an unknown frontier. Every centimeter of his crack that I explored subjugated his moans. His kiss became more passionate, and his body gave into my digital vulgarity.

By the neck, I forcefully pushed him against the wall opposite the wonky door. I focused his face on mine. I want us to be naked and fully engaged. I reached under his dick, between his legs, and my finger found his hole again. His face, still looking at mine, reacted with surprise and anticipation. When I pressed my finger against his hole, I could feel him tighten it up then relax. We were finding a rhythm that suited us. His face cosigned.

"Oh, look at that. I think I found your spot, John."

"You never told me your name," he asked, trying to be casual about being willingly violated.

"You do not need it for what I am going to do to you," I shot back. "We are not going to be having a long conversation, John." The more I directly called him by his name the more I could physically see him become submissive. It was a great turn-on for me. My aggression toward him became equally intoxicating for both of us.

I kissed him again, hard, shoving my tongue into his mouth, and making him suck on it. My hand continued to probe his ass from the front, massaging his hole. I could feel him tensing up, then relaxing, ready for whatever I had in store for him. His dick was a good seven inches, thick, cut, dark blond pubes. For me, that was just the right length and width to be a bottom or a top. He was thin and toned, with damn near no body fat on him. He had a great mix of youth and natural thinness while peppering in an air of maturity to his persona. Any body fat he had was allocated in his bubble butt and his cock.

I grabbed him by the shoulders, and spun him around, shoving him face first into the wall. I held him firmly in place with my hand on the back of his neck. He was not going anywhere. Somewhere during our aggressive making out his towel had left its home around his taut, tanned waist and was on the floor. I spanked his ass with my other hand, hard. He jumped from the unexpected lashing. His whiteness jiggled from the impact. Another slap to his butt forced the surrender a pink handprint.

I leaned into him, my body against his back. My dick lodged between his butt cheeks. I put my mouth near his ear. I wanted to be heard over the dance floor music.

"I heard you enjoy your ass played with, John. Is that true? Do you like your ass toyed with, John?"

I reached down in front of him and grabbed his hard dick, squeezing it in my hand.

"Fuck yeah, I do," he submitted.

"I am not asking permission, either. You have something I want, so I am going to take it."

"I understand, Sir."

"Do you understand fully, John?"

"Yeah. You are going to use my ass all you want, huh?"

I did not feel the need for a Sir moment this time. His willing submission to my anal whims was enough. I had no clue this was going to turn into such a dominant moment. John was very much his own man, except when someone was toying with his hole. But since Gad had described him as such a willing bottom boy, my inner dominant side came roaring out with John.

"Good, because I am not in the mood to get fucked today. Not by you, or anyone." Only partially true. I was almost always down to get fucked at the club. I also kept my options open and went with whatever opportunity at before me. Today, that opportunity was John's perfectly pale and peach-shaped ass.

"You got it," he responded.

"Spread your legs for me." He obeyed. When the threat of his ass being played with became a reality, he turned into another person. I massaged his eager hole, holding him in place by the neck. I leaned into him again and chewed on his exposed ear. He melted where he stood. He let out a huge moan, and I knew I was on the right path. It seemed that John and I both had our ears hardwired to our dicks. It was familiar territory that drove him crazy.

Without warning, I slowly pushed my finger into his hole. His sphincter tightened up around my knuckles. I kept working his hole fighting against the tension. I got one knuckle deep, then two, then all the way. Immediately, I felt his prostate. No matter the guy, the prostate always felt like a solid walnut with a rough yet pliable texture of a marshmallow. It is every man's hot button, and John was no different. I steadily massaged it. He dug his fingernails into the wall. His back arched naturally like a wild animal displaying to potential mates that he was in heat. I was hitting a sweet spot. I knew it, from my own experience, very well.

"Fuck," he moaned out loud.

"I thought you would like that, John," I said into his ear, as I kept kissing the back of his neck.

"That is just one finger. Let us make it two, shall we?" I was working him into a tizzy.

"Yes, please," he begged me. I obliged. I pulled my forefinger out, then slid it back in alongside my middle finger. I stretched his hole a little wider. With my fingers pointing down, I did a reversed "come here" motion inside his hole to continue stroking his prostate. His knees started to buckle. I continued to hold him against the wall by his neck against the wall; although at this point he was not going anywhere. He was my finger puppet and would not be easily detached. I also knew his dick was hard as granite against the wall. The more I massaged his golden nugget, the more he responded. I wanted to take him to the brink and pull him back. I dug into stroking his A-spot with slow and intense gusto. I could have made him cum just like that. I resisted.

I slowly pulled my fingers out of his hole. Keeping my grip on his neck, I guided him toward the bed and shoving him into place.

"Now, get on the bed, John." He moved in quick succession to his spot.

"All fours and spread your legs." He never uttered any word of resistance. I rolled up a towel and put it on the floor next to the bed. I had every desire to eat his ass but none to wreck my knees in a prayerful position. One had to improvise for padding and safety in strange places. A rolled-up towel turned knee pad did the trick.

I parted his ass cheeks looking at his beautiful hole. It was pink then naturally dark, furry, and winking back at me with unfettered anticipation. I smacked his ass a few times. His bubble butt turned darker pink. I massaged around his hole with my thumb, practically making him beg me to infiltrate him. His dick dangled between his legs like a cucumber on a shoestring. I slowly worked my thumb into his hole. It was a different move since most guys would use their fingers. But I liked the angle of this and if his quivering thighs were any sign he had no objections. His moaning was honest and did not feel like he was auditioning for Randy Blue or Falcon. I reached between his legs with my other hand and grabbed his rod. Holy fuck, he was as hard as the innards of a skyscraper. I toyed with his dick, caressing and squeezing it, taking mental notes of the details my fingertips logged. I never jerked his dick or masturbated him properly. It was part of my plan to keep him on edge the whole time we were together. My dick was suffering a bout of rigor from being so dominant. But my focus was on John.

I continued to thumb-fuck his fleecy entryway, licking all around his crack and kissing his cheeks. Watching this misplaced beach bum squirm in front of me kept me motivated to give him more and more.

I pulled my thumb out and proceeded to drive three of my fingers into his hole slowly.

"Oh my god, is that your cock?" he asked.

"Never mind what it is," I came back at him.

"It just feels huge."

"I can stop if you want me to, John."

"No. I mean, ignore it. I will shush. Please! Do what you want. I can take it."

I finger-banged him with three digits, dragging across his prostate every time. I fucked him just like it was a dick. It was keeping me hard. I loved getting men off, and this had gotten my dick's attention.

I pulled my fingers out, and spit on his hole.

"I am about to eat your ass, John. I am going to bury my tongue in your hot hole as long as I want."

He laid his head down on the bed and perked his ass higher with nothing but a groan of approval.

Before he even finished his short declaration, I pulled one of his cheeks back and buried my tongue in his hole, flicking my tongue across his furry pad. His ass was so clean and soft it made eating him out even more enjoyable. The more I ate, the more we both loved it. I licked around his hole and stuck my tongue as far in like it was my mission in life. The tongue fucking came easy. I freed his dick from my grip to let him do whatever he wanted with it. I paid attention to my dick now while being tonsil deep in his beautiful butt. We were both jerking our meat. My cock which was now as hard as the floor beneath me. Neither of us wanted to accelerate our climaxes too soon.

I decided to flip the script.

"Get the fuck up, John," I told him.

"What?"

"Come on," He stood up, dazed and a bit confused about my sudden command.

I laid on the bed on my back, legs spread, dick straight up in the air. "Sit on my face."

"What?"

"Sit on my goddamn face, John." I did not care how he sat on it, as long as he did.

He got up on the bed. With a bit of maneuvering on both our parts, he eventually straddled my mouth. He was facing my body so he could see my raging hard cock. It was a modified sixty-nine position with him being upright instead of sucking my dick.

He gently lowered himself onto my face so I could flick my tongue against his ass. He was not smothering me, but he got close enough that I quickly had my tongue all the way up inside him. His ass squirmed with every puncture of my tongue. His muscular and toned thighs gave gentle squeezes on either side of my head with every vibration of gratification. He was an expert at it. He braced himself with one hand on my chest and stomach while jerking his dick with the other. He forgot he was riding my face and treated it like he was getting fucked by a dick. He was, and had, a great bottom. His ass was a perfect place to spend the afternoon.

A few times he stopped jerking his dick, putting both hands on my hairy chest and just rode me. I felt his dick bounce against my chest. I wanted to fuck him so bad. It only persuaded me more to deprive him of a full-on fuck. I continued to dine on the feast above me. Truth be told I am sure I would not have fought the idea of him jumping on my dick for a while. My dick ached to be touched. A few times he tried to reach down and jerk me off, but I would guide his hands away. I wanted to feel the ache of being so hard and aroused and not being pleased. We shared that common experience. He ached to be fucked, and I hurt to burst in his throat. But that was part of the whole experience. I wanted to make him beg me. I wanted him to writhe in bliss and ask for more. He continued to rub and stroke my chest while riding my tongue. I was relaxed, yet aroused, happy but needy. I do not know how long we were going at it like this but time did not matter anymore. My tongue in his hole quickly became my only focus.

∞

"Roll onto your back," I told him.

Without hesitation, he did as I asked. I put his legs on my shoulders and put my face in between his cheeks. I continued to tongue fuck his fuzzy hole. He tasted so clean and sweet. We spent almost just as long with him on his back and my face in his hole as we had with everything else to this point.

In this position, I was finally able to get to my dick and masturbate. I had to time my strokes and the pressure just right or I would surely cum in a second, thereby ending our bathhouse fun.

Ultimately, I had to cum, or I was going to implode. I grabbed my meat harder while tonguing his hole. I knew I was getting closer.

"I want to watch you cum on me." he half-asked.

I raised my head. "What?"

"I want to see you cum on me, man."

I quickly got up on my knees as if to fuck him.

"Lift your legs. Let me see that hole, John."

He raised his legs and held him in place with his arms. He damn near folded himself in half. His blue eyes pleaded with me to plunge my cock into him. I refused us both that great pleasure in favor of something else.

I jerked my dick a few more times until I could feel the inevitable rush over me. My legs locked up and I aimed my purple-headed monster at his hole. I jerked with all the energy I had left in me until I whitewashed his cheeks. I had not cum so hard from eating a guy's asshole or masturbating. It was the overflowing a man has when a big dick is fucking them for a long time. My spunk slammed into his dick, soared onto his chest and even hit the wall behind him. I did my best, mid-orgasm, to aim it right on his asshole.

I was sweaty and slightly stiff from being on my knees so long. My muscles screamed while I was upright and they were involuntarily constricting around my frame struggling to balance my weight in the midst of painting John's ass. My sauce was everywhere.

"Fuck!" I do not remember who said it.

"Now it is your turn. Keep your legs up, John."

I laid down between his legs and ate my cum out of his ass and off his butt cheeks. I pushed some of it into his hole with my tongue. I was eager to lap up my jizz out of his ass. It found a new sense of excitement from it. I had never eaten my cum out of a man's asshole before so John was a first for me. I could feel my freak level go up a couple of notches. There was something almost overwhelming about a guy making you cum on himself, then sucking your cum off his warm skin. It took me a couple of minutes, but I cleaned up his hole. I had messed his hole then brought it back to the immaculate state that I found it. He was feverishly jerking his dick the entire time I was playing the role of anal housekeeper.

I got up on my knees and rested on my legs folded under me. I took two fingers and sunk them back into John's hole. He started jerking his dick even quicker. He was on edge. He was using some of my rogue spunk as lube.

I dug in further. He rested his legs on my shoulders. He was using me as leverage to hoist his hips upward. I surely added to the sensation by lifting him up from the inside, pressing firmly against his prostate again. Then it came. He was ready to cum.

I felt his legs harden like steel beams. I took it as permission to continue to double-finger fuck him.

He let out a huge groan, which I am sure most of the Creek Court Club heard. His ass tightened up against my fingers clinching with the waves of orgasmic gratification raging through him. He probably was not going to break my fingers with his hole, but for a second it sure felt like it. It was a battle to brace against the natural strength in his legs. He shot buckets of spunk all over his chest, even hitting his face and the wall behind his head as mine had minutes prior. He was baptized in his cum. His muscular body wiggled, pushing out every spark of satisfaction.

Finally, his legs collapsed on either side of me. His chest was flushed red with rushes of blood and spotted with gooey white debris.

I readjusted to sit upright between his legs, his thighs over mine. I rubbed his legs on either side of me. I teased his dick and his body convulsed with rejection, but I overpowered to get in a few more strokes. His laughter burst out with such joyful glee. It was nice to see him happy, living in the moment. He was not getting that kind of attention in the hot tub.

"Stop. Do not touch it!" he begged me. I giggled and chose not to torture his dick any further.

Both of us were still in a daze of afterglow. We enjoyed the silence between us. Neither of us had much to say. The boom-boom of the music pulsated through the club just loud enough to hopefully drown out any moans, gasps, and yelps. I grabbed a towel nearby and wiped my face down knowing I probably still had jizz somewhere on me. I tossed his towel on his chest.

"I think you will need that more than me. I cleaned up mine," jokingly referring to having cleaned his ass with my tongue.

"That was so goddamn hot!"

"Fuck yeah it was. You have one hot ass, John."

He blushed. "Thank you."

I kept my hands on him exploring his body as he tried to wipe his jizz off his chest.

"You never told me your name," he non-asked.

"I do not plan on it either. You have more than enough to remember me."

"Yeah, I guess that is true, huh? But really, what is…" Before he could finish, I hoisted myself up to kiss him. The towel still on his chest and belly, I rested some of my weight on him. His legs bent at the knee to wrap around my thighs. I am sure he was hoping I would tell him my name. I never would.

"Hit the showers, you need it," I said.

He chuckled. "I do. I am a stupid mess."

He stood up, wiped himself down one more time. He balled up the towel in his hand.

"Thank you, again. I will not forget that."

"I am glad, John. It was a lot of fun for both of us."

"Oh shit," he exclaimed.

"What?"

"The door has been open this whole time?!"

I thought we had closed that wonky door. I misjudged that. The door had never fully closed.

"Well, how about that?"

"We probably gave people a fucking peep show," he wondered. I could not tell if he was worried or happy.

"Did it matter?" I asked slyly.

He thought about it for a moment.

"Not one fucking bit."

"It is kind of hot thinking dudes were watching," I confessed. I had not planned on giving a peep show, but I could not change it now.

"They can watch me," he said dismissively. "Maybe they learned something. A lot of the guys in here are lame." He was right in his defiance. "Not you, though," he finished. I appreciated his sincerity.

What shame does a guy have after getting worked over like John just had? It was not like anyone would be shocked to see naked guys in a bathhouse jerking each other off or eating and plundering some ass.

Butt naked with his towel still wadded up in his hand he turned on his heel and started to leave.

"Hey," I called out to him.

He paused and turned around, his dick still slightly erect. I noticed a wad of cum still on his treasure trail.

"Yeah?"

"If anyone asks you what happened in here..."

"Do not worry," he interrupted. "I am a slut, not a gossip."

"No. That is not what I meant," I countered.

"What then?"

"Tell everyone."

The smile on my face was all the affirmation he needed.

With a smirk on his face, he walked down the hallway to the open shower area tossing his towel in a laundry bin just outside my room. If I listened hard enough, I could almost hear him whistle while he walked. I watched his proud strut down the corridor until he disappeared. He had no shame in his body or the fact that he still had splashes of cum on him. Other guys may have wanted him, flirted with him or been rebuffed by him. But today, and maybe only this day, I had had him.

I sat there for a few moments, quite satisfied with myself. I dried off my sweat, made sure my face was cum-free, then got dressed. I stripped my bed and rolled up the linen and my towels. The staff would clean the room for a new customer. It was their job. But I always tried to take the initiative to pull the linens off myself. I dumped them in the bin on top of John's cum soaked towel. I gathered my things and headed home.

As I passed the wide opening to the showers, I saw John standing there under the hot water. His body was still red from our excursion. The water cascaded off his toned surfer body and the track Halogen lighting, set to a dim number two, caught every ripple of his shiny muscled frame. His hair was wet and partially hanging in his face. His blue eyes peeked out from behind the strands of his sun-lightened blond hair. Gad and two other guys were wet under their respective shower heads cleaning up from whatever adventure they had been a part of in the club and sharing anecdotes that only they thought were hysterical. Gad was friendly enough that his shower mates could have easily been strangers five minutes ago. Throughout us getting to know each other at the club, I noted how easily Gad was able to make friends and engage other men. Between the water flowing and the ever-present dance music, I could not hear anything Gad, John, or their buddies were saying. John glanced up and saw me. His body profiled perfectly. His dick sloped downward easily holding no secrets. He nudged Gad with that same smirk on his face. His head jaunted toward me, turning Gad's attention in my direction as if to say "there he is, that is the guy I mentioned." Gad already knew.

He said something to Gad. John smiled while keeping his eyes on me. He grinned at me, and I winked back. He ran his hand over his chest and abs like a titillating goodbye. I kept walking, a smile on my face, dropped my key at the front desk and made my way to my car.

The look on Gad's face was what I exactly wanted when I told John to tell everyone what we had done together. I had no shame.

John surely did not.

No one should.

† David †

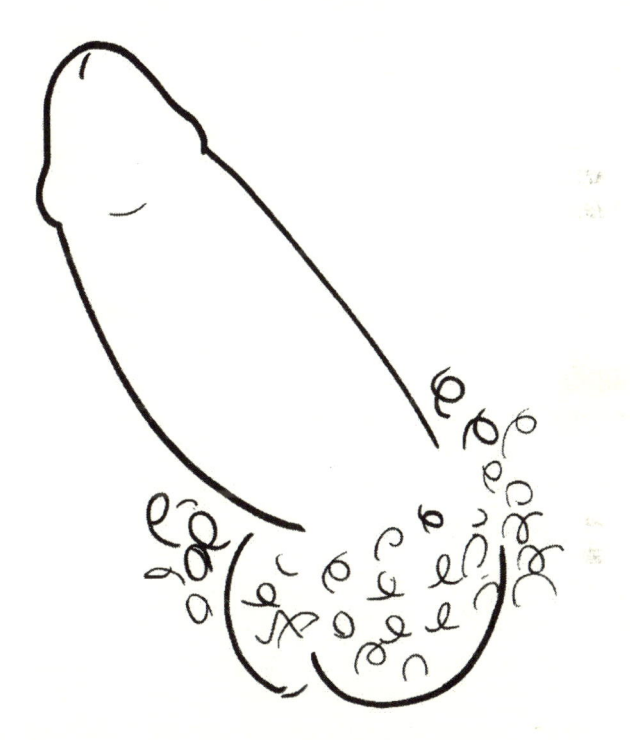

I had been out for most of the evening with friends. I had been drinking, so my buddy Kenan was my designated driver to get home. He was almost double my age and often called me son. Now while many have a fantasy for a daddy-son relationship, but with Kenan, I did not. He was a great pal who was always more than willing to let his young friend ride along, get tipsy and keep him in check. Kenan was in his mid-forties, divorced, drank a bit too much (but not tonight), and had a huge dick. I knew that because he had a faded spot on the front right of all of his jeans from his dick pressing against the denim. It was kind of like how people have that faded ring shape on the back of their jeans pocket from carrying a round tin of dipping tobacco. Even in a new pair of denim pants, the bulge was undeniable. His cock was often in the door before the rest of him.

After everyone disbursed from an hour-long chat in the parking lot after dinner, Kenan dropped me off at my apartment just outside downtown Cottam's Bend. The sun had long gone down, but the late-night news had not queued up just yet. I planned to head upstairs, get comfortable outside of my clothes (which always seemed to be an obstacle to true comfort in humid weather), have a nightcap with myself, then eventually go to bed.

It was such a beautiful night. Summertime was my favorite time. It was warm, people wore very little clothing, and nothing felt like the good old air conditioning on my skin when I arrived home. Tonight, it was no different. It being summertime, even that late, there was still a tiny bit of light in the sky. Dusk was offering its farewells to an otherwise beautiful day. The street lights were waking up for the evening shift, unapologetically looking down with their amber eyes illuminating a path for night people like myself.

My apartment was a little efficiency on the second floor of a building – owned and operated by the business on the ground floor, McGee's a local sewing machine and vacuum cleaner repair shop – which was probably built 100 years before I ever laid eyes on it. Its character and charm were as evident as was its need for repairs. I made the best of my little place, with its original hardwood floors, a bathroom that had no door, and a kitchen that was the size of most bathrooms. It was nothing to write home about, but it was mine.

I walked around from the parking lot to the front of the building. I heard Kenan drive off down the back alley leaving me to my own devices. Pedestrians and automobiles had long deserted the street. For a moment, I wondered if this is what it felt like to be the last man on earth; totally void of not only humans and their noise, but of judgment, strife, and conflict. It was the most peaceful time of the day for me. I stood there on the sidewalk, the dandelions making their quiet proclamations of independence from their cement oppressor next to my sneakers, and wondered what I would do first if I were the last man on earth. Maybe I would take my clothes off and streak naked up and down the road without an eye on me. Perhaps I could sing out of tune as much as I desired and no one winced at my flat or sharp tone. Maybe I could relax and enjoy the silence.

But I was not alone on earth, or even within a hundred feet. A guy meandering at the other end of the building caught my attention. He did not look familiar (nor should he). I presumed he was waiting for someone or otherwise occupied under the ambient street lighting. It was an odd place to wait for someone at this hour but who was I to judge? He was pacing around in his Timberland boots and khaki shorts. A tank top hung from his back pocket. His dark brown skin simmered under the day's last ribbons of light. The humidity, and the amber eyes above us, laid on his skin like the shimmer of a fresh cup of coffee next to a campfire; glowing with a sincere, warm invitation, rippled, and steam rising from the surface.

We noticed each other, and I nodded a general unspoken "how are you doing?" head tilt. He returned the courtesy. I entered the main door and headed upstairs to my little apartment. By the time I was at the top of the stairs at my front door, I had forgotten the dark stranger downstairs. As I pushed the door open to my apartment, the cold rush of air conditioning hit my body. It always seemed to catch me off guard despite me looking forward to it since leaving Kenan's truck. It was like a great friend greeting you every time you come home from your day. My nightstand lamp glowed from the bedroom area across the apartment. I do not know why I always left a light on when I left the house. Mom always did that. Maybe to make people think someone is home and not to rob us. It was a habit I did not consider.

I was sweaty from the humid and warm Oklahoma weather. I closed and locked the door behind me and immediately pulled my shirt off and tossed it on the floor near a pile of laundry.

I need to do laundry tomorrow.

I kicked off my trainers and socks. I enjoyed the cold air on my damp, bare skin. I had one window cooling unit across the room near the bed. Since the apartment was just a large room, the one air conditioner I owned was more than sufficient to turn the place into a virtual deep freeze. It was a necessity in Oklahoma summers. Even though the kitchen and bathroom were partially walled off, the cold air somehow found its way to invade those places. I did not usually leave the air on while I was not home. Tonight, I just wanted it to be cool after dinner. The utilities were included in the rent, so I indulged at the landlord's expense.

I clicked on a lamp over the couch on its lowest dimmer setting. I tapped on my iPod to shuffle whatever through my Bluetooth speakers. I headed to the kitchen and raided the fridge for a beer. I needed to shower before bed to wash off the Kenan's cigarette smoke and the restaurant's aroma. I turned on the hot water in the shower stall. It was an old building, and the water would take a short eternity to run hot enough. I knew once I got comfortable in my chair I was going to be down for the evening. I paced around the apartment enjoying the music playing shaking my bare ass as the beat dictated. I hustled my way to the front of the air conditioner to get some cold air on my tits. I looked out the window down to the street. I guess the stranger found his ride home. I did not see him anywhere.

I made my way to a hot shower and took my beer with me. I was under the water long enough that I made it almost all the way through my lager. I stood there naked under the water, my head bent forward almost like a prayer and let the day wash off of me. I soaped up and got as clean as I could, giving my dick a few extra swipes with a soapy hand. I was never one to jerk off in the shower, but I did pay more than enough attention to my cock while under the hot water. You never know when the urge would hit to get on an app and find a hookup for the night. One has to prepare for these things since guys seem to show up at your door wanting to fuck you. In the future world we now lived in, a piece of ass is never far away. I got the soap up between my ass cheeks and made sure my hole was clean, too. Pits, check. Dick, check. Ass, check. The rest, check. I kept my beer on a shelf at the other end of the shower and took the occasional swallow in between soaping and rinsing.

Eventually, my beer was gone, and my shower was finished. I got out, patted myself mostly dry and hoisted the towel over its rack.

I took myself to the kitchen and traded a now-empty beer bottle for one that was full. I had a half-dozen in there yet to be opened and guzzled. I did not plan to go through all of them tonight.

Damn, this is good stuff. Buy local.

Creeeaak. BANG!

I felt the floor shake a bit under my bare feet. It was the door downstairs. Someone was coming or going from the building. I listened for a minute but did not hear footsteps. Despite the wood and plaster walls, the building was still very audible at times. The insulation consisted of the concrete, stucco, and paint. It could stand another hundred years, but unless someone refurbished the place, it would forever be noisy.

I fumbled through my fridge considering a snack or something that was not too heavy before heading to bed. I did not find anything that suited me, so I grabbed a beer. I was off tomorrow, so it was the adult thing to do.

I plopped my self in my chair, legs apart to air out the bits, and leaned my head back. The cold air felt welcome on my naked body. I sat in the peacefulness of my little flat, the music playing whatever mix at a low enough volume, so I did not feel like I was suddenly jarred awake while trying to wind down for the night. A shower and a beer are all it took, that night, to relax me. I closed my eyes and let my mind go blank.

KNOCK! KNOCK!

The guy across the hall, a gay guy who went by Shadrach and could put any drag queen's runway strut to shame sometimes, apparently had company.

KNOCK! KNOCK!

Maybe he was out for the evening, too. The knocking continued which made me think whoever was out there was not getting the point.

Shadrach is not in his apartment right now. Please stop knocking on his fucking door.

I needed another beer.

I got up, dick swinging, and shuffled to the fridge. I tossed my empty bottle in the recycle bin on the way. Just as I closed the door to the refrigerator, the knock was suddenly louder; it was at my door.

Who the hell is that? Is it Kenan? Did he forget something? No way, he had not even come in with me when he dropped me off a half-hour ago. Well shit. Should I get dressed? I should get some clothes. It cannot be a salesman or a nun, right? Do Mormons or Jehovah's Witnesses do missionary work this late? Girl Scout cookies?

I decided against getting fully dressed. Why bother? I mean, who could it be this late? It was my house, and I did not necessarily have to dress up to answer the door. I jumped in my mesh shorts and aimed for the source.

New beer still in hand, I opened the door.

It was him. It was the guy from downstairs. I did not know this guy from a can of paint. He did not look threatening or crazy, but I had no idea what he wanted.

"Hey there."

"Hey, what is up?" I asked. God knows what we looked like standing there; me still dewy from my shower, holding a beer, sporting a pair of shorts that were probably revealing more than I bargained for when I bought them; him inherently dewy from being out in the hot, humid air meandering around the building.

"Sorry, man. Have you seen Shadrach tonight?"

What, was I his secretary?

"No, not since yesterday. I have been out, so who knows."

Shadrach and I had met up at the mailbox yesterday and talked for a few minutes. I had not heard a peep out of him today, though. Me telling the stranger where I had been all evening was probably more information that he was bargaining for right now.

"Oh..." he trailed off for a minute.

"Sorry, man."

I figured that would be the end of it. I started to close the door and get back to my relaxing.

He continued. "What is your name?"

I told him.

"I am David."

"Cool, nice to meet you, David. Sorry but I do not know where Shadrach is tonight."

"Hey, it is cool. Maybe should have called him first."

"I guess so," I offered, a bit at a loss for words.

"Well, thanks. Sorry to bother you," he almost apologized.

"It is alright, man. Have a good…" I did not get to finish.
"Hey man…" he half-heartedly said.
"Yeah?" I took a swig of beer.
"You gay?" he asked.
His prodding caught me off guard. It was a bold move on his part. What if I was not gay? I wondered if he went to random guy's homes and asked them if they were homosexual or not. There is cruising then there is flat out being nosey. Maybe he was on a mission. Did he want to hang at Shadrach's house or was it an excuse to get to my door? I felt the latter was the more significant possibility or maybe I ended up being a backup plan. David was just a few inches shorter than me. He had on those shorts, and his undershirt was still hanging out of his back pocket. He was clean, trim, solidly built. His skin was still slightly shimmering from the humidity. It was dark brown and beautiful. His darker nipples stood like guards on the front of his muscular chest. His abs were making a greeting of their own, and his shorts had been pulled down just enough to show off his hip-flexors and the first two inches of his boxers. None of that was a mistake, I am sure. He wanted to be seen.

I gulped almost feeling like I was being interrogated although I know I was not.

"Yeah, I am. Why? Do I look gay?" I took a bigger swig of my beer. I figured I could hide my awkwardness with some sass. The beer was just liquid courage.

"Sort of…" he offered.

Did this guy just say I looked…

The twitch of my head must have brought his eventual punchline to the forefront much sooner than expected because I thought he had not come to my door to pass down some social sentence of impropriety.

"Just kidding. But yeah, you cute as fuck, bro." I was a bro now. I had been a bro with Mark, but I knew him. I did not know this guy from a hole in the wall.

"Oh, you got jokes, too, huh? You taking a survey of gay dudes in the area or something?" The beer was loosening me up, and I felt my improvisational comedy skills soaring. I also felt my guard dropping with this guy.

"Yeah, I guess I am." he chuckled while glancing down at his dark chest running his long fingers down his overtly flexed abs. Was this guy flirting with me? I had deduced he was not there to sell a box of cookies or get me to buy magazines subscriptions.

There was a pregnant pause. He looked at me in some way that riled me. He was confident, but not cocky. I smirked at him not only giving him a sign that he was cute but that I knew what he was trying to do. He was going to have to work for it. It would be foolish not to consider inviting this beautiful guy into my house or my bed. But could I be a fool for doing so? Debating the conundrum's pros and cons was a luxury I did not have while standing there. We were working in milliseconds, not hours or days.

"Too bad Shadrach is not home, huh" he offered in small talk, still trying to be slick. My neighbor's absence seemed to be his jumping point for a conversation.

"Yeah, I have no idea what he is up to sometimes."

"He is crazy, man." He would know better than me.

"He is a nice guy, though," I offered. "He is a good neighbor to have around here."

"Sorry I asked if you were gay. I guess I am just nosey."

"I get it, man," I relieved him of his game.

"You two ever..."

"Oh, God, no," I gently barked back. Shadrach was a stitch to hang around, and he was a kind person. To think about sleeping with him just was not on my radar. We maintained an unpretentious friendship. We were the two gay watchmen or gatekeepers at the top of the stairs. One black, one white, both gayer than a holiday parade.

This was one of those moments where your brain runs formulas for about twenty scenarios, answers, possible outcomes, and overall situations.

"Have you?" I was suddenly dead curious.

He paused for a minute, and his face sent the affirmative that I sought.

"Hey, forget I asked. Not my business, man." I saved him from having to admit anything out loud. Since they were probably friends with benefits, it was no surprise who the top was and who played the role of the bottom. If tonight went right, I knew I would be sitting in Shadrach's proverbial chair. It was not a bad idea.

I had a decision to make, and quickly. After all, I was standing in my doorway, barely dressed, yakking it up with a guy who was marginally dressed more than me and only because he was wearing shoes. It was actually out of character for me, but I decided on our rapidly intertwining fates. Instead of gossiping about the neighbors I should go for it.

"Hey, how about you come inside? Maybe Shadrach will show up soon. You can wait here."

I knew Shadrach was probably out with friends for a while or just elsewhere for the evening. He often went out for what seemed days at a time.

"Sweet. Thanks, man. You alright," he affirmed, tapping my bare chest with the back of his hand as he came into my little abode.

"No problem," I said as I closed the door behind him and locked it. "It is way too warm out there to just be hanging out like that. How long have you been out there? Were you waiting on Shadrach?"

"Yeah, for a while. I was supposed to hang out with him then get a ride home. Not sure what the fuck he is doing."

"You look like you have been out there for a minute," I said, hoping he would pick up the subtle flirt. I had no answer for him regarding his friend and my neighbor. I suspect his exasperation was equally feigned and genuine. I was in no condition to drive a vehicle even if he did need a ride home. And he was tired of waiting around for his friend to come back. Maybe I was a last-minute backup plan for him.

Then it hit me.

What the hell am I doing? I do not know this guy from Adam, and now he is in my apartment.

I had surely just lost my mind. I had done worse in life, but this was up there with some of the more random shit I had pulled out of my gay hat. My freshly washed dick was thinking for me.

"You want a beer or something, David?" I offered.

"I would love one, thanks."

"Have a seat, hang out," I motioned him to the couch. I walked into the kitchen to get him a beer still totally questioning what I was doing. It was a bit strange inviting a stranger in my house, yet the danger of it was proving to be equally exciting.

I handed him his beer, and he took the first drink of it.

"Thanks again," he said.

He had found a seat on the couch, just left of center, and I sat opposite him. It was close enough that I could smell him. He had a gentle male musk about him. With the lamp gently beaming down on us from behind the couch, his brown skin practically glowed under the warm incandescent light like the hardened top to a crème brûlée. We talked about whatever - sports, music, guys, our families, even about Shadrach – also making smart remarks with light sexual innuendo. It was enough to break the ice between us. We were sitting just close enough that our hands touched when we were making jokes or laughing. David was engaging, sexy, smart, and had a forward air of confidence. It is always a delicate balance between confidence and vanity. So far, he was doing just fine. I kept my body turned toward him to let him know I was open to him and interested. Despite wanting to jump on him and kiss him, I was enjoying our conversation. Hookups rarely possess a preamble beyond a contrived interest in the other's apartment or something equally arbitrary and pointless.

An hour would pass between us, and we would get through most of the other beers in the fridge.

"Beer should be cheaper because you do just rent that shit," I announced as I got up to go to the bathroom.

He laughed. "I hear you, man."

I got about to the doorway of the kitchen, stopped and turned on my heel.

"I need to piss. How about you meet me in the bedroom? I will see you there." As if the bedroom was a whole separate area he would have to search out on his own. It was not, but it sounded nicer than "can you meet me twelve feet to your right?".

"Hey, I am down," he answered without hesitation. Something about his willingness and confidence to approach a stranger, as he did with me, had entirely captivated me this evening.

"Right through there," I pointed to the bed, humoring only myself. It was the only bed I owned. I do not know if he got the joke. He certainly did not laugh.

I pissed, washed my hands, and headed to the bed. When I came back around the corner, he was laying on my bed. He had his shorts on, top snap unfastened. He had long since kicked off his boots during our couch talk. He was leaning back on his elbows. His abs were naturally tensed and making themselves known again as they had through our whole time on the couch. It became a chore to keep my eyes on his eyes and not on his beautiful body. But now, there he was in all his dark-skinned glory. His swagger was in fifth gear.

God, he is so beautiful.

"Come over here. Let me look at you."

I walked to the side of the bed and started to get on the bed figuring he wanted me to join him.

"Stop. Let me see you."

What?

What was I supposed to do? Spin around like a prom girl in a new gown? We had just sat and talked for an hour – all that conversation while I was still in just shorts. Had he not examined me enough? Somehow, I felt a terrible smirk crawl onto my face. I was trying but failing amazingly to be coy about the whole thing.

"Take off your shorts, slowly," he said. I was in no position to argue. "And look at me while you do it."

I backed up a couple of feet and locked eyes with him. I put my thumbs down inside the front of my shorts and pulled them away from my waist. Technically, I was exposed but from his angle, but he could not see anything. I was going commando so there would be no second act to this impromptu striptease. I had to milk it. The music playing throughout the room became my muse. I used one thumb to lightly pull down my shorts in the middle and expose my pubic hair. I swung myself around, feet apart, and lowered my shorts to reveal half of my hindquarters. I wiggled my ass and gently pulled my shorts back up to hide my giggling buttocks. I turned back to face him. My shorts were failing in hiding my now growing erect dick. I pulled the shorts down all the way around, exposing my pubes and my part of my ass. I turned away from him again bending over and slowly raking my shorts down my legs. I stepped out of them and grabbed them with one hand. I let him drink in my bare ass for a minute. I put the shorts in front of my groin and turned back around to face him. I was fully naked and exposed all but for the shorts in my hand hiding my cock from view. I let go of the shorts and let them hang on my dick, hoping to God the trick would work. It did.

"Drop the shorts, man. I want to see all of you."

I decided to be bold.

"How about you lose your shorts, first?"

"Nah, man. Drop your shit." He is in my house, right? Fuck it. I will play this game.

I fastened my stare to his and slowly raised the shorts off my hard cock moving my free arm in place as a barrier. I was teasing him. He sat up on the edge of the bed for a better view. I gyrated my body, moving closer to him, as I pressed the shorts against my chest and slowly rubbed them down between my pecs, down my treasure trail, my pubes and eventually hung them over my dick again. I put my arms behind my head as if expecting to be frisked. My naked body was right in front of him. He was enjoying the show. To even my amazement, my dick felt like it was still getting harder and harder. He had not touched me yet, and I was already rigid. I glanced down at the shorts, then back to him, back to my shorts, back to his eyes. He was practically salivating. He grabbed my dick through the shorts and pulled the shorts off of me dropping them to the floor. I kicked them across the room sacrificing any last-ditch relief from being embarrassed and naked in front of him. I wanted to be vulnerable and without an exit. I could not reach for cover even if I needed it. My heart was pounding. He could see I was nervous. I think he liked that even more. He licked his lips like he was ready to devour me. I thought he was going to suck my dick right where I stood.

"Turn around," he commanded. I obliged.

My beefy white butt was right in front of him, and I could not see what he was going to do.

SLAP!

I jumped.

"Damn boy, that is a fine ass you got. You going let me hit that?" he asked, continuing to caress it. His hands were warm and dry. Soft yet strong.

I reached around and grabbed both my ass cheeks with either hand, clawing at them.

"You want this, huh," I said trying to entice him.

He just rubbed my ass for a minute. He was firm, and gentle at the same time. He stood up behind me pulling my back against his bare chest. He still had his shorts on, and I could feel his thick dick against my butt cheeks. His shorts and boxers were the only things that separated our bodies. He grabbed me by the waist and started to grind his crotch into my ass getting himself worked up even more. His arms wrapped around my waist and torso from behind, hugging me.

He whispered into my ear. "Yeah, I am going to tear your shit up, boy. You think you can take it?"

"I was going to ask you the same thing."

"I got a big dick. You not going to cry, are you?"

"Are you going to stop if I do?" I asked.

He knew I was toying with him as much as he was with me. We had an understanding now.

"Fuck no!" He reached around and slapped my ass harder. He could see the rush of pain and joy on my face. His hands made their way to the small of my back, and he pulled me against him. His dick was earnest and unrelenting. At some point, in the very near future, it was going to be in me.

With one hand, he grabbed the back of my neck and kissed me. He had those firm, but slightly puffy lips that you could get lost in for days. His tongue invaded my mouth. His taste was intoxicating. We both had beer on our breath. His fingers spread out across the back of my head and then closed in to grab my hair.

"Take my clothes off," he commanded. As I reached down to unbutton his shorts, he pushed down on my shoulders as to guide me to my knees. With both fists, I grabbed his shorts, and underwear, and yanked them down to his ankles. His huge, black dick bounced out ready for battle.

He grabbed the base of his dick and slapped it against my face. He was teasing me more. I needed to suck him.

"Take this dick and suck it," he said, guiding it right to the edge of my mouth. He was full of instructions tonight.

I grabbed his dick with one hand...

"No. I did not say touch it. I said suck it." He had firm ideas about how he liked to start the ball rolling. I rested my hands on his thighs. I opened my mouth, and he put the huge head of his dick in my mouth. It was monstrous, and I was not sure I could handle it.

I glanced up at him and saw the stern look on his face. He wanted his dick sucked, so I was trying to do just that. While still trying to maintain eye to eye contact he fed his dick in and out of my mouth, little by little. I sucked on it and played with it a bit. He moved his hips around in reaction. I took more of his massive meat. It was a solid nine inches of pure dick. I was determined to swallow as much of it as possible.

He pulled his hips back and yanked his dick out of my mouth. His hands were on the top of my head, holding me in place, as he waved his dick from side to side, slapping me with it. It was what both of us wanted. I would try and catch it in my mouth, but he was toying with me. He wanted me to beg for it; to work for it.

"Please let me suck your dick. Let me lick it." He stopped mid-swing, aimed it at my open mouth, and shoved it in, pulling my head toward his groin. Fuck, it was nine inches, because I almost immediately gagged on such a full complement. He pulled it out then shoved about half of it back. I continued to suck his cock as much as possible. It was like no other cock I had had in my mouth. There was little room for tongue movement or to even close my lips around it. He kept his grip firm on my head and kept face fucking me for a while. My dick was so hard through it all. I was straddling nothing on the floor but air. I was fantasizing about him fucking me. Would he

shove it in me? Or would he take it easy? Should I ride him? Should I get on my back and let him hover over me?
Gheezus, stop overthinking. Just suck his dick. This is not rocket science.
After a time of enjoying his dick in my mouth, I started to get to my feet. He tried to keep me in place, but I grabbed his forearms, and not only moved his arms away from my head but used them as leverage to stand.
"Why you stop?"
I did not answer. With both my hands, I forcefully pushed him back on the bed. His dick, glistening with my spit, bobbed up and down like a soldier saluting the crowd. I crawled up to him, and settled my crotch over his, our dicks fighting for dominance. I rested my hands on his chest and started to grind my dick against his. He did not say a word, but I knew he was enjoying it. I leaned into kissing him, and he initially resisted. What – he did not kiss after I sucked his dick? I do not think so. I wanted to experience every part of this god in my bed.
With one hand, I grabbed his jaw. "If you want that, you are going to give me some of this."
He eventually relented, and we locked lips again. The more I kissed him, the more he ultimately kissed back. He liked it. Any protest escaped him.
I suddenly felt his hands on my hips again, and we caught the same rhythm, grinding our bodies together. His hard chest and flat abs against my somewhat normal pasty white body felt amazing. He seemed to like my body as much as I was enjoying his. I ran my hands all over his muscled arms as they flexed while letting my mouth explore his nipples or lick the ridges of his six-pack abs. He loved me worshipping his body. In the dim glow of the nightstand's lamp, I was hypnotized by his sublime shadowy sheath laid against my chalky surface.
"I need to fuck you," he announced.
I thought we covered that already.

"Yeah?" I inquired.

Before I knew what he was doing, he had grabbed me and flipped me on my back. I know the missionary position is boring for some people, but I love it. I like to see a guy hovering over me, in control, with me being a toy at his whim while he is deep inside me.

He grabbed my legs and raised them. I rested them on his shoulders. His hand grazed my rock-hard dick attempting to play with it.

"Do not touch it," I begged him. "Just use me."

I reached over to grab the lube on my nightstand and handed it to him.

"I am going to fuck the cum right out of you," he confidently declared.

"If you think you can," I challenged. David's head seemed to tick. Did he accept the challenge?

I leaned over to turn off the nightstand lamp.

"No. I want to see you," he said. I left the lamp untouched.

He squirted lube on his dick. I reached down to get his dick ready. He poured more into his hand and made sure my hole was wet.

He looked down, and as he grabbed his dick that he was so proud of (and who would not be?), he pushed the head against my hole.

Shit, here we go. That thing is going inside me. Even if it hurts, stay cool.

I was so horny and ready but still tight. David pulled back and re-centered himself. He got his body closer to mine and his big fucking purple head of a dick against my hole.

"Do not fucking cry like a bitch, you hear?"

For a split second, I wondered if he often made grown men cry. Was his big dick just a bit too much for most of his partners? Maybe he was just tired of hearing people say "Oh shit, too much, slow down" or worse.

"Bring what you got, son," I countered. But really, all I could do is look at him and wait. He pushed it in a bit more, and I flinched. My hands pushed against his chest as if to slow him. He paid no attention to my signals. Inch by inch, he pushed inside me without apology.

"Ahh!" I could not help it. It was a bit too fast, too soon. He leaned his body down against mine. My legs fell into the insides of his elbows, his chest flat against mine. His legs adjusted to compensate. One of his arms rested on the bed right next to my head. His other hand was now firmly over my mouth.

"I said do not cry. I told you I am going to tear this shit up, you hear? Do not be a pussy."

I knew he was serious. He was an alpha, and it was showing. I wanted to get through the pain to the goodness that I knew was mere inches away. I wanted him to force his way into me. I knew the pain would be temporary and the rest would be incredible. I wanted him to hurt me a bit. I wanted him to force himself on me, and into me. Eventually, I knew my hole would relax enough for both of us to slip into our own private Promised Land.

He looked at me, his hand over my mouth, and slowly worked his cock in and out of my tight ass. My legs would tense up a bit when he would push all the way inside me. He loved it. He liked knowing I wanted his dick as much as it hurt. And fuck did it hurt. The pain lasted for a few minutes, and I did not want to be a pansy ass about it. Or as Luke so elegantly put it, I did not want to be a pussy faggot. I endured and went on while he started his fucking. Eventually, his hands went elsewhere freeing my mouth from its temporary purgatory, but he was still very much in control. My hole gradually relaxed and opened up for him. I gave myself to him without hesitation. He found a rhythm that was neither too fast or too slow. It was aggressive enough to maintain a seamless intensity.

He raised back up, grabbed my ankles, held my legs high and like a fucking jackhammer, and pounded my white boy hole. He was a fucking machine. His body would harden with every push. I had not seen a guy fuck with such concentration since Mark. I dare not tell him, but I think David was beating Mark's intensity. David's attention was explicit and focused on fucking me. At first, I was in awe of his prowess to get to it so quickly and smoothly. He worked hard from the first push. He had confidence in knowing what he wanted which then allowed me to give it to him willingly. His hips pivoted forward, back and forward again with his upper body barely moving. His core strength was more massive than I had ever judged before now. He liked to work, and he liked to fuck; one went in tandem with the other. The sweaty quickly oozed from his cocoa skin accentuating every hard curve of his muscles; the dim light offering just enough pictorial echo to make him insatiable. You could not get this sort of lighting in Hollywood. Frankly, you could not get this sort of fucking either. David was not out to prove himself or make a statement. He knew who he was and what he wanted. Confidence is sexy.

After almost an hour of pure unadulterated fucking, he took a pause. Both of us were almost out of breath. Our dicks were as rigid as when we started and neither of us was anywhere near cumming.

"Hey man, let me shower? I need to cool down a bit." He was working so hard that even the air unit not far from us was not enough for him to stay cool.

"Sure. Go ahead." I replied. I let my legs fall to the bed. They tingled from finally relaxing. My body was covered with my sweat. He used the bathroom, and I heard him start the shower. I wanted to join him, but he had worked me up and down, side to side. I needed a minute to be sure I could still walk under my own power.

Almost immediately he appeared from around the corner. He was naked, partially hard, and wet. A real vision of manhood.

"You coming with me?"

"In a sec..."

I took a few deeper breaths and staggered to the bathroom joining him in the shower. We enjoyed the tepid water against our skin. I was glad to rinse off and be in any position other than on my back. It was a nice break. We took turns washing each other slowly, keeping the sensuality between us. We kissed between washing. Neither of our dicks had returned entirely to flaccid.

"You are not finished," I said.

"Oh, you want some more of this, huh?"

"I am not going anywhere," I retorted. "I live here, after all." I was half-fucked and still sarcastic. I pulled his wet body to mine and kissed him. I reached down and grabbed his ass and gave it a friendly squeeze. Damn, even his ass was hard. He never asked, but I would have let him sit on my face for a while.

"Mmm, nice ass you got there, Bubba."

"Thanks, baby," he said as he kissed me. We kissed deeply with the water trailing over us. I was hard again, and after a minute I realized he was, too. A couple of his fingers wandered their way to my hole and massaged my brown eye, teasing it to open for him.

"Your fucking hole is still tight, baby."

"You sound surprised," I said trying to be coy again. I clinched a bit to keep his fingers from invading me. The lockout did not last long. He continued to massage and prod my hole. He got a good thrill attempting to invade it with whatever method was available to him. His digits eventually found their way in as he shoved them inside me. I let out a guttural moan that echoed off the tiles in the shower. My ass had slowly, and naturally, started to tighten throughout our time in the shower. He was keeping it agape and ripe for another ingress while methodically finger fucking me with however many he had in me. It was driving me crazy standing there.

"You want some more of this dick?"

He wanted me to beg him to fuck me again. Even in the midst of the intermission shower, he was working my hole. I figured it was a given since neither of us had cum yet. What is the use of a good pounding if there is no happy ending? I wanted some more of his thick, brown, meaty piece of manhood inside me. I would be a fool to send him home now.

"You got some more to give me?"

"Fuck yeah, I do."

"I want you to fuck the cum out of me. You said you could, right?" I challenged him.

He had big words to live up to right now.

"Fuck. Yeah, I guess I did," he said, reminding himself of his promise from earlier. He was on notice.

∞

Just as I got to the foot of the bed, he told me to stop. He was staring at my ass again. I was already ahead of him. I slowly bent over, putting one leg up on the bed, hiked my ass up a bit to expose my hole, and jiggled my butt. Then I pulled myself up on the bed with my other leg. I was doggy style, ass up, right on the edge of the bed. I knew I was exposed because I could feel the cold air hitting my hole. Such an interesting sensation.

"Come get it, big man." I craved for his black cock in me.

He walked up to me. Without missing a beat shoved his dick inside me.

"AH! MOTHER OF GOD!" I screamed. "Just fuck me!" Even in the midst of my second ration of being pounded my mind made a note.

He still smells great after the shower.

My exclamation was all the motivation he needed to ensure his penile aggression would endure. He grabbed my hips and pounded my hairy gorge. Stroke after stroke, thrust after thrust, it was better and better. My dick was rock hard and bouncing against my belly under me. I shifted my body in tempo to push back against his dick when he pushed forward. As big as it was, I could have taken it all night. Using every position known to mankind, we easily fucked away another hour.

∞

I was finally on top of him, riding him. It was a perfect position. I could see his hard, beautiful body relaxing and heaving at the same time. I could also control just how much of his dick went inside me. I have to be honest, at this point, I was still letting him go balls deep. I gladly bounced up and down on his dick. I arched my back, leaned on his legs behind me, and let him pound me. His thrusting got faster as did my ricochet. His cock was rubbing my prostate through the whole experience. I knew the moment was on its way like the four horsemen of the apocalypse except now there was a mysterious fifth horseman: ecstasy. I started to feel the tingle. You know – *that* tingle. That tingle when you know you are getting close to that point of no return.

"Oh, baby, do not stop fucking me. Just like that. Goddamn, that feels so fucking good."

I knew I would cum if we kept our momentum as it was; he knew it too. He wanted a notch in his proverbial headboard of making another dude cum by his fucking. He loved the idea of fucking the cum out of me. He did say he was going to do it and I was holding him to that promise of sexual perfection.

My back was arched, my chest elongated, and my dick bouncing up and down between us. The more he fucked me, the closer I got to never coming back. I wanted so badly to reach down and jerk myself to completion. I ached to release all my spunk. My body screamed with joy and my balls begged for relief. It took everything I had not only to maintain the right position of his cock ramming into me but do not touch my dick. It was screaming for more attention. I resisted that urge in favor of something better to come very soon. My thighs were already quivering from the mini-orgasms running through me. Every push of his dick kept them coming.

Just a few more minutes…. oh my fuck…

"Come on, motherfucker. Come on!" he said, reading my body language. He was close, too. He was hard and fast, concentrating on my body. I squeezed my ass to wrap around his dick even tighter. The momentum was almost too much for a physical body to handle. I thought I might pass out right there. I just had to let go and let it happen. I could not save it anymore. He was about to fuck the cum out of me, a moment I longed for eternally.

"Shoot on me, boy! Give me what you got!" he ordered. Now I felt obligated. I was here to please.

Then it happened. The rush started with my legs tightening up; my breathing got faster. I could not see anything. My head started to get light. I let out a huge roar that, even to me, did not sound entirely human. I am sure the whole building heard us, but I did not care. An even bigger ball of energy shot through me. I had no idea what was happening until I looked down and saw I was cumming. I was cumming so quickly and in significant quantities. My body had moved to a new plane of sexuality; I had reached a new plateau of utter bliss. I was cumming without touching my cock. White, hot, creamy streams shot over his magnificent ebony body like fireworks. There was no rhyme or reason to their trajectory or their landings other than it was what we both wanted to happen. My thighs quivered more, and I felt no pain, no regret; only pure joy. But I was not nearly done before he announced with a force I had not heard yet from him. His fucking was at its fiercest – keeping my near-eternal orgasm alive - and about to culminate inside my tight and well-used hole.

"I am going to spit in you!" he yelled.

I could only utter noises to endorse his carnal oath. I screamed as I was still squirting cum. My body shook uncontrollably with a full body orgasm.

He let loose.

His hands gripped my thighs with all the strength he had in him. I felt him cumming inside me. Every pulse of his dick was as evident as his first assault inside my hole hours ago. His cum consolidated inside me. It was not the first time I would feel that sensation, but it was a formidable moment. I continued to ride his dick. I wanted to milk every bit of him into me. I was on auto-pilot riding him while the energy of my orgasms pulsed through my body. I slowly started to regain control of myself, but the frenzy of orgasmic waves was to continue their presence for a time.

Our rhythm of give-and-take, our synchronized in-and-out - still in concert - slowed. We both twitched from the aftershock. I wanted him to stay in me forever. I milked his dick as best I could manage. He shuddered from being over-sensitive right after cumming, but I did not let up from riding him. I held him in place and getting every last drop. Every nerve ending in my body was alive and pulsating. My heart was beating out of my chest, and my eyes were blurred. He reached up aggressively caressing my chest which only sent more chills through my body.

I was afraid to move. The energy between us was so beautiful and real that I felt any counter-movement would only diminish it. He remained inside me. I could feel his hands rubbing my chest or thighs. My hands were still resting on his legs behind me. I found it within myself to swing one arm around toward him. He pulled me forward a bit to break me out of my near-frozen position. I felt so free and perfect that moving ruined it.

I opened my eyes and tried to focus on him. I looked down at both of us dripping with sweat, trying to catch our breath, wondering what to do next. His face was one of pure satisfaction, as I am sure mine was, too. He looked down at his chest, and his abs naturally flexed. I was shocked at how much jizz I had deposited on his body. I still had not touched my dick. It was up and down and not sure where it was going. The feels I had were more than just on my dick. I decided that I could not feel any embarrassment at how much cum he had fucked out of me. He kept his word, after all.

"Shit!" he said.

"You fucked it out of me," I told him in between still heavy breathing. We were both charmed by our production. "You were insane."

"You made a pretty mess," he admitted.

"It was some of my best work yet," I lamely joked.

We both surveyed the damage. I squeezed the inside of my hole against his dick still inside me.

With two of his fingers, he wiped some of the spunk from his chest down to his abs and put his fingers in my mouth. I dutifully sucked my nut off his paw. A few more swipes maintained the feeding.

I slowly pulled my ass away from his dick, still partially hard. I leaned down to feast on the remaining debris left on his chest. I licked my nut off his nipples, his firm pecs, his incredible abs; anywhere I came on him. Voraciously, I took it back into my mouth without humiliation. This

was something he had not bargained for but was enjoying, as evidenced by the look on his face. He put his hand on the back of my sweaty head and gently guided my head around to get every possible drop left from his encouragement. The last swipe of my tongue was on his dick. I ran it up the shaft, and over the head, giving it a gentle suck like a straw, extracting any remaining juice.
He flinched.
I collapsed on the bed next to him wiping any extra spunk from my mouth and face. The silence between us was beautiful; the only noise was the hum of the air conditioner. The music had long since stopped. Our bodies were deluged with the other's exudation. No words were needed as a verbal language almost felt secondary. The thick, cold air sunk into our pores, every surface sensor confirmed this was not a hallucination but rather an acute existence. In the quiet, we stared at the ceiling occasionally touching hands or shifting our weight. Our breathing regulated itself, and our heart rates dropped back to normal. We both needed another shower at some point, but I had no desire to rush the moment. We spent a long time just enjoying the afterglow of what we had accomplished.

∞

I set myself up, the fitted sheet peeling away from my back. I swung my legs over the side of the bed and sat up, feet on the floor. The blood rushed to, or from, my head. I gave myself a minute to find my balance. I felt his hand stroke the small of my back. The expected goosebumps ran a quick course across my back. I leaned back resting my head on the side of his chest. We were some malformed letter T from another angle. He stroked my walnut-colored sweaty hair.
"You were pretty fucking fly, man."

"Was I?" I questioned. "I do not know if I have ever been fly before, with anything."
"You ever ride a dick like that before?"
"I have been known to pounce on a few here and there."
"You sure you never pounced on Shadrach's?"
"Dude, no way. He is a nice neighbor, but anything more is just weird. It is not like that. I do not think we have even watched a movie together. We usually stand outside and judge people."
We both laughed.
"I am just kidding you, man," he said as he patted my chest. Despite his detective work, his hand felt great.
The fuck you are kidding. You are digging.
"The fuck you are, man. You are digging. You worried someone is fucking your girlfriend?" While I did not always refer to men with feminine pronouns, Shadrach was overly feminine, which was a trait not always in my sexual wheelhouse.
"Nah, man. Just asking."
"Uh huh. You want a beer?"
"Please."
I hopped up as best I could simultaneously hiding that my legs still felt like warm pasta and my body had never felt like it did right now.
"Hey," he said, getting my attention. "Meet me in the shower? I am funky all over, man."
I continued to the kitchen, singing out loud to myself, *"He is a funky, funky man..."*
Another shower. Another round? Whatever it would become, it was after midnight. I had every intention of meeting him in the shower. I could only hope when he left in the morning that Shadrach would not be coming home at the same time.

After round three when the sun was coming up, Shadrach was the furthest thing from my mind, just as he was every time David came over after that.

120 † Ernest Sewell

† Eli and Daniel †

He rented a small room in a big building downtown called the Horton Building. It was a men's only sort of facility, and it served his purposes for him being in between apartments for a couple of months. It was a cheap alternative for him to crash while he settled things. It was more like living in military barracks without the drill instructor. The rooms were one person and private while each of the floors maintained a community bathroom & shower area.

Frankly, a place like the Horton would usually scare the ever-living shit out of Eli. It was just an odd in-between place for him to inhabit instead of crashing with the few friends he had in the area. Eli, like everyone else there, had his room – his being the first just off the elevator landing – and was eight feet by eleven feet. It had a small closet and a window that faced a courtyard which went mostly unused by the tenants of the building. It was barely a view. His room was on the third floor, which was a nicer floor than the second. The second floor had its own vibe and housed men who had probably been there a very long time. The fourth floor had rooms and beds that went virtually unused. The fifth floor was empty and had never been used or furnished. The guys on Eli's floor were friendly and kept to themselves. Common courtesies were extended as an unwritten rule. Should someone be in the shower area, others waited them out, if possible. It was courtesy of privacy in an otherwise very public and vulnerable space. Eli was not, nor were most of the other men there, an exhibitionist nor cared to shower in front of other men.

Daniel was a guy as young as Eli, five foot seven tall, blond hair, thick and furry hair on his chest (which always seemed to peek out and make an appearance through the pastel tank tops he favored), blue eyes, slightly stocky, loved his rum and sodas in the evening, and had a smile that lasted for days. There was never a quiet moment to be had with Daniel in the room. He was almost always the go-to funny guy. His humor always puts people at ease proving to be a bright light in a place that could be rather dim at times. Eli had no idea how Daniel ended up there for so long. He had recently mentioned his residence at the Horton was approaching its year anniversary. Eli never pried to ask the how or why of Daniel's situation. Even though Eli's room was far enough away, he could often hear Daniel from his room (which was on the just on the other side of the bathroom and shower area) laughing or talking to some poor soul he latched onto and dragged into his room for some late-night chatter. He relied on sarcasm, not cynicism, and would crack a dirty joke at the drop of a hat and not caring who heard it. Eli appreciated the gentler side of Daniel's good chiding humor and clever wit. Daniel was also a flirt with most guys he met. To his credit, Daniel was a good judge of character with the flirting because not every good old boy is going to take a gentle nudge-nudge-wink-wink when it came to sexual innuendo. Most men were secure enough to take it, but there were always a few who were not.

Eli usually got up around 6:30 a.m. for work during weekdays. The weekends were quieter and more laid back. Eli, and Daniel, and a thinner, dark-haired guy named Isaac (whose room was adjacent to Daniel's), would hang out in one another's rooms to drink, tell jokes or watch television. On the weekends, Eli would often work out, enjoy a late afternoon shower, and otherwise take care of his matters before they all gathered at Selena's Café for supper. It was a local diner during the day but turned into a little hub of drinking activity after 7 p.m. most evenings, and especially on weekends. Their breakfasts and blue-plate specials enticed patrons as much as their Monday dollar drafts, Hump Day three-dollar drink specials, and Thursday Therapy karaoke with Todd.

This Saturday, after Eli slept late; late for him was 8 a.m. He got dressed in his Saturday bum-wear, and the three of them left to get breakfast around 9 a.m. at Barb's Cafe. Their biscuits and gravy were the excuse to go, but the pancakes were the reason to stay. After some socializing and guy banter, they broke up for the afternoon and planned to meet up again around 8 p.m. Eli ran a few errands to get an apartment in order, check on his things in storage, and maybe swap out some clothes he had there with the ones he had in his room. Daniel napped, and Isaac disappeared somewhere. Eli could never quite figure out how Isaac vanished on weekends for a few hours at a time. Eli was sure Isaac did not have a car to travel long distances. He never pried enough to find out Isaac's meanderings while they were out of each other's company. Eli had only been here for a short while and was not going to be here much longer. The friendships were convenient and appreciated, but the probability of them being long-term was thin, at best. Wherever Isaac wandered off to, hopefully, he was having fun. Eli enjoyed Isaac's company in a different way than Daniel's. Isaac was the boy next door, grown into his late twenties. Daniel was the rowdy boy at the party. It was a balance that Eli found comforting during his sabbatical from a standard lease agreement. He wondered if he would strive to maintain either friendship once he moved out of the Horton.

Eli made it back to the building around five in the evening to workout in the downstairs attached gym. The gym was included with room rentals. Free weights, machines, a pool, a small sauna; not too shabby for a couple hundred a week in rent. Some people paid that for a gym contract alone.

After a long and sweaty workout (Saturdays were cardio), Eli needed to shower and get himself together before dinner. Instead of taking the elevator, he took what bit of energy he still had in him and ran up the three flights of stairs to his floor, skipping every other step in his sprint. Once in his room, he kicked his shoes off, hung his sweaty muscle shirt on a chair to dry, and dropped his shorts & jockstrap where he stood. He grabbed a towel and wrapped it his around his still-sweaty waist. He slipped into a pair of flip-flops - a necessity to avoid anything undesirable on the shower floor - tucked his shower kit under his arm and locked the door behind him, shuffling his way down the hall to the shower area. He passed Isaac's room, which was on the same side of the hall as his own. Both Isaac and Daniel's doors were closed. Eli had no idea if they were around or not.

The shower room had ten shower heads in one large tiled room, much like any high school, military boot camp, or prison. The building was old and the architecture, inside and out, reflected its age. The tiles in the shower were probably original as were the old shower heads and faucets. A few tiles were cracked but were mostly in excellent condition considering they had withstood decades of soap, hard water, scrubbing, and the occasional caulk repair. For a reserved guy like Eli, a public shower could be a social nightmare. He felt no shame in wearing a speedo to dive or swim. It was his uniform. But to shower with other people was something he would rather avoid. Sure, he was just a guy, but he still had a modicum of reticence. No one was in there and mostly kept out if someone else was in there. The unspoken consideration, a simple human gesture among like-minded men, did not go unnoticed by people like Eli; a bit of discretion was a constant on his gratitude list.

He went to one of the shower heads near the back-left corner of the room. It was under a long, narrow horizontal window located near the top of the back wall. The window on the rear wall faced south. The late afternoon sun, what was left of it, beamed into the room. He turned the now-vintage knobs and started the water flowing which was a good three minutes away from being hot. In an old building, hot water takes a while to get from the source to the spout. He had brought a fresh pair of shorts with him to slip on in case his towel got too wet. He left his shorts, and towel on a bench outside of the showers where he could see them. He took the room key with him, along with his loofah, body soap and shampoo. While the guys were nice here, Eli never really trusted anyone to not snag his items; at least not in a place like this. If he had his key, he could at least make a mad dash to his room should someone steal his items on the bench. He had no aspirations to streak in the buff down a long hallway to get to his room safely. It had not happened before, but he was one to always be careful instead of careless. He was glad he had the shower area to himself; that is unless someone else decided to join him on a mid-Saturday afternoon. It was unlikely, though.

After what seemed an eternity, the warm water started to flow. The warmth of the water felt welcoming hitting the palm of his hand. He slowly eased himself under the water and adjusted it to a perfect temperature.

He took his time standing there letting the hot water hit his head, run over his face and neck, race across his chest with its budding hairy new growth and eventually down his legs and feet. It was winter in Oklahoma, so the warmth was welcome to his usually warm-weathered body. Oklahoma winters were short but always proved to be as intense as any other in the mid-south. The radiant heat in the rooms kept tenants, including Eli, finding the perfect balance between a hoodie and shirt or shorts and no-shirt. Eli stayed active, so he always told himself he did not have time to get cold. The single digit wind chills kept that fantasy in check. His workouts kept his body warm today, and the water felt just as good on his skin as a fleece throw from his mother's couch. He leaned back to let the water fully engulf the front of his naked body. The water trickled off the end of his dick like he was pissing. He turned around and backed into the water. It hit the back of his neck with a vengeance, and he quickly succumbed to it. He looked down and watched the water run down his abdomen and off the tip of his cock. He could feel the warmth run down his back taking playful visits in the crack of his ass. It felt good. Having been raised near the ocean until he was seven-years-old when his father then took a job in Cottam's Bend, Oklahoma, he felt a kinship with the water. He was a starting junior swimmer in school and quickly found the swim teams in Oklahoma to be a worthy challenge; an academic activity he maintained through his college years. Eli's affinity with water ran through his life, so even the simple act of taking a shower proved to be relaxing and centering.

It was his Zen.

He grabbed some shampoo and lathered up his head. He kept his dark hair short but long enough to brush. It was already dripping wet from cardio beating his ass earlier, a challenge he always welcomed. Cardio kept the heart healthy and the body leaner. Resistance training kept him healthy and toned. He closed his eyes, tilted his head forward and felt his way through a slow and methodical head washing. Before the soap rushed from his forehead to his eyes, where the burn would be swift and painful, he ducked under the water and rinsed it away. The sweat and dirt of the gym washed down the drain.

What was that? Is someone in here with me?

Eli did not hear another shower going. But he was sure he heard something rhythmic like footsteps.

Fuck – is someone taking my stuff?

He tried to open his eyes, but the water proved to be too much, his vision blurred. He dismissed it.

Probably just the echo against the tile.

He put his hands out to feel for the water and blindly maneuvered his head back under the powerful shower head. He shut his eyes tighter and ducked his head under the hot water to rinse his face. He turned around to rinse the soap off his neck. He tilted his head up and back, letting the water run through his hair and down his backside. His face and head were clean once again. The warm water found its way around his tight swimmer's body including his bubble butt and muscular legs. He took a moment before washing the rest of his body. Half of his stink was gone having camped out under the shower for so long.

He felt like he was not alone. When he opened his eyes, he realized his instinct was right. He had company.

For a fleeting moment, he almost thought he saw something. Was there someone in the shower with him all this time? He felt vulnerable in a strange place; not in control. He quickly wiped the water from his eyes and focused on the blurry vision in front of him. Someone was way too close in his unseen personal space.

Who the fuck is that?

"Daniel? What the fuck?"

There stood Daniel as naked as Eli. It was easy for him to pop in the shower since his room was next door. He had a smirk on his face like he had just done something or pulled another joke. Eli's body twitched from the shock of being caught in the shower, exposed. He glanced over at his items on the bench. They were still there from what he could tell. He never knew what prank Daniel might try to pull on him, although Daniel had never really attempted that with Eli. But Daniel hiding Eli's items would not be out of the scope of possibility. Eli was painfully aware he was wet, vulnerable, and very naked. He was also irritated by Daniel's invasion.

"Dude, what the fuck are you doing in here?" Eli asked, trying not to come off too perturbed.

"It is a community shower. We can all be in here." Daniel said in a softer voice; one Eli had never heard him speak in until now. It disarmed Eli. He could barely hear Daniel over the water running and its reverb on the tiles.

"Um...sure. Yeah, sorry. You startled me. I am almost done." They were now shower-buddies as they were both naked, making small talk in a shower. Is that not what locker room buddies do? Talk to each other naked in the shower stalls at a gym?

"Sorry about that," Daniel apologized.

"It is fine, man."

It would be better if you would let me wash my ass in private and leave.

Eli was blinking through the water in his eyes, as he was still backed up to the shower, and it was hitting the back of his neck. The misty splatters of water bounced off his head in the beams of sunlight that filtered into the room creating a show of affection for the intruding sunlight. The steam from hot water and the ricochets of water bouncing off old tiles, and men's bodies, always gave a subtle yet striking light show. The water was keeping Eli's eyes clinched more than not. He tried to keep doing what he was doing and figured Daniel would either shower or go back to his room. Admittedly, he was not looking for friendly banter right now. They were due to go to dinner with Isaac later.

What did Daniel want that could not wait?

Daniel moved closer to Eli. There were ten shower heads. Did he need to use the one next to Eli in the corner? Daniel took another step toward him and put his hand on Eli's smooth chest. His reflex was to pull back a bit, and he did. He was against the wall. He instantly felt the cold tile behind him send a shock through his backside. Even though he moved backward, Daniel kept his hand on Eli's chest toying with his hairy pecs continually violating Eli's personal space. While the inanimate shower maintained its position above him, Eli's back pressed against a cold tile wall. Daniel stared at Eli challenging him to stop.

"Your heart is pounding. I did not mean to frighten you." He almost seemed to giggle inside at the thought of scaring Eli. Maybe that was the joke.

Even when swimmers were not swimming, they often kept shaving their bodies. Eli had not shaved for a few weeks, so the thick hair between his pecs had started to return. It was just as sexy on him as a totally-shaved chest, but old habits die hard in the swimming world. He kept his hand on Eli's wet chest toying with his chest hair and feeling the hard tone pecs that Eli had proudly procured throughout his life. The warmth of Daniel's palm over the sternum felt hotter than the water itself. Eli tried to brush Daniel's hand away. Daniel kept a firm pressing on Eli's toned smooth chest.

"Dude, you are still touching me," he said.

"Yeah, I am."

"Can you stop, please?"

"If you want me to stop, make me," came the challenge.

"Come on, Daniel. Stop fucking around, man."

While Eli had a swimmer's body, he still had muscle under it. Daniel was not as muscular, but he had the heft of being a cub type body type. It would be an equal match if it came down to scrapping.

Eli took the challenge. He tried to be as non-offensive as possible. He grabbed Daniel's meaty wrist and tried to push it away again. Daniel finally relented, and his hand gently fell to his side as did Eli's. They were still in their staring contest.

"That felt weak," Daniel challenged the sport.

"I am not in the habit of men accosting me while I take a shower. I thought I was alone."

"Is that what I did? Accost you?"

"Well, no. You did not," Eli rethought his words. "But you did surprise me. So, there you go. You got me. Ha, ha. Very funny. Now can I finish what I came here to do?"

"Maybe, if you let me finish what I came here to do, first."

Daniel's eyes seemed to stare at Eli's chest, where his hand had been, almost as if he missed having it there. Eli was not sure where this was going, but his dick had an agenda that he was unable to hide from anyone.

Eli followed Daniel's eyes as they traveled down Eli's tight and wet torso to his waist and stopped on his cock. Eli noticed the desire in Daniel's face. He was there for a reason. Following his lead, Eli looked down and saw his dick was getting hard fast. He had not realized, through all these little awkward moments and being confronted, that he was almost fully aroused. His dick was sticking out and engorged with blood. It was thick, his pubes trimmed to a respectable length, his balls dangled from the hot water and his workout. Eli was cut, and his dick was a perfect color that dicks like his were; no two-toned shit here. Eli's erection was not entirely Daniel's fault. The gym always worked up Eli's already strong libido, and cardio-day was no exception to that rule. The more testosterone he worked up, the more likely he was to be hard in the slightest of breezes. Running pushed endorphins through Eli's body weekly and that only alerted the arousal center exponentially. It was not uncommon for Eli to jerk off after a long run or an intense weight-day workout.

Daniel's other hand returned to Eli's chest. This time Eli felt the surge of blood flow through his body making his heart beat faster; his cock got even harder. He immediately took a nervous inhale.

"Hey look, man, I am flattered," Eli offered, as he tried to move forward and out of Daniel's snare.

"I can tell you are flattered because your cock is pointing at me. They say it is not nice to point."

Daniel reached down, and gentle wrangled Eli's dick in his soft meaty hand. His words were blunt and made Eli try to cover his boner, to no avail. Daniel's hand was keeping its place and not letting go just yet.

"Christ man, someone could come in here and catch us," Eli warned. "If they saw us like this..."

"Are you afraid of someone finding us? It is a shower, not a lion's den," Daniel countered.

"Yes, Daniel, I am! You know guys have gotten kicked out of here for that shit, man," he said finally brushing Daniel's all-too-warm hand from his cock.

He pushed Eli backward until his back was against the tile again. Unrelenting cold tile shocked his hot, wet skin.

"I am not worried," Daniel declared. He stepped closer to Eli until their chests were touching. Was this a dare to move out of his way?

"Kiss me," Daniel said.

"Daniel, come on, man. This is silly. I get it; you were pranking me. Funny, man. You even got a boner out of me, but seriously…"

Daniel had heard enough. Before Eli knew what was happening, Daniel kissed him. The water ran over both of them. Eli felt his dick rub against Daniel's thighs. He realized he was getting even harder. Daniel pressed his stocky, hairy body into Eli's thinner frame. Eli could feel Daniel's dick pounce on his own. Eli had not looked down at Daniel because he was not interested in seeing his dick. He just wanted to finish his shower. Eli noted to himself that Daniel's dick felt thick and meaty. They both felt the other's dick grow between them. Eli was not sure whether to push him away again or just let it happen. His instincts were to stop it. He could not afford a hotel for the next few weeks before his apartment was ready. The risk was too high.

Upon check-in, the management had stated, "no homosexual activity allowed." Eli, led by Daniel, was breaking those rules hard and fast.

Daniel's kiss was intoxicating which says a lot since he was sober. Daniel's furry barrel chest pushed against Eli, his chest hair – thick and curly – was wet and intertwined with the minor amount of hair Eli had right between his firm pecs. Eli would breathe in, his chest heaving and full of steamy air, and Daniel's would exhale, relaxing. Then Eli would subside, and Daniel's would puff up and become hard. It was a give and take. Eli could feel his dick dueling with Daniel's for domination. Eli started to reach up to grab Daniel. This could not go on; it was dangerous. He was not sure if he was going to push Daniel away out of fear of being caught or pull him closer to submit to the momentum between them. Daniel quickly stunted his plans. Before Eli could stop him, Daniel grabbed either of Eli's hands mid-air and pressed them against the wall on either side of his body. More shock to his system and more of a rush of endorphins running through his body. With his arms out and fighting Daniel's inhuman cub strength, Eli's body flexed showing off his natural lifelong muscle toning. His biceps were strong, and a vein was visible running down his arm. His shoulders were full and flushed from the hot water. His body was accentuated in the sunlight and shower water, his dick horizontal to the floor. Daniel kissed Eli harder. He had a plan, and he was fully executing it with Eli braced against the wall held in place and rock hard. The sense of excitement that came from the danger of getting caught only enhanced their interaction. Eli was conflicted equally by the fear of being ousted from this place for having sex in a public shower with another man and the thrill of having sex in an open shower with another man. Eli kissed him back, but his grip and his arms were strong. Daniel was a thick guy and had that lovely natural brawn about him. Eli suspected that before Daniel lived here, he worked out in his regular life. He was not a jock, but someone just as comfortable with a power tool in his hand, a beer, or another man's wrists.

He toyed with Eli. He kissed him, bit his lip, sucked on his tongue. He moved his mouth to Eli's neck and chewed on it a bit leaving Eli weak and utterly helpless. Eli's neck and ears were always a big erogenous zone for him. Daniel did not know that until he started kissing Eli there, then he knew it. Eli reacted in the only way he knew how – immediate and intense. Through the rush of sensations on Eli's neck, he still took a second to look up to see if anyone was watching and if his clothes were still there. All was well on the bench.

Daniel pulled away from Eli. Eli was not sure what would happen next. Was he done? Was it just a big tease moment to get the testosterone going? While Eli was participating, he was still just a passenger on the Daniel crazy train. They both took a deeper breath, trying to regain their composure. Daniel let go of his wrists. Eli was not sure what to do with his arms, and they slowly lowered on their own accord.

"That was nice, man. Thank you."

"Thank you? I am not dropping off take out, Eli. We just made out naked in a shower. I think I deserve more than a simple thank you."

"Uh…I.." Eli was not sure what Daniel wanted to hear. Eli felt disarmed entirely and caught off guard.

As Eli tried to conjure a proper response, Daniel dropped down to one knee, then both. It was as if he was bowing before the gods and sacrificing himself for their pleasure. This time, the god was Eli's stiff cock, and the sacrifice would be his seed. His strong hands grabbed Eli's narrow hips, clinching them just enough so he would know they were there. Eli's dick was bobbing up and down, ready for something to be done with it.

Daniel's mouth was as warm and wet as the shower. His scruffy goatee grazed against the softer flesh of Eli's groin. Daniel's lips searched for the lowest base point of Eli's shaft, while the head of his cock throbbed against the rigged roof of Daniel's mouth. His tongue moved, wet and textured, against the bottom side of Eli's pole. The sensations were varied, intense and consistent. Eli leaned into the wall behind him, using it as a brace, and spread his feet apart just enough for Daniel to find a home between his legs. What started as the cub being forceful now turned to him being submissive yet aggressive, but who was in charge here? Eli realized it should be enjoyed. Fuck! Daniel's mouth felt so fucking good on his dick. It had been a good month since Eli had his dick sucked.

Moving and putting things into storage had sidetracked his usual routine of hookups and fun with friends. His sex drive had not changed, but he had relegated his boners to jerking off a few nights a week. Daniel's mouth was proving to be a much-needed yet unexpected release.

Eli's hands seemed to naturally find the top of Daniel's head, pushing his face into his fleshy groin. Daniel sucked hard, and then he sucked soft. He went slow, then fast. It was never boring. He had never felt Daniel pull back for air or gag. Daniel had a notable lack of a gag reflex. The water from the shower was still hot and ran down Eli's chest and no doubt onto the dick that Daniel had in and out of his eager mouth. Eli's penny-sized nipples were hard and pliable. Eli kept one hand on Daniel's head to hold it in place while stroking his chest with the other.

Eli grabbed Daniel's hands off his hips and put them on his chest. He obeyed Eli's lead, grabbing and clawing at his chest eventually reaching up far enough to find Eli's erect nipples. He gave them plenty of attention which all but released Eli from caring if anyone caught them having sex in the showers. He wanted – no, he *needed* - his dick sucked until he was ready to cum down Daniel's willing throat. He missed having his dick sucked lately. Life got in the way. Fuck it; he was recouping his losses.

Eli held onto Daniel's head and fucked his face without apology. Daniel's hands fumbled around Eli's chest and eventually landed back on his legs. He wrapped his arms around Eli's upper thighs, hugging his ass. He palmed either of those swimmer's ass cheeks pulling Eli's body into him. He had wanted to suck Eli so badly before but never mentioned it. Now he was getting his chance.

Eli's head stayed back against the wall; eyes mostly closed enjoying the wave of indulgence. When he opened his eyes, he was jolted out of his fantasy of a shower room blowjob and realized he was still having sex in a place that frowned on homosexual activity. He feared that they were making noise and anyone might hear.

We could be caught at any moment and thrown out on our naked asses. What in the gay fuck am I doing?

At some point, while one's dick is buried in a guy's throat, one gives up worrying about that sort of bullshit. No homosexual activity? Not even the Catholic priests believed that much less a young Christian men's housing facility. Whether foolishly or not, you throw caution to the wind and embrace your inner savagery. Life was meant to be lived. Eli had lived a great life despite his weird spell at the downtown Cottam's Bend habitat. Eli stayed focused on the situation. The element of danger did nothing but enhance the continually unfolding moments. He realized that aside from a bucket list fantasy playing out, it was a genuine threat. He was in a men's shower room, water running over him with a husky and hairy cub on his knees in front of him, sucking him like it was his last time. The water, the mouth, the fucking blowjob - it was all too real.

Eli's thrusts into Daniel's mouth became more frequent, almost furious. He became unwavering in shoving every inch of his seven-inch swimmer's dick into Daniel's mouth, whether he was ready for that impact or not. Daniel may have wanted to blow Eli during his shower time, and goddamn they were going to do it Eli's way. Eli was mostly a top in his life and knew how to sit back and receive a great blowjob. His moans echoed back in the vast room where he stood. Eli felt it coming. He was getting close.

Eli's legs started to tighten up, and his breath became the heaviest it had been. He grabbed the hair on Daniel's head and offered no mercy.

"Fuck. Fuck! FUCK! I am going to cum! Oh shit..."

Daniel looked up at Eli's firm body, flexing and tightening, highlighting all those trim and defined muscles he had hidden under his skin. Eli's six-pack was perfectly lit in the sunlight and sparkled in the shower water. His biceps flexed still soundlessly bragging with that one vein that runs down the inner arm. Daniel felt Eli's real strength as he gripped Daniel's head like he was about to do shoot from the three-point line.

"Mother fuck... Here I .... here I cum..." He never finished the warning before he blew a boatload of white matter into the back of Daniel's throat. Daniel caught every bit of jizz in his mouth while gazing up at him in the throes of passion. Daniel dug his fingernails into Eli's ass locking them in an almost-forever position of dick-in-mouth, hoping for the continuous orgasm. Eli's torso heaved forward as he came. He grabbed the back of Daniel's neck, hugging his head, and braced himself against him as not to collapse on top of the cub. Daniel never moved his mouth as Eli continued to empty his seed into Daniel's throat. Eli could feel Daniel latch onto him not wanting to miss any of his liquid pearls. Daniel sucked Eli's pulsating dick like an infant with a bottle, milking the cum out of Eli's baby maker. As his swells of self-indulgence slowly subsided, Daniel kept Eli's dick in his mouth.

There were a few moments of silence, the only noise being the shower water still coming out at high pressure against Eli and the floor around them both. Eli was dizzy. The steam in the shower was thick and had warmed Eli's body, flushing his torso with an all-telling and unforgivable redness. It was undoubtedly redder from getting a fantastic blowjob. Eli steadied himself, gathering his senses. Daniel stood up to face him.

Eli was wet, euphoric, and satisfied. Daniel slyly wiped the side of his mouth with his left forefinger as not to let anything escape him. They stood there for a minute wondering what they should do next. Eli's dick was going flaccid. He did not know if Daniel was able to jerk off while down there or not, but he did know his hands were busy most times.

"Hey man, let me catch up with you later," came a stranger's voice from the hallway leading to the shower. They were about not to be alone anymore.

Eli's heart raced with anxiety.

"Fuck, someone is coming. I told you," Eli aggressively whispered. "Get out of here!"

Daniel grabbed Eli's shampoo bottle and quickly jumped to the shower on the opposite corner of the back wall and turned on the water. It was warm instantly, as the hot water had been running for a while now. Daniel dropped some shampoo into his hand and lathered up his head to mimic being in the middle of showering. Eli felt awkward, suddenly standing there alone. He still had tingles running through his body. Eli saw a shadow of someone coming to join them. He turned away from the opening to the shower, as to hide his still partially hard cock to whoever was about to join them. He grabbed the shower wash quickly lathering his body. It was hit or miss to give the appearance of showering and not one of afterglow.

Only showering. Nothing to see here folks, keep it moving. Thanks for stopping by, please exit through the gift shop.

If Eli washed anything, it was half-assed at best. He was distracted by just getting out of there, but his motor skills had yet to catch up with his brain. Eli stayed turned away until his dick went down enough that it would not reveal the near-criminal activity of what just happened.

Eli heard someone step down into the shower area. Whoever was coming for a visit let out a slight cough that served as a warning that the shower roster was growing by one. Eli turned around to see a young, tall, and athletic man step into the doorway of the shower. He had beautiful, brown skin that looked like velvet and probably felt like it, too.

"Hey guys, how goes it?" he nodded toward Eli. He nodded back only out of sheer obligation.

"How are you doing?" Eli offered up, almost stammering over such simple words.

"Hey there," he heard Daniel say. He forgot for a moment that Daniel was still in there. Eli was too busy trying to project his own 'nothing to see here' illusion.

Their visitor found a shower three heads over from Eli's self-assigned zone. Little did he know that it was a crime scene and that a significant "no homosexual activity" violation had just taken place.

"Looks like the sun is finally warming it up a bit out there," the visitor said, motioning toward the sunlit window. Small talk in the shower. It was a welcome respite from everything going through his mind.

"Oh yeah? We could use it," Daniel gregariously offered.

"They call me Jeremiah," he explained, taking a couple of steps over to fist bump Eli with an arm that seemed to be longer than a broomstick. Eli noticed Jeremiah give him a quick up and down look, but is that not what guys do in locker rooms? They are cool with the nudity, but everyone is still checking out everyone else's dick. Eli wondered if his dick was still bouncing around or had drained itself of the blood that kept it hard earlier.

Eli gave him his name and kept rinsing his body. "Good to meet you, man."

"I hope that is your name then, or that would be pretty awkward." It seemed Daniel's sense of humor was back.

"Yeah, man. That is what my mama named me. You are the funny one, huh?" Jeremiah chuckled.

"And my mother named me Daniel."

The conversation and the awkwardness, at least Eli's, continued with their fellow shower mate after a brief introduction. He hoped that maybe Daniel would keep Jeremiah talking long enough for him to escape. But he could not count on that. Eli quickly rinsed and finished his shower. He snagged his key from the shower taps and exited the area.

"Have a good one, man," he nodded toward Jeremiah.

"Hey, you too man. It was very nice to meet you. Maybe we can hang out somewhere else next time."

That was an odd offer, Eli thought. "Sure thing." It was not meant to be dismissive, but Eli was not there to plan a banquet either. His goal was to get back to his room.

At the bench, he did a quick pat down with his towel, then wrapped it around his waist. He grabbed the shorts with his loofah and body soap and quickly headed down the hall. He is surprised he made it out with both shower slippers on his feet.

As he walked toward the main hallway, Eli heard them talking about everything and nothing as Daniel did with strangers or new friends.

What did he say was his name? Jason? Jeremy? Gherkins?

He got back to his room, his towel barely staying in place on his body, but was happy for making it out alive.

Eli locked the door behind him, shutting out the now-distant conversation coming from the showers. Without even turning the light on he collapsed on the bed. He laid there, his towel loosely draped over his legs, breathing heavy, his abs tightening up with every inhale. He could still feel the tingles of jubilation sparking through his body, albeit mixed with the fear of company suddenly appearing. Anxiety on every level, and rightly so. He rested for a few minutes taking a few deep breaths. He always relied on the breathing he had learned from being a swimmer to relax outside the pool when he needed it. He had the time. He was on auto-pilot and wanted to get back to normal.

Deep breath in, hold it. Slowly release. In through the nose, out through the mouth.

He had time before Isaac would come looking for him and Daniel for dinner. He laid there, still damp and naked. He let out a little chuckle under his breath.

"What the fuck just happened," he exclaimed in the dark to himself. "That motherfucker!"

He did not know whether to slap or thank Daniel for his boldness. Another chuckle revealed itself.

He reached under his towel and grabbed his dick. He gave it a little squeeze relishing the whole experience. He still felt his body reacting inside, the blood rushing in and out of his groin. Sure, it was dangerous, and he was in a spot where he did not need to be thrown out of a place he had only been renting for a few weeks. He was not going to be here forever, but he had to keep a low profile until moving day happens for fuck's sake. This was not the way to accomplish that. He stopped beating himself up about it. He did not regret what happened. How could he regret a great blowjob?

No more shower sex, man. Stop it. That was fun, and all but you cannot risk it again.

He hung his towel on a rack-mounted near the closet door. He had some time to hang out by himself. He could benefit from meditation before dinner. When he learned that his swim coach was into Transcendental Meditation, Eli laughed. Most of the swim team did at first. But eventually, he learned how it paid off for him as a swimmer and in his everyday life. The rug always proved to be a perfect place to sit and meditate. He cleared his mind of the stress in the shower room and pushed the resulting anxiety out of his head. Twenty minutes of uninterrupted and steady breathing would calm him.

He would make his way through half of it.

∞

The knock on his door shattered his final quiet moments. He was not expecting a visitor.

Who the fuck is that?

Maybe he dropped something in the hall, and someone noticed it. Although, he did not have much with him to lose with his quick exit.

He ended his meditation and quickly shuffled himself into a pair of boxer briefs and his cargo shorts; his favorite pair still on the foot of his bed from yesterday, ignoring any need to wear a shirt.

He opened the door just the width of his own body.

"Hey there. Sorry to bother you. Your friend told me you left this in there."

Jeremiah presented Eli the shampoo bottle that Daniel had snagged earlier, never having gone into the shower actually to shower; only to suck Eli's dick.

"Oh wow, thanks, man. I forgot about that. You did not have to return it. I could have just bought a new one."

"No problem, man. Hey, I hope I did not scare you out of there earlier. I just got back from a run and…"

"No, it was fine, man. I was just back from a run, too. I was finishing my shower when you came. I was just distracted," he confessed, which was not a total lie.

"Good. I know folks like to shower alone. Jeremiah," he said, extending a hand for a shake. "just in case, you forgot. You are Eli, right?"

"Yeah, that is me. It was nice to meet you."

"You too, man. Do you play sports? You look like it."

"Oh yeah, I used to swim. High school, college, varsity, all that. Tried out for nationals a couple of times and made it. Did not place as high as I would have wanted."

"Right on, man. It is hard not to notice you have a swimmer's body. You look good, man. Maybe we could run together sometime. No pressure or anything."

"That might be cool, yeah. And thanks, man. You look good, too," came the half-hearted call and response. Eli was too lost in his thoughts earlier to notice just how tall and muscular Jeremiah was when he had come into the showers. He certainly took notice now. Jeremiah was a few inches taller than Eli and did not have an inch of fat on him. His skin was dark as coal, and his muscles were that of someone who preferred to stay bulked throughout the year rather than trimmed down like Eli's body. Eli had taken a quick note that a stereotype was true. Even in the midst of their awkward greetings in the shower, Eli noticed Jeremiah's overly-endowed member wagging like a dog's tail between his legs. Eli had certainly enjoyed his share of bottoming while maintaining a healthy dose of topping, too. His libido was too big to limit himself to just one or the other. He considered himself a top with a propensity to bottom at an almost equal number He had been with many men, even a couple of those were with brick houses like Jeremiah. And in another situation, he would have considered Jeremiah as a probable hookup. Eli's taste stayed varied, but he always enjoyed a similarly athletic man as much as he enjoyed a cub of Daniel's ilk.

Jeremiah stood there in a pair of shorts that were possibly a size too small and a yellow cut-out shirt that was more of a joke than a piece of clothing on his hulky frame that almost glowed against Jeremiah's dark skin. His nipples peeked out either side and did nothing to add any modesty to his appearance. His chocolate skin was still moist from his shower.

"Listen, I need to go," Eli said, trying to end the hallway small talk. "I will look you up the next time I am going for a run. I am meeting up with friends later, so…"

"Jesus, are you going to open the door all the way or not?" a familiar voice taunted. Jeremiah took a step back.

Daniel, hiding around the corner, dropped into view with that usual grin on his face.

"Open the door already," Daniel nudged.

"Sorry, man. Daniel said you were cool," Jeremiah offered, obviously leaning to something else.

Eli tried his best to give Daniel a firm "you fucker" look while not giving anything up to Jeremiah.

"Listen, man," Jeremiah started, stepping closer to the door and lowering his voice. "I could tell something was up when I walked in there. You were not hiding anything. Your dick was hard."

"Oh fuck," Eli said. "Sorry about that."

"It is cool, man. I am not here to snitch on you. I liked what I saw." Jeremiah was genuine in his discretion.

"Oh, well thanks. I appreciate that. It is not something I usually do around here."

"Yeah, the rules are fucked up," Jeremiah agreed.

"Get dressed, dork. We are going upstairs," Daniel said, clearly excited about a pending excursion.

"What? There is nothing up there."

"Oh yes there is," answered Jeremiah.

"Like what?" Eli was confused.

"Privacy," Jeremiah countered.

"Come on, doofus. We are going to have some fun," Daniel taunted, albeit with a high note of legitimacy.

"Some of us go up there and play. No one checks up there, so it is safe," Jeremiah explained. "I would love it if you came up there with me. I think you are smoking hot, man. It is a safe zone. That shower is not." Jeremiah glanced at Daniel with a subtle side-eye that only Eli could appreciate from his vantage point.

"A few guys are coming up soon. You can hang out if you want, but..." Jeremiah trailed off, hoping Eli could finish the rest himself. Jeremiah was forward but did not want to offend. He certainly tried to make it known that he had a substantial internal boner for Eli.

Eli had to make a quick decision. Was he up for round two with a larger group of guys? Did he want to do this again, in the same building? Despite Jeremiah's claims, there was always a chance someone might take a trip up there and find them. It was unlikely but…

"Look, man, I would be lying if I said I did not want to get with you. Have some fun. You are not uptight, are you?" Jeremiah was prodding him to new adventures, taking a risk that Eli could handle the joke.

"You know you want to, silly faggot. So, get a shirt and bring your towel just in case," Daniel ordered him.

Just in case? Just in case what?

It was a great chance to have some more fun before dinner. Eli could certainly use it. This place could otherwise wear a person down after a while; relief in some form was almost a requirement.

"Fine, but if we get caught…"

"We will not!" Daniel interrupted.

"I will take the heat, man. I have been up there a lot. It is safe, trust me," Jeremiah assured him. "I have been going up there for months. I tell you, I was not the first. Besides, I work here."

Eli was shocked. "You work at the Horton? Then why are you showering up here?"

As Eli's voice trailed off with his question, Jeremiah's expression told Eli everything he needed to know. He remembered Jeremiah around the gym area almost every time he was there. He rightly assumed Jeremiah had been quietly watching him, for weeks.

"I go where the pressure is best." Jeremiah retorted.

Eli grabbed a clean shirt and his towel and locked his door behind him.

"Besides, I cannot very well hit on you in front of a hundred other people while working out down there. I figured if you liked what you saw in a shower, maybe you would like to see some more."

They headed to the stairwell near Daniel's room. It was faster than waiting for the elevator.

"I forgot to tell you," Daniel started. "Someone else you know will be there."

"Who?" At this point, Eli had no idea what to think.

"Some dude named Isaac," Jeremiah finished. "You know him?" Jeremiah had been entirely unaware of the existing friendship between them.

"Yeah, I know him," Eli admitted. "Wait, you..."

"He has a fantastic ass, man," Jeremiah confessed. "The guys up there love them some Isaac."

So that is where Isaac disappears to sometimes.

Two flights of stairs and some time later, Eli began to learn what, and where, Isaac had been hiding.

And no one ever found them.

† Cain †

Do not ever doubt that gingers are anything less than hot property in and out of bed. I have yet to meet or see not-hot gingers. I believe everyone has a hot factor in their way and is attractive to someone. There is something incredibly alluring about a red-headed man. They are ridiculously handsome, often pale, and adorable to a fault. Cain was no exception.

I met Cain online years ago, as I had most of my male conquests (or I was his conquest?). He was a bear type, furry, cute; he possessed the build of a ranch hand, with lean muscular legs, a thick neck, and broad chest, rusty colored beard; he was red-headed from top to bottom. His pale skin was sprinkled with freckles which jetted in and around his farmer's tan. During our chats online, I quickly came to realize he was mostly a top. I was down to get fucked, so I kept the conversation going with him. After trading some pictures, and talking about all the things we loved in the bedroom, I hopped in my Rubicon and drove out to his apartment in Sugar Lake, the suburb immediately south of Cottam's Bend.

Cain had a pleasant disposition that immediately put me at ease. He dismissed himself to the bathroom, no doubt to empty his bladder before he emptied his balls.

I took a moment to walk around and observe my temporary surroundings. Cain's interior decorating skills were lacking a certain finesse, but his bear fetish was glaring. There were bear tchotchkes all around his house. He took the bear thing seriously. Television console, bookshelves, end tables, and almost every other bare surface was occupied by bear figurines in fireman and police uniforms, bears with smiles, holding hearts, and bear couples kissing. I began to wonder if he had raided a bear bauble outlet mall in Missouri or Texas. One had to assume that I fit into some bear category myself since I was now puttering around his home with the inevitability of adult activities. I was never a twink or super thin nor was I on the extreme thicker side of life. I had maintained a fair middle ground. With my natural body hair, I probably qualified as a cub. It was apparent he identified with the bear community and loved the model of big, hairy men. I could only imagine that since he was huskier with muscle hiding under his bulk, and a few years older than me, that I was a cub to him. I did not explore the labels, but the assumption was a safe one. Something felt comforting about being his cub.

I was near the far wall of the living room examining Cain's bear paraphernalia and tchotchkes when I heard the toilet flush followed by eventual footsteps.

"It seems you like bears," I called out, assuming Cain was within earshot.

"How did you guess?" he asked.

Suddenly I felt his warm breath on the back of my neck. His hands gently slid around my waist from behind, and he pulled me near him with my back to his chest. His arms were big and strong. Even in the gentle tug from behind, I knew I would feel when it pleased him. His fuzzy face - which had likely never been cleanly shaven in a decade and barely had the ends of it trimmed in half that time - nuzzled against my nape and sent instant tingles across my shoulders and down my back. The skin on my arms bristled to attention. He kissed the back of my neck. I scrambled to savor the moment.

It was one of those moments you see in movies where a wife or girlfriend is up early, making coffee and toast, and the man comes up behind her, usually in just his tight-whiteys or less and slips his hands around her waist. She is loosely wearing one of his shirts and no panties. She tilts her head to one side simultaneously flinging her bedhead hair and exposing her neck allowing his pending kisses to land softly on one of her most sensitive and alluring spots. Her skills are impeccable as she does not miss a beat of swiping the crusty bread with its dressing. His hands reach around to explore her furry caldera. And as the camera pans away, he puts her on the counter – damn the toast – and fucks her before breakfast.

I stood there living the all-male version. I was, for this moment, proverbially buttering my toast. Cain's big arms bordered my mid-section. I put my hands over his arms, letting him silently know not to rush it. Since Cain was taller, his slight paunch fit the natural curvature of my spine. I could feel his dick getting erect, but I still had no idea if he was even dressed or not. He was hiding behind me, and I had not laid eyes on him yet since his trip to the lavatory. I had only worn a favorite rock t-shirt with the sleeves removed and blue cargo shorts to his house. His hands rested on my stomach. He held me close yet did so tenderly and gently. In a single move, he grabbed the hem of my t-shirt and pulled it off over my head. It found a place to land somewhere. As he leaned back into me, it was then that I realized he was naked – or had, at least, left his shirt in the other room. Having had my back to him when he came back from the bathroom, he could have been wearing a clown suit for all I knew. I felt his muscular pectorals against my shoulder blades. The bristles of his chest hair dug into my smooth back sending flushes of prickly happiness through every one of nerve endings. He kissed and licked the back of my neck which all but melted me at the knees. His hands were all over my torso rubbing my furry belly finding their way to my hairy chest. His hushed moan vibrated in the back of my neck. If he had stripped me naked at that moment and taken me from behind, I would not have fought it.

I reached down to unfasten my cargos. Without missing a beat, Cain's hands ran down my sides, his fingers effortlessly slipping into the waistband of my shorts and underwear. His rough but warm hands felt intrusive yet welcomed on my bare skin. He pulled down my remaining clothes with one fail swoop. I stepped out of my shorts and haphazardly kicked them out of the way. His deep voice rattled me to my bones.

"Put your hands up against the wall."

What did he say? Was I being arrested? Fuck, was this guy a cop? It was not against the law to fuck dudes, was it?

"What?" I started to turn around to him. He stopped me. He grabbed my arms from behind and raised them up toward the wall in front of me.

"Put your hands up and spread your legs."

I did not argue.

He was giving me raised hairs all over my body. He kissed my neck again, then methodically worked his mouth down my spine kissing every inch of the way before stopping at the top of my hips. He nuzzled his nose into the small patch of soft hair on my lower back. Inch by inch, he fetched my attention. His chapped hands splayed across my achromatic hindquarters and spread them as far apart as they would travel. His nimble thumbs prodded my hole which acted like the on-switch to my libido. I could feel his tongue flicker around the perimeter of my hollow. Involuntarily, it winced. He wasted no time burying his tongue into my needy valley. He loved to eat ass, and I was here to let him maneuver his way through that to the fullest. The coarse hairs on his face taunted the soft flesh between my buttocks.

It was only moments until I became fully aroused, dick bobbing for attention, but getting none; not yet. This ginger god was behind me eating my ass out with an enthusiasm I had not felt in a long time. Sure, some guys are exuberant and eager to please with the anilingus efforts, but few truly knew how to hit the right spots. Cain was hitting the right places. His method, which was more controlled and purposeful rather than chaotic and random, was one of the hottest things I had experienced with another man. There is nothing like getting your ass eaten. It is one of the most amazing feelings aside from putting your dick in something wet and tight or getting plowed. His copious beard prickling the inner parts of my ass made it feel like divinity in motion.

One of his hands reached between my legs from behind and up to my dick. He cupped my balls in his palm and toyed with my dick. I had lost track of where we were in this because I was concentrating on the tossing. I forgot about my dick. It sounds odd, but when you are in that sort of moment, you go with it. Other things, like your cock, take a backseat for a while. Sometimes living in the moment is sacrificing your selfishness. His touch on my balls and dick made me want to explode straight away, but I was in control enough to dampen that urge.

He stopped. Had he had enough of my ass? He grabbed my hips with both hands and spun me around to face him. With the same quickness he had exhibited earlier with removing my attire he pushed me back against the wall of his apartment. The bears, on their small, big box store shelving, shook as a warning toward our rambunctious activities. Cain was still on his knees, leaning back on his thighs. His alabaster body was flushed dark pink with rushes of blood. I saw his dick, thick and short, hard as a rock protruding from between his legs. His pubes were bushy with that beautiful orangey rust color that gingers sometimes have in their nether regions. He looked up at me. I am sure I had a ridiculous expression on my face since I was still processing the feels he was giving me. He kept me at a disadvantage as he took my dick in his mouth. I let out an inarticulate noise that neither of us was interested in trying to interpret. My knees almost gave out under me. He seemed to take a moment and sat there with my dick in his mouth, his warm spit encapsulating my cock. He moved his tongue under my shaft only to send my senses into a higher dimension of gratification. Faithfully locking his lips around the shaft all the way from the head down to my pubes, he started to suck my dick slowly. Slow and steady, he pulled back just to the head never fully letting go, then swallowed all my dick again. He never used his hands to jerk me off while sucking me. It was like having my cock swirling in some wet tornado.

He happily sucked my cock not nearly as long as I would have wanted but certainly longer than I anticipated. He methodically worked my dick into a graduated frenzy. It was like a slow burn. You knew the bigger side was coming, but it was as excruciatingly slow as it was perfect getting there. One of his hands reached between my legs, this time hunting for my hole. Two of his fingers found my man cave, massaging and playing with it. It was already wet and anticipatory of more intrusions from his assiduous tonguing earlier. I knew what he was doing, and I was going to let him. I rested either hand on top of his head while guiding his face into my crotch (as if he needed help). That was just enough for his finger to penetrate my asshole. He finger-fucked me while sucking my cock. My torso lurched forward, and I found myself bracing my weight with my hands on either of his shoulders, a simple move to me but one that was mostly spontaneous. He did not let up despite my buckling knees and quivering legs.

Then, I felt it. Cain suddenly had two fingers in me. I felt that feeling, just like you are going getting ready to cum, and reach the point of no return.

"God, fuck, Stop! Stop!" I pushed his head away.

"Oh my God, I am sorry. Am I hurting you?"

"No bubba. You are going to make me cum. You have no idea how fucking intense you are making this."

"Or do I," he taunted. "Baby, I want to make you cum," he said, doubling down on hand, making a big wager.

"I know, and you are so goddamn hot, but I want it to last." I pleaded. He had slowly pulled his fingers out of my opened ass. But not before sucking my dick some more.

He stood up, and his knees popped. We both reacted to it and had a little giggle under our breath. It was unexpected and slightly unnerving.

"Old is as old does," he excused.

"You are not old, buddy. You are just right," I reassured him. He was only a few years older than me, but his blue-collar occupation in construction and its resulting manifested physiological change not only gave him his daddy-bear vibe – that he played perfectly with nearly no effort - but had also taken a toll on him physically. This was not the first time his knees popped.

"I am going to get more of that ass in a minute, just know that," he demanded.

"Yeah, I do not know if you can handle it again. You are pretty old." My coy statement was met with a stern eye.

His hand grabbed my throat and pressed against it. He immediately leaned in nose-to-nose with me.

"We will see who is telling who to stop when I am done with your ass."

"You do not scare me," I challenged him, grabbing his arm just as tightly.

"I do not want you to be scared of me. I want you to want me so bad that you are begging for more."

"Big talk from another soulless ginger." It was all I had to offer in playful banter. I wanted him to keep his tongue deep in my ass for hours. I doubted that would happen. His macho forcefulness combined with his tender touches from earlier made me forget any roles we would typically inhabit. I just wanted to be with him.

I had no more than finished my quasi-cocky comeback than he grabbed my head and started kissing me. Our facial hair battled for dominance, the one poking the other's face. But that was part of the stimuli with two hairy men colliding naked, full of testosterone and endorphins. He was a great kisser. He did not try to inhale my face, and his tongue was doing due diligence with just enough curiosity in my mouth. I returned the favor as best I could, but parts of me felt like a wet noodle in his arms. I was losing myself in his touch.

He grabbed my hand and led me to the couch. I stumbled backward just a few feet trusting him to get me where he wanted me. I felt the sofa touch the back of my calves. His gentle nudge and pushed me onto the leather sofa.

Leather?! Yes, please! I had not noticed anything particular about his décor other than the bears. I had never had sex on a leather couch. For a quick moment, it felt so stereotypical. Was John Holmes or Jeff Stryker going to walk in and get in line for this shindig? We should face the facts here – leather is just easier to clean.

My legs opened, and he found his way between them and leaned in to kiss me. My rock-hard dick pressed against his belly. No doubt he felt it push into his abdomen. His warm mouth and willing tongue found their way to my chest. He kissed wherever he felt like kissing and eventually found my nipples. He sucked on one adding little bites into it. It sent me near the edge again as his hand toyed and pinched the other. He worked back and forth between the two freely. Eventually working his way down to my belly, rubbing his nose and tongue over my natural pelt, my dick was next.

He went down on me again and, without missing a beat, gobbled up my dick. I had slumped down a bit on that leather sofa, so we were in a perfect position together. I wanted him to know I still wanted him to fuck me. If his mix of aggression and tactile perfection were any indication, his fucking would be just as stellar. While he was devouring my cock, I raised my legs and rested them on his shoulders. He did not mind. I held onto his head and kept his mouth on my cock. He took great care in repeatedly swallowing my dick. I swear the guy had no gag reflex. He tongued my balls, and under my balls slowly working his way back down to my ass again.

He flicked his tongue on my hole taking notes from my reactions prior. I could have let him do that forever. All the while I never touched my dick. I knew I was close at any given moment that just a couple of strokes would have me jizzing all over him and his couch. I would rather just let the tension build. If he was not paying attention to my dick yet, then I was not going to either. He was eating me alive. He raised up and walked on his knees closer to me. His dick was still a hard, fleshy pole between his legs, insistent on being let in on the action at hand.

"Want me to suck you, baby?" I asked.

"No. I invited you here. I want you to enjoy it," he said.

"You sure, cuz I would…"

I did not realize he was already guiding the head of his dick and pressing it against my hole.

"No, buddy, I want you to feel this," he said, as he slowly pushed his pale pink rod inside to penetrate me.

I let out a huge gasp and moan. I thought it might hurt, and it did, but he had also gotten me more than ready to be fucked with his fingering and rimming. It was a mix of foreplay and preparation all in one. Cain had the moves, and I did not realize it until I was being moved, top to bottom. My hole was always tight, and guys loved fucking me. I can say that with a certain amount of pride. Sometimes I wish I could fuck myself to see how it feels. Cain had been prepping me this whole time, so when he did enter me, it felt as natural as breathing air.

"Like that," came the punch line. Like that, indeed.

Goddamn, he felt good inside me. His girth filled me entirely and stretched me out just enough. He kept my legs on his shoulders, holding them with his big man hands. He began to slowly and methodically fuck my hole. It was official – I was in ginger heaven. I was laid out on a leather couch with a hot blue-collar ginger inside me. He had already eaten me out, fingered me, and sucked my cock. And he was a great kisser. It was a half-dozen bucket list items filled ten times.

His dick, while not huge, was just right, and he knew how to use it. He fucked me for a good half-hour straight without stopping to reposition or otherwise feign a break. He never let it entirely escape from my hole. He knew exactly how far to pull out before almost-violently shoving it back in me. He was aggressive but respectful. He seemed to love an intense hot fuck with another guy without a lot of hoopla of dominance or game playing. A little manhandling was fine, but he was otherwise a closeted romantic. I could see him as husband material were it ever to go that far.

Sweat began to form on his forehead, and his shoulders were shiny in the sunlight beaming through his living room. His breathing was rapid but consistent. He was not out of breath, but he was working. We both were doing our jobs. I kept him engaged with kisses when it pleased him to lean in to demand one. I played with his nipples, and he loved to have them tweaked. The more I played with them, in between times of pure unadulterated euphoria, the hornier he became which meant I got fucked longer and harder. I loved reaching up and finding his chest, full of burliness and puffed up with testosterone. I wanted to please him. I caressed his furry chest and kept my eyes on his. He steadily pounded my hole making each stroke feel better than the previous.

Just over a half-hour later, and without warning, he pulled his dick out of me. I wondered if he was done. I do not remember him saying he was going to cum. Was he tired? Maybe he just wanted to take a breather for a minute. He was not out of shape, but he also was not a marathon jock that could go for hours on end. If he wanted a moment to take a breath, then I could deal with that. I was wrong on all of those counts.

He lowered his face to my ass and started to eat me out again. Was this real? Was he eating me *and* fucking me? He buried his face and burrowed his tongue into my fuck hole as deep as genetics would let him. It lasted only a couple of minutes before his dick was inside me again, relentlessly pounding away. He switched back and forth countless times, driving me crazier with each change. He leaned against my chest as he fucked me, kissing me or teasing my nipples between his teeth. Then he gave his dick a rest, alternatively grinding his tongue into my disheveled hole again. Another half hour passed, then another. We were both sweaty, horny, and built up with enough cum to fill a bus.

He had finally settled into a steady rhythm fucking me. This was the final stretch, and we were about to hit a home run that any crowd could not help but cheer for us.

I shifted my hips upward just a bit, so now his dick was hitting my prostate on the upstroke. The plus of the couch is that there is support almost anywhere you need it despite your position. Our sweaty bodies slid around on the leather hide which only made us work harder to keep our momentum intact. One of my legs was still on his shoulder, and I was holding my other back against my chest. We had altered with him pushing against the back of my thighs folding me in half, him holding my legs by the ankles, and whatever else we felt like exploring. He never let me up off the couch. He was in control, and he loved fucking me. We found a great balance between top and bottom and just hot fucking between two grown men the way God intended it.

His breathing became labored, and he started to grunt with every other thrust. He reached down, wrapped his hand around my dick, and began to pump it.

"You know you are going to make me cum faster that way," I stated.

"Yep. I want us to shoot together."

"Are you getting close? Because I am." I asked.

"I am close. You want to cum with me?"

"Fuck yes, I do."

"I am going to fill your fucking ass."

"Then fuck me, goddamn it." I was ready.

That set him off tenfold. With just a few more strokes his orgasm was coming hard and fast. He was still jerking my dick in near perfect rhythm. My legs started to tense up, and I knew this was it.

"Oh, shit – oh.......oh fuck, I think I am going to cum." And I did. He never lost the rhythm, tightening his grip in the process. I came all over my belly and chest.

"Oh, fuck yeah. Look at that cum, boy. Fuck yeah!" I have to admit it sounded like the script to a porn film but at the moment, it felt right.

I could tell by the look on his face that he enjoyed seeing me spray my seed onto my padded midsection. I took over milking the final bits out of my dick. He grabbed both my ankles and pushed my legs up and outward a bit. He was in a pure beast mode which reminded me of my times with Mark, my former jock roommate who had gone onto conquer more gym time, more women.

Most guys cannot take getting fucked after they cum and I am one of those guys. We tend to tighten up, and the stimulation of being fucked quickly dissipates after we orgasm. It is easy to go from contentment to quick pain if a guy is still inside you after you cum. Not always, but it is a common trait. But this time, I did not care. It might have hurt a little bit, but I did not want him to stop until he came inside me.

"Come on, you fucker, cum in me. Cum in me!" Instinctively, I slapped him, hard. He was stunned for about a millisecond but never lost himself.

"Again!" he ordered me.

I slapped him again, harder.

"Fucking fill me, dude! Come on!" I prodded him.

Another slap.

He shook off my aggression as his moans became louder and more consistent. He fucked so fast, so hard. My ass was hurting from it, but I was also incredibly turned on that he was using me like that.

Another slap, even harder.

I grabbed his face from under the jaw like he grabbed mine earlier. That way when you want someone to look right at you, and you wrap your fingers around either side of their jaw.

"Do it, come on, Cain! Fucking fill my ass, man."

"Aaahhhhh!!" came the yell from him. I let go of his face and just watched him orgasm inside me.

"God fucking damn it! UUUUUHH!" I could feel his hot seed planting itself inside me. Every collision between my hole and his dick coaxed out more of his nut. I squeezed down with my sphincter as much as I could to tighten around his meat. I drained every bit of him into me. The exaggerated look on his face showed me that he appreciated it. His natural huskiness was bloated when he came. His body constricted on itself. His grip on me was right, and there was no way I was escaping it. His thrusts slowed, and his breathing struggled to regulate itself. He kept his cock inside me. His broad chest was engorged from blood and oxygen. The sight of Cain still in me and between my legs was nothing short of seeing the face of God, at least a ginger god.

"Mother fuck, that is a hot ass," he declared.

"I have never met someone who knew how to fuck like that." I retorted.

He slumped forward to lay on top of me. I tried to stop him from making contact.

"I am covered in cum, man."

He did not seem to care about that. He collapsed on me.

He settled his head on me. My legs had fallen to a sitting position on either side of him. Both of our breathing slowed a bit, in unison. His sweaty head was in the middle of my chest, and no doubt he could hear my heart beating wildly. He dug his arms between my back and the cushions behind me and held me. He was still on his knees, but he seemed comfortable for now. He was also probably wedging himself, so he did not just fall backward. I stroked his ginger hair, wet with sweat, and ran my fingers down his back a bit. All of my jizz was now not only on me but him as well. I could feel it squishing between us.

"Come here," I said as I pivoted around to lay on the couch normally. "Get up here."

His knees popped again as he stood. He crawled onto the couch and laid on top of me.

"Old is as old does," I said.

"Hmph," came the only note of acknowledgment.

The silence between us was beautiful. We listened to each other breathe. We could almost feel the other's heartbeats in the quiet air of the room. Either of us drifted in and out of consciousness as our bodies went into a short-term hibernation mode We napped. The feeling of Cain on top of me, relaxing and melting into me, felt like laying in the lap of heaven. He was not so heavy that I struggled to breathe. The top of his head was right under my chin. His fingers twitched as he went in and out on sleeping. I felt like we could have stayed there forever. We were a pile of sloppy gay, albeit temporary, garbage. It was a good mess to be part of with him. The inanimate bears in the room seemed to form looks on their faces. I wondered which ones gave their stamp of approval and which ones might protest the love Cain and I had created. Our afterglow endured for a while since neither of Cain nor myself had to rush anywhere.

"You are the first ginger I have ever fucked."

His head still laying on my chest, "You mean the first ginger to fuck you."

"Noted."

He raised his head to look at me. "Did you enjoy yourself?" Was he serious right now?

"It was terrible. No rhythm, sloppy kissing, no ambiance whatsoever," I did not get to finish my humor. He hoisted himself forward the few inches that separated our mouths to kiss me.

"Bullshit, you liar. You loved it."

Another tender kiss.

"Hey there," I said in quieter tones. "We should go shower. There is a lot of mess we have created here."

"We will go together. I got a big tub, big enough for two."

"Well hell, why the fuck we been in here this whole time fucking around?"

"Because I wanted to hold you. I could have fucked you all night, baby boy," he teased.

"On a good day, I would let you," I teased back.

"Was this not a good day?" he asked.

"It was. I wish we had more time."

"You are not exactly hurrying to get out of here."

"No, I guess I am not, huh?" I admitted.

"I am glad you came over today, man," he confessed.

"I am glad, too, Cain," I confessed. "You see this couch and my belly? That is not from a bad time. I look like I have been glazed at a bakery."

My humor always seemed to show up at the worst times.

He pushed himself up to land on his own two feet. He offered his hand to help me. Both of us let out a little groan as we stood. Our muscles had been so tensed up and worked out they did not want to cooperate. We stood there, embracing and appreciating the afternoon we spent together. He grabbed my hand and led me through his kitchen to the bathroom. He turned on the water faucets and toggled on the shower head. I stood there, somewhat awkwardly, waiting for the water to get hot.

He turned around to me, put his hand on the back of my neck, somewhat forcefully and pulled me close.

"You! You are perfect," he announced.

I must have turned ten shades of red, because I knew I was not anywhere close to, nor aspired to be, perfect. I shook my head a little bit, with that "aww shucks" demeanor. I enjoyed hearing that, but it still felt strange actually to accept it.

"Aww. Thanks, but no, I am not ...."

He put his hand over my mouth. "Do not argue with me." He gave me a playful slap on the cheek, grabbing my ass in the process.

"Ow! I suppose I had that coming," I relented. No doubt a now hand a red hand mark on my butt from his scolding.

"Yeah, you did. I might let give you another for a small, nominal fee." He knew a good metaphor.

"The bank is closed," I countered, playfully tightening my buttcheck in his hand.

"I thought you were open late?" he joked.

Are those bears on the shower curtain? Son of a bitch, those are bears on his shower curtain.

"Now get in here, so we can get you clean. If you are good, we might do that again."

"And if I am bad?" I challenged.

He furrowed his brow and growled under his breath.

† Abel †

Youth offers a lot of benefits when it comes to sex. Abel was no exception to that rule. I was almost thirty when he was barely twenty-one. We were both eager for more sex in our lives. Although I did not have a lot of experience, I was sure his list was even shorter. What we both had was desire. The desire to shepherd a deeper connection and frequency in our sexual lives.

In the early days of online internet services in the United States, there were plenty of chat rooms for almost any subculture of people, whether it was gay related, sex-related, or for a more dominant guy like Luke. In the chat room of my city is where I found Abel. He was young and had a serious girlfriend. He was from a political family who was well established in the community. He was the second and youngest child. His older brother, who succeeded him by seven years, was a prominent up-and-coming builder in the community; taking significant roles in literally changing the skyline of Cottam's Bend. Abel slid into the same field in a lesser position. Him being gay and out at that time would have been a massive scandal for the family. The father was in politics direction, his brother a builder, and his mom on the same floor of the city building where they both worked. To his credit, Abel found that hiding out in plain sight and looking for some fun in a chat room to be a much easier process, for the time. He could see someone he did not know but hopefully trust to keep his secrets. Discretion always plays a hard and fast rule in most hookups. It was not that gays were mere sheep to the slaughter with no regard for anyone else; instead, it became a courtesy the good gays extend to others in the pastures of dick. I had no real desire to out anyone to their family or the neighborhood. I, like many other guys, just wanted to fuck around with men.

I did not have a computer at home, so I stayed behind at work, locked the doors and jumped online, hopping in the Cottam's Bend M4M chatroom. It brought almost immediate results. Abel came into view.

```
Abel: Hi there. You are cute
Me: Thanks, man. So are you
Abel: thx. what up
Me: hanging out at work, you?
```

Typical start to a private chat as this was not English Literature 101 at the community college. It was nothing more than screening for a hookup. Chat rooms were consistently an audition process. I took the opener with a grain of salt. I was as new to all this online cruising and chatting as anyone. At least he was making the first move. I took a gander at the handful of photos he had uploaded to his profile. He had dirty blond hair, glasses, and that ever-youthful glow that most twenty-one-year-old people have sitting in their skin. He was a mix of a local Senate page boy and a geek-in-training with a very straight-laced look. He was restlessly exploring his sexuality, which resulted in an internal budding accompanying every orgasm brought to his loins by another man.

```
Abel: do you want to meet?
Me: sure
Abel: can I come to your place? I can not host.
Me: yep I can host
Abel: are you a top?
Me: versatile
Abel: cool
Me: you like to suck dick and get sucked? Kiss?
Abel: where are you
Abel: yeah I like that, get fucked too.
Me: I am on Westerlo. Do you know that area?
Abel: downtown right?
Me: cool
Me: yeah, between S. Ferry and Herkimer, south of Green Lane.
Abel: yeah I park down there for work. Address?
Me: 103 Westerlo. #2, bottom buzzer
Abel: be there in 15
Me: Give me 20, but cool. Shower time for me, see you in a few
```

He was soon in his car with directions to my house and a need to get naked. I quickly locked the office door behind me and power walked home. I lived two or three blocks from the office, so I was back home within three minutes.

I ran upstairs and started the shower water. In the interim, I straightened my bedroom, sprayed some air freshener, and lit some sandalwood and vanilla candles. I had not lived there long, so I did not have a lot of furniture or extras in the apartment. What I did have needed to be put away including clothes, a couple of take-out containers on the coffee table. I jumped in the shower to wash the undercarriage and wobbly bits and get myself in fucking order; literally and figuratively. I threw on a pair of running shorts and a sleeveless Prince t-shirt.

My wait was short-lived. It was only a couple of minutes before the door buzzer interrupted the silence of the house. He was right on time. I pressed the button near my front door to unlock the door downstairs. Just before he got to the door, I made a quick peek through the peephole to get the first glimpse. Amazingly, he looked just like his picture.

"Well! Hey, there!" I greeted him.

"Hello," he said, almost sheepishly. He was nervous. Any guy meeting another for the first time will have a certain number of jitters. I would make a fair wager to say that the power of getting our dicks wet almost always overpowers the neurosis. Good odds.

"Come in, man," I said.

He had on a pair of faded jeans, basic nondescript sneakers, and a blue pullover shirt. Through his tight shirt, I could see the outline of his young almost waifish body. He was a slim guy and probably ran track in school for a while. He did not have any facial hair and did not seem to mind my goatee.

"Can I get you something to drink? I have tea, beer, water, hard cider, soda, purple stuff," I trailed off waiting for his response. If anything, I was an excellent host.

"Nah, I am good. Thank you." Points for politeness.

I realized that even I, too, was nervous. It was nice to know that we were on equal ground.

"Did you find your way okay? All these one-way streets can be confusing down here."

"Yeah, no it was fine. I work downtown and park around here, so I knew where to go." Two demerits from me for not remembering our conversation earlier.

"Oh right. You did tell me that."

He chuckled at my awkwardness. I walked to the kitchen, and I pulled two hard ciders from the fridge.

"Here, have one."

"No, I am okay."

"Take it. You look as nervous as me. It will calm us both down a bit. You do not have to finish it."

"Thanks. Maybe it will take the edge off a bit." He seemed relieved to have the drink in hand. We both took a big gulp of the hard apple cider.

My assessment was heartfelt. Abel's hesitance was evident even more knowing his backstory. I figured he could use a liquid salve on his internal fidgetiness.

"Come with me," I told him.

I led us outside to the deck. Traffic was non-existent, and the shuffle of state workers getting to their cars had long been silenced. The sky was beautiful, and I already had the patio door open enjoying the evening's breeze. The night air in downtown Cottam's Bend was magical. Sometimes you could hear salsa music from a block over spilling from a boom box and reverberating off the sides of buildings and bouncing up from the asphalt. If there was an event at the convention center a few blocks away, herds of people came scattering back to their cars in no-charge parking lots around the neighborhood, wearing and carrying memorabilia purchased from street vendors profiting from the event. My patio faced a community garden and a parking lot where only residents were allowed to park. Even though it was open to anyone else within eyeshot, the sheer vacancy of downtown after 5 p.m. made it virtually a private deck. I had older neighbors in the brownstones on either side of me. To see them outside this late was a long shot. Plenty of nights I showered and walked outside on my little deck unclothed, still slightly damp, without a worry about who would see me up there. It was only the night sky and the big dipper that saw my full moon.

Abel shadowed me as I walked through the second bedroom toward the attached deck.

"What do you do for the state?" I inquired.

"I work in project bids. It is pretty boring stuff. I hate it."

"Sounds like a party waiting to happen. Why do you do it if you hate it?"

"My mom works there. She helped get me a job. It is good money, but it is not what I want to do forever."

"Make that money now and party to take the edge off," I suggested. What did I know? I was still partying and living my twenties as well.

Another chuckle. The conversation was short lived. I finally gave in to Abel's charm. My desire to plow this guy was growing with each passing minute.

"Do you want to go to the bedroom?"

"Yes," came his quick reply accompanied by a restive nod of his cute blond head.

"Bring your drink." Because if we needed to take the edge off of the conversation, we were sure as hell going to need it to take our clothes off and copulate.

I left the doors to the deck open behind me and moved to my bedroom. We sat our drinks on the nightstand. Neither of us knew what to do at first. Is that not always the problem, where to start? Do you jump right into kissing? Do you take off your clothes before you start? Do you undress the other person? I had to break the ice quickly, so I decided to get started by choosing the latter. I yanked my shirt off and threw it on the floor.

I turned to face him. He looked at me wondering what I would do next. I took a step toward him. I ran my hand down his chest over his shirt. I could feel his heart beating. With both hands, I grabbed the bottom of his shirt and gently pulled it over his head. His arms, without thought, raised to cooperate. He stood there with his pale and mostly smooth chest exposed. His relative modesty became apparent as he involuntarily trembled at the sudden discomfort of being susceptible to my fancy. I sat on the edge of my bed as I grabbed his pants at the waist and gripped his belt buckle to pull him closer to me. I tried my best to get his pants open gracefully. The small patch of dark blond hair rising at his waistline and encapsulating his belly button made the job even more enjoyable. Leaning forward, I kissed his flat stomach and let his treasure trail tickle my nose. His skin was soft under the little pelt of fur. I felt him tense up as my goatee tickled his stomach. Whatever abs he had in his thin frame were relatively undeveloped beyond what youth naturally brings to the young. His body was supple and pliable. I gently licked his enticing trail, an act to which he did not object. I lightly blew on the same spot sending a new sensation over his midsection. One of his hands slid up my arm and onto the top of my head. He was not forceful but proactive. For someone who started the online conversation, he seemed incredibly apprehensive about continuing it on a physical level. I pulled back and went to work on unbuckling his belt. He attempted to help me, but I stopped him. I looked up at him while fiddling with his belt and undoubtedly had a silly, satisfied grin on my face. I looked him in the eye and realized something. He was scared to death.

"Is this your first time?"

"No. No, why?"

"You seem nervous."

"I...," he almost seemed embarrassed.

"I have not been with a lot of guys," he confessed.

I put my hand on his belly as a way to comfort him.

"You are okay, buddy. I am not here to judge you. We are here to have fun. Just relax. We do not have to do anything you do not want to, okay?" I reached up to cup the side of his face.

"Thanks."

"And listen, we have all had first times or newer times with a man. Everyone goes through it."

"I guess you are right," he relented.

"Do you want to continue?" I did not want to push him into something he did not feel like doing.

He released a sheepish smile and nodded in the affirmative. It was then that he knew I would not push him into anything he did not want to do tonight. I had gained his trust. I had no reason to betray that, not for the sake of a quick lay.

His belt was undone, and I quickly finished unbuttoning his jeans. He kicked off his shoes. I leaned inward as I pulled his jeans down to his ankles. He stepped out of them. I sat there for a moment and just admired his near-naked body. I pulled his body toward my face, and I buried my nose and mouth into his abdomen. I worshipped his midsection with kisses. He had no choice but to react. The sensation of my tongue wrangling with his body hair was more than he had probably felt all week and had not from any quasi-girlfriend he toted around with him. He smelled nice like he had just showered. Slowly, I worked my mouth up his chest, and over to one of his nipples. My arms held him close while my hands were firmly planted in the middle of his back. I let my mouth revere his nubile body. His nipples reacted to being licked and sucked becoming erect in mere seconds. His muted moans of pleasure tried to hide his embarrassment of finally giving in to his sensual side. I could feel and see his dick getting hard through his underwear. I wanted to savor every moment with him. He was so pure, almost untouched. He was indeed old enough to be here. Dare I say he almost had a virginal quality to him. I was not busting any cherries tonight, but he was closer to it than not.

I moved one of my hands to the side of his neck, slightly wrapping my fingers around the back of it, then I pulled his head down to mine, and kissed him. He was a little awkward at first, but we soon found our rhythm. It was a ploy to lean back on the bed and pull him on top of me. My feet were still on the floor, helping to balance his body weight on top of me. He probably did not weigh more than 140 pounds and was only about 5'9. His maturing body felt so good against mine. His smooth chest battled my hairy chest. My dick was rigid and leaking precum in my shorts. I reached into his tight-whiteys and cupped his ass. I pushed them down to expose his perfectly white ass. He lifted his midsection up and somehow, we both got his underwear off his body.

"Get back over here," I said, playfully.

"Should you take those off?" he asked, motioning to my shorts. I could not argue the point. He was naked, and I was not. I had to even the playing field.

"Yeah. I guess I should, huh?" I pulled off my shorts and got him back on top of me.

His naked, sleek body laid on mine as if it were meant to be there. His dick was longer and thinner than mine. Both of our cocks were making their introductions. I shuffled myself up onto the middle of the bed. He, legs straddling me, followed in succession.

We took a moment slowly, kissing and exploring each other's body. Abel grazed his hands over my hairy chest exploring its coarseness and enjoying the sensation on the pads of his fingertips. It felt like Michael the archangel was giving me the once-over before approving my move to heaven.

His rested his legs on either side of my thighs, I laid there with a note of disbelief that this blond-haired angel was naked on top of me. Our groins found an amicable cadence during our amended and enhanced frot. We continued to kiss, feeling each other's bodies in the process. I kept reaching down to hold his perfect butt in my hands. I could not get enough of it. I pulled his ass cheeks apart to tease his hole with my finger. His body responded naturally, and he did not question my efforts. He would arch his back, giving natural rise to his hips which begged for more attention. I ran my fingers along the inner part of his ass where it gets dark, furry, and warm. I resisted every urge I had to plunge my fingers into his near-virginal hole. I could have easily finger-banged him, and I could have sent him home happy. There was no rush, though. He did not seem fragile, but to be overly aggressive or rough would have been an evident miscalculation on my part. Teasing was always a safe option to judge someone's sexual dexterity.

I rolled him over on his back and laid on top of him. He kept his legs open, and I put myself gently between them. He was so beautiful and pure laying on my pillows. The candles in the room lighted his body. His alabaster skin pulled in the amber tenors of the flame and warmed his tone. I held him in my arms and put as much passion into my kisses as possible. He responded in kind by wrapping his long gangly legs around my waist, holding me just as close to him as I was holding him to me. Making out is always a favorite thing to do with a man. Neither of us was in any hurry tonight. We took our time.

He wanted to roll back on me, so I obliged. He raised up from kissing me and looked at me with those fucking blue eyes. I grinned at him. He knew what I wanted. He shifted himself downward. I put my hands on his shoulders and nudged him into position. With his non-calloused hands – hands that felt so warm and soft I almost a compulsion to check his driver's license because no adult I knew had hands that soft - he grabbed my dick. There was not one blemish or rough spot on his hands. Of course, one does not get callouses writing bid proposals for the state. He was not someone whose hands were that of a manual laborer that could easily prove the signs of a hard day's work by the palms of his hands. His youth and a decent skincare routine were evident with his grip on my cock.

It was the middle of summer and, although it had grown dark just after his arrival, the air outside was still thick with eighty-degree heat. I had no doubt it was just as warm in the house. The windows were open to let any breeze freely travel. A couple of fans were oscillating across the room keeping watch over us like little soldiers at their post. A newly forming modest glow of sweat on our bodies reminded us of the heat in the air. I felt the dewy softness on his back. His hair was matted with perspiration through our make-out session.

I glanced down to watch his mouth envelop my cock. I knew he had not sucked a lot of dicks before as he fumbled around with it a bit. There were a few swipes of his teeth, but I kept my senses about me. Everyone starts somewhere, and he was trying. He sucked it like he was licking up a red, white and blue bomb popsicle in the middle of a southern heatwave. Every touch of his tongue against my shaft was my own personal Shangri-La. He slowly worked himself into a fervor sucking my dick. His eagerness to appear more skilled highlighted his lack of experience in giving oral gratification. The teeth scrapes were gone. All I felt was his mouth massaging my cock from all angles. His warm, wet mouth knew no bounds.

"Hey, slow down, buddy. It is not going anywhere. Relax and enjoy it."

"I am sorry."

"Do not be sorry," I offered as I cupped the side of his face. "There is no pressure to perform here. It is not a movie. It is just you and me. You can trust me. I am not here to use you like that. Just do what you enjoy."

That seemed to calm him a bit.

"I want to suck you," he offered.

He redirected and endeavored to go down on me again. I guided his mouth up and down the length of my pole at a slower tempo. He understood and found a regularity that pleased us both. I watched him for a while. He was diligent in his cock sucking and seemed to enjoy honing his skills. I wondered if he was as voracious with his girlfriend's cunt. He glanced at me from time to time partially embarrassed that his skills were not better while also seeking my approval. I continued to caress his head and gently thrust my hips into his mouth to soothe him, letting him know he was doing something right. If my dick was a pacifier, he was sucking that thing like it was an instinct. He settled into the creation of pleasuring another man which, in turn, gave him pleasure. I smiled at him relaying that he was on track.

I steadied my gaze at him. My purpose as not to humiliate him. I wanted him to drop any inhibitions he had and realize sex is just sex. It is meant to be enjoyed and exploited by both parties. This was not a time to be shy or hide in the dark. I alternated my thrusting between passionate and playful to aggressive. The dominant moments were punctuated with me holding his head over my dick and fucking his willing mouth. Other moments I would let him do whatever he wanted to do. Either way, I was going to enjoy this as long as I could and make damn sure he was along for the same ride.

I pulled him up toward me.

"Get on your back. It is my turn now," I ordered.

He found a comfortable spot where I had just been. His long and evenly colored cock stood straight up in my face. I hovered my mouth near his dick slowly licking the underside of his shaft, teasing him with a preview. I kissed his chest and unexpectedly tasted the salty sweat that we both had excreted. My tongue continued down his tummy to his treasure trail, a place of recent familiarity. I felt like I could have just stayed in an eternal holding pattern kissing his belly making him shiver and twitch every time my tongue tasted his skin, his heart skipping a beat with every kiss I gave him.

His college-aged cock was eight inches if it was one. A puffy blond bush surrounded it. It was longer than it was thick; veiny and had a nice little mushroom head on top. It was sleek and perfect, like him. His dick exceeded the overgrowth of hair and towered out on its own, begging for something to be done with it. His groin was shallow and flat. I would imagine any other time his dick rested there like it was a custom cushion. I lowered my mouth over his thickness and used my tongue to wrangle it into my mouth. His whole body seemed to tighten. I was going to show no mercy at this point. I took the head of his cock in my mouth and sucked it like the nipple on a bottle. I pushed the tip of my tongue into the frenulum; that little part where the head of the dick wraps around the underside. Some guys get that waft of skin pierced. But I have found that a man is susceptible to great moments of pleasure when it is manipulated just right. When I latched on with my lips and gently sucked it, his legs immediately quivered with approval.

I got you.

As I toyed with his dick, sucking it and licking it, I gave his balls a proper amount of attention. My fingers found their way to tease his hole again. He responded by pivoting his hips up for me to further torment his fuzzy cavern. I massaged it with two fingers while keeping his dick in my mouth. I pressed on his taint provoking his prostate which, in turn, prompted a response. I took all of his cock – a feat he seemed to be as flabbergasted by as he was captivated - until my nose once again found the pelt of pubes at the base of his young cock. His hips immediately discovered their tempo as he attempted to fuck my throat. He was finally letting loose. His inhibitions dropped as he gave himself over to the moment. I can only imagine that he felt freer than he ever had with his female cohort gallivanting at political fundraisers and state-sponsored dinners.

With all of his unit in my mouth, I bared down with my tongue to suck harder. He was in heaven, and he let me know it when he let out a huge cry. I thought for a second that he was going to cum. Thankfully he resisted. I repeated going all the way back down on his dick, held my mouth there for a minute then I looked up at him. His eyes were closed as his body gesticulated. It only made me harder knowing what I was doing to him. I sucked him and made him feel like it was his first time. I worshipped his cock with every bit of my mouth. I purposely edged him, bringing him close to orgasm then backing off from it. I let him settle, sucking on his balls in the interim, before slowly working him back into a near-frenzied state before relenting yet again.

I sat up in bed and got him to sit on my lap with his legs wrapped around my waist. This was one of my favorite positions to make out in, or fuck in, or whatever. My dick was upright, and hard, and pressed against his brown eye. I had my arms wrapped around his torso to keep him upright in front of me. He was trying to grind up and down to get my dick inside him. His arms were around my neck and helped leveraged himself to stay in place. Our kisses grew passionate, hard, and I could feel his inhibitions continue to fall off little by little. My fingers dug into his back or grabbed his ass and moved him up and down over my dick. I wanted to fuck him so badly. His hard dick was upright against my soft belly. His legs would tighten up around me, and his arms would stiffen. He was ready.

"Get on your stomach."

He rolled over face down on the mattress. I grazed my hands over his perfect ass and parted his cheeks. I blew on his hole sending an involuntary quiver through his body. I crawled up parallel with his body, my chest tickling his back. My dick was cradled in his crack again, purposely teasing his hole.

"Have you ever had your ass eaten before?"

He paused for a second. Did he even know what that was, I wondered?

"No, I have not."

I sunk down between his nubile pegs and buried my tongue into his wooly hole. His moans changed from that of amazement to ones of imploring of me. He was compelling me to eat his hole. His arms stretched out and grabbed handfuls of bed linen. His legs parted leaving everything about him open. He was willing to let me do whatever I wanted to him. I flicked my tongue against his wrinkled entry point, allowing the hairs to catch my tongue as they dared. He immediately tensed his hole then released it. I continued to tease his ass while gently massaging his cheeks. I pushed my tongue into his hole which still had a scent of soap and fresh water. The deeper I drove my tongue, the more he hiked his ass up to me, silently begging for more. It was clean and inviting. The more he squirmed under the tutelage of my tongue the more it made me continue to lick his hole in every way I could imagine. He loved having his butt eaten. I continued to give him what he loved.

I reached between his legs and pulled his dick downward, so it pointed at me. He submitted to all of it. I licked his dick from behind alternating back to tonguing his hirsute cavern. We were both in comfortable positions, so we felt no great need to move or change it.

"Oh, God," he moaned.

"Oh sorry, are you not enjoying this?" I said as I popped my head up from his crack. "I can stop."

"No, please. Do not stop, please." He reached back and pulled open one of his cheeks. He begged for more which is what I wanted from him. He was an angel, and I wanted him to want me. Usually, a hookup is just that – a reason to have sex. But for some reason, I was drawn to his innocence and his proverbial shell opening with me. I was surprised at him being so verbose. Thus far he had been a quieter lay, but now he was like a new puppy barking for the first time. Every moan that came out of his mouth felt fresh like it was the first time he had ever uttered a guttural sound based in pure, unfiltered sexual pleasure. I could only surmise that - not only did I truly love eating his ass but that, as I did - his groans told on him and how much he loved, even craved, being with an experienced man.

"Please fuck me." Not just fuck, but *fuck*.

"You sure," I asked from between his legs.

"Yes, I am sure. Please fuck me."

I got on my knees and right up to his butt, my dick within centimeters of his ass. With one hand in the middle of his back, I used the other to guide the head of my dick right to the top of his hole.

"Do not go too hard." Now he wanted leniency?

I gently pushed my purple head into his tight hole. He started to crawl up the bed to get away from it. I grabbed his hips and held him in place.

"Do not worry, baby boy. I am not going to hurt you." He looked back at me for reassurance. "But I am going to fuck you senseless."

"Yeah, but pleas...." I did not wait for him to finish. I slowly and steadily push my thick dick into his wet hole despite any objections his ass might have had.

"Oww!" he yelled.

I leaned forward until my chest was touching his back. I rested my chin on his shoulder so I could whisper.

"Easy, buddy. Just breathe through it."

"It hurts."

"It always does at first, breathe. Deep breath. There you go, another. Breathe."

He took my lead and took deep breaths waiting for the pain to pass. I knew we would soon arrive at a better moment of pure pleasure.

I slowly pushed myself further into him. He continued to wait out the pain. I pulled out a bit then pushed back in noticing just how tight of an ass he was carrying. It was insanely hot. I could not figure out which felt better: his soft hands and wet mouth around my rigid cock or his warm, fuzzy ass wrapped around my dick like a set of forceps on a newborn's head.

His body writhed in a conflict of temporary discomfort and pending gratification. My meat spreading his hole open probably did hurt. He wanted this as much as me. We had an understanding that narrow was the road to the kingdom, but wide was the hole spread to open the gates of unadulterated pleasure.

"Mmm, that is better, huh? Yeah, you are doing okay."

He moaned, and I knew the pain was leaving. I resisted the urge to thrust myself back and forth as I wanted into his near-hymeneal posterior. Instead, I just stayed inside him for a minute. I laid on his back with my arms around his and our legs locked together. Neither of us was going anywhere. I was patient enough to wait.

"Squeeze your ass."

"But it hurts."

"No, it does not. Squeeze your ass," I commanded. "Squeeze like you are holding in a piss."

Although this was not a dominant scene, someone had to take the reigns.

"Baby, it will not hurt if you relax. Breathe through it. I am in you. Tell me you want it to stop and it will stop. Just say the word."

He pulled forward, hesitating. I thought he was going to make me pull out, which I did not want right now. But had he asked, I would have kept my promise. Maybe he was too inexperienced or young to enjoy a moment with an older man. Perhaps a moment of youth versus maturity was just too overwhelming. If it were, I would respect that. I promised him I would not hurt him. I intended on keeping that promise.

"No," he mumbled, barely audible.

He squeezed his ass as I instructed. I felt the inside of him close in on my shaft. It was already tight, and now it was unworldly. I pulled my dick halfway out of his hole.

"Now relax your ass." When he did, I shoved my cock all the way back into him. He took the initiative to tighten up once I was all the way inside his butt. Again, I pulled back, and he loosened his inner grip. He was learning the rhythm. He was starting to relax and enjoy being fucked, which is what he wanted. Each time became more natural than the former. He was learning. I was loving.

"Still hurt?"

His moan was enough of an acknowledgment, and the only one I needed. My rhythm became steadier, forceful; his dick was still poking out from under him. Seeing his ghostly white ass ripple with every thrust only turned me on more. My pace increased, and the inertia kept me fucking him like it would be the last time for either of us.

He became more vocal, moaning with every push I made. We were sweating in the black summer's night air. At times, it dripped from my nose or forehead onto his back. His white skin was shiny with sweat.

I put my legs on the outside of his and plunged my dick into his butt; my chest was over his back. I hooked my forearms across his chest and pulled him up onto his knees, back arched. I held him against me hugging him from behind while pushing my cock inside his tight, furry cavity. I thrust my dick into him relentlessly, kissing and nibbling the back of his neck. His legs would buckle under him then he would find the strength to keep himself upright so I could stay inside him.

"You okay, baby?"

"Uh huh," was all he could utter.

"You feel like an angel right now."

He turned his head to kiss me. He proved to be flexible.

"I love you..." he said. It surprised both of us.

"What?" I replied, calmly.

"...inside me. I love you inside me. It feels..."

"...like Eden?" I finished his statement. My heady verbiage might have been too much for him in the heat of the moment. I was not here to edit myself, either. Fucking Abel did feel like a favored sacrifice to a higher power. The beauty of the shadows we created in the candlelight was an enchantment. We breathed together, that night, in unison. Our breath on the other's skin felt like a wisp heaven's wind butterflied by an angel's wings.

∞

"Let me ride you. Please?"

"Really?"

"Yes. Please?"

"Come on, then," I said.

He got up, turned around, and was standing on the bed. He walked and stood over me. I reached down to grab his ankles. We both stopped and took notice of the other.

"God, you are so perfect right now, Abel. Do you know that? How did I get so lucky?"

Despite already being flushed with red, but I could see him blush. His chest was pink and radiated from his towering stance. His long dick teetered straight outward and cast a long shadow.

"Let me fuck you. Come, sit on my dick," I said, getting us back into the groove.

He squatted down over my dick and guided me into him.

"Remember, take it at your own pace because I do not want to hurt you," I told him, ardently.

He had proved to be flexible and willing. Once he got himself into a good position, he lowered himself onto my dick. He felt amazing in a whole new way. I enjoyed watching him bounce up and down on my dick. His legs were bent, and I helped hold him in place by grabbing his knees. He braced himself with his hands on my chest. I let him ride me. He had to learn somehow as it was clear he had not been a bottom on top very often, if at all. It was a particularly vulnerable position to be in for any bottom on top. For him, it seemed to be an especially true form. Him being as exposed and vulnerable as he was with me seemed to let me wholeheartedly earn his trust.

"Bend your legs, and sit on it," I told him. "You might be more comfortable."

He paused and quickly negotiated that in his mind. While squatting over a dick is great it can become more laborious than enjoyable. By bending his protracted offshoots under him, he could rest his ass on my lap and use his whole body to rock back and forth on me.

One leg, then the other, bent down on either side of my hips. My cock rubbed against the thick fur in the crack of Abel's ass. It was almost too much to bear. His torso, long and slender, hung over mine as he reached back and guided my dick into him.

I manipulated his chest with my hands exploring every inch of his body. His chest was crimson and feverish from the rushes of blood. I put my hands on his waist and fucked him from my prone position. I loved seeing his still-developing young body tighten up with every gesture to massage his insides. He now fully trusted me. He leaned backward, his hands on my legs, arched his back, and just rode me. His torso was bent backward, and I could see his little ribs over his tummy that went even flatter; his firm abs showed through, and his huge cock bounced up and down against my hairy belly. Being one with him was exquisite. It reminded me of my own dick riding experience with David.

I reached down and grabbed Abel's dick.

"You want to cum, baby?" I asked.

"You want me to make you cum?"

"Yes," I deferred. "I want to cum with you." That seemed to energize him in a whole new way.

I continued to bulldoze his ass. He leaned forward, resting his hands right on my pecs, and let me fuck him.

I reached up and pointed his face right at mine.

"Look at me when I am fucking you. Look at me."

It was an intense move I learned from Luke; keeping eye contact with your partner, whether fucking or getting fucked, it lowers any last barriers.

I had the impression he had never done that before and probably felt awkward about it. Hookups often remain anonymous even in the midst of the act. Faces were not examined, and experiences were kept below the neck. I like to see the guy I am fucking or who is fucking me. I want to look at his face. Eye contact is just as hot as a blowjob. It was a nuance that Abel had not learned. Yet.

"No. No – look at me. Watch me when I cum inside you. I want you to see me cum."

"I want to cum so bad," he urged.

"I want you to, baby." I wiped sweat from my brow and chest, grabbed his dick and started stroking. It was not long until he was squirming more. His hips attacked my hips, his hole unrelenting in its hiding of my dick.

"I want to cum with you, but you have to look at me. Look at me, baby. I want to see your face when I make you cum. I am so close."

"Yes. I will, I promise. Please let me cum" Abels petition was clear. I put all I had left inside me into pounding his ass. In sync, I pulled on his cock. He reached down to assist, but I pushed his hands away.

"Eyes on me," I told him. "Watch me while we both cum, okay? I got you, baby. I got you."

"Yes. Yes, I will," he promised. My fucking got faster, as did my jerking off his dick. I was close. It was inevitable that I was going to cum. I could tell he was close, too. His moans started to incorporate a whimper and pleading.

"You close, baby?" I asked.

"Yes. Oh, God!"

I knew he was seconds away. His legs tightened on my hips without concession. With only a handful of thrusts, I let loose with whatever restraints I had and blasted inside his hole. The spasms assaulted every nerve ending I had. I screamed my bliss at the top of my lungs. Instinctually, my hand gripped his dick tighter. Two seconds later, it pulsated in my hand. He was cumming with me. He shot his serum all over my chest, hitting my goatee and face. I continued to shake as I thrust my dick into him. Through his screams, his face told me the real story. He was having the best orgasm of his life.

It was indescribable not only to see his face but to feel myself depositing every ounce of liquid I had into his ass. I felt the cum all over his hole and inside it. It dripped back out onto my balls and between my legs. Both of us were out of breath, sweaty. I was covered in his jizz.

"Oh God, do not move, please," I begged him.

"Are you okay?"

"My dick is so sensitive." Every micro-motion he made, the hairs around his hole void of mercy, felt like a million fingers tickling my dick. It was too much to handle.

"Okay," but he moved a little bit. I happily winced.

"Sorry."

"It is okay. You feel so good right now. I want to stay inside you for a minute."

"Fuck, I am sorry," he said, looking down at me. "I came all over you."

I laughed. "That tends to happen when someone gets fucked like you just did."

He chuckled a little bit. I realize my hand was still on his dick. I had not released my grip. Assuming he might be sensitive as I was, I gingerly let go of his young cock.

"This is not a mess; it is beautiful."

He had not heard cum on a belly quite described like that. I could see him process it in his head.

"That is all you and just how turned on you were, right? Nothing wrong with that."

"I guess you are right," he conceded.

"You are so adorable. Do you know that?"

"Thanks, again. You told me." he insisted. "You are hot, too. I like older guys."

"Less than a decade. That is not too far off, is it?"

"Nah, it is not. But to me, it is older," he said.

"I get it. I do not have much of an age preference," I said. In your early thirties, it is a sweet spot up and down the age scale of gay men.

"I do," he said, annoyed. "Guys my age are dumb fucks. Not all the time, but sometimes they are so stupid."

"Well, you are no dumb fuck," I demanded.

"No, not me. Computer club, choir, some track my freshman year. Pretty much anything that gets your ass kicked on a weekly basis."

I hoped he was mostly joking about the violence.

"You are still cute as fuck. I insist. Besides, did you hear me complaining?" I asked.

"It was awesome when you licked my butt and fucked me." His glowing facial expression echoed his sentiment.

"Have you ever had your hole eaten before?"

"Uh, no."

"Did you like it?"

"Yeah. It was great."

"When I saw you, I knew I wanted to do that to you." It was true. I wanted to taste every bit of him.

"You did?"

"Are you kidding? You were a fucking cherub the minute you walked in the door, Abel. The way you got sweaty and intense when I was eating your hole. I could eat that little peach butt of yours for days."

He squirmed from the barrage of compliments.

"Kiss me," I asked him.

He leaned down, keeping distance between the jizz on my chest, and kissed me. My softening dick slid out of his ass without either of us taking note of it. I patted the mattress beside me.

"Come, lay here," I said.

He made himself at home. I reached down under the edge of the bed and grabbed a towel that I kept there for just such occasions.

"Always prepared," I joked. He giggled the way only he could which did nothing but endear him more to me. I wiped his spunk from my torso as best I could, catching most of it in the blue terry cloth. I tossed it back to the floor. I put an arm and motioned for him to get next to me. I wrapped my arm around his mild frame. He laid as close as he could to me, his arm over my chest; his head rested on my shoulder. I kissed him on his sweaty head, raking my fingers through his hair. I alternated lightly grazing my fingers down his svelte back, feeling his soft and damp skin on my fingertips. The fans oscillated cool air over our bodies inviting welcomed chills and goosebumps. He leaned up and kissed me. I pulled him closer, him still wrapped in my arm, and tried my best to convey the passion I felt for him that evening. He caressed my chest, still exploring his touch on another

man's body. We craved each other's attention, and I was glad to let him use me to explore that part of himself. We both enjoyed the moments we were creating. We were naked, well fucked, and entirely at peace with each other.
I heard his breathing change, and he was letting out little snores on my chest. I chuckled inside thinking how insane this whole evening had been between us. He was worn out, and a nap could not be resisted. He found my body comfortable to sleep against, but I was the winner that night. I was the one who felt unfettered joy and (dare I say it) love for Abel. I loved his kindness, his willingness to explore and be explored, his curiosity and bravery in confronting it. I wanted him to stay forever, but I knew he had a schedule. I knew he had a girlfriend. I knew he was not resting on her sweaty body like he was sleeping on mine. I knew he did not let loose his inhibitions and fully sink into the joys of someone fucking his ass. I also knew he would probably never be a man I could call my own because his loyalties to family and appearance trumped moments like this. I could not blame him for maintaining a life that he felt offered him other opportunities by being around the right people. I blamed society's need to push gay men and women back in the closet. I tried my best to stay in the moment and enjoy his presence in my bed. I knew it would not last forever, so I savored every moment. I do not know how long he napped, but he eventually woke himself because of his adorable puppy snores.
"Hey, baby. You okay?"
"Yeah. Was I snoring?" He seemed embarrassed, propping himself up on one elbow to face me.
"Um, yes you were."
"Oh God..." he started.
"It was adorable. Do not over think it."
I grabbed his hand and pulled him back to me. I ran my fingers through his damp hair; it was another excuse to

touch him. We kissed without thought of time or any presumed schedules.

"Did you have a good time?" I wondered. If a young college type like that showed up at anyone else's house, there was a good chance the guy would have used him and sent him home. The real joy comes in taking time and exploring the inexperience and pushing a few limits.

"Do you hear me complaining?" he said wrapping his arms around me again.

I did not. I would not for the next two rounds, either.

† Nicolaus †

After going to the 3C bathhouse for a time, you begin to know people, at least by their face and the way their towel hangs. Wednesdays were half-price cover charge days, which means that was the day I hopped on the train to sexy town. I started seeing a handsome guy there on a regular basis. Ours was strictly a bathhouse-only relationship, but it worked for us. We were both there for only a few reasons, the biggest of which was to seek out the pleasures of the flesh directly. One does not go to a bathhouse to resist lust or sexual relations; instead, one goes to indulge in them wholeheartedly. I never asked if my bathhouse friend was married, fully gay, closeted or otherwise. It did not matter. A bathhouse was our own local Las Vegas: what happened there, stayed there.

My adventures with Nicolaus, the Greek – who looked like he was dropped straight out of an ancient city like Antioch or Athens and would have won every physical event in the original Olympic games - will always stand as one of the great examples of how random sex can turn into something entirely different. The Greek was not the only man I would encounter at 3C, but he was arguably one of the best. I learned from each encounter I had in life and paid it forward to another willing host. Nicolaus became a Wednesday regular.

Nicolaus was swarthy, and probably in his mid-fifties. I was barely thirty myself, so he was right up my alley. I never minded an older man. In my twenties, I tended to be attracted to men in their thirties and early forties. Once I got into my thirties, I felt like I was in my sweet spot with men my age and up to a couple of decades older. I quickly learned never to underestimate someone based on their age. The experience, the familiarity, the ease of it are all pluses that a younger gay man can take for their future years.

The Greek's body was firm and stout. He was thick with a natural brawn to him. His curly chest hair had hints of gray and differed little from the hair on his head. His eyes looked like two raw olives; lush, green, soulful, ripe with stories that only he had seen and only he could tell. He was just shy of a full six feet tall which was slightly shorter than me. He seemed tall as a building the way he carried himself. He was worldly, confident, a real stallion. He had been raised old school where people had few real hang-ups about the natural definition of their body. Those who lifted weights and built themselves up to then-abnormal-looking-bodies were the exception, not the rule as we would see just a few decades later. I had no doubt his brawn came from hard work. Men did not need to go to the gym when they worked in factories, at construction sites, on tractors, or in woodshops. The muscle came naturally from physical labor; a hard day's work showed on the face and the body. The Greek had that look about him. The first time I ever saw him come around a corner - his skin lustrous and shining no doubt from a quick trip to the steam room or sauna - I felt paralyzed, unable to move, to speak, or to wipe the stupid "wow" look off my face. If anyone watched me, they could indeed conclude that I was instantly attracted to him. He was so striking that in any other situation, I would expect to find him making furniture or something else steeped in hands-on manual labor. His dark skin seemed to pulse with light from the inside and contrasted beautifully against the white towel swathed around his thick waist and thick thighs. With every step he took, his calves flexed showing off their muscle definition. His ankles were thin, and his feet were shorter with a perfectly symmetrical sloped toe line from big to small. Dark hairs hung out on his legs holding their droplets of moisture refracting the dim light in the club.

I was soaking in the hot tub. Nude, of course. There were two other guys in there, but they were way more into each other than me. I did not care because I was there to relax. If they were going to fuck, they could do it in their room. Them making out was no big deal for me. They mostly chatted in hushed tones that were still audible over the hum of the jacuzzi motors and swishing water currents that swirled around all of us. The Greek had passed the hot tub a few times. The 3C floor plan was rectangular in nature with no dead end so one could circle through the club and never run into a wall. Most guys walked around or hung out on a bench to watch guys come into the club area after having checked in at the front desk, surely sizing up who they would hunt next. I was not sure if the Greek kept doing laps every couple of minutes out of boredom or that he was trying to get my attention. The guys making out in the hot tub departed to other places. I was the only one not in the sauna, steam room, or a private room. Secretly, the Greek had my attention from the first time I saw him a few weeks prior. I had just never made it a point to interact with him; probably out of fear of rejection. When you are walking around in a towel, and nothing else you either go into it with full on confidence and bluster or you go in hoping for the best. After a while, you lose your inhibitions and go with the flow. If one guy rejects you, another one will appear soon enough.

When the Greek was doing his laps this time, he seemed to eyeball me purposely. Did we happen to catch each other's eye or was there more to it? Men work quickly. Looking straight at someone for more than a millisecond was deemed a visible sign of cruising.

Having been in the hot tub for a good half hour, I was starting to pickle around the edges. I grabbed my towel from the hooks on the wall nearby and wiped my head and chest. I loosely wrapped it around my waist and went to take a quick piss in the nearby bathroom.

As I came out of the bathroom, he was doing another lap around the joined hallways. I followed in his direction, although he had already rounded another corner by the time I got to the first.

I always rented a room when I went to the club. Some guys would just rent a locker, but I liked a little privacy if I was to get lucky. As a rule, I was always out to get lucky. I figured I would walk around the hall to my room, the one with just a big reflective *15* sticker on it – one obviously picked up for a song at the local hardware store around the corner - and maybe he would find me. I unlocked my door with the key issued by the front desk.

There was dim lighting throughout the club, and someone a few rooms over had their light on, so any extra light in my room was unnecessary. The walls were a foot shy of the ceiling, so I had ambient lighting. I left my door slightly ajar, partly because if the Greek did not show up I would head back to the steam room. Aside from cruising for dick, finding my Zen moments in the steam room or sauna, eyes closed and enjoying the hum of the building, was almost as satisfying as getting a blowjob. Either way, I left the club happy. If I shot any DNA down a guy's throat, I was happier.

Leaving my door ajar is also a silent cruising code. If you are in your room and leave your door open to any degree, you are inviting a man (or men) to join you. I hoped the Greek would find me before someone else did. Not that the other men in the club on this day were not good looking, but I saw no one queuing outside my door. The Greek was in my wheelhouse that day. He was just the kind of guest I wanted to share some time with between these walls of room fifteen.

I realized I needed a fresh towel. We are issued two when we check into the club. This one was a bit too wet for me after drying off from the hot tub (and the steam room before that). I tried to dry off a bit more before hanging it on the back of my door to air dry. I could toss it in one of the laundry hampers in the hallway and get another one. I had a second towel, so I vetoed a trip to the front desk.

As I opened the door, towel still in my hand and standing there naked deciding whether or not to head back out into the common areas, something caught my attention from the corner of my eye. I looked over and there he stood. The Greek. It was clear to him from the body language that he had unintentionally startled me. I do not know how long he had been standing there watching me fumble with towels, keys, or whatever else. I held my towel in front of me to maintain some level of modesty, trying to cover my dick; but mostly out of a knee-jerk reaction to being caught naked.

"Hello," he greeted.

"Oh hey."
"I am sorry. I did not mean to startle you," he apologized.
"No, it is fine. I was swapping towels. The hot tub obliterated the other one. They are not exactly Egyptian cotton?" I was terrible at small talk with strangers.
He chuckled at my ridiculous attempts at friendly banter.
"How are you?" I said, almost involuntarily continuing the conversation.
"I am good. I am Nicolaus."
I returned the favor of putting a name to my face.
"Would you mind if I came in?" he asked, ever-so-politely.
Fucking hell yes you motherfucking can!
"Uh, sure. Absolutely." I tried my best not to make "absolutely" not sound as giddy on the outside as I felt inside my gut. It was more of a southern "absolutely, partner" kind of approach.
"I do not want to intrude if you are busy…"
"No. You are fine. Get in here so I can shut the door. You caught me standing here naked, flashing everyone." I added a giggle to relieve my inner awkwardness.
I took a step or two backward to let him in the room.
"You just caught me off guard. I saw you walking around earlier. You are hard to miss."
"Thank you."
He shut the door behind him. Instantly, I was mesmerized by his dark, olive skin against the stark white towel around his waist; like a child's first time gazing into a crystal ball. I found myself at a loss for what to do next. I could not offer him a drink or a piece of fruit. He smiled at me which instantly melted my insides. His eyes pierced into me like they were looking into every part of my soul where I hide all my dirty little secrets. I had been wrapped in a towel for the past few hours, yet at this moment I felt the most vulnerable I had all day. His face was one of acceptance and non-judgment. Even if

I were a child being scolded by him, I could tell he would still care for me in the midst of my verbal lashing. I was instantly at ease with him; more than I expected to be in this situation. He took the towel from my hands and hung it on another hook on the back of the door. It left me naked and exposed in front of him. Thank God for the dim light. I was not ashamed of my body but the introductions while naked, opposed to the nudity coming after initial greetings and salutations, certainly escalated the momentum. He stepped closer leaving us inches apart. He reached out and caressed my chest. I returned the favor quickly, feeling the thick, furry hair on his barrel chest. I ran my fingers through the bristled hair trying to remember every strand. We took a moment to examine each other's bodies, both of us finding elements of the other than we enjoyed. I hooked a couple of fingers in the wrap of his towel and pulled it loose. It fell on the floor around his feet. He did not flinch, whereas I was a jittery mess when I had been exposed. His massive uncut dick was already getting hard. He stepped in closer to me until our chests were touching. I could feel his dick poking at my upper thighs. He pulled my hips toward him and leaned in to kiss me. I put my arms on top of his shoulders. We felt each other's soft lips press against those on the receiving end; our tongues exploring our vocal caves. My dick almost instantly got hard. He had a man's kiss, you know? He knew what he wanted, had it before, and he was going to have it again. This time it was going to be me. He pulled me tight against him, and I practically melted into his strong, burly arms, giving him every bit of snogging action that his embrace demanded. His big hands were clapping onto my ass, which heightened my awareness that I was now lip-locked and in the throes of foreplay with this Greek statue come to life. His strong and rough hands ran up my back all while holding me closer.

He pulled away and knelt in front of me. He turned me around and had me sit on the bed in my room, legs apart. He buried his face in my crotch, immediately swallowing my dick. His beard stubble rubbed achingly across my inner thighs sending tickles of pain and flushes of gratification through me. He engulfed my manhood. He hungrily licked my dick sucking me like he was trying to pull my soul through my cock. The more he sucked, the harder I got, which I am pretty sure was not physically possible at this point, but it sure felt like it. He pushed my legs further and further apart, licking and kissing and sucking all over my shaft and balls. He dipped a little lower and started to lick my taint bringing to life that flab of skin that none of us ever see on ourselves with the aid of a mirror and good yoga position. Often overlooked in daily life, it comes to life with a tongue pressed against it. He sucked on my balls, gently taking them in his mouth. He was hitting every exit on the highway. His tongue spun around my scrotum and across my taint sending unexpected tremors through my thighs. He did not stop until he reached my hole. He was voracious as he buried his face in my ass cheeks. I could only see the top of his head while he initiated a non-verbal tongue lashing.

His tongue penetrated me. I reacted with a huge groan, as my hands – already on his head – pushed him deeper into me. My whole lower region prickled with cheer. He came back up to my dick and kept sucking it. He had moved one of his hands off my leg, and his finger teased my tight hole. In mere moments, he had one finger, or was it two, inside me, pushing deeper and deeper. He was finger fucking me and was purposely massaging my prostate. The fulfillment with him felt like a dream.

When he came up for air, the look on my face must have been one he had not seen. He smirked, and I saw an inner chuckle happen.

"What?" I asked. "Do I look ridiculous? Be honest."

"No, you do not. Do you like me finger fucking you?" The fact that he felt he needed to ask the question seemed insane to me.

"Your mouth is amazing," I countered.

"Can I fuck you?" he asked.

I found I could only nod my approval and gladly chose to approve the request.

I stayed in the same position. He stood up and grabbed a condom off the shelf in my room. Much unlike the seventies or eighties, all the rooms in 3C were well stocked with male and female condoms, the latter for the discerning bottom. He ripped the package open with his front teeth and started to roll it over his meat.

"Here, let me." I sat up and took the condom from him. I leaned forward and took his dick into my mouth, wetting it as much as possible, making sure he remained fully erect. I expected to gag on his thick, uncircumcised cock but it fit wonderfully between my cheeks and on my tongue. The groan that emanated from his chest was deep, resonating throughout his body. His hands rested on my shoulders, and he lightly thrust his hips toward my mouth. I gladly took his meaty slab as far as he wanted into my mouth. I would have happily sucked his dick for an hour if he wanted me to do so. I spent as much time pleasuring his mature manhood as he desired.

I rolled the rubber over his cock taking special note to do it as sensually slow as I was able. I dressed his dick with the latex barrier we both silently agreed to use. I looked at him with nothing but proposal and desire in my eyes.

"Now, fuck me," I demanded.

He got between my legs, putting them on his husky shoulders and maneuvered the tip of his dick against my asshole. My first instinct was to tense up because you never know how it is going to feel, even if you are in the mood like I was right then.

"Go slow, please. You are not exactly packing a pinky finger down there," I joked. I still felt relaxed with him, so I hoped his entry would prove to be smooth.

"Do not worry lovely, I will not hurt you," he assured me as he continued to massage the entry to my hole with his dick. With each breath he pressed against it more, alerting me to the inevitable.

I had never been called lovely before then. It was endearing, and I was wearing it well. While we were both out to have a good time, he was still a gentleman; as much as you could be one in a bathhouse fucking a stranger. His assurance of being gentle fell on my ears like water on a dry tongue. It soothed and quenched any fear I might have harbored. His dick was asking for entry, and I knew I was ready for him.

"Just push it in and take me," I begged him with a quick change of heart. So much for being gentle. I was ready, no matter what his thick, hard, uncut Greek cock would feel like violating my hole. I was determined to take it. I felt my hole naturally opening and readying for his cock.

He pushed the head of his cock inside me. I knew the pain would pass soon. Nicolaus inside me, stretching me open as my muscles fought to constrict against this shaft was nothing short of exhilaration likely akin to jumping out of a plane. Unlike most men, he did not start pumping right away. He took a pause and just held it inside me. My anal muscles tightened involuntarily trying to reform into their natural state.

"Does it hurt?"

"A little but it is okay."

"Here, I will..."

Please do not pull out of me.

"No! I mean, stay where you are. I will be fine. You feel nice. You want me tight, right?"

"Yes, I do. You are very tight but tell me if you are hurting, promise?

"I promise."

He leaned in to kiss me, my legs still on his shoulders, his big arms holding himself up on either side of me. He was slow and passionate with the right amount of pressure against my lips. His tongue breached its way into my mouth. Kissing was always a huge turn on for me, and he was pushing all the right buttons the way he kissed me. He slowly pulled his dick out, but not all the way. Every inch sliding out of me felt like something I am unable to explain. He kept his wistful kisses coming as he pushed his meaty cock back into me as far as either of our bodies would allow. I could feel the friction from his dick. My anal muscles screamed for relief, but I was not giving it to them. I loved him stretching my hole out with each thrust of his cock. He kept his eyes on me while slowly making me his for the afternoon. He wanted to see my face and my reaction. In such an intense moment I found myself afraid to even look at him. It was so personal.

"Stay with me," he chided, grabbing my chin and making me focus on his face.

Once I locked into his gaze, I could not help but look at him. I was happy to show him what I was feeling. The dominant way he commandeered the situation left me breathless and under his spell. My dick had grown so hard it felt like it was not mine anymore. I did not know dicks could get that hard. Do not get me wrong – an erection is my favorite thing, and I never let one go to waste. This was something different, something special. Every time he leaned toward me my cock rubbed against his belly. It kept me seconds away from cumming. I certainly did not want to reach down and jerk off just yet. I just wanted to feel him inside me. His thrusts got steadier pushing in balls deep. Every move he made was so purposeful as to not only please himself but to drive me utterly insane.

"You are so handsome," he said. Again, I melted. Who does not love to hear that they are handsome, especially in the middle of being nailed by a mature Greek warrior? He grabbed me by the neck and pulled me closer to kiss me again. I lifted my legs more and wrapped them around his torso to show him I was ready for more. He was not going to cum anytime soon. He was having as much fun as I was and neither of us wanted it to end. We were in this for the long haul. We were enjoying every moment. I also knew with a condom on it might take him a bit longer to cum which was great for both of us.

Today, not unlike other days, I was a power bottom with an upgrade. I had no shame.

∞

Nicolaus's fat dick continued to fill me for almost another hour, a near record at a bathhouse where fucks are as quick as people checking in and out at the front desk. He never half-stepped it either. Every push inside me was balls deep almost from the tip. I felt like we both entered another dimension of making love, or fucking, or whatever this was that we were doing. The world did not exist anymore. The door to my room could have been wide open with everyone there watching, and I would not have noticed or cared. It reminded me of my time eating John's ass in this very same room with no regard for the wonky door which decided to remain accessible through our anally-charged tryst. I felt secure and open with Nicolaus. His eyes looked into mine while my hole greedily wrapped around his cock belayed any intention of putting up a wall or hiding something.

During the hour of fucking, he turned me around to get me on my knees on the edge of the bed. He stood on the floor and reentered my gaping, wet hole. My hard dick flopped under me with every one of his advances. I did not dare touch myself lest I cum too fast. I had been oozing precum almost the whole time of him fucking me so perfectly. I glanced down below me and saw precum dripping on the sheet-like syrup out of maple tree. The head of my dick was shiny from the wetness, and so was my belly. Although I had not noticed, I am sure he had some of my precum on his stomach, too. I had my hands against the wall in front of me, bracing my body upward, instead of being on all fours doggy style. His dick knew precisely where it was going and how to get there each time. He never missed a beat. It was effortless for both of us. Our bodies seemed to fit together perfectly, and for that stretch of time, we existed as one person.

He wrapped his arms around my chest from behind, holding me close as he fucked me. It is an excellent position because if the bottom is fully braced up against the headboard or a wall, then the top can have more body contact by holding onto the bottom's torso. It is even sexier because it is two men using their muscles, flexing, sweating, and helping each other. They are using each other as leverage. It is a team effort. It was a position I learned to appreciate more after fucking Abel so earnestly just a few years prior.

Much like Cain, the curve of Nicolaus's belly nestled into the small of my back. My ass cheeks braced themselves against the top of his thighs. Our breathing became the same; our thrusting was monumentally synchronized like divers at a national sporting competition. It had been a long time since I felt so connected to another man.

I gladly held myself in place and let him take me as long as he wanted. His hands explored the front of my body, grabbing at my chest, my stomach, and even down to my thighs. Every time he reached for my dick I let him stroke it a couple of times but then moved his hand away. He was teasing me, edging me closer to an orgasm only he wanted to provide. It also exasperated my body into releasing exponentially more precum. It felt like we were made to fuck each other; to be joined every way possible. Despite it being our first time, it seemed as though we knew each other's body from years of experience. He reached around and grabbed my dick again.

"Do not touch it!"

He paused, still deep inside me

"What is wrong, lovely?" he said, knowing better.

"I am so close, and I do not want to cum yet. You feel so good; you got me real close. I do not want it to end."

As much as I wanted to feel myself in his grip, it would have to wait a while longer. With one finger, he swiped the precum off my dick and fed it to me.

"I want more from you. Will you give it to me?"

"I will do anything you want," I confessed.

"I want you to feel good, lovely."

"Good is not a word worthy of this right here."

"So, then, I will keep fucking you," he said as he swabbed more precum from my dick. I gladly sucked it off his rough chubby cigar-like fingers, submitting to his every whim. Every man has tasted their precum or cum, but it is an entirely different sensation when another man – who is still inside you and possessing every part of you – feeds your own pre-jizz back to you. There is a feeling of total abandon when small things like that happen. You have no choice but to trust the other guy, honestly and freely give into him, and he to you, to do anything you want. I was all his and did not care who heard us.

"Yes, please, keep fucking me. It is yours, use it. Please do not stop." I begged him.

With that, his thrusting became faster. I could not seem to arch my back anymore or offer my ass up enough that satisfied my greed of his cock inside my hole. I shifted my hips down a bit, and he instinctively made a small adjustment to his position. It was then that I felt him hitting my prostate directly. His arms stayed wrapped around me from behind, sometimes touching the hair on my chest, or taking another swipe of pre-cum off my dick to feed me. My thighs started to quiver uncontrollably. I almost could not keep my balance. My hole continued to constrict and released; all of which I had no control. I was having orgasm after orgasm. Not ejaculating yet, just having orgasms repeatedly. When he would lean in so his chest was on my back and the more body contact he gave me, the more intense it felt.

"Lay face down for me, lovely," he asked. So, I did. I was face down on the bed; legs spread eagle as best I could. He knee-walked up between my legs, then closed them. He straddled my butt, and his dick took a nose-dive right back into my ass. My dick was flat under me, against the sheets and me. He laid face down on my back, and ground his shaft into me, repeatedly. My thighs and hips started to percolate. He was insatiable at this point knowing he was giving me mini orgasms. He kissed the back of my neck and chewed on my ear from behind, which only made me more nuts for him. My ears are such a big turn-on zone. I have always wondered if my ears were directly hard-wired to my dick. For now, I had no doubt they were connected end to end.

"Oh my God, fuck me. Please fuck me. You feel so goddamn good!" I urged him.

He was fast and heavy slamming his dick into my ass, his body slapping against mine, covered with sweat and breathing heavy. His grunts and groans were as loud as mine. I have no doubt anyone within earshot could have heard his balls slapping against my ass and our mutual guttural moans echoing through the bathhouse. But that item was nowhere to be found on the list of things to give any fucks about that day. I was delirious and wanted to shoot. My balls quietly screamed their aching rage of agony to be relieved, seizing higher and higher into my groin and abdomen. They were relentless much like the Greek's thrusts and anal violations.

"I want to see you cum, lovely." And with that, he had pulled out, turned me over, and had me on my back again. I pulled my legs up and to the side. His sweaty body lumbered between my legs, and he entered me for the last go-round.

"Can we cum together?" he asked.

"Fucking yes we can!" I agreed.

"I am so close. I will wait for you, tell me when you are close, okay?" I was close. *So* close. Just a few yanks on my rod and it was going to end it all. I was still surprised that my dick was this hard. It felt like steel. Maybe I had never had a man fuck me like that. It is entirely possible this was one of the best fucks I had ever had in the three decades of my life thus far.

The point of no return was upon us. His grunting and thrusting were aboriginal. Our conversation grew quiet, yet our communication was clear. The constant sound of our bodies thrashing together in untampered devotion was peppered with the carnal sounds emanating from our mouths. I tried not to distract him. I just watched him fuck me and watched all his inherent manhood flow freely through his dick which clearly showed on his face.

"I am getting close, lovely. Very close."

I started jerking my dick. Fuck, I was close, too! Closer than I thought.

"Goddamn, Nicolaus. I think I might cum!" I said.

He looked at me. "Cum with me!"

He reached down and grabbed my dick from me with a grip which matched the look on his face. He started pumping my cock.

"Oh fuck, I am getting close, papa," I said.

"I am too. Cum with me!" he commanded.

With a few more strokes my legs tightened up, and I felt the surge of elation coming to my dick. My whole body locked into some obtuse unhuman form. I could not see anything in front of me. It was as bright as it was dark. My ears rang with sounds I had never heard yet the room felt incredibly silent. I was not in control of myself as I exploded. I came everywhere; then I came some more. If there is a thing as pure joy, I had no doubt this was it.

In the midst of my body doing tricks seen only in cartoons and orgasming to no end, he pulled out, ripped off the condom, and jerked off onto my belly. His seed was like thick white gravy. It covered me and left me soaked with his juices. When it hit my gut, I could feel how warm it was, and I loved it. It was not just semen; it felt so much more personal. When a man's jizz is that warm, more than usual, you know he is aroused. His body shivered from every wave of orgasm he was having. His arms were fully flexed, and his bulky body was like a superhero – confident, almost brazen.

His body lurched over mine, sweaty and heaving to catch his breath. He was milking every bit of seed from his shaft onto me. His dick seemed to stir the deluge of our expulsions on my gut. The cum blended as quickly as we did for the last however long.

"Stick it in," I said.

He looked at me in disbelief for a moment. He soon realized I was serious.

"Nicolaus, just stick it back in me."

My ass had tightened up from cumming so hard. His re-entry was painful, but I did not care. I needed him to be back inside me for a while. I also wanted to have his seed inside me as well as my own. How many guys have their jizz back inside them? It was an erotic moment.

"Fuck, you are so gorgeous right now, Nicolaus," I said. It was manhood personified.

"Thank you, lovely. You are beautiful."

I squeezed my ass muscles around his dick drawing out any remaining cum. I was still hard and tingling from the eruption barely catching my breath. He slow fucked me until both of our dicks softened. Eventually, I could hold my legs up no longer. We were both spent.

"Come here. Lay next to me, handsome," I offered.

He seemed to relish the invitation. He politely, thinking ahead, grabbed my wetter towel from the hook and tossed it to me to clean my chest.

He laid next to me and put his arm under my head. He wiped my chest with the towel doing his best to tidy up the mess we had made. Him taking care of me was another notch in the plus column. He tossed the towel, now covered with the evidence of an otherwise beautiful afternoon, on the floor and turned to face me. I was too hot to cuddle, but our bodies were touching, and that was enough for now. We were still breathing heavy, our bodies sweaty, and hearts pounding in our chests. The Greek resting next to me felt special. I know it was just a bathhouse excursion but even those can be special moments between two men who connect. It felt like no one else existed and only he was supposed to be there with me. Whatever this particular thing was between us, we dared not speak about it. It was temporary so why spoil it? We just enjoyed it equally. We were officially in the afterglow, and it was splendid. I laid there, our bodies slowing down to a normal heartbeat and breathing. I stroked his sweaty head. Neither of us had to say a thing. It was insanely quiet in the bathhouse except for the club music on the sound system. We were still tired enough to slip into a quick nap that probably lasted ten minutes.

I felt him move.

"I should go," he whispered in my ear. "I am actually on a break from work."

A break? That is one hell of a break.

"That is one hell of a break," I said out loud this time. What kind of job was that?

"Yeah, it is a split shift, and I go in soon for the second half," he explained.

"Ah. Well, I am sorry you have to go. Because whatever all that was…" I jokingly motioned to our dicks and my belly which still had some cum on it, "it was pretty fucking amazing."

"Do you come here a lot?" he asked.

"I try to every Wednesday."

"Well now, I guess I will have to as well," he said.

"That would be lovely, would it not?" I jokingly offered. I had to work 'lovely' in, at least once.

He gently grabbed my chin with his hand. "You, little one, are the lovely one here."

He wrapped his towel around his sweaty waist.

"Maybe we can see each other again," he offered. He opened the door and paused a second. He turned around, bent over and kissed me as deeply as he did the first time. "You were the best I have had in a very long time."

Before I could respond, my venerated cohort was out the door, quietly closing it behind him.

I laid there with a certain look of satisfaction on my face and in my heart. I was sure I would never have another time as good as this one. I hoped I would, though. I expected that if I came back again that the Greek would be here and we could have another great session.

I was not sure if it would ever reach that intensity, though. I was not sure I could ever cum like that again. But a week later, we sure fucking tried.

† Thomas †

I had seen Thomas online throughout a few years on different dating apps for bearish gay men. We traded a few messages here and there, but nothing ever manifested to meet in person. He was cute in his photos, naturally body confident, and distinctly younger. I wagered he was in his mid-twenties, likely played football or lifted weights in high school and had the youthful brawn to prove it. He was also another ginger barking up my treehouse. It was flattering considering I had a considerable advance on his years. I would learn that Thomas had no judgment in him about anyone, was accepting of, and sweet to those he met. He hounded me off and on for those few years to meet up with him. He was drawn to huskier guys like myself (a feat easily achieved but not readily on my grown-up list of things to accomplish). The problem was that he was not from my area. He lived just across the border in the next state. A casual hookup had to be planned and coordinated more than usual with so much distance between us. I put him off for a long time. Something about him scared me. I did not feel like I could handle my own with him, so I just kept ghosting him and ignoring his messages. I do not know if he ever took it that personally. From the looks of him, he certainly could have any slew of men that crossed his path. My intentions were never meant to be impersonal toward him. My reluctance was rooted merely in my insecurities; ones I wholly owned and knew sabotaged me on regular occasions. I entertained them anyway. I did not understand how someone so deftly athletic and drop-dead hunky would repeatedly attempt to sleep with me.

Fast-forward a few more months and Thomas, again, showed up on the proverbial gaydar showing he so many miles from me. His heat seeking pits were fully engaged. The app on my phone dinged with a message from him. He was persistent; I will give him that. He was passing through town on his way to St. Louis, Tulsa, or some other godforsaken midsouth charter-township-village-hamlet for a bear pride event; no doubt an event that would bring more men to the area than any congregation of Promise Keepers and gun show vendors combined.

```
Thomas: Hey stud
Me: Hey.
Thomas: Woof. How are you?
Me: Good. U?
Thomas: driving and horny lol
Me: Not a great combination. Lol
```

```
Thomas: I am going to be in your area soon
Me: oh yeah? what is going on?
Thomas: Fuzzy Bear Pride
Me: Is that a gay thing here?
Thomas: lol not in your area. It is a bear
event. I go every year
Me: ahh I see. I am sure you will have fun.
Thomas: I was hoping you would want to get
together. I would love to meet you.
Me: me? Really? I am sure you have plenty of
men waiting at the event.
Thomas: anyone I had is not in your town.
Me: lol
Thomas: I thought maybe we could hang out
Me: hang out meaning fucking
Thomas: woof! Yes.
Me: you do not mix words do you?
Thomas: haha Nah man, I say what I want
Me: and that means you want me?
Thomas: woof yes!
Me: you are sweet
Thomas: could I come over?
Me: where are you now?
Thomas: I am on I-40 coming up on I-270. You
close to that, right?
```

Well fuck, he was right, which means I would not have long to prepare.

```
Thomas: I left str8 from work. I could use a
break from driving
Me: wow, that is a long drive then
Thomas: lol yea
```

It all happened so quick. I had no idea what to do. Should I avoid Thomas, or allow the football player to make a pass and possibly tackle me?

```
Me: well I am free until 5 p.m. then I have to
get going
```

> Thomas: where do you live?

I knew that since he was looking at me on an app with a built-in GPS location that I could not lie about how far out I lived from where he was driving. The damn technology was trying to get me laid.

> Me: I only have a couple of hours. I do have to meet up with my roommate just after 5 p.m.

I was trying to be verbose enough to blur his vision and want to keep driving. Self-sabotage at its worst.

> Thomas: sounds cool. Address?

I relented. I also reiterated that I was on a schedule. It was the truth. My friend and I were headed to dinner around 5:30 p.m. and I would need time to clean up and get myself together as if I had not been fucked by a young linebacker while acting as his wide receiver and making a few touchdowns. I even tried giving him a deadline, but he was flexible.

> Me: If you can get here at 2 p.m. that will give us time to do a lot of stuff.

It was three hours. If it did not go well I could send Thomas to his destination and not think twice about it. He met the challenge head-on like a real pro player. He typed the address into his phone and said he was about twelve minutes away. This was going to be a very quick shower. Maybe light a candle or spritz some air freshener through the house.

First things first: shower.

∞

He was poised on my porch like an oak tree resisting a tornado's attempt to level it. He wore glasses, tennis shoes and nursing scrubs.

A nurse! We could have some fun with this.

His Navy-blue scrubs wrapped tightly around his muscled chest, the sleeves of his uniform were losing the battle brought on by his biceps. He was built like a brick house and had a physique I had not seen on a man since the Greek. His photos did not do him justice. He made a quick up and down glance of my half-wet body with a brown towel wrapped around my waist and smiled.

"Woof. Hello there."

"Hey man, come on in," I replied, ignoring the flattering yet awkward woof. How does one answer to a woof? Do I woof back? Growl? Purr? Turn around and spray? I could not say much since I was answering the door in a towel. I did not feel up to flashing the neighborhood today, so I quickly ushered him in and shut the door behind him. He stood in the entryway of my apartment and already had his hands on me. Suffice it to say; he was very tactile. He rubbed my belly and even flicked at my nipple.

"You are sexy," he exclaimed.

This kid had his moves down pat. I blushed.

"Thanks. Come in while I pat myself dry."

"Need some help?"

I led him to my bedroom making small talk.

"Easy, tiger. Unless you want to help me brush my teeth."

It was a rhetorical comeback.

I had lit a big candle, opened the windows and made up the bed beforehand. I was not a total heathen. My mother taught me the more delicate points of entertaining.

"Make yourself comfortable, man. I will be back in a sec."

I gestured to the bed and left him to his own devices, literally and figuratively.

While I did need to brush my teeth, the moment alone also served as a vehicle for me to regain myself before I went back to the bedroom. I sometimes needed that moment to gather my senses and mentally size up a guy. I required it this time because Thomas was just as lovely as I thought. It is always a little awkward first meeting someone. It is even more awkward to walk into the bedroom and get straight to it. I try to avoid the impersonal slant that a hookup can sometimes create. While I always endeavored to be cordial to anyone in my home, hookup or otherwise, Thomas made it easy. He was charming and had a quiet spirit about him which proved to be disarming. I could drop my defenses with him. Talking to him was easy.

As I walked back into the room, I lightly smacked my tongue in my mouth.

"Much better."

Thomas was already undressed down to his underwear. He had even taken the initiative and found a plug to charge his mobile phone.

"You do not mind, do you?" gesturing as he laid his phone on the floor under the plug.

"Not at all."

"Thanks, stud."

I was a stud; at least he made me feel like a stud. I only offered him a wall socket. Imagine what I could be if I were contributing more.

His shoes were the foundation for a pile of dark blue scrubs, hospital lanyard, and any extras on the floor. It was the first time I was able to take a visual drink of his youth, near-nude body. His body was agile, buff, with a furry chest, muscular legs; his big biceps did not disappoint any more than did his curvy calves. His neck had a thickness that one would only find on a linebacker. He crawled onto the bed on his knees. We had three hours, and it was clear he wanted to waste none of it.

I felt I had to break the ice a bit. I motioned toward the towel around my waist.

"Well clearly, I have overdressed for this occasion."

It was not much of a lie either as my towel was about ten times the fabric used for the white briefs wrapped around his wide hips.

"Come over here. We can change that." I took a couple of steps toward the bed and met him at the edge. He grabbed the front of my towel and gently tugged at the wadded up pseudo-knot in front.

"You are so fucking sexy," he said. He had such a deep soothing voice. It is the kind of voice that when a guy calls me "buddy" and I lose all sense of self.

That.

"Oh stop, I am just a regular guy, man." I was halfway fishing for another compliment. What guy does not want to hear they are a stud? I also never believed I was that much of a stud or fucking sexy. I looked down at his chest because I had become embarrassed. I was blushing again.

I put my hands on his pecs, and they were as solid as ice yet warm as fresh bread. As I caressed his chest, he grabbed the edge of the towel and released it in one quick move. I remained for a moment waiting to see what he would do next. I was naked in front of him, nervous and feeling a tad unworthy of the attention of yet another jock. I had been with Mark long ago; a guy who was a statue of health and masculinity; one of my first Brosie Greers. I always thought maybe Mark was a fluke with his chants about being straight and fucking bitches. More and more, I would find thin guys or jock types attracted to me. Thomas could have anyone he wanted, but he was here in my bedroom.

The next move is yours, buddy.

"I love your body," he said. "And your ass is perfect." I refused to argue the point.

He wrapped both hands around either of my buttocks and pulled me into him. He planted a surprise kiss on me. My dick practically sprung into third gear. He grabbed me by my back and pulled me onto him on the bed as he fell backward. My thick body laid on his husky frame, my legs straddling his redwood-esque thighs. Our cocks were pressed against each other. He held me tight and kissed me deeply. His tongue started slowly finding its way around mia bocca instead of being a typically quick tonsil search. My groin was naturally grinding into his without me even realizing it. My instincts seemed to override my logical thought process.

Then his football player past came into play. Without warning, he grabbed me and tossed me on my back. He muscled his way between my legs and pinned me against my memory foam mattress. He grabbed my hands and positioned them above my head. This guy was not only young and limber but strong as fuck. He was easily overpowering me despite my play-resist efforts.

I do not mind a bit of wrestling or strong-arming in bed. Men are men and our testosterone blends well beyond just fucking for an hour. When we are flexing and using our strength, there is a whole new level of fun and danger in our sex. He had me laid out and defenseless to whatever he wanted to do to me. He shoved his tongue into my mouth. His chest was heaving against mine, and he fervently kissed me. His hips were already thrusting as if warming up for the unavoidable.

"I want to fuck you, buddy." Oh sure, use "buddy" to melt me at the knees. I could not find it in myself to flag the play as illegal.

"Yes, I have noticed." I had heard this story. Most times men meet the task and sometimes they failed miserably. I was reasonably sure he could fulfill his challenge.

"Question."

Right now?

"Uh, okay. Sure." I had no idea where this was going.
"Why have you always avoided me." he asserted.
Fuck. I had to think quick.
"Have I?" Me being coy was not going to work.
"Yeah, you have."
"I... well... " I was struggling to be honest.
"Come on, man," he promoted. "We have been talking for years. At least I have tried. You avoid me every time."
I had to concede to his question. I could not avoid it.
"I do not know. I have no answer for you."
"Well, if you did have an answer, what would it be?"
It was a Dr. Phil-worthy, witty comeback. Was this motherfucker trying to use reverse psychology on me?
"You scared me."
He did not have to answer. The look of "what the fuck?" on his face said enough.
"I guess I thought you were too hot for me," I confessed.
"That is crap, man. I do not believe that."
"I am serious. I am nothing that special. Look at me and look at you. I am older, never played sports or have muscle bulk. You are like a linebacker full of piss and testosterone. I am not sporty or getting modeling gigs. You could do either."
"Oh, fuck off, dude. I am here now. I have wanted to be here for years. No one is too hot for someone else. You do not believe that, do you? It is bullshit. I love all men."
"Yeah well, not all men love me," I again confessed.
"Then you do not need those men anyway. Fuck them."
"Listen, man. I do not get many guys like you after me, so I figured maybe you needed eyeglasses. Or worse."
"What is worse?"
I knew I should not have said that.
"A pity fuck."
"A what?" he asked.

"You know. Guys at Pride will find some low life to fuck as a pity fuck like they are doing the gay world a service. They fuck them knowing the lesser guy is going to do everything to please them. Then the guy never talks to him again."

"Shit, man. You think I would do that to you, or anyone?"

"No, I guess not. But like I said, guys like you do not typically pursue guys like me."

"Okay well like *I said*, fuck those guys. Men are coming out of the woodwork. Do not concentrate on the ones that disrespect you. I would never disrespect you."

"I believe that, and I know you would not do that. I guess it is my insecurity."

"I am here because I want to be here, not because I feel obligated to you or anyone else. I think with both heads, and they both lead me here."

I felt horrible about having avoided him this long. He was well-adjusted and knew who he was as a person. I could only hope to emulate that at some point in life.

"I am sorry for being a dick about it," I continued.

"It is okay. I forgive you and your dumb ass," he joked.

"Oh, I am a dumb ass now?" I was teasing him.

He laughed. "Shush."

"Can I get a do-over?" I was trying to get us out of our awkward tête-à-tête and get a pass for being a dickhead.

"Oh, trust me, you are about to be done over, under, sideways, and any other way I want."

I believed him. He already had me pinned down showing his inhuman strength over mine. The rest seemed an obvious progression.

He grabbed both of my hands at the wrist with one of his hands. With his other, he turned my head to the side and buried his tongue in my ear. Now while everyone has their erogenous zone, the ears are mine. The neck comes in a close second. If a man wants to drive me nuts, squirming for relief, all he has to do is chew on my ears.

My response was instant and involuntary. I let out a scream, and my legs tightened around his waist. My arms writhed to get loose, but he had them firmly trapped under his grip. He used the weight of his frame against mine to hold me in place. My dick was also throbbing for attention. My insides quivered knowing his pole would soon invade me. I tried to free my arms, but his grip was too secure. I wanted to touch him and manhandle him. I wanted to participate. But he was overpowering me without much effort. His tongue kept abusing my ears trading off between either one. He eventually let up on my ears and moved to give my nipples a lot of attention. He had relocked my wrists under his meaty paws at the side of my head. He sucked on my erect nipples biting them at his whim. It hurt, and I was not entirely comfortable with that. I convulsed my torso to try and free my nipple from his toothy grip.

"Ow, fuck! It hurts! Ow, easy, easy!" I pleaded. It was all for naught. "Please!"

He put a hand over my mouth to silence me. I did not think my nips were ever that sensitive or were an erogenous zone for me but he proved that wrong.

"Do you want me to stop? If you do, I will."

He took his hand off my mouth.

"I had never had someone chew on my nips like that before," I confessed.

"I play rough. I am sorry if I hurt you."

"You did not hurt me. I guess I was caught off guard."

"I just want to eat you up because you are so sexy."

"The eating part is apparent."

He laughed. He kissed me again making me instantly forget why we were even having a conversation.

He laid back into my nipples. He throttled his aggression, but his rough play was not going away. It was only moments before he accelerated into more uneven combat. His nip action was so intense and methodical giving me no room to complain anymore. If I asked him to let up, I could end up looking like a pussy. I had to step up and take the pain and learn to see it as pleasure. I always said I believed in having my limits pushed and this was the time for me to demonstrate that rather than be labeled a hypocrite. Could I handle this, though? Nipple play had not always been my thing. Maybe I could learn to love it; perhaps I just never gave it a shot. I had no choice but to give myself to his oral mauling. He felt my surrender. It was all he needed to consume all of me.

My muted howls continued under his grip. I begged him to stop, but he knew I was only half serious. Surprisingly, my nipples were so hard they could have cut glass. My body betrayed my pleas for mercy. The more he lightly tortured them the more I gave my power to him. My wrestling was an involuntary reaction but, in reality, I wanted him to continue. I wanted him to overpower me. I wanted him to hurt me and test me. I wanted to see just how far I could be driven.

"Sit on my dick."

I was so distracted by my pleasure that I did not even hear what he said.

"Huh?"

"Come, sit on my cock." I had heard that request before Thomas. Before I could answer, he jumped off of me and found a spot to lay on his back. I was dizzy with my endorphins in full effect. He pulled all the blood and energy from my body into my chest by way of my nipples and into my head by kissing my neck and ears. He laid back, and I saw his dick. It was uncut, thick, and standing straight up like a flagpole. I wasted no time in the attempt to join our bodies for the ultimate journey.

"Stretch your legs out and just sit on me." Thomas's dick was glistening with precum that was probably mostly his but surely had some of mine, too. Our dicks had been rubbing against each other the whole time he was molesting my nipples and making out with me. We had undoubtedly generated a lot of precum between us. I grabbed his dick and wiped the precum into my palm. I redistributed it back onto his dick, using it as my lube.

I crawled on him, bent my legs and guided his dick into my hole. The mix of pain and joie de vivre reminded me of the nipple play minutes earlier. I pivoted left then right and pulled my legs out from under me. They extended toward the headboard, my feet on either side of him. I braced my hands on his thighs behind my ass and ground his dick into my hole. I wanted all of him inside me.

Thomas and his cock were so perfectly synced with anything I hoped to be as a bottom. His relaxed attitude coupled with his shameless attraction to me made me question my sanity. Why had I ignored this guy in previous years? This was going to be one of the most intense fucks of my life; how and why had I put it off for so long? What was I scared of with him? My only defense, as I continued to take all of his jock cock inside my ass, was temporary insanity.

His hands explored my legs and belly, never once not touching me somewhere. My back was slightly arched, and I was riding his dick in a way I had never ridden any man's dick before now. I dug my heels into the memory foam on either side of his shoulders giving myself incredible traction.

Memory foam beds are not only great for sleeping, but their lack of sliding and slipping around make them excellent for fucking. Whether you are the top or bottom, it is easy to get in a position and not have to readjust every few minutes. I was perfectly positioned to take his cock long-term. I wanted to make the pass and go for a touchdown with the linebacker turned nurse. His dick inside me was nothing short of perfection. He laid back and let me do the work. I was happy to do it. We both felt we had the best view. He eventually made his way to my dick. If he did not have my attention before, he did now.

"You are so hot," he let me know.

"I think you have the advantage here," I countered, not missing a beat with the grinding action.

He let out a moan as I continued to cover his ivory tower with my hole. He teased my dick. He grabbed it, stroked it, then let it go. I wanted him to make me cum so bad, but he was going to make me wait. I could have ridden him past supper and into the late-night talk show lineup had my schedule not interfered. Despite my pending meetup, I was quickly losing track of time.

"Get on your knees." I felt like we were going through a list of positions, all of which I was willing to try master in a new way for him.

I jumped up and immediately got into doggy position on all fours. I put a pillow under my chest to give me leverage. Thomas got on his knees behind me. He reached around and grabbed my dick. He stroked it once to milk out any precum I had oozing. He spread it across my hole and nuzzled his dick into its new favorite place. There was no warning, no slow motion. It slid in without a hitch. My hole stayed tight but was willing to take anything Thomas had to offer. I had no resistance. I kept myself present in the moment. I wanted to be fully present and not checked out with Thomas. I owed him that much. He had shown nothing but affection and kindness toward me, and that is often a hundred times sexier than a tight ass or an unusually large dick. The way he hugged me or held me down while he dominating me kept me a willing player in the game. My bed was the pitch, both of us were opposing yet allied teams, playing against each other; or were we aiming for a common goal? The more he showed his raw masculinity and used his athleticism to fuck me, the more natural energy I was able to relay back to him. I did not have to act or put on a show with him. The interaction between us was organic and felt primal.

I braced myself by holding an arm against the headboard. Thomas was fucking me so hard we were moving the bed with every push and pull. We were locked in our semi-permanent divots in the memory foam, but the wheels on the bed kept us, quite literally, mobile.

"Man, your ass is so fucking sweet."

"Is it? I have worked on it all my life. God delivered, I just signed for it." Old joke, but what is sex if not funny?

All I could do is continue to grunt and moan with every one of his forceful thrusts. Every push felt more profound than the one prior. I did my best to clamp my anal muscles around his cock more often than not. I wanted to bleed him into me. I felt the sweat from his brow drip onto my back. He held me by my shoulders and rammed himself into me without pause. His breathing was heavy, and he was working hard to fuck me. It felt as though he needed to fuck as much as he could while he had the chance. This guy was a fucking machine. I glanced at the clock and realized over half an hour had passed already just with him behind me.

"Whew, how about we take a break, ok?"

"Sure." I was glad to get the breather.

I collapsed onto my stomach, sweaty and tingling. He leaned backward with his feet now facing toward the headboard. We just needed to catch our breath.

"I will be right back," I said. I wanted to go to the bathroom to splash my face with cold water. We were already sweating like crazy from the making out and first-round fucking.

"Do not be gone long."

"Where am I going? Green Bay?"

He chuckled.

I splashed my face and head with water barely bothering to pat either dry. I cupped my hand under the pewter faucet to grab a few gulps of cold water. I dried off a bit with a hand towel and took a piss.

∞

The sight of Thomas stopped me in my tracks. Despite having copulated with him for an extended period, I had not seen him quite like this. His eyes were closed, so he did not see me standing in the doorway as I drank in the sight of his body. The afternoon sun bullied its way through the sheer curtains in the bedroom. Some of it landed on his body which did nothing but compliment his form. The whole room had a warm filtered hot yellow glow to it. The light felt welcoming and new. I could smell us when I stood in the doorway. I felt reinvigorated by the musky pheromones that lingered. His muscles were highlighted from the sun bending through the beaded prisms of sweat that stood rank and file over his body like Seamen on the flight deck of a carrier. It seemed every inch of bulk and brawn was perfectly illuminated, glistening like morning dew on the front lawn. His legs were stretched out - rigid, long, and hard - like trenches of cured cement. His arms were swollen from our wrestling, engorged with blood, ready for another bout of sexual audacity. Testosterone and passion still pulsed through the veins in his arms. If I looked hard enough, I could almost see his heartbeat. His chest was flushed with a fleshy pink hue that gave revelation to just how turned on he was today. His breath was steady but slightly labored; his heart rate inevitably higher. His dick had not gone flaccid nor did I expect it to anytime soon. He had pitched himself in such a position that head draggled off the foot of the bed. His neck was thick and elongated and begged to be kissed. His eyes were closed I had little doubt he was reenergizing for round two. I cursed myself for not having a camera nearby to capture the sheer essence of manhood and male beauty. Even with Mark's gym rat body, the Greek's natural factory-driven brawn, or David's genetically privileged stamina, they all paled with the sight of Thomas in front of me. I would surely find another moment like this with another man. If I were a betting man, I might have sidestepped that bet today. The evidence of Thomas being the best longshot I ever took was irresistible; it would prove to be a substantial wager.

He must have heard me move. His eyes suddenly opened and his head quickly turned in my direction. Caught! He spotted me leaning on the door frame, in all my sweaty nudity, staring at him.

"Hey stud," he greeted me.

"Hi there," I said, with a coy smirk.

"Come over," he prompted extending his arm and open hand toward me. I took his lead.

"I have an idea," I offered as I walked toward him. He started to ask me what it was, but before he could finish, I grabbed his head with my hands and shoved my dick into his mouth from where I stood. I put one hand under his chin and the other on the far side of his head so he could not turn away. I was not going to let him go. He started to move away, and I tightened my grip. He pawed at my hips or torso trying to wiggle free. But I had the upper hand. I slapped his cheek.

"Shh, shh, shhh. This is happening, so let it."

He continued to struggle, even if just a little bit. If he wanted it aggressive, then those were plays in the book. I could only conform to them.

"Come on, let it happen. Come on, now. There you go, buddy." I coaxed him as I kept my dick in his mouth, slowly pumping against his attempts to free himself.

He finally submitted knowing this might be the only way to get his dick back in me. It may have been a small consolation to him, but it was well-deserved to me. The last thing either of us wanted right now was a stand-off in negotiations. He bore down on my shaft with his tongue and mouth. I face-fucked his mouth making him taste my sweaty meat from tip to balls. It was still covered with both our precum. Despite his pleas for freedom moments earlier, I found him quite willing to suck my cock. He put himself in that vulnerable position, and I took advantage of it. Either he enjoyed it, or he was doing it to keep me happy for the moment. My dick was getting sucked regardless. I had become as insatiable as him, pursuing every avenue of pleasure available to us.

"Shit, that is good." I wanted him to continue. He tried to pull his head back. I slapped his face again.

"No, no baby. Not yet. This is my turn. Just keep sucking my dick," I commanded. I rode his face shoving my dick into his mouth. He might have fought it, but his dick divulged the real truth. Within thirty seconds of me fucking his mouth, his dick sprang back to full attention. I kept my dick deep in his throat and tweaked his nipples with my free hand. His whole body came alive. His nipples acted like a power switch. He let out a huge moan that vibrated against my cock which was still housed firmly against his tongue. I dug in harder with twisting and pinching his nipples. They got erect almost as fast as his dick had seconds ago. He might have been a big quarterback or whatever in school, but it seemed he liked being dominated sometimes. He wanted to be on top and in his star quarterback position, but he could also be easily coaxed into sucking another man's cock.

∞

I was lost with Thomas inside me. I had failed to realize that over two-and-a-half hours had passed between us. It was when I glanced at the clock I saw it was twenty minutes before the next hour would ring present. I was meeting my roommate in less than an hour to get dinner. Thomas nowhere near wanted to finish. He and I had become one person in the last couple of hours. There was no separation between us anymore. There was no jock, or chubby guy; no football player, no fan. His thrusting had become deep and purposeful. His body was full of electricity, and he had plugged into the biggest power source in the world: me. Sweat rolled off him like he was under a showerhead. We were intoxicated by the pheromones still lingering in the pungent bedroom air.

The afternoon sun had shifted. His chest glinted from sweat to the point that anyone else might have considered him to be oiled up for a photo shoot. My legs were apart, and I felt so agile, lithe and free. He had situated his hands on the back of my thighs to brace himself. It kept me vulnerable to his animalistic fucking. His prick ruled every part of my being. He was taking me to heights that I knew would make short time to reach orgasm. He had me bent in such a position that he was already hitting my little acorn with every dynamic lunge. He had the energy and stamina of a younger guy coupled with the carefully paid attention to detail of someone close to my age. He was the best of both worlds.

I reached down to grab my dick. Time was not going to stop and had I been without a pending appointment; he would not have either. I knew he had another hour in him given a chance.

"You getting close, man?"

He either did not hear me, or he just wanted to keep fucking and not break his concentration.

Suddenly his eyes fixated on mine; like the Terminator zeroing in on Sarah Connor.

"I am going to fill your fucking ass."

Well shit man, get at it!

"If you think you can..." I trailed off, trying to challenge him even more.

I tightened the grip on my dick while simultaneously squeezing down on his dick with my innards. I clinched with all the strength I had left in me after being fucked over two hours straight. My legs fought to go rigid. I could feel the tinging in my ass, my groin, my back, my hips, and my dick. I could loosen or tighten my grip as necessary to time my orgasm with his explosion.

"You want this load?" he implored.

"Fuck yeah I do," I pleaded.

"I am going to cum in you…fuck…"

He leaned forward, and I thought maybe he had cum and was going to collapse on me. He moved one of my legs to his shoulder. Then he leaned in more and wrapped his fingers around my throat. He kept his eyes on mine as the conflict between fear and fantasy came crashing together. I trusted him at this point, and he knew it. I gave the slightest of smirks, and he rightly took it as permission to release any further inhibitions. He leaned the heel of his hand against my manubrium; that is the top of your sternum before your Adam's apple. His fingers continued to wrap themselves around my neck. His strength had never manifested itself more. He was not letting up. He was finding eroticism in choking me.

"You are going to take my fucking load… fuck… FUCK."

The room seemed overly hazy.

I heard him groan like a hungry bear waking up from hibernation. I felt my cock pulsing with energy and DNA landing on my torso. Everything was blurry, and the room sparkled as if I had sweat in my eyes. We had synced our detonations perfectly. Hearing our groans together was like a symphony to my ears. His was loud and gruff practically muting mine. His face contorted into what could only be described as beastly. I felt his body shake and jolt from his orgasm.

His strokes were long and hard giving no pause to any pain he may have been inflicting on me. I felt everything but pain. My head was dizzy. The surges of orgasm were not isolated in just my cock. They invaded my thighs, swam through my stomach, and galloped up to my spine like a herd of wild stallions.

Whoa, is it getting dark?

I felt like it should have been much lighter in the room. Had the time passed later than I anticipated? Was it late evening? Was it just before dawn?

If I could just... turn... to see... the clock...

Thomas's face grew dark, almost black like coal. The whites of his eyes disappeared in front of me. I could not move my arms or legs, but I could still feel him emptying his seed into my hole. I tried to look down to see my spunk hopping up on my stomach. But I could not see anything. It was just so dark.

I was confused. What was happening?

Why is it so dark in here?

"Oh fuck!" he said.

∞

Dreams are sometimes so vivid and lucid that you struggle to separate the fantasy from reality. I am sure we have all fought to know if we were naked at the grocery store or not, or whether our mother had become a lizard while we asked for gas money. I was still trying to differentiate between what I thought happened and where I was right now.

I could almost feel the smack of a hand on my face. I could not see anything in the dream, but I could feel it. I heard something faint, almost jarring. Was someone yelling at me? My level of clarity was increasing exponentially. The noise I heard became clearer. It was a voice. Who is that? What are they saying?

"Hey, buddy. Hey, wake up, man. Fuck. Come on, man. Hey man, wake up...shit!"

I finally started to find a grip on the reality I was in with Thomas. Was I not woke? How did I get not-woke?

"Dude. You in there? Come on, man."

The sun took me from darkness to overwhelming light. Maybe I was being born, again. I fought to gain focus visually and mentally.

There he was, Thomas. He was sitting next to me. I felt him touching me. It was not sexual. The last thing I remember is still looking into his eyes and face as we were orgasming together. It was ...was that real?

"There you are, stud. You alright?"

"What the..." I asked, confused.

"Whew, thank God," he said under his breath.

"What the fuck is going on?"

"You came and went." He chuckled, no doubt trying to elevate the weight of the moment.

"I did what? We were fucking..." I trailed off, still trying to figure out what happened.

"We were fucking. We came, and you left."

"I what?!" I tried to sit up, but he nudged me to stay put.

"Stay there; you are fine. Yeah, you were gone, man. I thought you were playing around until you went limp."

"How is that even possible?"

"I think I cut off your air supply a bit and when you came, and you just lost consciousness."

I tried to sit up again. The nurse had other ideas.

"Stay put, man. Give yourself a minute or two. You are fine, I promise."

"You mean I passed out?" I asked. It was something I had only heard about from my brother and his many conquests with women he picks up at bars. But this was hitting it all the way to home base.

"Yep. You are good, though. I checked your pulse."

Well great, because this is not the way I want to exit life. Then it hit me.

"Oh fuck, what time is it?!" I glanced at the clock. 5:15 p.m. Whew, I was not out long at all.

"I should get myself together. You have somewhere to be if I recall," he said.

"Yeah, I do. That," I sat up to continue, "has never happened to me."

"You were hot, man."

"You certainly knew what you were doing. I hope I was not a total goof." I offered.

"I hope you are not freaked out by it. I just really got into fucking you, man."

"No. It is okay. I am fine, I think."

He looked at me with a look that was either of concern or wondering if I was lying a little bit to make him feel better about what just happened.

"You are probably the hottest sex I have had in a good while," I told him, quite seriously.

The accidental erotic asphyxiation aside, Thomas was probably one of the best times I had with a guy in a long time. Not that my other visitors were less-than, but I stayed awake with all of them. My goal was not to always lose myself to the point of unconsciousness. This one, though, I had to give this one a pass.

"I need to get myself together," I hurried the situation. I felt perfectly fine. Amazing what a little oxygen and a quick Propofol-free nap can do for a guy.

"I hear you. I still have more miles to cover."

We scurried around to pull ourselves together. THomas threw on his scrubs and shoes and gathered his stuff. I found my towel from earlier and wiped my head and chest with it. He stepped over to me and grabbed my hand with the towel in it and pulled me close. We kissed.

"Sorry I made you faint. Forgive me?"

"To quote a friend, 'you are good.'"

I wrapped my towel around my waist and walked him to the front door. We promised to meet up again sometime. A promise we kept.

† Simon and Peter †

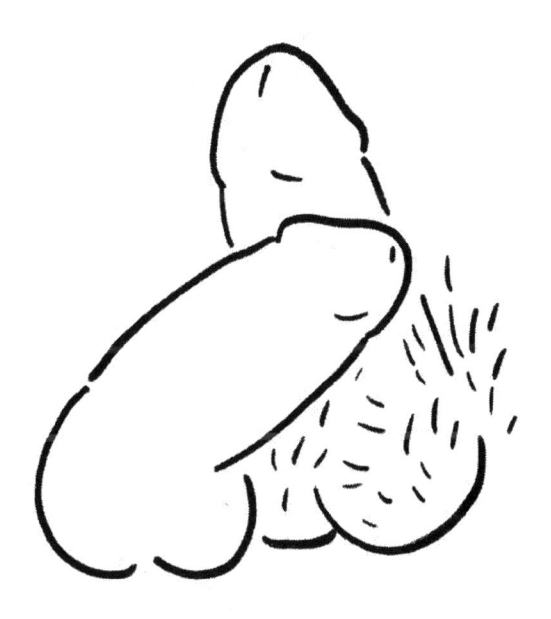

While he was temporarily living back home at his folk's house - after a job across the country had transferred him back to Sugar Lake's south coast of the town's namesake body of water - Peter was excited that morning. He stayed busy, and he enjoyed his job, but he always needed some extra-curricular entertainment to take his mind off the nine-to-five. He found comfort back in Sugar Lake enjoying time with dear old mom. His dad died a half-dozen years ago, and the adjustment to living alone was tough for her. Peter hated that he had been so far away up to, and after, the funeral rendering him unable to look after his mother. So, while he would eventually find his place back in his hometown soon enough, the home time was what they both needed. His mom was still independent, so he did not have to care every single day. It was the companionship that mattered the most.

He was more than thankful his job had not called him for one of those fucking phone conference meetings on his day off work. He hated them, and they often seemed to lodge themselves in the middle of his day aborting any plans to have a life before the vampires crawled out of their caves at dusk. It left his free time to do with as he wanted. Excursions outside of work or family functions were an appreciated relief of feeling like a teenager living at home with the parental units.

Peter had gone partially deaf at a younger age. Although if there was no outside noise when people spoke, and he was able to see their lips, he did fine with understanding them. Asking people to speak up was as much a part of his life as taking a piss. It was such a part of him at this point that he did not think about it too much. It had never played negatively in a hookup. He told people about his condition, and no one made it a point of contention when considering his proposition.

Peter was twenty-three, decent credit, no marriages or divorces, no stray offspring wandering the earth to and fro, nor a caretaker for the elderly. His life was still his, for now. The moments he did have to himself were often spent hiking, working out, watching sports with new pals and while getting to know old friends. A night out to a gay club for some drinks was just as typical of a routine as hiking on a sunny day or biking up to Pleasure Point on that goddamn motorbike his mother and late father despised so much.

For the past few of years, he had been slowly exploring facets of his sexuality and what appealed to him. A slap here, a tickle there never hurt anyone. If it did hurt, it was a good hurt. More intense than leg day at the gym, but less robust than kickboxing or CrossFit.

Through the course of many hookups, some great and some less than stellar, he had found a guy that might take him to new places. Last year, he had his limits pushed and explored with a guy he respectfully called Sir Luke. However, the Sir seemed to be pretty busy at times. That, coupled with living out of town for a while made meetings infrequent at best. Sir Luke once told Peter that he had a new guy to train and work with so he might not be around much in the following few months. Peter said he understood yet remained quietly disappointed. The couple of times he played with Sir Luke were never lacking in extraordinary insight into his limits. He learned some things he liked and some things he did not enjoy. Peter always wanted to be pushed further, so maybe the things he did not like would become new things to enjoy. Luke was not the first man Peter had explored extreme sex, and he would not be the last.

Luckily, today Peter knew someone that was only slightly new to the things he liked, those being bondage, domination, submission and almost anything that went along with it. He needed to get moving as he was already running late for his appointment with his new friend.

Simon was someone Peter met online via the usual vehicles of internet chat. They chatted via video just once to know neither was being lied to by the other. Simon was familiar with the things Peter found arousing and erotic. Simon had certainly been around and talked a good game. Delving into BDSM still felt like a neutral territory. It was something Simon often thought about but had never entirely acted on himself. What he had done was participate in bigger scenes. In Canadian Falls - in the northeastern edge of Benton County, his home for the past twenty-five years - he had attended plenty of orgies where there was extreme play. He took mental notes and often assisted the masters in charge, learning everything there was to be a submissive or a dominant. Sometimes he felt more daring and assumed the role of guy number three of six in a gangbang of some twink strapped in a sling, and whose hole was already blown out and dripping with lube, spit, and cum. In his personal mono e mono encounters, Simon kept his actions on a less intense level; anything from vanilla to a strong espresso. But in a group setting, he often found great pleasure in watching a group of dominant daddies control a willing submissive man-boy. When Peter found out Simon's willingness to explore with him, he was more than ready to bring Simon into the fold of extreme playing fully. Peter thought it was a mission, but Simon viewed it as the next step in his sexual journey of intense play. Not everyone gets off with being tied up and abused. Peter did. Simon wanted to put to use the things he had learned from his observations throughout recent years. Peter was either brave or just really easy to let himself be the proverbial whipping boy for Simon's dark exploration as a total dominant. Simon felt he had a good handle on the ins and outs of BDSM and jumped at the chance to extend his knowledge into a real-life experience finally. Being the lead manager at his job, Simon certainly knew how to take charge of a situation and be the boss. Perhaps Peter would pose a challenge to his managerial skills, or maybe it was just the perfect situation waiting to happen for both of them.

Peter set about packing up a bag to take with him. He ran down his mental checklist.

Keys. Wallet. Toys. Dildos. Lube. Rope. Duct tape. Clothespins. Restraints. Blindfold. Towels. Jockstrap.

The toys in his bag are things people might find to be somewhat pragmatic. To the laymen, most of those are not tools for sexual play. They were essentials of a well-stocked workbench or tool shed. To someone like Peter, they were fodder for a great time.

He continued the internal recital of the list as he drove under the late morning sun. It warmed his car on an otherwise chilly April day. The forty-five-minute jaunt from Sugar Lake up to Canadian Falls would be ample time to mentally prepare as best he could for the task before him. He considered some of the things he might let Simon do to him; although when you are tied and helpless the list of "yes" and "no" dwindles quickly. One of his favorite things to use his leg and arm spreaders. They were roughly three feet in length, with a cuff at either end which usually fastened with a lock and key or a buckle mechanism. They kept a person's hands and feet separated. They are used in many ways including standing and tied to a door frame, on the bed or hogtied on the floor. Maybe today they will find a new way to keep Peter's ankles as far apart as possible. The feeling of vulnerability with having no way to protect yourself incredibly alluring for Peter. He had a long list of responsibilities in his life and to be able just to let go of it all had become an attractive relief. He also brought his leather gloves. The leather was well used, and the aroma on them was a mixture of sweat, and a little spunk.

Peter took the on-ramp for I-270 north straight to Canadian Falls. While it was a bit of a drive, anything under an hour was reasonable for a good and rough time. He followed Simon's directions to the letter as typed out in an email, now printed and in the seat next to him.

```
Get on 270N, take exit 22B.
At the end of the exit is a light. Turn left
onto South Lynn Ave.

Stay on S. Lynn Ave. (going west) four blocks
until you see Jacob St. Turn right (north).
```

```
Go to the end of the block, park on the street,
or in a parking lot called Franklin Ave., just
before the apartment.
The address is 73. Push the bottom button, #2.
```

Easy enough.

Simon had been watching out the window for Peter to arrive. He liked to see the person before they came to the door just so size them up, eliminate some of the surprises because God knows there were plenty more surprises in store today. They had a whole fantasy to work out; an entire scenario right out of a good movie. Sort of a mix of a sexy hostage scene and a porno. There you have it. Bondage 101. Simon had been sorting out what he wanted to accomplish today as the first-time dominant. He had seen plenty, done even more, and felt confident in today's forthcoming activities.

Simon sized up Peter right off the bat when he saw him walk towards his two-family building. He stood in his living room window poised and ready for his new venture. He knew he could handle Peter.

"You little toad, you have no idea what you are walking into, not one bit," he said out loud to himself.

When Peter came up the steps on the stoop, he obeyed the directions and rang buzzer number two.

Simon headed to the door buzzer but paused for a moment before hitting the release button. He wanted Peter to wait and know who was in control. Simon slowly counted to five then pressed the button. He heard the foyer door buzz and then Peter pushing it open.

Peter proceeded up the steps to the second-floor flat unaware of what waited for him.

Once Simon heard Peter was in the building he briskly headed to the bathroom and hid in the darkness. This was part of their plan; a planned surprise attack. It seemed like an oxymoron – two words that are the opposite of each other like jumbo shrimp or controlled chaos – but it was all part of the experience. Simon's heart was beating through his chest. He was as excited to exercise his dominant side as Peter was to submit to someone exploring it in full for the first time.

Just breathe, idiot. Relax, it is just sex. And you can do this.
Great self-pep talk.

Peter got to the top of the stairs and stood outside Simon's front door for a minute. He took a deep breath knowing, or not, what was about to happen. He had agreed to all of what was about to happen, though. Only a couple of boundaries had been set beforehand. Everything else he relinquished over to Simon. He understood that control of his own body, and the situation as a whole was entirely in Simon's realm of power. He gave up any rights to say 'no' unless Simon felt it was too much. Some would argue that to be a good dominant, you must first know what it feels like to be submissive. Peter felt perhaps that was not always the case. It certainly was not the normal way of introducing someone to the world of Bondage, Domination, and, Sadomasochism. But then again, the world of BDSM was not new to Simon. He had been there done that, mostly. Peter loved to be tied up and used, and after weeks of conversation with Simon on the computer, planning, negotiating, just talking, and even a phone call or two, they had drawn enough information to conclude Peter could trust Simon with whatever he wanted to put into the mix. Simon had no reservations about pushing Peter's limits, and his own in the process. The blue-collar aggression that Simon possessed was a trait Peter was pleased to learn in their chats. And for Simon, Peter offered a much more enticing and different level of kink and exploration. That trust would either grow or deplete itself by the end of this meeting. Both had hoped the latter was not true.

Peter slowly exhaled preparing for the unexpected. He turned the knob, and the door freely opened. It felt very odd walking into a stranger's home with no one to greet him, even if he was invited. He breathed in and took in the smells of Simon's apartment. Was it musty? Did it smell like lunch had just been served? Did it smell like the people who lived there? In a nanosecond, Peter summed up what he thought about what he felt or what he did not. Simon had aired the house out and straightened it up a bit before his company arrived. The rub was that Peter was going to see so little of it, being possibly blindfolded for the bulk of his stay, that it did not matter what décor Simon had chosen for his flat.

Peter shut the door and took a minute to gain his bearings. From the entryway, there was not much to see. To his left was a small hallway, if you could call it that, that led to two bedrooms. He knew that probably was not the way, so he followed the narrow corridor to the right. As he turned the corner, he saw the living room. He heard nothing, although he could not hear that well anyway. The house did look like there was no sign of life in it. He walked through the hall, each step building up his sense of impending excitement and anxiousness of what was about to happen. The hallway ended in the living room. He dropped his bag of toys and focused on a wooden chair in the middle of the floor. A few candles were lit, and a couple of random extension cords were on the floor behind it. That was the last thing he noticed before he felt the brute force of him being knocked to the floor. It surprised him, although he knew it was coming. It almost knocked the breath out of him. Simon had tackled him from behind holding Peter's head to the floor while laying on top of him. He grabbed Peter's hair, pulled his head back, and lowered his face to Peter's ear.

"Who the fuck are you and what do you want?"

"I, I....I am not sure," Peter said, immediately slipping into the fantasy he had craved for so long. He would be lying if he did not admit that part of his response was based on pure fear of actually being in the wrong house.

"I must have found the wrong house."

"You found the wrong house? Are you that stupid that you do not know where the fuck you are going? You walk into a motherfucker's house, and you get fucked!"

"I am sorry, will you please let me up? I will leave."

"Oh no motherfucker, not today. You are going to pay for this shit. Do you understand?"

Peter panicked. Was the fantasy that real or what had he walked into a stranger's house?

"I am sorry," he said in strained breaths under the weight of Simon's body.

"Please let me up, Sir," he begged while struggling.

Simon grabbed his hair harder and put a knife in Peter's eye line.

"I said you are not going anywhere, you little prick! Your ass is mine."

There was a pause as Peter wondered if he could make it out of this unharmed. He realized his chances were slim that he was in the wrong house as much as him getting out unscathed. Fear and doubt enveloped his body.

Simon pushed Peter's face into the plush pile and quickly reached over for one of the extension cords. Simon had chosen extension cords rather than rope because they had a more industrial feel to them. Simon had enough rope on hand – and had prepared another phase of torture for Peter with it - but preferred the extension cords method right now. The cords felt more sinister, harsher on the skin. Simon put his knee on Peter's back like he had seen on some cable network, to keep him in place. He wrapped the cord around Peter's neck then quickly tied Peter's hands behind his back.

"Do not even think about moving, or I will gut you like a fish." Peter's fear of the unknown was growing. Simon grabbed the duffle bag.

"Bring me a present?" he said sarcastically.

"No, it is just..." Peter started.

"Shut the fuck up," came the retort from the big man with the knife as did a backhand upside his head. Peter was stunned. Simon opened the bag and immediately saw a pair of leather gloves. Perfect. He put them on, rechecked the bag and found a roll of the duct tape. He quickly pulled a leader piece off the end to make it easier to wrap as much as he wanted over Peter's eyes. He made sure the last thing Peter saw was that long, shiny knife on the floor next to his face.

"Do not forget I have this, you piece of pig shit. It is real, and it is very sharp. Do not give me a reason to show you just how sharp, got it?"

Peter dared not even look at Simon's face. He cowered and tried to stay as submissive as possible including not making direct eye contact with Simon.

Before Peter could get any words out, Simon was wrapping the duct tape over his eyes. He had thought about screaming, but why bother. No one would hear him now. Not in this upstairs apartment, with brick and mortar between either wall.

"Oh God please do not hurt me," Peter begged. It threw Simon off for a minute. Did Peter think he was being kidnapped? Simon knew Peter would realize soon enough he was in just the right place. The thought of Peter's fear seemed to rile Simon up, and the movement in his pants was the evidence.

"God is not here, faggot. Or is he? Is he here and I do not seem him? Did you ride here with you?" Simon shouted.

"Now get up!" He grabbed Peter's shirt from behind and pulled him to a standing position in the middle of the floor, with his hands still tied behind his back, and part of the cord around his neck. It was way too tight for Peter's liking, but he did not have a choice. He knew that a captor did not accommodate their victims by making them comfortable. He quickly surmised he should not ask to loosen the cord. He would have to deal with it. He would not be able to relax his arms behind him because they were on a terse lead. If he dropped his arms, it would pull the cord tighter around his neck and start to choke him. Simon walked around to stand in front of the blind Peter boy. He turned Peter around and unfastened his pants, yanking them down to his ankles. He pushed Peter into the wooden chair and moved the pants and his shoes out of the way. Peter would not need these for a while. Simon put Peter's hands over the back of the chair, so they were not close to his body. He quickly checked the extension cord and made sure it was tight around Peter's neck and hands. He took another cord and wove it through the chair legs and around Peter's legs, rendering him all but helpless. Peter's calves were secured to the legs of the chair. Simon tied him apart at the knees so he would have full access to Peter's dick. Peter knew better than even to move. The knife had to be close. The last thing Peter wanted was to bleed to death from a laceration.

After Simon had him secured to the chair, Peter became obediently quiet. His breathing was heavy with anxiety and fear rushed through him. He sat there, straining to hear what he could not. It was times like this he cursed the fact he had lost so much of his hearing as a child. All of his other senses should be sharper, more on point. He was unable to surmise the situation beyond actually being restrained. He suddenly felt a hand grab his hair and pull his head back. Simultaneously he felt cold steel against his neck. He felt the hot breath of Simon in his ear again. Simon did not say anything. He was letting Peter know he was still near and was not about to let him out of his sight. Peter's breaths grew quick and shallow from the strain of having his head positioned backward. With the pain of having his hair pulled, it was all he could do to stay sane. Simon slid the dull side of the knife slowly across Peter's neck from ear to ear. Peter felt every inch of it and only hoped it was not the sharp side of the blade. Simon had no intentions of hurting Peter by way of a sharp knife. It was mental, but Peter did not know that. What Simon wanted was not to scare Peter to death, but get him as close to it in his mind as possible; just this side of the reaper's flat.

Only slight relief came from Peter as he felt the knife slip away from his neck. He had no idea what else Simon had planned for him. This was Simon, was it not? Of course, it was. He hoped. Simon kept one hand on Peter's head and had quietly put the knife down with the other. He loosened his grip on his victim's hair, and for a moment Peter was grateful.

Simon rifled through Peter's duffle bag to surmise what he had available. Peter was quickly out of earshot to hear anything. He left Peter to sit in the chair, totally untouched and curious about what was coming. He was pleased to see what Peter had brought much of his equipment. Simon did not mind using his toys, but it was indeed an easy clean up afterward if you send the stuff home with their owner.

Peter felt both of Simon's leather gloved hands on his head again, but he was not pulling his hair. He was rubbing his head slowly, almost massaging it. Simon moved down either side of his head, quickly caressing the ears that would hear much of nothing today. His hands ran down Peter's face, over his taped eyes and even brushed his lips for a minute. Simon felt his hands had never been more tactile as they were right now, even through the gloves. He made notes of every inch of Peter's face. He made his way down to Peter's chest and reached inside his T-shirt. Even though Peter was still scared to death, the caress of the leather hands relaxed him, if ever so slightly. The smell of leather intoxicated Peter. It is part of the reason he was here. Simon reached further into the T-shirt and found the nipples. He pinched them slightly, not hurting them. He slowly slid his hands back up Peter's chest and without warning. Peter suddenly felt a violent outburst from his subjugator. Simon wrapped his fingers around Peter's neck, protruding into Peter's Adam's apple, the first knuckles pressing down on the juggler's veins; the palms and the heel of the hands pushing in from the side, thumbs interlocked against the back of his neck. Peter began to gag and gasp for air. He could hear the saliva gurgling in his throat as the grip got tighter. Was this how he was going to die? Or worse yet, was this just the beginning of something much more cruel only to be found in the mind of his detainer. Simon held the fat neck in his hands for longer than either expected. Peter's body tensed up and strained to try to wiggle free of the grip around his neck threatening his life. Simon held him in place easily loving the struggle Peter gave him. Just as quickly as the death grip had started, it stopped. Peter took a deep breath, coughing in between, hoping he was still conscious.

"There is more where that came from, do not worry," said with a taunting and dominant tone.

"Let me go, please. I promise I will not tell anyone."

No response.

Simon grabbed a well-worn pair of underwear he had nearby. He wore the same pair of underwear six days straight as he visited the gym, knowing exactly where they would end up today. He grabbed Peter's chin with one hand and started to shove the bikini shaped underwear into Peter's mouth. Peter twisted his head from either side, begging his defeater not to do it. Peter was afraid of being gagged and fought it as much as he could. He tossed his head back and forth more than that little girl did on the bed with the demon inside of her.

Simon tightened his grip, pulling Peter's head back toward him.

"No! Do not do it! You shit head, do not do it!" Peter said, as he suddenly grew increasingly defensive. His fighting was futile. Simon had tied him tightly to the chair, and Peter was going nowhere. Simon straddled Peter to hold him in place.

"I have wrestled more worthy opponents, you faggot." Simon loved taunting Peter. He cared little about Peter's reaction to any of it.

With only a few struggles the underwear was in Peter's mouth. Peter fought against the sweaty and well-worn smell of Simon's exercise odor. The stench of a week's working out and whatever else Simon did while wearing it overwhelmed Peter's senses. The funk infiltrated his nostrils, and the bitterness sat on his tongue, permeated the inside of his cheeks and the back of his throat. He heard the rip of duct tape. Another strip was being wrapped around his head, keeping the bikini in his mouth. Not only was he blind to his impending torture, but he also could not beg for it to stop at this point. He almost wanted to cry but did not. Simon wrapped the tape across Peter's mouth again and again. He reached down and grabbed the bottom of the front of Simon's t-shirt. He pulled it up and back over Peter's head, creating a hood of sorts. Simon stepped out from behind the chair and stood in front of Peter. He took a moment to take in his handiwork thus far. He had done this before to some degree. It felt much more gratifying doing it on his own and in his apartment. The rush of total and complete power was intoxicating. He would be responsible, but it was deceptively exhilarating. Peter struggled to breathe through his nose and the shirt. Through his heavy-handedness, Simon made sure Peter could breathe.

He emptied Peter's bag onto the floor nearby making anything in it easily accessible. There was plenty ahead for both of them. Simon was just getting started.

Simon put his hands on his prey's thighs and leaned into him to be heard once again.

"You are the biggest pussy I have seen in my life. Your mother must hate you." Harsh but they were not here to have a kumbaya moment. This was pleasure and business, and neither was too far gone to see that.

The very extent of the insult and disrespect was enough to confuse Peter's senses temporarily. Simon reached over and grabbed one of the burning votive candles from a table. He grazed the hot glass across one of Peter's nipples just fast enough as not to cause him any severe damage. The stuffed underwear absorbed screams that would never be heard behind them. Only a slight noise came from Peter's nose. Simon derived great pleasure in the pain inflicted upon poor Peter boy. He quickly repeated the action against the other nipple. The same muted screams came from the body. Again, and again, the heat of the candle pushed Peter further and further into a world of pain and the unknown. If pain was a great hotel in which each room held a different form of torture, then Peter had barely made it to the front desk. Simon was announcing his reservation. But, as the song goes, he could try to check out, but he could never leave.

Simon tipped the container and slowly dripped hot liquid wax onto Peter's chest. Peter felt burning all over his torso. Hot waxy splatters tortured every nerve ending they found. He could not localize where the burning sensations were coming from; he just had to endure them. A little more wax spilled onto his bare chest. And again. And again. And again, until the candle was all but gone. One last press of the hot glass against his chest sealed this chapter in the torture. Simon stood up, and let the wax harden. Peter sat there alone for a time he could not measure. His body twitched from the hot wax and in desperate expectation of what was coming next. Simon wanted him to wonder if it all stopped. Peter was left to his imagination going into overdrive.

Simon took another inventory of Peter's toy bag. He was impressed that Peter had been just thorough enough to include items not only of pleasure but ones that could inflict great, unrelenting pain.

"Spreaders? You are asking for it today," Simon said not caring if Peter heard him or not. He took them out and inspected them. He had helped attach them to willing orgy participants in the past, but it was only him being dutiful to a larger scene. This was direct action, and he had to not fumble his way through it. He would get to any other articles in the bag as he needed them. Today was a good day and the possibilities endless.

He got behind his victim again and cuffed one of the sides of the spreader to one of Peter's hands. He quickly untied the extension cord and grabbed the other hand and put on the other cuff. Peter struggled to break free still exerting subdued screams through the bikini in his mouth. Simon was stronger and quickly wrangled Peter's arm into submission and the other cuff. The cord still being around Peter's neck had temporarily loosened enough that his sense of an open airway did not feel as threatened. He was wrong. Simon pulled it and wrapped the end of it around the spreader bar, creating similar tension against Peter's throat. By default, he lifted Peter's arms way behind him, in quite an uncomfortable position putting a strain on Peter's muscles and joints. So, what could he do? If he allowed his arms to relax then he would pull the cord tighter against his neck; if he lifted his arms behind him to keep any tension off his neck, it would be an impossible task for more extended periods. Both choices were meant to be equally brutal on Peter's physicality and mentality.

His hot breath was caught between his mouth, and the T-shirt still pulled over his face. Through the shirt, he felt a hard slap come at him like a train. Then another from the other side. Then with his gloved hands, Simon slapped Peter's wax-ridden chest. Some of the wax flew across the room. A few more slaps to the chest would dislodge more of the wax taking some hair with it. It stung like hell. The rest would stay there for the remainder of the day until Simon decided to remove it by force. Simon stood in front of Peter, poised for his next strike. He reached up and pulled the shirt off Peter's head. He then grabbed the knife and cut the shirt down the middle, leaving it hanging on Peter's arms. The now-cut up shirt left Peter's bare torso fully exposed and vulnerable to Simon. Peter was glad he was not struggling to breathe through 100% cotton anymore.

Simon grabbed Peter's crotch feeling the sub's dick through his underwear. He squeezed down with little mercy. Peter's breaths became quickened and anxious again. Simon leaned in and took one of the exposed nipples between his teeth, and bit down ever so slightly. Then harder, and harder. Peter squirmed to pull away. There was nowhere to run.

"If you move or kick me, I will end you. Do you understand me, faggot?"

Peter's sweaty head nodded in agreement.

Simon slapped Peter from his kneeling position. "Do you fucking understand me?"

Peter nervously shook his head faster to acknowledge Simon's question.

Simon found the second spreader in Peter's duffle bag. He untied either of Peter's legs, quickly replacing his ankles in either cuff in the spreader's cuffs. Peter realized that somehow Simon had not only gotten him unclothed but tied in a chair in spreaders. Between the apparent fear and the enjoyable pain, Peter was impressed.

Simon grabbed Peter by the hair and pushed him out of the chair to the floor. With nothing to stop him but the floor itself, Peter fell hard to the rug. Peter found himself kneeled on the floor, blindfolded, gagged, hands behind his back in a three-foot spreader, and his legs followed suit. Simon sat the chair behind Peter, grabbed him with a choke-hold from behind wrapping his stiff muscled arm around Peter's neck. Peter felt like he was being lifted off the ground by his neck.

Simon had undoubtedly been able to always hold his own at work, at home, and in the bedroom. He lifted weights and worked out enough that his mature muscle was developed and an asset. While his body was lean, his arms were defined, and the gun show was never far away. It felt more than easy to wrap his arm around Peter's neck in a chokehold from behind, cutting off his air supply. It probably did not cut off much, but Peter had the sensation that he was suffocating or being choked. Simon knew half of the intense play is the act of it, and the other half is mental. The knife, the questioning of being in the right house, the strangling – it was all part of the larger puzzle Simon put together. Whether Peter fully realized any of that to this point was irrelevant. Simon had a plan. It was going wonderfully.

Simon leaned into Peter's ear once again.

"I am going to feel you from the inside, fucker. You think you might like that? You think that might be on your list of things to do today in between picking up some crackers and lemon soda for your mom, or whatever shitty attempt you make at working out? Look at you. You are fucking disgusting. Why am I even bothering with you? I have shit out better piles than you."

Peter knew he was in trouble. Simon held his arm around Peter's neck for a minute tightening the muscled hold. He was left-handed, so it left his right-wing mostly free. He played with Peter's nipples and pulled at his waxy chest hair. Peter was struggling to breathe through his nose. He felt utterly helpless. Despite the sweat on his forehead, the duct tape over Peter's eyes did not seem to be giving way. It paid to buy a professional grade gear.

Peter could do little to respond to the taunts. He struggled to stay on his knees while in the most awkward of positions. Few people could remain in a kneeling position while both hands and legs were in spreaders. Simon let his arm loose from around Peter's neck, caressing his exposed skin. The leather felt strange yet comforting to Peter.

Maybe he is going to let up now.

Simon nuzzled the back of his victim's neck. His gloved hands ran over Peter's body. Despite being scared, Peter's dick was coming to attention. So was Simon's, but he was not going to let Peter know that. Not yet. Simon nibbled Peter's ear from behind sending chills through Peter's body. He kissed the back of Peter's neck sniffing the musk forming through the sweat glands under the hair on Peter's head. Peter started to relax a bit and tried to enjoy the oddly gentle nuzzling from his master. Simon untied and released the extension cord from around Peter's neck and tossed it out of the way. Enough of that.

"There you go, baby. Is that better?" he taunted. He knew Peter was unable to respond. As Peter stayed kneeled on the floor in front of the chair, tensing his legs to remain upright, beads of sweat running down his forehead and off of his chest, Simon continued to caress him from behind in his sitting position in the chair. He ran his gloved fingertips over Peter's sweaty body, bringing up goosebumps across his skin.

"Calm down, buddy. You are having a good time, right? I can tell you love this. You want this so much. You were asking for it, begging me for it. Such a good boy. Oh yeah, look at you."

Simon continued to stroke Peter's face and body eliciting a false sense of calm and reprise.

"You are quivering, struggling to stay upright and alive. You are an animal. I can smell your scent. I know what you want. You do not have to say it. Of course, you cannot say a word, can you? How do those underwear smell in your gullet? That is what a real man smells like, buddy. Never forget that smell."

Peter let out a slight muffle. He feared if he said no then Simon would taunt him more, or worse. Peter was glad to be able to breathe without taking a blow to his body.

Simon got out of the wooden chair leaving Peter in the middle of the floor on his knees.

"Stay right here, okay buddy? I will be right back. Do not go anywhere, okay?"

Another taunt.

Simon walked to his bedroom, removed his jeans and tank top. He could hear Peter moving around, pouting through the underwear shoved in his mouth. Simon chuckled to himself taking a moment to regroup and make sure his dick was sitting nicely in his red jockstrap. He put on a pair of white socks and slipped into his favorite leather boots; a costly pair thank you very much. He tried to resist the Rusty Rebel Leather salesman, standing in the shop that he had operated for over twenty years, leather vest on with no shirt, jeans, chaps, and nipple rings that teased even the most pretentious of customers. The argument of leather versus pleather (a faux plastic-y imitation leather) was a debate both Simon and the salesman enjoyed. Simon was helpless to resist the daddy's suggestion of real leather boots. It set him and his charge card back a bit more than he planned on spending that day. He later realized how appreciative the subs in his life would be when licking those same boots or polishing them on Leather Weekend at Sterling's; the local gay bear sometimes-leather bar.

Simon had even surprised himself so far. He walked back into the living room; his chest puffed out with a sense of pride. Peter looked helpless and hopeless. His dick communicated that he was having a good time. His cries for mercy were a distraction from his dick's truth. Simon removed the gloves and tossed them on the floor near Peter's bag contents. He picked up the knife and held it against Peter's cheek. The blade had grown cold, and the shock against Peter's hot skin sent his heart rate back into the stratosphere. He ran the dull side across Peter's chest and down to his abs. Peter began to panic. A knife was moving quickly and dangerously close to his privates. Simon grabbed Peter's dick and pressed the blade against it. Simon pulled Peter's underwear away from his body and used the knife to cut them loose. Peter's erect dick flopped out betraying his outward fear-baiting. Simon slapped at Peter's dick, grabbing his balls and squeezing them, and otherwise abusing it. Peter was fully naked, afraid, and vulnerable to Simon. He took a seat in the chair behind Peter again. He wrapped his bare hands around Peter's neck and pressed harder this time. Peter's muffled yelps for relief were ignored. Peter shook where he was still on his knees. His body trembled as his muscle screamed for relief from his oppressor's sadistic whims. He pushed Peter further each time he strangled him, and it scared Peter more every time. Simon doubled down and, while still choking Peter, nibbled on his ears again from his sitting position. Peter's body betrayed him as it stressed to find a better airflow from the throat while the endorphins of the ear nibbling confused even the keenest of senses.

"Oh baby, you feel so good. Give me more, baby. Oh, that is it baby, do not stop. Fuck, you are so hot," he whispered into his slave's ear making goddamn sure he was heard through Peter's aural affliction.

Simon released his grip on Peter's throat and held him upright by his hair. Peter's legs struggled to keep him in the position he needed to be in to feel any sense of control. Simon put his boot in the middle of Peter's back.

"Later, bitch." He kicked Peter to the floor leaving a size ten boot print on his back. Peter had nothing to stop him. He fell like the walls of Jericho. Only this time, Simon did not have to march around Peter's body for seven days. The impact knocked the air out of him. His feet flailed up behind him then landed spread-eagle on the floor. His arms were still struggling in their spreader prison. Simon got on his knees and straddled Peter's legs, leaving just enough room to see and play with Peter's ass at-will. Although Peter's hands were in a spreader behind him, Simon still had plenty of room to do with Peter what he wanted. Simon grabbed a bottle of lube he already had on the coffee table and squirted it into Peter's crevasse. Simon eyeballed the various penetrative devices on the floor. Peter must have been sending silent signals with his bag's contents. Simon could only assume Peter wanted his ass used and abused. Being mostly a top, Simon knew his way around another man's hole. Simon snagged a flesh colored dildo from the pile of contents on the floor. He poured some of the lube on it, stroking it and making sure it was wet and ready to violate Peter's ass. He slapped Peter's ass a few times to be sure he was paying attention while face down and damn-near hog-tied on the floor. Simon used the dildo to toy with the hole in front of him. He taunted it with the tip of the seven-inch monster that looked intimidating to even the most seasoned of professionals. Feeling his toy press against him, Peter squirmed to try and avoid the inevitable, but to no avail. He was in no position to get away. He was fearful of just how forceful Simon could or would be with his bare butt. Peter was versatile and had taken a dick as much as he had given it. A significant part of him enjoyed the submission, the fear factor, the element of the unknown when it came to another man having total power and control over him. He had been slapped before, spanked, man-handled, pushed around, tackled and almost anything else that went along with this type of scenario. There would always be an element of surprise with every guy like some new experience waiting to happen. Could that happen tonight with Simon and his overtly alpha-male takeover?

He felt the full open-handed slap on his ass. Simon was keeping Peter alert and engaged quite well for his first time going this far with domination and sadism. Just like using his dick, Simon slowly maneuvered the head of the dildo into Peter's hole, poking its way past the dual contracting sphincter's natural resistance. Penetration had been accomplished, but the whole thing was not going in, not yet anyway. Peter tried screaming for help and wanted to beg his Warlord of Pain to stop. He would do anything to make it stop. As the head of the fake dick went in and out of his ass, every time it went back in, it would go a little further. Watching the dicky dildo go in and out of Peter's ass made Simon as horny as he had been since jerking off in bed last night. A new hard-on was a hell of a way to start the day. Simon moved up and put the other end of the dildo between his thighs. He laid his body on Peter's back. He moved as if he was fucking him. Peter was in tears and his version of bliss. He was uncomfortable with the spreaders keeping him in an awkward position yet the dildo inside him was hitting every right spot. Simon decided not to give Peter's ass any more time than necessary to loosen up to comfortably take the dildo or a dick. He knew he was being violated and he could do nothing to stop it. The man on top reached up and bit on the exposed ears of the bottom. His hands reached around and would occasionally envelop the neck as they had before, nearly choking the air out of him, then he would release his clutch. Just as Peter regained some breath, while trying to forget about the pain of being fucked in the ass with a dildo, the hands would regain their grip for more deprivation of air. Simon lost himself abusing Peter's hole. He was rock hard in his crimson jock strap; the hardest he had been yet today. There was no way Simon was going to let this moment pass without showing Peter what bottoming felt like tied up on the floor.

Simon penetrated Peter, fucking him without recourse; all in between trying out each dildo in the bag on Peter's weak and sore ass. No one heard his muffled screams, saw his tears, or cared about his discomfort.

∞

How long have I been down here? Did he leave? Should I try to get up? Is this part of the game? He could be watching me. If I move, he might come after me again.

The shadows in the house had significantly shifted since Peter arrived some odd time ago. Simon had left him on the floor to suffer in silence. Peter let his face sink into the carpet and had been weeping fiercely. Simon had taken his time abusing Peter's ass with all three dildos from the bag, and his cock.

Eventually, Simon got up to get a drink. He was shiny & soaked from his perspiration akin to someone who had run a half-marathon; slight rug burns showed up on his knees, and the familiar rush of endorphins that running or sex propagated filled his body. Thankfully the burns on his knees were minor since his boots helped him keep traction while waylaying Peter's hole. With a drink in hand – a little whiskey never hurt anyone; it was afternoon after all – he sat in his favorite chair to relax, leaving Peter on the floor to his own mental devices. The sub's discomfort was of no great consequence to Simon. He was not able-bodied or going anywhere as long as Simon was in charge; which, arguably, was the rest of the day. Peter writhed in pain, his muscles begging for relief. Simon enjoyed watching the struggle on the floor, this homunculus blob of pig shit gasping for air through his nostrils while still being violated with wafts of foul-smelling underwear and his sweat. Is this what Agent Smith meant when he told Morpheus that humanity smelled of a stink that saturated and permeated everything? Was it that Peter or Simon's existence was defined through misery or suffering; that a perfect world of love and sex does not, cannot, exist without pain, fear, and violence? Both had contemplated in the past if their lives would be as fulfilling without scenarios like the one they both wrangled themselves into on this day.

Simon finished his whiskey neat and found a second wind to finish the job before him. He removed the spreader from Peter's ankles. The ones on his arms stayed. Simon grabbed Peter from behind and lifted him to his knees.

"Stand up, fucker." It was the first words Peter had heard from Simon since before he took his break.

Peter pushed himself up to his feet. His muscles ached in silent agony. Simon walked him to a double-door entry to the dining area. Peter was sure to watch his footing since he had no way to brace for another fall, nor could even see where he was being taken.

"Step back and up," he heard Simon say. "Do it. Step back and up, one foot at a time."

Simon had set up two pillars of wood blocks; scraps from a building project last year. Each was a seven-inch square and about one inch thick. Each pillar, or pile, was comprised of six blocks. Anyone standing on their pillar of blocks would be a half foot taller.

He had placed them at calculated width apart to accommodate Peter's feet. Simon could have used anything to stand Peter on, but the wooden blocks were purposely tricky. They are not made to stand on or use as a lift. So, for Peter to stand on them would prove to be another level of willpower and self-control, and mental torture, that Simon put on the table.

"Step. Back, up, step again." Peter had no idea what Simon was trying to guide him toward, but he played along as if he had a choice otherwise. His legs still screamed with burning pain from being spread and sat on by Simon. He had not been able to stretch or move the whole time Simon had been raping his ass with artificial dicks. Peter struggled but got both his legs onto the two sets of blocks acting as platforms. Without the benefit of a visual inspection, they may have well been ten feet apart. Simon had retrieved some rope from the duffle bag (and his utility closet) to tie and secure Peter's legs in the double-wide doorway in the living room. Extension cords were nice sometimes, but it stood to reason that Simon had his supply of rope on hand. Just enough. The French doors that were there had long since been opened and furniture set in front of them. They became décor and unusable. Simon had prepared for today by feeding the rope around the door hinges and putting every inch where it was needed. With Peter now in place, he snaked the cord around Peter's thighs starting from his crotch down to his calves and ankles. Simon had strung another long piece of line over the top two hinges of either door and across the top of the doorway. The rope was pulled down and doubled around Peter's neck. The long loose ends hanging from under the hinges were pulled tightly and wrapped around Peter's arms, tying and suspending them on either side of him. Peter stood there, tied up, standing on a pair of uncertain blocks feeling more vulnerable than he had yet this morning. He was susceptible to everything.

Simon leaned up to Peter's ear.

"The more you scream, cry or try to yell, and I will remove a block from under your feet. And you already feel the rope around your neck. You do the math on that one. You do not have far to travel if you start acting like a pussy. You got it, boy?"

Peter paused in a moment of terrified realization that if the blocks were removed, he could slowly be strangled. How much of a masochist was he that he was letting Simon do all of this to him? Simon's sadism seemed to know no limits. What the fuck was this guy thinking?

Simon let him stand there and adapt to his new prison in the doorway, helpless like a newborn. Simon teased Peter's nipples, getting them as erect as they could be at that moment. A little biting on the areola would not hurt – or maybe it would. Peter writhed from the damage being done. Simon enjoyed inflicting any pain on Peter. He had retrieved a couple of nipple clamps from his bedroom while changing out of his clothes. He placed them on Peter's tender and overly sensitive nipples. Peter squirmed again from the pain. The constant pinching and teasing were almost too much. He put a few on Peter's scrotum; after pinching up some skin on top of his dick, Simon put one there as well. Were they clothespins or nipple clamps, or those binder clips you can get at the store? Whatever they were their presence clinging to Peter's delicate body felt like small spider bites made to torture its victim.

Simon lit another candle. Without telling Peter, he placed it on the floor directly between Peter's legs centered under his dick. It was far enough that no pain would hit him just yet. It was more like putting a fish in a bowl of cold water, then slowly turning up the heat. He would soon learn just how much Simon was increasing the heat.

Simon sat down and reviewed his work. He sat at his desk on the other side of the room. He poured himself another whiskey. Peter stood straining to stay steady on the blocks, clamps bringing the blood to strategic parts of his body; all ones made of the same erectile tissue. The candle was already promoting its agenda, heat quietly and rapidly rising between his legs.

Simon grabbed the digital camera on his desk, turned it on and let it load. He took photos of Peter from the front and back. He wanted proof of his work and for his collection of partners, or victims.

Being in his mid-somethings, Simon knew the importance of surprise and was not afraid to instigate it with a partner. Peter, being younger, was often more out to have fun and explore sex, fucking, or being fucked. While not all of his dates were this extreme, they did prove to be a nice change up from the routine of copulating with the like-minded menfolk. Peter had delved into the divergent shenanigans early on in his life. Simon had experienced his share of what some would deem as abnormal or deviant. But he never made apologies for anything he did sexually or otherwise. Life was just too fucking short to rain on your parade and carry shame for being pissed on one time or being number four in a line of seven who fucked a more-than-willing bottom at an orgy in a barn a few summers ago. There should always be more people enjoying pleasure than any religious or societal based guilt promoted in opposition. Simon's motto was 'more men less sin.'

After a sip of whiskey and a swig from a bottle of water, and a few more photos – both of which were arguably out of Peter's realm of hearing or general knowledge for the time being - Simon went to the kitchen and pulled out a small bowl from the freezer. It contained a pre-frozen ice cube. It was not just any ice cube. This ice cube, frozen in a long banana-shaped cube tray was unique. This ice cube had a crushed and oddly potent breath mint dissolved and frozen in it. Simon had no interest in freshening anyone's breath today. But he did have a great interest in torturing Peter's ass more.

He stood next to Peter and ran his fingers along Peter's back. The endorphins raced to the surface while still fighting the pinching clamps on his front side. Simon glided his fingers lightly across Peter's skin. Goosebumps checked in for roll call again across his back and up his neck. Peter knew it was not a sign of good things.

"I will make you a deal, okay?" Simon offered. Peter nodded with desperation.

"I will remove this tape and take my dirty underwear out of your mouth. But if you scream one time or beg me to stop, I will only make it worse for you. You get that, right? Do you understand?"

It was no surprise to him that Peter quickly approved.

"Do you agree to these terms? I will take the tape off your mouth, and you behave yourself, yes?"

Peter nodded furiously with his affirmation. He just wanted the shorts out of his mouth.

Simon grabbed the tape around Peter's head and over his eyes from the back and lifted it off his head. The sweat had finally weakened much of the glue anyway. With the knife, always on standby, Simon carefully cut the tape from around Peter's jawline and pulled the bikini out of his mouth.

"Oh my God! Oh my God!!" Peter exclaimed. The bright noon sun beaming in had all but blinded Peter for the moment. His vision was bright and distorted. Was that a spotlight in his eyes or was it just the sun that he had not seen in a very long while?

Simon slapped him.

"Hey, no yelling and screaming like a bitch. We have an agreement," Simon reminded him, grabbing Peter by the back of the neck.

"Man up, pussy. Do you want to go down like a bitch? Huh? Do you?!"

"No."

"No what?"

"No, Sir."

"Better." He walked around to face Peter. "Looks like you got yourself into one hell of a fucking situation, huh? I mean, goddamn, look at you, son! You are sweating like an unarmed cop in the middle of the zombie apocalypse! You are all but a puddle of pig shit right now. The difference is that pig shit has somewhere to go. It has a purpose. People think pigs roll around in shit, but that is untrue. Pigs roll in the mud to stay cool on warm days. They are relatively clean animals with a good sense of self. Do you have a good sense of yourself, faggot? Do you know why you are here today? I am not sure you fully realize just how much power you gave up and who you gave it up to, honestly. By the way, I would not even think about stepping down from those blocks if I were you. Go ahead, look at them.

"Look at yourself. I will give you a few seconds to take your inventory. You are naked in a stranger's apartment. You have been tied up and restrained the whole time, punched, slapped, burned, fucked with God knows what. My God, son; how much are you willing to take? I wonder just how far your limits go. I say we should find the fuck out, what do you think, huh? You could not be in a worse position, although stretching your body over a barbeque pit might be a fine afternoon snack. It just seems to me that you have done gone and got yourself into a big fucking mess!"

Simon was not inclined whatsoever to eating Peter. Simon was kinky, but he was no cannibal. It stands to be said out loud. He was there to physically torture and mentally fuck with his victim. If the thought of being fricasseed alive happened to frighten Peter, then Simon would play that card, but only verbally.

Peter glanced down, still trying to make his eyes work, and saw his feet on the blocks and the candle under him.

"Yes Sir, I guess I have."

The ice cube was counting its seconds in Simon's palm. He swaggered back behind Peter.

"Do not even think about turning around, punk."

He did not. Simon stuck his finger between Peter's butt cheeks and massaged his hole.

"How is that ass of yours, anyway? It has taken a lot today. I wonder if it could take some more. They say more is not always better but then again who are they anyway? Who put a limit on indulgence?"

"Yes, Sir. It hurts."

"Sorry, what? Was that a complaint?"

"No Sir, just being honest."

"Oh, honesty. Well, I like honesty. It pleases me to hear you speak your truth. We are not done yet. And you are not exactly in a position to bargain for your freedom. Of course, I do not have to tell you that."

Simon continued to prod around Peter's butt.

"Your hole is nice and opened up for me. I guess you must be ready for some more. I have to admit your hole is mighty entertaining to use. And your screams...," he took a deep breath relishing his next words, "your screams are like nourishment to a starving man. They quench me."

Simon was near Peter's ear again, stroking his body from behind and soothing Peter.

"Your cries for pain are like blood to a vampire waking up at dusk. The sun goes down, and the fear of the people rises knowing that the dark lord is circling for his meal. I never realized how much I needed to be quenched inside until I heard your pleas for mercy. The more you whimper and whine the more I am drawn to your fear. It is like nothing I can explain."

"No, Sir. Please no!"

"Uh-oh. Tsk tsk. I hear begging. That is going to cost you."

"No, please! No!" He did not know what he was begging Simon not to do. He was trying to save himself.

Simon inserted a couple of fingers.

"Keep your ground, boy. There is a rope around your neck, or did you forget that part?"

"No Sir, I did not. But..."

"Good. Now because you have violated our rules, I have to punish you."

"Sir, no! Please?"

"If I give you a pass then I have to give everyone a pass, and that is not very fair to anyone, is it? It is not reasonable to me, and I am the one in charge.

"I am begging..." he caught himself. Wrong choice.

"I am growing tired of your pandering. It bores me. Rules are rules, and if you break them, you must suffer the consequences. I have told you this, but maybe you need a harsher reminder that I mean business."

The ice cube was still remarkably solid; more than it was liquid. He slowly dragged the ice cube down the middle of Peter's spine. His heated body involuntarily jerked away from the cold. Simon moved with him keeping the ice on Peter's skin. Peter felt the ice at the nape of his neck slowly moving down his back. It was at the small of his back, then nudge into his intergluteal cleft. That is the little indention at the top of one's crack right on the tailbone. Peter figured there would be no reason to go further. He miscalculated Simon's next move.

In one quick movement, Simon pushed the ice cube between Peter's buttocks and into his hole. Peter let out a big yelp and squirmed to get free. The noose around his neck tightened as a harsh reminder he had no wiggle room. He had nowhere to go.

"Hey, stop. Stop!" Simon commanded grabbing Peter by the face. "You hold that and do not fucking let it go, do you understand?"

"Sir, it is..."

"No complaining," Simon barked holding his finger against Peter's hole.

"You hold that in there until it is gone, do you understand me?" Simon pushed his finger down to the base knuckle assuring the ice cube was well inside Peter's hole.

"Your job is to keep that in there. Even as it melts, I do not want to see one drop coming from your ass. You see that candle below you? If it goes out because you dripped, it is over for you."

Peter was utterly speechless.

"Good. Now we are on the same page. I like when we are on the same page, my dear faggot. It keeps me calm and that works in both our best interests. You do want what is in my best interest right now, yes?"

Peter had no words.

"I will take your silence in the affirmative," Simon said as he paced around the living room ignoring Peter's strains to keep the ice cube hidden.

"Do you remember that joke when we were kids? Oh, it is a funny one. You find a girl who has a small chest or a big chest. Size is irrelevant. You dare her to look down her shirt and spell attic. Have you ever done that? Attic. They never get it. The girl looks down the blouse her daddy picked out for her and says 'a-t-t-i-c.' Get it? A tit-ty I see! It gets them every time! I always say 'I do not.' That always killed me."

Simon laughed out loud at his joke. Peter had no choice but to listen to Simon's monologue. His long diatribes were not mean to inspire or educate. They were to torment his sub, giving him moments of confusion or distraction. Simon liked a slow burn. He relished Peter's the trembling as he tried to assess the scene. But the speeches were always on point.

"Speaking of tits, yours seem busy right now." Simon flicked at the nipple clamps which were still doing their job. The pain they were inflicting was real and ever-present. Simon rubbed Peter's bare ass. He put his body close to Peter's and felt his flesh on his own. He took note of the heat coming from Peter. Simon was a few inches over six feet, and because Peter was almost a foot shorter and standing on blocks, their bodies lined up almost perfectly. He had Peter on those blocks for a reason. Partly to make him strain and fight to stay upright, and partly to be in line with him in case things took another turn. Simon repositioned some of the nipple clamps to new random positions around Peter's dick. Peter's body twisted in pain. Simon ran his hands back down Peter's chest and belly, then down the sides of his hips and around to his bare ass again. He stepped back while still gently rubbing it. His caress mutated into scratching, digging his fingernails into Peter's sweaty flesh.

SLAP!

Peter was not expecting that but then again why would he not? The day had been full of more surprises than he bargained for so what is a slap on the ass at this point? Simon continued the impact, and almost immediately Peter's butt started to turn a pretty shade of fleshy pink. Another slap came to the other cheek. Simon unleashed a dozen more slaps each in a different spot and each a little bit harder than the last. It was a lead-in to his next weapon of choice.

Simon had a few belts hanging on hooks just inside the door frames. It was doubtful Peter had looked over his shoulder and saw them. Simon grabbed a favorite brown belt that was his father's before he died years ago. Simon's dad had used it on him a few times, and he felt it only natural to use it on others. Simon was always a tough guy, a dude's dude. So taking a punch, or even a belt, was just part of being a man. He received his lumps and moved onto the next thing. The belt was not a style he would usually wear, so he upcycled it into a tool for pleasure. He tossed the belt on Peter's shoulder.

Peter's heart rate skyrocketed. He had flashes of his father taking him into his bedroom and making him lay across the bed to receive lashes from a belt. His mother always disapproved of such punishment on a young boy but his father was much tougher on little Peter. Peter always mentioned the irony of having such horrible memories of being spanked by his dad yet totally enjoying being flogged or otherwise whipped and beaten as an adult. Funny how things change like that. But today, he felt like a child again. His fear of Simon's whimsy was magnified by his insecurities of being a child who suffered his father's belted punishments.

"Oh fuck, please, Sir! Not that! Please!!"

"Do not pander to me; you pile of dog shit. You wanted this, and you got it."

"But Sir. You cannot…"

"Are you telling me what I can and cannot do?"

"No Sir, but …" his pleas trailed off into the ether.

Simon grabbed the roll of duct tape and wrapped a few new strips around Peter's head covering his eyes.

"You will learn before I am done with you that I will do whatever the fuck I want to you or anyone else in my house. And you do not want to know what I will put in your mouth next time. My advice is to shut your mouth."

"Yes, Sir."

"What?"

"Yes sir," Peter said louder.

Simon moved to grab the belt and tightened it around Peter's neck.

"Did you have anything else to say? Anymore pandering or that pathetic baby girl begging thing you do?"

Peter strained to get any syllable out, but it was all for naught. Simon pulled the belt just enough to cut off Peter's ability to say anything and have it sound coherent. Peter struggled to focus and breathe.

"I told you there would be repercussions, did I not?" he asked. He let the belt loose. Peter coughed catching his breath. It was more out of fear than any real injury.

"I think you need some help here. But I want you to do something for me, okay? I want you to think about your time here. What have you learned? Who are you that you let this happen to you? You put yourself in my capable hands, and you have lost everything. Your pride, your comfort, your joy. I have taken all of that from you. I have fucked you, brought you pain, fear, probably a dash of despair if my senses are correct. You have just really done nothing but put yourself in a position to be used as an old doormat. How does that make you feel? I want you to think about that for a while."

"Sir, I.."

"Nope, not out loud. I do not care what you think."

Simon walked over to his desk and grabbed a set of wireless headphones. Simon put the headphones on Peter's head. Peter jerked away not knowing what he was feeling. Simon forced his way past the objections.

"There, there now. Easy. I know... I know. Just take a deep breath, asshole." The taunts and sarcasm were inherent in Simon's syntax.

He went back to his desk and opened his music app.

The sound immediately flooded Peter's ears. Simon had already pre-adjusted the volume. He knew Peter was partially deaf. Peter heard white noise through the headphones. Not too loud. Simon had no desire to add to Peter's hearing loss. But he also wanted Peter unaware of any movement or sound. The noise swelled intermittently distracting him from the pain of the clamps on his body and his arms locked like the Catholic church's founding father's execution.

Communication was only by touch now. The headphones buzzing in Peter's ears were to desensitize him to oncoming torture yet keep him fully aware that anything could happen at any time. Simon grabbed the belt from around his victim's shoulders and folded it in half. Not hitting too hard, he delivered a perfect swat to the buttocks. It was enough to alert Peter that this was his new reality. This was all he had to worry about for now. His rump immediately clenched up, which only assured the ice would melt in perfect union with the torture going on outside his body. Another swat landed with slightly more force. Then another, and another. Peter's ass went from that bashful pink to a deeper pomegranate. The lashings, worthy of any visit to the garage by dad or a principal's office, varied in intensity and frequency. His fingernails across Peter's butt only antagonized the pain.

Peter cried out for it to stop. It would fall on deaf ears, ears that chose to be deaf this time. The ears of the abuser enjoyed the screams. The more he begged for it to stop or at least lighten up, the more that Simon laid into Peter's ass. Simon switched up weapons of abuse by exchanging the belt for a leather flog.

A flogging was due to this piece of filth. As the numbing noise flooded through the headphones, the flog made its presence known to Peter's already sore butt. With Peter's body temperature being higher because of the abuse, the ice cube had already quickly dissipated in less than half the time it should have melted. The crushed mint was moments away from being exposed, giving Peter that unexpected minty fresh feeling. The cold had slowly numbed his innards, and a little water had run down the inside of either of his legs. He found himself hot from underneath as the candle started to slowly warm him from its position on the floor between his legs.

Throughout however long, with the white noise in his ears, Peter's body continued to flinch and twitch in pain with Simon's effortless and merciless flogging. He was battling between just enjoying the very-present threat of the candle and Simon's seemingly insatiable desire to inflict pain. Time became a stranger to Peter. He had no idea how long he had been up there or how long this would continue. The struggle was real. The pain ever-present and the fear was crippling.

The crushed mint bits were relentless as they released themselves into Peter's sensitive rectum. Simon knew when the ice had melted inside Peter and he took it as a queue. He grabbed a thicker butt plug from Peter's bag, surely to be as violating as that bastard dildo used earlier, or his cock, and inserted it all the way into Peter's minty hole. Peter could not remember if he had been fucked by Simon earlier or if Simon just sat there and abused his hole with various dildos. At some point, they all felt the same, and they all inflicted the same pain.

Simon pulled the headphones from one of Peter's ear, the other still covered.

"Hold onto that plug, you understand?"

"Yes, Sir...but..."

"Your hole is never going to be the same."

"Sir, it is burning."

"Your hole is burning?"

"Yes Sir, something is wrong."

"No, it is not. It is what I planned for you. You are not chickening out, are you?"

"I... I am not sure."

"Aww son, you have come so far and so have I. You do not want to upset me and stop now, do you? I do not think that is what you want in your wheelhouse."

Peter was not sure if he wanted to find out or not. Maybe he should go with it. After all, he had come this far and was still in one piece.

"No, no Sir."

"Hold that plug, or you will get another thirty minutes of non-stop flogging, do you understand?"

"I do not want that."

"Then hold it, asshole."

Simon walked around to the front side of Peter with a flog in hand. He stood back far enough that the flog would barely hit the clothespins still attached. Simon whipped the fringy leather ends of the flog against the clamps on Peter's nipples forcing their release. Peter let out involuntary screams of pain as each one ripped away from his body with a pinch and a pull.

"What did I say about screaming?"

"I am sorry, Sir. The pain is..."

"Too bad." He replaced the headphone on Peter's ears. One by one, or sometimes two, the clamps were forced to release their pinch on Peter's body. The red marks left behind were dots of shame or pride, depending on how he wanted to think about them. Simon saw them as marks of accomplishment. The shock of the pins being slapped off his nipples was painful, yet almost a relief to Peter that the flog or belt was not coming at his backside anymore. Simon purposely missed and let the flog land on Peter's thighs, belly, and sides. The flog made a vicious swipe at his dick, knocking most of the pins free. More swipes came to whatever devices remained. Simon walked around to push any of the butt plug planning a secret escape from Peter's worn out hole. A slap on the ass was a quick reminder of his duties as the sub.

Simon got near his ear. He pulled off the now sweaty headphones. Peter's ears rested in temporarily silence, a moment he appreciated.

"You want me to stop?" came the taunt.

Peter quickly nodded his head in affirmation, thinking he might get relief.

"You want me to untie you?"

He nodded again. Simon reached down and slowly scraped his fingernails across Peter's reddened ass.

"I want to keep going. What do you think of that idea?"

Peter started to whimper as tears formed behind the blindfold still guarding his eyes viewing his abuser. He shook his head.

"No? Oh. That is too bad. You do not have a say so in all this do you, pig?"

No response.

A bare-handed slap woke him up to reality.

Simon knelt down and removed two blocks from each pile under Peter's tired feet and quivering legs.

"I said you do not have a say in all this, do you?"

Peter felt the rope around his neck grow tighter. He found himself standing on the balls of his feet to compensate for the decrease in lift. His arms were stretched further making it a bit harder to breathe.

Simon yanked the butt plug out without warning.

"Enough of that."

"Thank you, Sir. Thank you so much."

His hope was short-lived. Still, behind him, Simon wrapped his hand around Peter's mouth. His other hand brought Peter's hole back to attention. Peter suddenly felt something new in his pit. It was the same dildo that had opened his tight hole to a gaping cavern. Peter tried to scream in shock and pain, but it remained relatively unheard through Simon's hand. Simon began to thrust it in and out just like a horny frat boy would his first time fucking someone. He tilted it more straightforward to assure it was rubbing against Peter's prostate. The thrusting became harder and purposeful. Peter enjoyed it as much as he hated it. His dick was well on its way to being more rigid than it had been in a while. Simon knew where Peter was between the screams and pleas for mercy. Simon's biceps and chest were flushed red as he endlessly fucked Peter's ass with the dildo. Peter's legs started to quiver, his breathing became heavier, and his previous whimpers of graveling became moans with gratification attached to them. Peter's whole body began to convulse, and he lacked the control to stop it. The moment was coming and so would Peter. The prostate had seen enough. Simon relentlessly fucked Peter keeping a steady rhythm and intensity. Peter felt a surge race through his whole body, his legs and arms already engaged for the past however long. Simon made sure the rest of his body had been on notice whether with nipple clamps, anal stimulation, or flogging. The waves of orgasm flowed through Peter like few other dominant men have been able to accomplish. In seconds, Peter's dick would spew its white gooey liquid. Simon reached around to let Peter's dick spit into the palm of his hand. Peter came hard while Simon exploited every drop. When Simon saw Peter was noticeably done, he left the dildo in Peter's asshole.

"Do not let it fall. I warn you."

Only heavy breathing was greeting his command.

Peter quickly clenched his backside to obey the order. It took every ounce of energy possibly left in him to do so.

"Open your mouth and stick out your tongue."

"What are you going to do?"

Simon grabbed his jaw. "Do it!"

Peter only partially opened his mouth, and Simon jarred the jaw again in his hand. "Open it!"

Peter's tongue came out a little bit more. Simon pressed his palm full of cum against Peter's mouth. Peter tasted the salty residue of his jizz and sweat on Simon's hand.

"Eat it. Do not spit any of it out, you hear me? You eat it all," he said as he kept his hand against Peter's mouth. He tried to turn his head, but Simon had already had his other hand in place firmly to keep him from moving. Peter obediently sucked and licked the palm of Simon's hand until all he tasted was his palm. Simon checked to be sure his hand was clean.

Without alerting Peter, Simon removed the candle from between Peter's legs, putting it on a nearby table.

"Now, drop the butt plug." Peter was shocked at the order but tried his best to unclench his ass cheeks enough to let the dildo free.

"Drop it unless you want me to fuck you more."

With a little effort and a big prayer, the dildo fell to the floor. Simon kicked it out of the way.

"I am going to remove your blindfold. If you scream, I will tape your mouth again and beat you twice as hard, do you understand?"

He nodded yet again. Simon ripped off the blindfold.

"You have done well. I will not hurt you anymore. Do you believe me?"

"Yes," he panted. "Yes, Sir I do."

"Good. Trust me." Simon left Peter to stand there on his own for a few. He went to get a bottle of water from the fridge. While there, Peter wetted a rag with cold water. He put the rag on Peter's head and wiped his brow. The coolness of the cloth soothed Peter's hot head and his nerves. Simon took the cold bottle and placed it against Peter's buttocks and ran it up his back, the opposite of the ice cube earlier. Again, the cold sent a shock through Peter's body.

Simon rolled the bottle back and forth, soothing the redness he had inflicted on Peter's back. He reached up and loosened the rope from around Peter's neck and eventually the ropes around his arms. Peter was glad to breathe freely. While the rag still lay atop his head, Peter felt hands on his back as Simon started to massage Peter's arms and shoulders and back, relaxing his muscles and his tense body. He maneuvered his hands down to each of Peter's sweaty and tired legs. Simon loosened the ropes from around Peter's legs. The untying took almost as long as the tying, but Peter gladly endured awkward positions for a few moments longer knowing he would probably be free.

"Stand up straight." He obeyed but struggled to stand up under his power. His muscles were doing their best to readjust to working again.

"How do you feel?" Simon asked.

"Relieved," came the all but too honest answer.

Simon stayed silent and continued to rub Peter's body. He reached for the water bottle.

"Drink this." Peter's instinct was to hesitate. "Trust me. Drink it." Peter tilted the bottle up to his open mouth and let a little water flow. When he finished, Simon put a bit of the cold water onto the rag and wiped down Peter's chest with it. The cold was another jolt as it had been on his ass, but his smile echoed appreciation. Simon dutifully wiped down Peter's chest, arms, and the rest of the front of his body to take the sweat off and cool him down a little bit.

Simon grabbed the wooden chair from earlier and put it directly behind Peter.

"Do nothing but sit down" he instructed.

"Yes, Sir."

Peter's arms ached and almost did not move at first when freed. They had been locked in that position for so long he felt as numb while simultaneously feeling the still-burning impression in his muscles and all of his body. He felt Simon's hand on his back and one on his chest.

"Sit." Peter trusted the command and did as he was told. "Relax. You are okay. I promise. Here, finish this," he said handing him the water bottle. He wiped his face.

Peter concentrated on catching his breath and getting all of the water into his body. Simon walked to his desk and picked up his camera and hung it around his neck. He walked over to and squatted in front of Peter.

Peter's eyes were still squinting from the sweat, and his mind was trying to find its normal again. He looked at Simon in front of him. They both smiled, albeit it one more than the other.

"Did you enjoy yourself?"
"Yes." came Peter's appraisal.
"Tell the truth," Simon ordered.
"Yes," Peter repeated. "I had to trust you."
The whole experience had been as thrilling for Simon as it had been for Peter, if not more.
"We are not quite done, though," Simon said with a smile.
"What?"
Simon stood up, his hard dick poking out of his jockstrap. He had oozed so much precum that it had damn near soaked the front of his jock.
"Suck my dick."
"Are you ser..."
"No complaining." Simon grabbed his dick with one hand and Peter's head with the other. He stuck his dick balls deep into Peter's throat. He grabbed the water bottle from Peter. Peter's hand immediately went up to Simon's waist to try and throttle the heated thrusts. He realized to resist at all would be an act of futility.
"Do not worry, baby. I am already close." And he was.
Simon poured the remaining water down his chest while his dick was engulfed in Peter's mouth. The fresh water felt sexy and natural running down his chest. He enjoyed watching it pour down to his dick and on Peter's still-stupefied face. Peter struggled to maintain himself and give a good blowjob on such short notice. He thought that Simon had cum earlier while fucking him on the floor. Was this round two for Simon or just prolonged foreplay? Despite Peter enduring a lot, Simon was not about to let him leave without shooting his load.
Simon turned the camera on and aimed it at Peter. The video captured all of Peter's looks of helplessness, and Simon's audible grunts and groans.
"Fuuuck yeah, suck that dick, you faggot. Suck it."

Simon put his boot on Peter's thigh to get a better shot of his dick going into Peter's mouth. He loved watching it go in and out of a guy's mouth or asshole. He loved his dick. He had been blessed with being well endowed. He had every intention, from early on, to let others be blessed with his dick, too. His balls were tightening up as they do when a man is about to open the floodgates. He held Peter's head with one hand, still focusing the camera with the other, and with his leg braced against Peter's chest; both men were locked and loaded. Simon looked down at his meat fucking Peter's pussy mouth. He pushed harder and faster giving no regard for Peter's comfort or even considering if he had a gag reflex. The bondage might have ended, but the sex was still in play, if only for a few more fleeting seconds. As Peter sucked Simon's cock, he wondered who had cum more. He certainly felt like he had let out a load of epic personal proportions when Simon fucked his ass. Despite all the fear and pain, he knew his dick had stayed hard. And if what Simon had in the palm of his hand was any indication he might be right. It only took a few scarce violations of Peter's throat until Simon emptied his load.

"You want this load, boy?"

An altered confirmation was all that would be heard on the MP4 later. Simon did not want to miss one second of him filling Peter's guts with his seed.

Simon's seminal expulsion seemed to go on forever, Peter thought to himself. He felt huge plops of Simon's milk shoot down his throat in batches he did not think humanly possible. Peter faithfully swallowed every bit. Simon centered the camera on his dick for a moment to enjoy Peter's mouth wrapped around it. Frankly, not to have Peter pitch a fit about something again was an equally appealing excuse. While dominating Peter had been a lot of fun he still needed to empty his balls, and there was no need for conversation. Simon looked down as he pulled his thickness from Peter's mouth. He rubbed the head of it against Peter's sweaty face then put it back in his mouth. Peter tasted the sweat from his face on Simon's rigid member. Simon humiliated him with his unit. Peter looked up at him with the eyes that only a submissive owned. Simon soaked in the view of Peter's weary face and still-willing mouth while he let his dick linger in and out of Peter's cakehole. It looked good on the camera's display, and it felt even better in person.

"Fuck, that felt good. You have eaten a lot of cum today," Simon prompted, the camera still recording.

"I do love eating cum," Peter confessed.

Simon chuckled. "You were in the right place today."

"Yeah, I guess I was."

"You want to shower?"

"Yeah, in a minute." Peter was thankful for the offer. If he went home now, looking flushed and sweaty, he would never be able to answer his mother truthfully. He looked up at Simon, who seemed to enjoy standing over Peter right now, both basking in their positions.

Peter reached to take the camera and pointed it at Simon. He panned up and down Simon's sweaty, tanned, and lean hairy body. His dick was still hard and hanging out of his red jockstrap. Simon waved his hips back and forth, making his dick wave in the wind. He gripped his dick and squeezed it for the camera. He ran his fingertip over the end of his cock, milking out a tiny drop of jizz. He pulled the finger up his treasure trail to his chest, smiling the whole time. Peter followed the direction with the camera until it reached Simon's face. He focused and centered on Simon's image in the camera's display.

"So, can I ask you something?" Peter asked.

"Sure, shoot."

"When is it your turn?"

The look in Simon's face was captured forever.

† Paul †

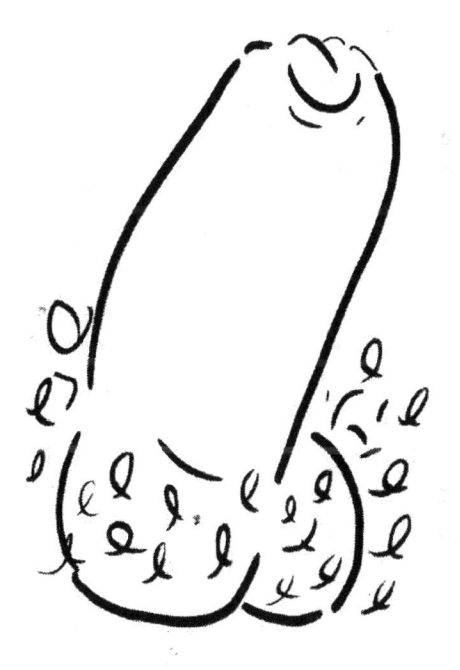

You never quite know what you are going to find when you cruise for dick on the internet. It is a protocol wild card; an understood play on the pitch that anything could happen with someone. People sometimes look like their photo, but it is always safe to assume they are hiding something from their current mugshot. Sometimes they are older or young, fatter or thinner, butch or more femme, taller or shorter. How someone can fake their height is a mystery. One's weight can undoubtedly fluctuate, but height is pretty standard on a day to day basis. You begin to wonder if it is the same person in the photo that is behind the chat.

How old is that photo, bro?

Paul's photo was not much better than a passport photo. It barely hit his shoulders, and the lighting seemed ungraciously harsh on his cheeks and forehead. He was also older. Fifty-two is not old, but when you are thirty-two, sometimes a twenty-year gap can seem like a lot of space. He sent another photo that was of his chest in a cheap t-shirt. It was enough to give me an idea of who was talking. I was drawn to him, and I was not sure why. I had never purposely sought out older men. I had plenty of men closer to my age, and younger, that kept a consistent shadow over the threshold to my home. Was it a daddy fetish? Did I suddenly have a thing for older men? I decided to overlook any shortcomings in favor of the stronger need to have my ass fucked. He said I could come over, but he wanted to keep it discreet and quiet. He mentioned that his job would not look favorably on him being gay. I was not sure what that meant, and it was not my business. I certainly was not going to show up with a camera crew – one that could easily have been part of a gossip television show that covered a thirty-mile zone for salacious stories and bloated tidbits - to try and out someone at their job. I always found gossip blogger's self-righteous practices of revealing someone's sexuality or sex life to the public very distasteful. Everyone had their journey; moreover, we all had to eat. We have to work and survive. And if keeping a lower volume about your personal life at work keeps the direct deposit active then so be it. I only aspired to be laid regularly, not hold a J. Edgar Hoover type file on people. This was not McCarthy-era homosexuality. It was modern day faggotry in which we all played openly and unapologetically giving little consideration for other's opinions of our encounters. I promised Paul that I was not going to out him. I gave him my word, and to this point in my life, I was pretty damn good at staying true to it.

When I arrived at his home in south Sugar Lake, his front door was slightly ajar. Perhaps he had the door unlocked so I did not meander outside too long; maybe he was peeking through the peephole to get a look at me. I had certainly done the same thing during my hosting frivolities. I felt his sense of privacy and concern so, after I parked, I made a brisk walk to Todd Glen apartments. He opened the door, and I walked into his little place. He was hidden a bit behind the door.

"Come in, please."

I did as ordered and stepped inside the door.

"I just got home from work and have not even changed yet," he offered, almost as an excuse.

I turned around, and I realized why he was worried about his job knowing he was gay.

"Surprise," he tepidly continued. Indeed, I was surprised at what I saw. His discretion made perfect sense. With a job like his, if his superiors found out he was homosexual, then it would surely be an end to his career in the Catholic clergy. It was not a job someone casually finds in the help section of the paper or on internet bulletin boards. And he had undoubtedly been a priest longer than the internet had been around at that point. It would be a sin and a lie to say that once my inner shock wore off that I was unaroused by the idea of a fifty-something-daddy-type-priest fucking me. Perhaps my instincts betrayed me, but I had the feeling that he battled being a priest and being gay. He was not cowardly or even sheepish, but his modesty for feeling like he may have lied by omission made him equally vulnerable and alluring at the same time. I felt for him. I had lived my life in the open, yet he could not do the same. There was a moment of suspense as he wondered how I would react to the revelation of the john before me.

"Oh, thank God. It could have been worse."

"Like what," he wondered.

"You could have been Baptist," I fired back.

"Well hell, I am not a monster," he popped, grinning through his witty comeback. The ice had been broken.

We walked through the foyer to the edge of the living room. His home was nice, simple in its décor but not without a subtle touch of class. An L-shaped sectional filled in the far side of the room. A large television stood guard on an opposite wall near a fireplace. A crucifix hung over the mantle, understated yet noticeable. Modern lamps, tables, and footstools rounded out the space. Comfortable, but not fussy.

"I would be in confessional for lying if I said the collar was not sexy as hell on you," I confessed.

"You would think after all these years they could make it less itchy," he said, tugging at the side of his neck.

"That bad, huh?"

"If you know anything about Catholics, they love to inflict suffering even if it is on one's self."

"Jesus. I thought Baptists were bad with the rules."

"Every group has their self-imposed languishing. I have a friend who is a rabbi, Joshua Bromberg. He has been a rabbi as long as I have been a priest. We met while both were interviewing for jobs in the same neighborhood. I was sitting in a cafe waiting for lunch. He walked in looking as young and green as me. I can only believe it was a divine order that every table was taken that day. I motioned for him to join me, figuring that two men of the cloth could share lunch. If we had a minister with us, it would have been the makings of a good photo."

Paul methodically walked around his living room, his hands behind his back. He was diligent in his concentration and storytelling like a college professor. His skills at being a public orator served him well. I found myself totally transfixed with his monologue, insanely curious what the next sentence would be.

"After introductions, we both realized we had been there to field a position at parishes just a block apart. I had never seen a chapel and a synagogue so close in a neighborhood like that. Rabbi Bromberg and I remain friends to this day. I eventually found my way to where I serve for a couple of decades. He has been the head rabbi at his synagogue for almost as long. We meet about once a month to catch up, talk about our flocks, swap ideas about God and sin..."

He paused standing in front of the fireplace, staring up at the crucifix. A candle burned below it. I could smell apple or vanilla in the air, no doubt from the candle's manufactured scent. He was contemplating his next words very carefully. They seemed exquisitely simple when I heard them.

"...and love between two people."

"Did you and him..."

"No," he chuckled, turning around to face me from across the room. "No, we did not. Not that I would have dissuaded him had it come to that. He is six ways of adorable. Shorter, stout guy, curly light brown hair."

"Like a Jew-fro?" I injected.

He laughed. "Yes and thick as a hedge with a beard to match. His beard is something they use to make legends. He has a funny giggle and an infectious smile. He is a solid friend. But to answer your question, no. We never did anything. I thought about it a few times if I am honest. He eventually married, had a family. He knows about me, as does his wife. They are discreet people. I trust them."

"It seems he got the better end of the deal."

"What deal is that?" he questioned, padding his way to me in his sock feet.

"Being Jewish. Rabbis are allowed to date and marry. Priests are not."

"That, my new friend, is true. I would like to believe I have lived a fulfilling life."
"Have you?" I challenged him. I immediately regretted the judgment call.
"Sorry, that came out wrong. I did not mean to imply..."
"It is fine. I know what you meant," he interrupted, graciously letting me off the hook of idiocy.
"I do not disagree with you. I have found other avenues to maintain a level of balance."
His words were still carefully chosen but clear as glass.
"They still put you in that collar, though."
"Yeah, this damn thing. Joshua and I have an ongoing bet as to which of us has the more cumbersome uniform. His yarmulke slides off more frequently than he would want. This collar sometimes catches a hair on my neck and tugs like it has a vendetta against me. I think I am winning the war of suffering."
"I hope you made it interesting."
"If I had a few C-notes back then, I would have," he said.
We both found humor in his statement. It brought us out of his solemn soliloquy about his friend.
"Does that mean you will not leave it on for me?" I was genuinely interested.
"Let us find out, shall we? Follow me, young man."
I suddenly felt like I was going to the principal's office. I kicked off my shoes where I stood. I followed him down a long hallway past two rooms and a bathroom into the master bedroom. His gate was long and strong. He walked with purpose making no game of his intentions.
I walked to the foot of the king size bed and waited for the next move by either of us. He walked up to me and put his hand on my collarbone.
"My God, you are a handsome, son."
The zaddy vibes were skyrocketing with this one.

"Thank you; you are too," I said as I attempted to return the compliment. Before I could finish the statement, I felt Paul's hand pushing down on my shoulder. He was stronger than I realized under his black shirt and that collar. His dark hair tussled over his forehead, and his dark eyes followed me as I knelt on the floor.

"Suck me," he commanded. He had somehow already gotten his pants unsnapped. I tugged on the waistband of his boxer briefs (also black). His semi-erect thick dick flopped out in front of me. I used both hands to pull down his pants and briefs even more and swallowed his dick in my mouth. He was uncut, and his almost-jet-black pubes were untrimmed. They tickled my nose on every intake of his cock. He groaned with pleasure as I swallowed his member. He guided my head back and forth as if he were laying hands on me. I kept my hands resting on his hips.

"Mother fuck, that is nice," he let out between groans.

His hands continued to keep hold of my head, his fingers digging into my hair sometimes grabbing it like a handful of licorice. An older guy in an authoritarian occupation taking control of me made my dick throb in my jeans. I had a jockstrap on under them. Jocks are made to hold your dick and balls, not just to serve as a protective layer between your body and your pants. My dick was hard and was battling the elastic stretchy fabric of the jock. I finally pulled his pants and boxer briefs all the way down while still sucking his dick. His legs were thick like a new punching bag at the gym. There had to be a lot of steps at his church. It was that middle-age dad-bod brawn that one could appreciate in moments like this. I ran my hands up his legs, his waist, and under his shirt to his belly. He was not too big although slightly stocky but without the big belly. This Father kept himself in shape. He may have lifted weights, otherwise worked out or been athletic in his younger days. The bulk had stayed with him. He started to unbutton his shirt from the bottom buttons first. He got three up, and I stopped him.

"Can you leave it on?" I begged.

"You are not the first guy to ask me that."

I felt bad. People had probably asked him this more than once just for the fantasy of it, but fuck. It was not a fantasy at this point. I was blowing him after all, and we had discussed anal.

"I am sorry. You do not have to if you do not feel like it," I paused for a beat, then added the icing, "...father."

Shit. Too much?

"Okay, but only for a little while. I have had this damned thing on since this morning."

I took his dick in my mouth, again.

I continued to blow him for what seemed a sweet and delightful eternity. His uncut dick fit perfectly on my tongue and between my cheeks. I felt no gag reflex with him. He was not trying to punch a hole in the back of my neck. He was enjoying being taken care of by someone. It would turn out to be one of the softer and gentler moments between us this afternoon. His mature gentleness recalled those times I had with Nicolaus, the Greek in our room at the 3C. Older men often took their time to enjoy the moment. They lived by the adage of life is in the details. It was a trait I would carry with me throughout my life.

He reached down with both hands and put them on my cheeks. He guided me up slowly to stand in front of him.

"Can I undress you?" he asked, while his hard dick bobbed between us, slightly glistening with my saliva.

"I would enjoy that."

I was wearing a button-down shirt not dissimilar from his own. He meticulously worked his way from the top button down to the bottom. He took his time, and I appreciated the brevity. I was so nervous standing there with this kind and handsome man (way better looking in person than his shitty photo online) undressing me, one button at a time. I took deep breaths and let him do it.

His hands slipped under my shirt and onto my chest. They were strong, longer than I expected; well-rounded. He explored my chest like a skilled carpenter using his hand to examine a piece of sanded wood. His eyes followed his hands as they surveyed the hair on my chest surely taking notes. I took pleasure in watching his curious visage examine me. Without missing a beat, he reached down and unbuttoned my jeans. He had done this before, more than once or twice. My stomach was filled with butterflies, knowing I would be just as exposed in front of him as he was in front of me. He was meticulous in how he unfastened every button on my shirt and unzipped my jeans. He treated it like a ritual of the highest degree. Every move was ceremonial, and nothing would be rushed. Everything had to proceed on its timetable. My jeans slid down over my rump and dropped to the floor. I kicked them to the side. My dick was solid as a rock; every throb was a plea to be let loose of the jockstrap which kept it bound.

"We are matching."

"What?" I asked.

"Your jock. It matches." He was not wearing a jock. I had no idea what he meant. I looked down as he ran one of his thick fingers along the inside of my waistband. I glanced at him to find the answer; then I realized it was right in front of me. I had on a black jockstrap with a white stripe on the waistband. It almost perfectly matched his clerical collar. It seemed appropriate although I never thought about it looking religious before this moment. Hell, it seemed downright planned. I snickered to myself.

"I did not plan that I swear."

"I know you did not. You had no idea who or what I was when we talked. I hope you understand I had to keep that to myself. Discretion keeps the lights on around here."

"Paul, I get it. I promised you I was not coming here to out you to anyone."

"I believe you. I am glad you are here."

"I am glad you asked me," I confided.

"Well, you were the pushy one, not me."

"God strike me dead if I am lying."

"Easy. I know people who could make that happen," he joked. I had no plans to find out if he was serious.

"You are a funny boy," he mused through a smile.

"Am I?"

"Yes, you are. I like that."

"Thank you, Paul. I am glad I came."

"Lean back," he said as he gently pushed me backward toward the bed. I felt the edge of the mattress contact the back of my legs. I sat down and laid back. His hands leaned on my chest, and he massaged my pecs and belly.

"My God, such a nice body."

"I do not exactly work out, you know," I tried to make an excuse. It did not go over that well.

"I do not look for perfection. It is overrated, trust me. I always look for something real in people. And so far, you seem genuine. I talk to a lot of people who are not real with themselves."

"I try. It is too exhausting to try and be someone you are not. I do not have the time for that."

It felt like an indictment of occupation versus sexuality. It was not my intention.

"Sorry, I did not mean…"

"Shh. I know what you meant."

I believed him. He took no offense to my statement, but it probably rang true in his head that he was living a double life as a gay priest.

His hands continued to rub my torso, and his eyes kept pace with them. He moved to my groin and crotch, rubbing my thighs. He pushed my legs apart a bit more and kneeled at the foot of the bed. His six-foot-five-inch height allowed him to tower over my dick. He caresses my upper thighs and pubic area with his lips. I could feel the warm breath hit my skin. My dick ached for the attention of his mouth as it continued to fight its way out of my jock, albeit unsuccessfully. He cupped it in his hands and slowly started to masturbate me over the jock. His hands were warm. My dick seemed to fit into his hand almost like it was meant to be held by him.

"You feel great. I bet guys love your dick," he prodded.

"I guess, but I wish I had more wanting to hold it as eagerly as you do," I confessed. I was with a priest, so the truth was required.

"Screw them if they do not. It is perfect," he demanded.

"Screw them, indeed."

"I could hold you all day," he confessed.

Before I could get a thank you out, he had maneuvered his hand up into my jock. His fingers pressed against my pubes and brushed against my dick. With one fail swoop, he lifted the front of my jock and moved it to the side and went down on me. It seemed that in an instant my dick was in his mouth. I knew he just wanted me to be in the moment with what he was feeling. His carnality dictated his actions. He held me in his mouth and let it simmer. I was throbbing. I know he had to feel that against his tongue. His mouth was so warm and perfect. I had never had a mouth feel like it was made for my dick like I did Paul's. I realized I had felt the same thing moments earlier. I had sucked a lot of dicks, but so few fit so perfectly in my mouth as Paul's did. His mouth felt like holy water. He seemed to salivate the more he sucked my dick. His mouth got wetter and wetter as it took in my cock. I reached down to grab his head and hold it in place. He came up for air.

"No, lean back and let me suck you for a while. Let me make you feel good."

The look on his face was all the convincing I needed. I was not sure how often he hooked up with other guys but he had a deficit in his love life. I assume most priests do to some extent. I felt like I should have been taking care of him. He was a giver by nature and profession. I was poised to accept anything he had to offer. I opened my legs more, threw my arms up over my head onto the mattress and left myself open and vulnerable to him. Whether he was a priest or not, I felt I could trust him to treat me right. He seemed to care about making sure I felt as good as what he felt from me. There was an unspoken gentleness in him. It was comforting. His low-key demeanor was engaging. It pulled me into his being more and more. He leaned his body forward, his mouth still on my shaft. His big hands went around my waist to the small of my back, almost as if to pull me into him. He hugged my waist while my dick was in his warm mouth. It was a struggle to relax my body to let him use it how he wanted and still naturally tense up while being sucked by a priest. He would sometimes pull up from my cock and gently suck on my balls working his mouth down to my taint. My legs opened further apart. I felt his wonderfully heavy hands under the back of my knees lifting my legs.

He continued to push my legs back almost folding me in half. With one hand he carefully replaced my jock back over my cock which was seconds away from exploding. I knew what was coming. There was a pause. I could not see anything but the ceiling. I thought maybe he had changed his mind, but then it happened. I felt his tongue trace my hole. He teased it. He tasted it like a snake flickers its tongue to smell prey. He let his anticipation of burying his tongue in my hole build up as much as he made me practically beg for it to happen.

"You taste so good," he said.

"It is yours," was all I could say to him to invite him to dine as he saw fit.

His RSVP was immediate. His nose squished against my taint, and his lips pressed around my hole. His tongue went in and out of my tight hovel. I wanted to tighten up with every lick. But I relaxed and let him eat me out any way he wanted. His tongue licking and kissing my hungry tunnel was not merely this side of paradise. It was the promised land. Before this was over, there would be milk and honey for all of us.

Eventually, he came up for air. I relaxed my legs a bit, bringing them back down to the mattress. He stood there at the foot of the bed, facing me with his shirt partially unbuttoned, his collar still around his neck. My chest rose and fell with every breath I took. He had me worked up so much from sucking my dick and eating my ass.

"You are good at that," I said, breaking the silence.

"It is easy when a guy is as hot as you."

He put his hand on my jock, my concrete thickness under it, and worked his way back up to my belly, then my chest, and my neck. Then he caressed my face, his palm on the underside of my jaw. His thumb toyed with my lips. I opened my mouth offering my talents. He moved the tip of his forefinger to my top lip and rubbed it from one end to the other. I leaned my head ever-so-slightly forward. He stuck his finger in my mouth. I pressed down with my tongue against the roof of my mouth. He moved his finger in and out of my mouth following the curve of my tongue. I locked onto his eyes and stared at him while I sucked his finger.

He brought his leg up and lifted himself onto the bed next to me. I laid there, in just my jockstrap, my dick still bulging. My shirt was still on although unbuttoned. It was splayed out on either side of me. I turned my body toward him and wrapped one leg around his waist and pulled him near me. He put his arm around my back and pulled me toward him. Our chests heaved against each other. I could feel the tip of his dick against my thighs. It was wet. He had been leaking pre-cum the whole time. We kissed deeply. Our tongues cautiously researched the other. The more I kissed him, the more passionate he became. This was more than a hookup, although if it was just a hookup, it was a fucking great one so far. We caressed each other's bodies as we continued to kiss. I felt his hand wander south again. Was he going to release my member from its black and white prison of a cotton/spandex blend? He grazed over it, but he kept going. His finger found its way to my hole. It was still wet with his spit from his tongue fucking earlier. He felt his way to the tightest pucker and pushed against it, almost knocking to gain entry. He was teasing me, asking me. The finger I had wet with my tongue made its way into my hole. I let out a moan giving him full access.

"Oh fuck. That makes me nuts," I panted. He was on top of my other arm since we were embraced. I pulled him as close as I could, using all the muscle I had to hold him. I want to be in his arms while he was inside me, even if it was his finger.

"That is just one. Do you want another?"

"Yes, please. Yes, sir, I do."

I felt his finger slip out of me as my insides pulsed with feeling. He pushed two fingers inside my brown eye. I felt so full. I gave myself over to him. He kissed me deeply, planting his tongue in my mouth while simultaneously massaging my prostate. I wanted so badly to touch my dick and jerk it. Instead, I held onto him and pulled him close. It was my version of twenty Hail Mary chants; it was my penance. My jock was still on and was keeping my dick in a sexual prison. It was begging me to let it loose. My body reacted to him instinctually. It was almost as if we both knew what the other was wanting or getting ready to do; the flow became second nature.

Since his pants had made their way off his body, he was naked except for his shirt and collar. His salt & pepper chest hair complimented the black shirt and white band around his neck. He pulled his fingers out of my now-wet, hole, rolled on top of me, and gave me a stern command.

"Move back."

I obeyed him and slipped out of my shirt in the process tossing it on the floor. I pushed myself upward on his bed, so we were closer to the headboard. He kneed his way up to between my legs. I lifted my legs because I wanted him inside me so badly. Finger fucking me brought me to a new edge of feeling, and I needed more. He grabbed me and scooted up to my gaping cavern.

"Guide me in, son." I am not always a fan of someone calling me boy or son although I did not hate it. Paul calling me son seemed organic, so I did not fight it. I reached down between my legs, and his dick was ready. I guided it to my own internal confessional.

"Push it in me."

And he did. His dick was long and thick, like his fingers. Because it was uncut, it had more girth than most guys I had experienced. I squirmed. It hurt, but it also felt great. He leaned into it and pushed himself all the way inside me. He hovered over me, his dark brown eyes staring into mine. He slowly began to pump my ass. I wrapped my legs around his lower torso and pulled him with each push into my void. His clerical shirt dangled on each side of my chest and the collar stared back at me. Holy hell! A priest was inside me, and it was not his freshman run at fucking another man.

He leaned down to kiss me while his dick still steadily fucking me; my legs still wrapped around him. I reached up into his shirt and clawed my fingers into his back. His kisses were firm. Wet. Manly. Feeling his tongue in my mouth and his dick in my ass at the same time made me feel alive and complete. Oddly, I felt safe. I felt l like this moment could go on forever. I do not know what heaven is like, but I did consider this could be one of those times when I was close to it.

My moans became louder and longer with each push of his holy scepter in me. His fucking was steady and intense. I had wholly surrendered my all to him, body and soul. But I had had enough of the collar. I reached up and pulled the plastic apparatus out of the collar of his shirt. He seemed not to care and continued to pound me with great passion. I struggled through the pushing and moving to find his top button to release it. He paused while still inside me, raised up, yanked it off and tossed it out of sight. His mature torso – tall, robust, and hiding a world of scars and hurts in his heart which was invisible to the naked eye – shadowed my hairy chest. His core flexed, and while his abdomen was not ripped, he certainly took care of himself. His stomach was strong and void of anything beyond a thirty-six waist. I was almost sure I saw a weight set earlier in one of the rooms I passed. His now fully naked body collapsed on mine. His shaft still violated my hole without any regard for penance. His belly and mine were pressed against each other, my jockstrap the only thing separating all of my skin from his own.

"You feel so..." he purred in my ear. He grabbed my hair from behind and locked me in his warm embrace. He never finished his sentence.

"Perfect?" I was joking. "I heard perfection is overrated, Father," I parroted back.

He paused, pulling back just enough to focus on my eyes.

"No. Not father. Say my name." With each push of his dick, he spoke the syllables.

"Say. My. Name." If I listened hard enough, I could almost hear a silent "please" come next. He not only needed to connect with someone sexually, but he also needed to be Paul, not Father, nor Reverend, not anything that the collar dictated. He needed to exist as a human. He needed to be recognized as a sexual being, not his profession. He needed to be seen beyond the collar. I doubt anyone beyond his family called him by his given name on a daily basis, except maybe his peers or coworkers. In front of a parishioner, he was Father.

"You belong inside me, Paul."

That seemed to set him off in a whole new direction. He pulled me as he sat up in the middle of the bed, spreading his legs in front of him. We were due for another change of position anyway.

"Come here and ride me." It reminded me of Abel and how we sat in the middle of the bed, with me inside him on that hot summer's night. I had not been fucked in that position in a long time, and I was more than happy Paul wanted to be in me like that. I squatted over his meaty thickness, and he guided it into place until I enveloped it. I wrapped my legs around his waist and held onto him around his neck. His arms wrapped around my torso and he kept me braced and close to him. I rode him so hard. Seeing myself be in a more prominent position, eye to eye with him, feeling us joined as one turned into the highlight of the whole afternoon. He kissed my sweaty chest and sucked on my nipples. He nuzzled his nose into the hairs on my chest, smelling me and tasting me. My back arched naturally, and I secured his head and mouth against either of my nipples to torture with his teeth and lips. We were clawing and scratching at each other's bodies, biting wherever our teeth landed. We had no shame in letting out howls during surges of satisfaction. It was clear to me that he rarely got to let go as much as he did here. I do not know if he was this passionate while naked with other guys or even how often he had other men in his bed. I did know that I wanted to be that sacrament for him. I want him to be able to sacrifice his inhibitions and expose his soul without judgment.

"I want to cum so badly," I begged.

"No, please. Do not. I cannot stop being with you, yet. I want to stay inside you."

"Paul, you feel so fucking good."

"Just do not cum yet," he begged.

"Then let me sit on you."

He got that my dick had been rubbing through my jock and onto his hairy belly this whole time. One wrong stroke and I would cum all over the place. I was able to keep it positioned so I would not cum until we were both ready. I loved how my balls ached for a release. My dick was oozing so much precum that it had worked its way through my jockstrap. It was hard to tell where sweat ended and precum began.

He leaned back on his king size bed and looked every bit the part of a man who knew what he loved. And at this moment, however you define it, he loved me. He, at least, loved being inside me. My body made no protests. He stretched out while he was on his back. His stomach pulled in just enough that I could see his muscles under it. His pecs were engorged with blood and testosterone. The hair on his legs was wet and stuck in weird patterns. His skin reminded me of the Greek's almost glowing aura. Paul had something extra. The love and joy he radiated while able to be himself with me was something he did much less frequently. I equated it with going through long winters, then finally being able to walk out into the sunshine and feel the rays warm your skin and brighten your soul. It was appreciated when it happened. Paul appreciated our time together.

I straddled his wide waist and guided his dick back inside me. This was how I was going to cum. I could pivot and position my hips just right so his dick would be in constant contact with my prostate. Not that it had not been already, but I could better control it in this position. I rode him as hard as I could. I wanted to make him happy. I knew the life of a priest could not be easy, being sworn to a life of celibacy (an age-old system for controlling people, I believed) while simultaneously longing for the company of another person, even another man, on a daily basis must have been torture for him through the years; not having who and what he desired so naturally. I had empathy for him. His passion in these moments, although I had no other experiences with him to compare, seemed so big and so intense. How did he hold it in between times of being with another man? Admittedly, he was not just jerking off on occasion to relieve the stress of his quasi-celibacy. Jerking off is great but what we were doing, and what he had done with other men as lucky as me, would undoubtedly prove to be more fulfilling. To love your spirituality and the intimacy of another human being is equally satisfying. It was also a problem only the church could create. What the church did not understand, or purposely ignored, was that spirituality and sexuality were never meant to be in a contest; a battle of wills. If anything, they went hand-in-hand. Paul was older than me but did not look much more than a half-dozen years difference. He kept himself in good condition. He had that brawn that Mark would have in another twenty-five years, and Nicolaus had a few weeks ago. I thought that perhaps it was these intense and almost-emotional times that kept the years off his face and the spark lit in his soul. It is not good that man should be alone – not even the clergy. This was a fundamental value he believed in, collar be damned. He fucked me like it was his last time. Frankly, if someone found out, it could very well be his last time as a man of the cloth. The upside of dismissal is that he could then be free to fully embrace who he was as a gay man and still keep a level of his spirituality as he saw fit for his life. The collar probably proved to be more of a tight leash than an easy yoke. I wanted to make him ignore all those burdens this afternoon. He was trying to forget, too. I could tell. He was not turning his back on God. Quite the opposite, I felt. He was honoring God with being what God created. To create a being capable of experiencing such an intense connection and endless pleasure then purposely deny the creature that would be an asshole thing for any entity to enact. It is like giving a chef rocks and sand or taking a painter's sight. He had grown past the traditions and embraced both his sexuality and his religion. He was trying to negotiable a modern existence in both worlds.

"Fuck, I want to cum in you so bad, baby." They always say 'baby' when they get near the finale, do they not?

"My dick is aching to get out of this jock and shoot."

He grabbed the waistband of my jockstrap, ripping the mesh from the elastic. The seventh and final seal had been released. Our day of reckoning was upon us. I loved that he was strong enough to pull my jockstrap and release my wild horses. I was also, partially, pissed he destroyed my jock. It was not cheap. But as far as we had gotten, I suppose it did not matter.

He pawed and grabbed my dick.

"Damn, you are wet as hell!" My dick was bathed in precum. I could have filled a shot glass with what he found oozing from my cock.

"You made me do it," I said.

"Does that make me the devil?"

"Not unless you want to be," I shot back.

"Have I told you how beautiful I think you are?" he asked.

"Yeah. But tell me again," I half-jokingly spit back.

"I will show you."

Even though I was still riding his massive shaft and doing an excellent job on my own, he started pushing up from underneath me. We instantly had our rhythm of up and down, in and out, any which way. My stick was captive in his palm with his fingers acting as the bars on the jailhouse door. He stroked it using my precum as lube. I felt a rush of tingling go through me.

"Paul, if you keep doing that, I am going to cum on both of us. I will not be able to stop myself."

"I want you to, son. I want you to cum," he pleaded. The seriousness in his face rectified any doubt.

"I am close. Will you cum in me? Please? Please cum in me, Paul?" I did not need to ask. I wanted to make him feel wanted because I did want him to cum inside me.

"I am going to cum in you, son... I ...oh fuck...*fuck*!"

His body tensed. His chest was hard and hot as the sun-beaten sidewalk. Every muscle in him clinched including the hand that was on my dick. The pressure made me react with a new-found zest. My thighs clenched his waist. I kept pivoting to move my hips. He did not let go of my dick. It was too late. It was happening.

"Oh, fucking God! Oh! Aahhh!!" My head had been thrown back by instinct, and my body released what had been building up for the past hour or more. I could not move yet I was somehow still moving. I could feel his sacred seed shooting inside me. It was warm and thick. I bared down more with any muscle strength I had left to leech every bit of it. My dick silently screamed with its release and the evidence was surely all over his chest. My legs were shaking and convulsing. I lacked any ability to stop them. I could feel his dick pulsating inside me still. The more he came in me, the more I came on him. He did not try to stop any of my cum from hitting his face or aiming in another direction. The power of our cumming together was overwhelming.

Through my years of having great orgasms, this was one of the few that felt rapturous. I felt like I was entirely in my body yet fully out of it at the same time. I lacked for nothing. His rod, his staff, comforted me. I felt the sound of heaven ringing in my ears. And I had knocked on heaven's door before, but this time I was able to peek through the keyhole at the glory that laid before me.

Jolts of energy continued to randomly jet through my body. I quivered and shook while he continued to push himself into me; the aftershocks of his release were still engaged. The beauty of the moment was too much for me to handle. As much as our bodies are made to experience pleasure, I often wonder just how much they can take before giving up the ghost.

I had taken a huge breath in, but I was too afraid to exhale. I thought it might all end if I did. If I held my breath, I could stay in this moment forever. I did not want it to end. Our bodies had been in contact for a while now, and any change scared me. It was too beautiful to let go. He had tiny trembles moving through him. I squeezed my internal butt muscles around his manhood. He felt it.

"Oh shit, what are you doing?"

"Hanging on to you. I do not want to let go of you."

He appreciated the sentiment.

Christ. I had cum buckets. My spunk was all over his abs snaking its way between the hairs on his chest. It was on the pillow and the duvet on either side of him.

"Look what you made me do," I teased.

"We are even. All of me is inside you." I relished that little comment because of the sheer truth of it.

I sat there, still straddling him and his dick still in me and relatively erect. We just stared at each other, enjoying the moment. We both felt the connection.

"Come here," he said softly.

I leaned forward slightly as not to squish the jizz between us anymore. I was, if anything, a considerate lover. He grabbed the back of my neck and slowly pulled me down toward him. He kissed me deeply. The hot rushes of pain and endorphins swept through my legs as I shifted my weight over his. My muscles scrambled to relax and repair themselves. Sweat rolled off my back while my seed found temporary housing in the hairs on his chest. I could almost hear his heart which was still beating faster than what was normal. Surely mine was the same. He let his fingertips glide over my back inciting the inevitable goosebumps that felt like an angel's kiss.

"That," he paused for dramatic effect. "was amazing."

I could only moan in agreement.

We both chuckled at the absurdity of it. We enjoyed the quiet in the moments that followed, almost drifting off into a much-needed nap.

After a while longer, he broke the silence.

"We should shower."

"Yeah, we have certainly made a mess of it," I said. The clean-up always felt like a chore. I often felt crummy for spewing so much DNA on a guy's belly. Then again, I was not alone in the shenanigans, either. I had plenty landing on my torso over the years. It is the dirt in the game.

"Hey, never apologize. It was nice."

"Paul, I lost myself in you. That has never happened to me before; not like that."

It had. To some extent with Nicolaus, or even Thomas, I had gained moments of a higher existence. I always believed sex is as close as we can get to feeling the universe's raw power, as mere humans. Right when we are about to orgasm, and then when we are in it, time stops. We have no recognition of anything around us. We do not understand time; spoken language is foreign to us, almost primitive compared to the stream of thought at that moment. Our brains do not short out; they open up. For a few brief clips, they bring us to a place that only spirit beings can genuinely appreciate and abide. We get a glimpse of it. We feel what it feels like to be out of our bodies. It was with only a few men that I had reached the upper levels of that existence. Paul was now one of them.

"You gave me what I needed," he confided. His candor struck me with a real understanding of his struggle. It was more evident than it had been in the couple of hours we spent together. The look in his eyes, his sincerity, and his honesty were all at the forefront. They stood taller and reached higher than any orgasm we just enjoyed.

He kissed me.

I moved off of laying on him. I sat up on the side of the bed kicking my legs over the side. I took a moment to myself. I was covered in sweat. The air from the A/C was cooling my body. Our clothes scattered on the floor reminded me of a tawdry movie from twenty years ago.

"Hey, you okay there?" he inquired.

"Yeah," I said, snapping myself out of my head. "I am fine." It was all I could muster.

"But?" he coaxed me.

"It…it was just intense. I am not complaining or anything. It was just unexpected."

"I do not get to…"

"I know," I interrupted. I knew where he was going. He needed the connection. I looked over my shoulder at him and touched his arm. He rolled his body toward me, propping himself up on his elbow, and caressed my back.

"I knew what you needed. I felt it. I wanted to be there for you, even if you are a stranger," I revealed.

"We are not strangers now, are we?"

"I guess not. I would say we know each other in a…"

"Oh God, do not say it!" he interrupted.

I could not help myself.

"…in a biblical sense."

He groaned, but we both laughed it.

"You are a silly guy; you know that?"

"I had heard that before," I revealed. "But you had fun?"

"Yes, of course. I am grateful you came to visit me. I think you read the room quite well when you got here."

"I hope so."
"You did, my friend. You did," he said, taking a deeper breath. "You were a good and faithful helper."
"Oh God, we are not going to have communion, are we?"
"I have some Malbec and saltines."
"You are funny for a priest," I shot back.
"I get that a lot."
"No, you do not," I taunted. "I am stealing a shower from you," I said, getting up from the bed and walking to his on-suite bathroom.
"You can try. I have others."
"You also owe me a jockstrap, old man," I blurted from the bathroom, as I started to turn on the water waiting on it to bring its warmth. I took a quick inventory of the large walk-in shower stall that was easily four feet in either direction. I had a nerd moment when I saw he had a shower head that possessed three nozzles mounted on the wall. It was all encased in glass. I am a sucker for a sexy shower or bathroom. I almost felt cheated if a date did not end with a hot shower and a possible second round of intercourse and broad-spectrum debauchery. Either knowingly or as an ingrained habit, I almost always assured a hot shower would happen for us.
The water ran warm almost instantly. I popped opened the magnetized door mechanism and stepped inside in front of the water jets. The water washed the afternoon off of me. I closed my eyes and ducked under the bigger shower head. I let it run over my skin and down my neck and back. It tickled me as his fingertips had a few minutes earlier. I stood there relishing the inertia of divine interaction that rippled its way through my being. I was happy but, moreover, I felt grateful. I was thankful for this afternoon. It was something I had not bargained for when I showed up to get my dick sucked. I was baptized by fire and water.
Then I felt it.

Those hands, that chest. They were behind me. He had made his way into the shower with me. He kissed the back of my neck and wrapped his arms around my chest. I tilted my head to the side where he rested his mouth to kiss me more. His hands run down the front of my torso to my waist. I leaned back just enough to feel as much of him against me as possible. He held me without reservation or guilt.

"I am sorry about your jockstrap. I will replace it," he whispered in my ear.

"It is okay. We were in the heat of the moment."

"I could not control myself with you. Being inside you felt like it was meant to be."

"Maybe it was," I speculated.

It felt like he was meant to hold me. His hunger for touch and connection did not make him seem desperate during our making love. Yes, making love. Somewhere through all the thrusts and grunts and moans, it went beyond casual sex. I could feel something ignite in him. His touch spoke without saying words. His body conveyed not just what he wanted, but who he was in his soul. When I saw that in him, it felt like home. I thought his embrace would keep me for all the days of my life. Together we had been purified. Our union was sanctified, and love approved it. They say God is love. If that is true, then we certainly felt the presence of God that afternoon.

He turned me around and kissed me. I wrapped my arms around his body and felt him pull me nearer to him. The love in him radiated from his person and into me like the steam from the shower itself. He nuzzled his mouth behind my ear. I knew what was going to happen next.

So did God.

We were okay with it. So was God.

† Acknowledgements †

This book came through a former blog of random short stories from years prior. I wrote "Simon and Peter" over a decade and a half earlier. I wrote two more stories exclusively for this book to round out to an even twelve tales. Much like Christ has twelve disciples, these are the twelve (or so) men with whom I found fun times. I wanted to take the on-going list of partners I had dutifully cataloged on a spreadsheet and put it into story form. When I was finishing up my first publication for 51st Street House Publishing in the early fall of 2017, I was already considering what I wanted to do next. I remembered my mostly un-read sex blog and decided those stories could be the basis for a set of gay erotica.

But, I knew I needed help. I did not know who to ask to read my stories of conquest and the eternal search for the best orgasm possible. Here they are:

Karen Bays-Winslow is my dear friend from our days growing up in Oklahoma. Karen majored in English, then received her Master of Library and Information Science degree. Karen, I knew I could trust your grammatical instincts, ultimately integrating your suggestions. Your support for a friend and writer coupled with your guidance in the structure of this book have proved more valuable than I could have imagined on my own.

A story: When we were attending high school together, I wrote a short story about two lesbians having unadulterated sex throughout a cabin in the rolling plains of the rural mid-west. It was mostly riddled with juvenile assumptions as what two women would typically accomplish in bed. I showed it to Karen. She decided to rewrite the story for her amusement with a pointedly G-rated approach.

An example:

> "Martha got on top of Veronica and shoved her tit up Veronica's ass."

The nuances of lesbian sex were lost on me.
Karen's rewrite read:

> "Martha got on top of Veronica's kitchen duties and shoved her teacup and saucer up Veronica's cupboard."

Another:

> "Veronica zealously licked Martha's hot pink pussy."

Which became:

> "Veronica eagerly licked the strawberry pink icing from Martha's freshly baked cupcake, still hot from the oven."

I am sure the young version of myself readily laughed at her edits for the next decade. Karen, through the years you have forever remained a source of joy and inspiration for me. I am so privileged to have you in my life. You proved not only to be the same sweet young woman today that I knew in my youth but as a source of help and a virtual living database of all things English. When I became paranoid about ending sentences with prepositions, I consulted you and conducted endless searches on the internet. While removing prepositions at the end of a sentence is not a hard and fast rule anymore, attempting to remove any violations did enhance parts of this book. It forced rewrites and made them, arguably, better. Your openness to my process, willingness to be a sounding board and patience toward an otherwise unhinged fledgling writer, (and possibly incorrigible, if your mother had a say), have never gone unnoticed. Your very presence in my life puts me at a significant disadvantage, forever sending me down roads searching for appropriate words to exhibit gratitude and love. You make me want to be a better writer and a better human being. From the pits of my heart, thank you.

Michele Hamilton volunteered to help with this book and became my first co-editor (as the missed spelling errors in my previous book proved how much I needed assistance). Some editors might shy away from the type of material in this book, but you did not. You gave me incredibly useful feedback, editing queues, and storyline suggestions. There were many pages added to this book based solely on your recommendations. I cannot imagine this book being as productive and engaging without your help. Thank you, Michele.

Patrick Stephenson is the man I initially wanted to write the Foreplay for the book (which is only half the reason why there is not one). Because of time constraints and schedules, it rendered impossible. Patrick, you are an immensely talented artist and creator. As much as I was delighted with this book, I felt it still needed another element. Your simplistic yet detailed homo-erotic art became a perfect fit. From your first drawing of the winged-ding opposite the Canon to all the final images herein, I cannot imagine this book without your timeless and classic input. You teach me more about being a human being than almost anyone. Thank you, Moose.

Russell Bowman, my friend to whom I feel more than a passing obligation to mention affectionately. While your help with this book was minimal and indirect, your history and knowledge of sexuality and relationship nuances directly affected how I wrote these stories. Long ago, when Russell and I still lived near each other, we had regular naked play dates about once a month. Russell, your touch was tender, compassionate, and sensual. Your hands were like velvet on my skin, and your approach to sex was like no one else's I had ever experienced. You called yourself an "ethical slut." (Reader: find the book and read it, it is life changing.) When you shared that word with me, it intrigued me. It was similar to the ideas in the sex-positive movement. Your subtle lessons of sensuality, polyamory, sexual ethics, massage, intimacy, and reciprocal affection while in my bed have proved to be an eternal forming factor in my approach to my sexual practices, and ability to be accessible to mew and exciting erotic explorations. In some ways, I could never have been so open writing about sex had it not been, partly, for you. You continue to be a positive influence in your community and the souls you encounter. I miss your touch, your tenderness, your body, your kiss, and everything you taught me. You have always been a teacher, and I will always remain your willing student. Thank you, Russell.

Lastly, it would undoubtedly be an indecent infraction if I were not to acknowledge **all the men** that have been the bones of these stories. They have not only given me earth-shattering orgasms, but they have also inspired me to be sexually bolder, to moan louder with the windows open, to be uninhibited and wilder while naked, and to aspire to some of my better sexual experiences in life.

My list of male partners is long. I regret none of them, whether they were stellar, awkward, embarrassing, or mind-blowing. They are all part of my sexual journey – a trip I am still wide awake and continuing daily. I am used to the snide remarks and disapproving looks from friends and relatives when I bring up my sexual itinerary. Their judgment motivates me. It is a win-win.

I hope your sex life is the same, that the jeers of your prudish friends only push you to have more and better sex; give them something to talk about, and pat yourself on the back. Success is the best revenge, and if you happen to be naked while accomplishing that, so be it.

By the way, if you have never slept with a chubby guy, you should try it. We are pretty great in bed.

† A Note from Ernest Sewell †

Thank you so much for reading *HYMNS Volume One*. If you enjoyed it, please take a moment to leave a review at your favorite online retailer, like Amazon USA or a review site like Goodreads.

I welcome and enjoy contact with my readers. At my website, you can contact me, keep an eye out for new projects, and find links to my social networking.

Please, tell a friend about my books.

http://www.ernestsewell.com

Ernest Sewell

† About the Author †

... at home

HYMNS Volume One is Ernest Sewell's second publication for 51st Street House Publishing and his debut in gay erotica and short story fiction. His first release, *Greatest Hits*, received great reviews from readers who were possibly high or otherwise altered.

Mr. Sewell lives in upstate New York with three cats, a friend, and an extensive collection of Prince music. He might also be having sex right now. Try not to picture it, just know it could be happening.

There are no contractions in this book.

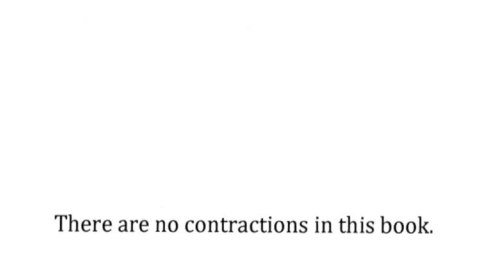

Made in the USA
Columbia, SC
27 September 2023